D0097297

"The perfect recipe for a deeply satisfying read—a wonderfully flawed narrator with an ax (and an ex) to grind, a fast-paced story set in the fascinating world of top chefs and restaurants told with an insider's knife-edge precision, an utterly believable and sympathetic cast of characters—all served up with delectable prose and refreshing insights into work, family, and love that linger long after the last page has been turned."
—**Liza Gyllenhaal**, author of *So Near*

"To say that *Aftertaste* is a story about food and love and resilience is like calling Anthony Bourdain a "cook." Readers are going to fall in love with Mira *and* Meredith Mileti. It's always a thrill to read a debut novel, but to discover a writer as great as this is pure treasure."
—**Jo-Ann Mapson**, author of *Solomon's Oak* and *The Owl & Moon Café*

"Serving up not only delectable cuisine but magnificent prose, Meredith Mileti's *Aftertaste* lingered on my tongue long after devouring the last page. Surely she is a writer destined for greatness!"
—**Lisa Patton,** author of *Whistlin' Dixie in a Nor'easter*

"A delicious debut."
—**Jamie Cat Callan**, author of *French Women Don't Sleep Alone* and *Bonjour, Happiness!*

aftertaste

{a novel in five courses}

Meredith Mileti

KENSINGTON BOOKS
www.kensingtonbooks.com

KENSINGTON BOOKS are published by

Kensington Publishing Corp.
119 West 40th Street
New York, NY 10018

All Kensington titles, imprints, and distributed lines are available at special quantity discounts for bulk purchases for sales promotion, premiums, fund-raising, educational, or institutional use.

Special book excerpts or customized printings can also be created to fit specific needs. For details, write or phone the office of the Kensington Special Sales Manager: Attn. Special Sales Department. Kensington Publishing Corp., 119 West 40th Street, New York, NY 10018. Phone: 1-800-221-2647.

Kensington and the K logo Reg. U.S. Pat. & TM Off.

ISBN-13: 978-0-7582-5991-2
ISBN-10: 0-7582-5991-3

First Kensington Trade Paperback Printing: September 2011
10 9 8 7 6 5 4 3 2 1

Printed in the United States of America

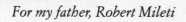

For my father, Robert Mileti

ACKNOWLEDGMENTS

Julia Child once observed that great gourmands are marked by warm and generous natures and that the people who love to eat are always the best people. My thanks are due to so many individuals who helped bring this book to the table—friends, readers, and great gourmands all . . .

My agents, Alexandra Machinist and Linda Chester, for zealously championing Mira and her story; Amy Pyle, my insightful and supportive editor, whose gentle hand and expert assistance helped guide *Aftertaste* to fruition; Debra Roth Kane, copy editor extraordinaire, for her careful attention to detail; and last, but not least, the team at Kensington, for giving this first-time novelist such a wonderful welcome.

Thanks are due as well to my earliest readers, Grant, Sonja, Holly, and Clara Schutte, Kathy Cienciala and John Lingley, for laughing in all the right places and for the inspiration of so many good meals shared around your tables. And to Betsy Levine-Brown and Patty Levine, Joan Vondra, Val Mittl, Debi and Bobbi Fox, Chanelle Bokelberg, and Mike Lynch, generous readers and wonderful friends. To Melissa Tea, Mercedes Goldcamp, Carol Fryday, Debra Schneider, and Sue Martin, my heartfelt thanks for their careful reading and helpful comments on later drafts of the novel.

A debt of gratitude is owed to Jennifer McDowell, equal parts coach, cheerleader, and dear friend.

To Sharon Oddson, owner of Trattoria Garga, in Firenze, *grazie mille* for teaching me to roll pasta with a rolling pin and for showing me what it takes to make a successful woman chef.

To my children, Stephanie, Amanda, and Mark, for loving good stories and allowing me my obsessions and who every day make me proud to be their mother.

To my father, Robert Mileti, the greatest gourmand I know, who took me to Italy and taught me to cook.

And, finally, to David, who makes all my dreams come true.

Antipasti

Cooking is a troublesome sprite.

—Pellegrino Artusi

chapter 1

The best thing about the location of the Manhattan County Courthouse is its proximity to Nelly's. Nelly's is a take-out stand that serves the best lamb burger this side of Auckland. Cooked rare, and topped with goat cheese and a fried egg so fresh its yolk oozes orange, it's the last meal I will ask for if ever I find myself on death row.

Climbing the steps to the courthouse, I imagine I am one of New Zealand's intrepid settlers, a nefarious wanderer let loose on the shores of a place new and dangerous, armed with the fortitude only a good meal can provide. I stuff the last delicious morsel into my mouth, savoring the finale, the unctuous tang of the cheese, the bracing bite of the lamb, wishing I'd ordered a beer to go with it. Maybe two.

The criminal division is on the second floor, and stepping off the elevator, I pass through security, where I'm checked for weapons before being let loose to wander freely among the drug addicts, street criminals, and those poor souls wrongly accused of being criminals (of whom, looking around, I suspect there are few). Everyone has a hunted look. They huddle in doorways and dimly lit hallways; some are handcuffed or shackled. The air is thick with the smell of unwashed bodies, of anger and despair. Police officers in various stages of disenchantment with humanity mill around officially, sipping burnt coffee provided free of charge by the grateful taxpayers of Manhattan.

The probation department is located in a slightly more hopeful annex, seven steps up and to the left of the criminal courtrooms. It is the third time I have found myself here, and I know it will not be my last. I have been court-ordered to attend a series of anger-management classes. We meet on Tuesday afternoons, a half a floor removed from the felons, but the smell of anger and despair is here as well. Although it is the third class of six, I think I've regressed. My anger is closer to the surface this time; I can feel it hot and palpable under the collar of my shirt, in the pulse in my neck, and in the palms of my clenched fists. Six of us sit in a circle on the green linoleum floor that looks and feels as if it hasn't been washed in years. The instructor, Mary Ann, is a licensed clinical social worker. She walks slowly behind us, repeating what are supposed to be soothing phrases. "Breathe in the clean, white air. When you exhale, picture your breath as black and hot. It is your anger. Release it, and let it go." It is how we began the last two classes, and it is, I assume, how we will begin them all. When she gets to me, she places a light hand on my shoulder and says softly, "Mira, you're very tense. Try to unclench your fists. Exhale that black, hot anger." She gives my shoulder an encouraging squeeze and moves on.

"Think of what makes you angry," she continues, in a hushed, singsongy voice. "When you feel your body begin to tense, take a cleansing breath, let out that black smoke, and repeat, 'I will not lose control.'"

So here I am, a person who's never so much as gotten a speeding ticket, a person with nary a youthful transgression to speak of, now a regular in the probation department, where I have been ordered to be by Judge Celia Wilcox, who one would have thought would have been more sympathetic to me—a woman scorned. I repeat, "I will not lose control," mantra-like, as if by some wild stretch of the imagination a mere verbal affirmation could make it so.

The truth is, I'm out of control and I know it. I'm out of control and justifiably so. I have just lost everything.

Mary Ann tells us to slowly open our eyes. Amazingly, the air around us is not cloudy with the black smoke of our exhaled anger, which can mean only one of two things: We have all kept it corked up inside to be released later when no longer under Mary Ann's watchful eye or, two, Mary Ann is full of shit. I know what I think and, looking around the room at my fellow miscreants, I know what they think, too. We are doing our time, all of us, thankful to be here and not downstairs, shackled in those orange jumpsuits.

We get up and stretch a bit, then move to chairs that are placed in a circle behind us. We do this more or less silently. The other people in the class, four men and one woman, do not seem to be given to lighthearted banter. They probably do not have good social skills, which might help to explain why they are in this class.

I, on the other hand, am a person with excellent social skills, a gifted conversationalist, a person used to lighthearted banter. A person who occasionally used to smile before rage and disappointment took up permanent residence, lagging in the pit of my stomach like an indigestible meal. I'm angry, and who wouldn't be? I'm forced to be here because the woman who screwed my husband is now trying to steal my restaurant. All I was trying to do was to protect hearth, home, and business, which in simpler times would have been a perfectly permissible and legally defensible option.

In fact, if I'd been a cave woman or even some medieval wench, I would have been considered the victor when I emerged, only slightly bloodied, and holding in my hands great clumps of Nicola's black hair—hair I pulled out by its roots while she sat naked, helpless, and sobbing, hands pressed to her bald and bleeding scalp. I would have won Jake back by a show of sheer physical dominance, and I, not Nicola, would now be presiding over the dining room at Grappa. That I am here, and she is in my restaurant and in Jake's bed is beyond anathema, and a testament to the decline of modern civilization.

A snort escapes me, and I look around, embarrassed. Mary Ann begins. "How did this week go for you all? Let's talk about triggers and what we did to address them. Larry, how about beginning for us?" She gestures to a large man wearing a New York Rangers jersey over white carpenter's pants who, we learned last week, beats his wife.

"I dunno. She got mad and left. So, since she wasn't there, there was nothin' to piss me off."

"Do you know what made her angry?" Mary Ann asks.

I squirm in my chair. I want to say, *How about being married to a guy who beats you? Isn't that enough for you, Mary Ann?*

"Who the hell knows," says Larry. Mary Ann doesn't say anything. After thirty seconds or so, the uncomfortable silence forces Larry to continue. "Might be because I didn't come home one night."

And I think, great, another adulterer, and because I have no impulse control where infidelity is concerned, I glare daggers at him, then wonder fleetingly if he is likely to turn his rage on me. He looks at me and then at Keisha, a large African American woman, an ex-professional boxer with a cauliflower ear and the only other female in the group besides me and Mary Ann (who, I guess, doesn't really count). Keisha is also glaring at him.

As if sensing our mutual disgust, he proceeds. "I had too much to drink, and I get mean when I'm drunk, so I thought I'd better not go home, just in case."

Mary Ann is all over that one. "Well, Larry, that is an important step. You recognized drinking is a trigger for you, and you were trying to keep yourself from doing some harm. I think you can see that as progress." She smoothes her limp, gray pageboy hair behind both ears, adjusts her cardigan sweater, and gives him a milquetoast smile.

Keisha, who may have even less impulse control than I do, says to Larry, "Hell, she's mad because she don't know where you been sleeping. I'd be mad. Miss Priss and Miss Chef over there"—she gestures to Mary Ann and me—"we'd be mad if our man don't come home, and we don't know where he is or who he's been sleepin' with."

Before I can jump in with a "Right on, sister!," Shawn, a middle-aged man in an expensive suit, waves his hand in a dismissive manner and says in a clipped and condescending tone, "Oh, come on, that really isn't the issue. It is not about what makes *her* mad. The point is, this guy, Larry here, is trying to get his act together. He knows there are probably a hundred little things his wife does that annoy the crap out of him, and when he's drunk those hundred things become a thousand.

"He's taking one step at a time, and if his wife doesn't see that, to hell with her. This isn't freaking marriage counseling. Larry's got other things on his mind besides other women. Why is it you can't understand it isn't always about you?"

Shawn's tone is full of disdain and thinly concealed misogyny. He hasn't spoken before, and I wonder what he has done and why he is here. One thing I'm sure about, it somehow involves a woman.

Mary Ann, a traitor to her sex, replies, "Thanks for sharing that thought, Shawn. Would you like to say some more about that?"

Shawn puts his forearms on his knees, buries his head in his open palms, and says in a tight voice, "No, that will do it."

Mary Ann turns her attention to Keisha and me and opens her mouth, poised to deliver a lecture, but before she can begin, before I even know it myself, I'm off and running. "Do you want to know what my trigger is, Mary Ann, Shawn, Larry?" I say, louder than I had intended. "Lying, cheating, scumbag husbands and their whores!"

I hear Mary Ann say "Mira," and I know she's about to tell me I'm smothering in the thick, black smoke of my anger. But I don't care, and I don't stop.

I blurt out my story, how I had hired Nicola to be the maîtress d'hôtel at our restaurant, Grappa, when I was seven months pregnant. How I suspected Jake and Nicola had begun having an affair when Chloe was just hours old; and how one night, when Chloe woke up and Jake still wasn't home at two-thirty in the morning, I bundled her up and strapped her into the portable infant carrier, walked the three blocks to the restaurant, and snuck in the side door.

The door was locked, but the alarm wasn't on, the first odd thing, because Jake always locks up and sets the alarm before leaving the restaurant. Chloe had fallen back to sleep in her infant seat on the way over, so I carefully nestled the carrier into one of the leather banquettes.

I crept through the dining room and into the darkened kitchen, where I could see the office at the far end was aglow with candlelight. As I moved closer I could hear music. "Nessun dorma," from *Turandot,* Jake's favorite. *How fitting.* On the marble pastry station I found an open bottle of wine and two empty glasses. It was, to add insult to what was about to be serious injury, a 1999 Tenuta dell'Ornellaia Masseto Toscano—the most expensive wine in our cellar. Three hundred and eighty dollar foreplay.

I picked up the bottle and followed the trail of clothes to the office. Jake's checkered chef's pants and tunic, Nicola's slinky black dress, which I hated her for being able to wear, and a Victoria's Secret, lacy, black bra. They were on the leather couch, Nicola on top, her wild, black hair spilling over Jake's chest, humping away like wild dogs. Carried away by their passion, they were oblivious to my approach. I drained the last of the wine from the bottle and hurled it over their backsides where it smashed against the wall, announcing my arrival.

Before Jake could completely extricate himself, I jumped on Nicola's back and grabbed hold of her hair and pulled with all the strength of my hot-blooded Mediterranean ancestors. Nicola screamed, and clawed the air, her flailing hands accidentally swiping Jake squarely on the chin. He squirmed out from under her and tried to tackle me, but I'm not a small woman. Armed with my humiliation and anger, I was a force in motion.

In desperation, Jake butted his head into the middle of my back, wrapped his hands around my waist, and pulled with all his might. He succeeded, pulling so hard that Nicola's hair, which I had resolutely refused to yield, came away in great clumps in my hands. Nicola's screams turned to pathetic whimpers as she reached to cover her burning scalp. She then curled herself into a fetal position, naked and bleeding, and began to keen.

My co-offenders are riveted as I tell them everything, right down to my fantasy of feigning a reconciliation with Nicola and then beating her senseless on the stage of *The Jerry Springer Show.*

When I stop to take a breath, I realize my hands are shaking, as my recollection of the events has triggered an adrenaline rush. I look around at the group. Shawn has removed his head from his hands and is looking right at me as if I have just confirmed all his worst suspicions about women. Keisha is smiling so broadly that I can see all of her white teeth. She shakes her head encouragingly and utters, "damn," under her breath with unconcealed admiration.

Larry does not meet my eyes. He has the look of a trapped animal, a typical bully who, once cornered, melts under the gaze of his captor. I'm receiving validation from my fellow thugs, and I begin to think maybe this group therapy stuff isn't so bad after all.

I do not realize the full extent of my blunder until my gaze finally reaches Mary Ann. Apparently the thought has occurred to her, long before it did to me, that an encore performance on national television would not provide favorable testament to Miss Priss's anger-management counseling skills. It is just one more time my temper has gotten the better of me, and I know, with an element of fatalism, it will not be the last.

I will not be graduating from anger-management skills training as planned, Mary Ann tells me after class. She can see there's much work to be done, and it doesn't take a licensed clinical social worker to see that an outburst like mine speaks of deeper issues to be explored. She then presses into my hand a white slip of paper on which is written the name and telephone number of a person she knows to be an excellent therapist. She adds, after a few seconds, that although she has no authority to order me to individual therapy, she hopes I'll seriously consider it. Then, with a depth of understanding I'd failed to credit to her, she deals me the coup de grace. "Mira," she says, looking fully into my eyes for the very first time, "you owe this to yourself, but more than that, you owe it to Chloe."

On the first floor I stop to buy a Diet Coke at the vending machine. It's now late in the afternoon, and most of the people awaiting trials have gone for the day. I'm spent emotionally and physically by my display in class, and I guzzle the Coke greedily on the way to catch my bus. By the time I get to West Broadway, I've finished the Coke and, as I run for the bus heading to the Village, I toss the empty can into the garbage, only to see the little, white slip of paper that has stuck to the side of the moist can, the piece of paper on which Mary Ann has written my ticket to sanity, disappear into the trash.

chapter 2

You cannot know the type of person you really are, I mean truly, deep down, appreciate the measure of yourself as a person, until you've felt the cold steel of a pair of handcuffs against your wrists. What does it evoke? Pain? Terror? Remorse? After my attack on Nicola, they had restrained me, in order to protect me from myself, the officer told me, her hand atop my head as she gently, and I'd like to think sympathetically, assisted me into the back of the cruiser. She had been kind, allowing me to call Hope, our downstairs neighbor and Chloe's sometime babysitter, and wait for her to trudge the three blocks in her bathrobe to pick up Chloe. She had even graciously removed the cuffs so I could hold her for an instant, allowing me to brush a trembling kiss across her forehead before transferring her into Hope's waiting arms. But the act for which I remain most grateful was her unexpected humanity—she had waited for Hope and Chloe to disappear around the corner before re-cuffing me, apologizing as she snapped the locks into place with a dispiriting *click*. Perhaps because I've spent my life working with my hands, I find it terrifying to have them immobilized. But, sitting in the back of the cruiser, my neck craned uncomfortably to watch the diminishing specters of Jake and Nicola out the cruiser's rear window—Jake's arm wrapped protectively around Nicola, a white tablecloth draped over her heaving shoulders—all I can remember feeling was a strange detachment, as if I were watching a Lifetime Channel movie of the week, waiting patiently for the next commercial break. It wasn't until Jake and Nicola had completely disappeared from view, and I struggled to turn around, the steel of the handcuffs uncomfortably chafing my wrists, that I found a piece of Nicola's long, dark hair had wedged itself firmly in between my two front teeth and was tickling my bottom lip. All I can remember thinking is, "How the hell did that get there?" No remorse, God forbid. No guilt. Just pure incredulity.

Now what does that say about me?

The thing is, you really can't know who you are, what you will do to get what you want, until you've been in trouble. Getting away with something makes it easy to hide behind the stories we tell ourselves, the lies we live with, often small and incremental, in order to secure our hearts' desires. But find yourself fingerprinted and photographed, forced to call a friend—of whom you have depressingly few, apart, of course, from your husband, whose lover you have just attacked and who is probably not, at the moment, inclined to post your bail—and you'll find you have some real explaining to do.

I've never been a person with big plans. Most of what I do, I do spontaneously, or as Mary Ann might say, impulsively. The only fruits of any serious planning in my life, in fact, are Chloe and Grappa. The trouble with planning things in advance, I've learned, is they seldom turn out the way you plan them. When Jake and I opened the restaurant five years ago, we thought we knew what we wanted. We were both tired of working under the direction of restaurant owners, bottom-liners, all too often loud of voice and lacking in vision or culinary understanding. We wanted to shake up the restaurant world, which we felt had grown complacent and mired in certain continental dining traditions. At one point, shortly after our return from Europe, we dreamed of owning a loft in the city. We imagined an expansive, multi-level space where we could live and work. Enough space to accommodate an open kitchen, where we would offer cooking classes and wine tastings during the day and where we could serve a few prix fixe dinners each week. However, when a cozy (real estate code for miniscule) basement space in the West Village became available, we took advantage of the opportunity, adjusted our expectations, and Grappa was born.

In its former incarnation it had been a small, dank pizzeria, or at least what passes for a pizzeria in the States, serving oil-drenched, over-sauced pizza Americans tend to love, which actually bears little relation to real Italian *pizza*. The kitchen was small by restaurant standards, and needed a total overhaul, stretching our budget and our borrowing capacity to their limits.

We picked up cheap stock tables and chairs at warehouse and fire sales, where we tried not to remind ourselves we were buying the remains of someone else's failed enterprise. White cloths and kitschy wax-dripped Chianti bottles dressed the tables in the fall and winter. In the summertime I loaded fresh flowers, which I grew on the roof of our apartment building, into the recycled aluminum San Marzano tomato cans that arrived at our restaurant weekly by the case. Our collection of vintage Italian food and wine posters was on temporary loan from our apartment, and Jake and I agreed they looked great against the exposed brick. The metamorphosis from basement slum to chic urban trattoria had taken only nine months, a surprisingly small amount of time in which to spend not only every dollar we had, but also every penny we could cajole from the First Manhattan Savings and Loan.

Within months of our opening, *Gourmet* did a piece on "Up and Coming" restaurants in New York, and Grappa was featured. It was a lucky accident they chose us, the kind of break that can make or destroy you in this town. The rave review on our food, however, we earned. The day after the magazine hit the stands, we had a line coming out the door at lunchtime. By the weekend, we were booked solid, two weeks in advance. We made money hand over fist, enough that by the end of our first year in business we were able to buy the first floor space above, enhance the kitchen, and expand the restaurant by eleven tables.

During those early years we weathered the storms common to all fledgling restaurants, particularly those in Manhattan. At the same time we engineered and oversaw a second comprehensive renovation. Jake and I lived, ate, and breathed Grappa. We had fully intended to start a family once Grappa had opened successfully, but we had to put those plans on hold, a decision not without a certain element of risk, given the fact I was already thirty-five and Jake was forty. Instead, we made Grappa our baby, its staff our family.

On my thirty-seventh birthday I bullied Jake into agreeing it was time to try for a baby, citing as evidence a now infamous article, published in the Sunday Magazine section and responsible for I don't even want to think about how many ambivalent conceptions, by scores of career women in their thirties, whose biological windows were much narrower than previously believed. Jake, rather reluctantly, agreed. In retrospect, he probably was secretly heartened by the news that perhaps my biological window was already closed.

Of course, I became pregnant almost instantly.

Chloe is sleeping when I get home from anger-management class. Hope, the sitter and our downstairs neighbor, tells me Chloe didn't fall asleep until after three, so not to worry if she sleeps a while longer.

I take out Chloe's dinner: veal mousse with shitake puree, creamed spinach, and, in order to balance the colors and textures, souffléed butternut squash. All homemade, frozen in the tiny compartments of blue plastic ice cube trays. Before Chloe was born, Jake and I agreed our child would have a sophisticated palate. No Happy Meals, no macaroni and cheese, and—God forbid—no chicken fingers. I make her food myself, at night sometimes when I can't sleep, as if being able to offer Chloe the pureed version of the best I can cook will somehow make up for what I fear will be all my other shortcomings as a mother.

Already at seven months Chloe has shown herself to be an adventurous eater. There's nothing she doesn't like. Jake, of course, has no idea. In the three months since he moved out, he's hardly seen her. He probably doesn't even know she's eating solid foods. And because he's never asked, I've never told him.

The few conversations we've had in the last three months have been about work: practical aspects of the changing of the guard from lunch to dinner, decisions about the seasonal menu changes at

the restaurant, how the last shipment of baby artichokes was un
characteristically bitter, and which one of us should be responsible
for calling the supplier.

Before Chloe was born we agreed Jake would supervise dinner
at the restaurant, while I would take lunch a couple days a week,
just to keep my hand in, until Chloe was a little older. Since the separation, however, and my forced compliance with the terms of the
Order of Protection that prohibits me from coming within two
hundred yards of Nicola, I've taken to cooking lunch five days per
week, while Jake continues to handle dinner. He has the harder job,
dinner being the more important and elaborate meal, and six days
instead of five, but I'm busy with the work of raising our child. Jake
tells me, mostly in writing through our lawyers, that he'll gladly buy
my share of the restaurant so I can stay at home and prepare
Michelin-worthy baby meals all day instead of just at night, that it
would be better for "the child."

What he really means is it would be easier for him and Nicola if
they didn't have to worry about my intruding into their private
lives, lives they've stolen for themselves right from underneath my
nose.

And so we try, or rather Jake tries, not to overlap at the restaurant, but sometimes we do. We are civil, and occasionally even
pleasant to each other, because there are usually other people
around. If nothing else, we are professionals who have a business to
run. I try, however, never to look directly at him because then the
ache will come and, unable to draw breath into my constricted
chest, I will begin to choke. Usually, it's fairly easy to keep from
looking at him because there are always several things that need to
be done in the restaurant kitchen, always something to occupy
one's hands and eyes.

Since Jake wouldn't agree to terminate Nicola's employment
(apparently he doesn't see quite enough of her, even though they
are now living together at her apartment), she still works the dinner
shift as maîtress. If I'm honest with myself, the vision of Nicola presiding over the dining room at Grappa bothers me as much as her
having taken my place in Jake's bed. Maybe more.

Chloe sleeps longer than she should, and when I get her up, she fusses and strains in my arms. Once I maneuver her into the high chair, she stubbornly refuses to eat, pounding the tray with her tiny fists and swatting my hand away whenever I offer her a spoonful of food. After I make several unsuccessful attempts, the tray of her high chair (and her hands, face, and hair) is covered in broad brushstrokes of orange, green, and beige, which she smears around the tray, like a manic little Jackson Pollock. Finally, arms straining, she reaches for me and makes little kneading motions with her fists, and I finally understand she wants to nurse. It is the only thing that seems to quiet her, and she sucks greedily, faster than she is able to swallow, the milk pooling in the inside of her cheeks.

Chloe's eyes roll back slightly in her head, and her previously clenched fists are now limp with exhaustion and relief. What hard and frustrating work it must be to be a baby. Being forced to communicate your needs without words to the people in charge of your care, people who mean well and are generally invested in your well-being, if occasionally dense and preoccupied.

I watch the almost imperceptible rise and fall of her chest, the halting tremble of her lips as they purse and then begin to suck sleepily and lazily at the air. Her movements are at once languid and deliberate, and I'm dizzy with the promise of who she is, this tiny person I have made. And I wonder if she senses I'm her mother and I'm here watching her. Defining myself in gentler terms, as Chloe's mother, seems necessary and, after seven months, almost completely natural. As if by doing so, I can erase all the mistakes I made in being Jake's wife.

Primi

Kissing don't last; cookery do!

—George Meredith

chapter 3

Mercifully, Chloe has always been an excellent sleeper, sleeping through the night when she was less than three weeks old. So it's unusual when she wakes at midnight, crying. She's hot to the touch and fretful. Cursing myself for not having sprung for the quick-read ear thermometer the pediatrician had recommended, I manage to take her temperature rectally. One hundred and four. I give her some Infants' Tylenol drops and a bottle of cool water, which she gulps down impatiently, but within minutes she throws up all over the two of us, mostly water, tinged purple from the grape-flavored Tylenol. We pace the apartment, Chloe's fretful cries becoming increasingly more piercing as I rock her, gently at first, then more urgently. With each lap around the apartment I become more and more nervous because I cannot stop her crying. Finally, when she shows no signs of exhausting herself and I can't take it any more, I pick up the phone and punch the pediatrician's emergency hotline number on the speed dial. I'm startled when, after several rings, I get the sound of Jake's recorded voice mail message. I listen, confused and mesmerized by the sound of his voice, until I realize I must have hit number one (Jake's cell phone) instead of number four (Dr. Troutman) on the speed dial. I hang up, but not before, blinded by worry and fury, I've managed to wail urgently and hysterically into the phone.

Chloe finally stops crying, but her body is listless and heavy, her eyes glassy. I take her temperature again, this time without disturbing her too much. Despite the Tylenol, her fever has climbed another degree. One hundred and five. I check the clock. 1:15 a.m. I hastily throw on sweatpants, socks, and running shoes, grab the quilt from Chloe's crib, and quickly wrap her.

Downstairs, Earl, the night doorman, is sipping his coffee from a paper cup, looking fresh and alert, when Chloe and I come flying out of the elevator. Without my having to utter a word, Earl flags down a cabbie, packs us in, and, leaning into the front window of the cab, shouts something to the driver in Spanish. By the time we reach the hospital, Chloe is in the midst of a convulsion brought about, I'm later told, by the high fever.

When caught in time, fever convulsions are quite manageable, the very young-looking intern tells me, speaking with an authority he could not possibly have earned yet. They bring down her fever with an injection and give her an IV of fluid to help rehydrate her. The needle looks enormous punched into her little arm. By 4:00 a.m. her fever is down to one hundred and three; by 6:00, an acceptable hundred and one. By 7:30 Chloe and I are back in the apartment. Diagnosis: viral infection, source unspecified. I should be relieved, but I'm not. I put her to bed and pace the apartment, picking up where I left off last night, imagining with each lap that I'm sinking lower and lower and that soon I will have worn a hole clean through to Hope's apartment on the floor below. I actually think of calling Hope, who has no children of her own and might not understand or fully appreciate my worries, but at least she'd have coffee. I imagine her expression as I report to her my litany of concerns about Chloe's health, how I've convinced myself that she has suffered permanent brain damage and might never learn to speak, or that she will be deaf. Hadn't Helen Keller gone blind, deaf, and mute from such a virus?

I let out an audible sigh. I'm totally spent, physically and psychologically, and yet, hidden under the thin skin of my exhaustion and worry lurks another raw emotion, one that I haven't had to fully identify until now. I'm angry. Furious, actually, that Jake wasn't there to help me, to help Chloe. And what about the message I'd left him in the middle of the night? Surely he recognized that the person bleating like a wounded animal into the other end of the phone was me. Why didn't he call me back? More evidence of his monumental callousness.

It would be so simple to hate him, but I haven't quite figured out how to, or at least how to sustain it. I'll make a heroic effort at it, like now, or during anger-management class, and then I'll remember something, some silly thing that weakens my resolve to inflict upon him the most grievous punishments, like castration or dismemberment. Now, for instance, as I imagine calling him on the telephone and screaming at him that his daughter almost died, suffering fever convulsions in a filthy Manhattan cab, all I can think about is how he shivers uncontrollably when awakened out of a sound sleep. When it happens he looks pathetic and boyish. It's hard to hate someone when you know the most intimate secrets of his sympathetic nervous system. If I could put half the energy into hating him that I had put into loving him, I'd be well over this man.

How had Jake accomplished it, this reversal of feelings, this decision to stop loving me? When did the little things he knew about me, things he had once cherished, or at least, minimally tolerated, turn into insurmountable annoyances? And how had I failed to notice?

But, regardless of how Jake feels about me, Chloe is still his child, and he should know about his only child's brush with death. Shouldn't he? And because it is my duty as the mother of said child to tell him, I pick up the phone.

Of course, *she* answers, and of course I've woken her. It is, after all, only seven forty-five. Early for them. On nights they close the restaurant, which nowadays is most nights, they don't get home until after two. Nicola's voice is deep and sexy with sleep. I wince, squeezing my eyes tightly shut as if I could block out the picture of them in bed together. Fat chance.

"I need to talk to Jake," I say with my eyes still clamped shut. Good. To the point, efficient.

I can feel her hesitate. I think there's a good chance that she'll hang up on me. We haven't seen each other, or even spoken, since that night, and I suppose she still harbors some residual bad feelings, to which, in my opinion, she is totally unentitled. I imagine her hanging up, murmuring in response to Jake's sleepy query that it had just been a wrong number, while quietly unplugging the phone, severing Jake's connection to Chloe and me. But she doesn't. Instead, stifling a yawn, she says, "He isn't here, Mira." Of course, a predictable lie.

"I need to talk to Jake. Could you put him on?" Note: I did not say please.

Again, she hesitates. "He's not here."

I stop dead. Not there? At seven forty-five in the morning? What did that mean? Was he not living there? Had he left her?

It isn't until I have Jake and me back together in an emotional reunion at Chloe's bedside that I realize Nicola is still speaking.

". . . left a few minutes ago. He's meeting Eddie." Eddie is our fish man, who occasionally asks us to meet him at the pier, although usually not this early in the morning.

"He's going in to the restaurant afterward to, ah, take care of some paperwork. You'll probably see him at lunch." Her voice is neutral. She could have been talking to anyone. The fact that she could treat me so evenly is perhaps the most horrible of all. Clearly, I'm no longer a threat. She's secure enough in Jake's love that she doesn't need to fear me in the least.

I'm silent. It's now my turn to speak, but the part of my brain governing the pragmatic functions of language is not working at the moment.

"Mira?" Her voice sounds strained, all vestiges of sleep now gone.

I don't answer her. Instead, I hang up the phone.

Paperwork. Going in early. Something doesn't sound right. First off, Jake doesn't do paperwork. That's my job. Jake and I usually shopped for fruits, vegetables, and fish, taking turns at the markets. Meat orders are phoned or faxed to our suppliers, and we are billed monthly by the various vendors we patronize. Spices, cheeses, olive oil, and condiments are ordered through Renata Brussani. Our bartender/sommelier handles the wine order, faithfully presenting his inventory and monthly statements to me for inspection. I take care of all the bill paying, as Jake considers such details mundane, and therefore beneath his notice. He fancies himself an artist and is perfectly content to leave all the details of running the business to me.

Lately, though, I've sensed Jake looking over my shoulder at the restaurant, trying to figure out what I'm doing. One day last week, I caught him in the office leafing through an inventory of our cookware. And Tuesday he had mentioned to me that we needed to replace the fire extinguishers in the back kitchen, a detail that typically would have totally escaped his notice.

I'll try him at the restaurant. Among other things, he needs to know that I'm not going to make it in for lunch. I don't want to leave Chloe, and I'm exhausted from being up all night. The only other thing I have scheduled today is my meeting with Renata Brussani, the importer who sells us olive oil and cheese. Could it be that Jake wants to be in on my meeting with Renata? Part of his grand plan to take over the restaurant? Luckily, I brought the paperwork home with me, so Jake will have no idea what we need.

I call Grappa and get our sous-chef, Tony. He tells me Jake isn't there yet, but he'll gladly supervise lunch. Tony seems surprised when I tell him that Jake is on his way in this early and promises to have him call me as soon as he gets there.

My next call is to Renata. She begins her days early, meeting with her clients, most of whom are chefs and restaurateurs, during the early part of the day, before they begin lunch or dinner service. I'll just ask her to meet me here, at the apartment, instead of at the restaurant.

For the second time this morning I'm taken aback, when this time a sleepy sounding male voice answers Renata's phone, and then I remember that she got married a few weeks ago. This must be her husband, whose name I have forgotten. They just got married in Vegas and then threw a huge party at Renata's Tribeca loft, after the fact. Although I was invited, I didn't go. I wasn't ready to celebrate the union of two idealistic people, full of the self-congratulatory tones of those who have found love the second time around. Not while I was still licking the wounds of my own failed marriage.

Renata picks up the extension. "*Buon giorno,* Mira, are we still on for ten thirty?" She sounds chipper, all business. She's probably already dressed to the nines and in full makeup, even though it's barely eight o'clock in the morning. Renata isn't really beautiful in a classical sense, although every straight man I know, including Jake, thinks she is. She is sultry and full-figured with a dark, Mediterranean complexion and great, full lips: a young Isabella Rossellini. What most women notice about her is that she dresses impeccably: Italian suits and silk shirts (invariably open to reveal an impressive décolletage), and I can't recall ever seeing her without a scarf and earrings. I look down with disgust at my purple-tinted, vomit-stained sweat suit.

"Sure, I'm all ready to go, but the thing is, Chloe's sick and I can't leave her. She was in the emergency room last night, actually. Would you mind coming to the apartment? I've got everything here, at home."

"Is she okay? Are you sure you don't want to reschedule?" she asks.

"No, no, we're fine. I'd just as soon get the order in. We would have to close our doors if we ran out of Parmigiano-Reggiano. You know, Jake has a liberal hand."

"Yes, I do, God bless him."

"Well, I wouldn't go that far."

She laughs. "Whoops, sorry, I forgot—the bastard."

Over the years Renata and I have developed a social relationship. She proved herself to be an invaluable advisor on a number of occasions throughout Grappa's early stages, and we've become good friends over the last few years. I nursed her through a couple of bad breakups, including one marriage, and she has been supportive of me during this recent unpleasantness with Jake, at least insofar as someone as self-obsessed as Renata can be. But she's also a shrewd businesswoman, and I suspect that if Jake ever did manage to wrest control of the restaurant from me, Renata would continue to make sure his needs, at least for oil and cheese, were spectacularly met. Nevertheless, it's hard not to like Renata. Among other things, one has to admire her business acumen. She broke into an incredibly tight market in a male-dominated profession through sheer smarts, perseverance, and impeccable food sense. Yet, despite her closet full of Fendi handbags and Ferragamo shoes, Renata comes from a family of simple people who were sheep farmers in the foothills of Abruzzo for centuries. At heart, Renata is a simple girl who, when no one is looking, likes to roll up her sleeves, eat big bowls of pasta with sausage, and spit olive pits out the window of her chic Tribeca loft.

I don't ask her about married life, feeling sure that during our meeting she will treat me to all of the details I can stomach. Renata has a way with men. She was actually the first to warn me about Nicola. At one of our meetings, shortly after I hired Nicola, I introduced Renata to our newest employee. They had greeted each other cordially, each appraising the other in the way that only women who know their own power can do.

"Mira," Renata had hissed when we were out of earshot, "are you out of your mind? What were you thinking?" I was seven months pregnant at the time and tired. Nicola was barely a whisper in my hormone-clouded head. In retrospect, I wonder if perhaps Renata had seen something in Jake, some evidence of his wandering eye. Attractive women always know when they have the attention of a man. At the time I considered what she said, but then dismissed it, so blind was I to the possibility that Jake could love anyone else.

We push back the meeting to eleven thirty, which gives me a little extra time to get cleaned up and feed Chloe, if she awakens before Renata arrives. When Renata volunteers to bring lunch, I don't refuse. I hang up feeling full of good intentions. After a shower I'll feel more human, and then there is the prospect of a sumptuous lunch. I'll even whip up a batch of hazelnut biscotti, which we can have with a little espresso for dessert.

My train of thought is interrupted by the ringing phone. The cordless handset slipped in between the cushions of the sofa when

I set it down, and as I fumble for it, the answering machine picks up. "Mira, it's Jake. It's almost nine. I don't know if I'll have another chance to talk before lunch—"

I switch on the handset. "Hello, Jake," I say, trying to sound calm and collected.

"It's Jake."

"I know, you said." Neither of us says anything for a few seconds.

"I got a couple of messages that you called. Tony said something about the baby being sick."

I want to tell him that she has a name and that it would be nice if occasionally he would use it. "Yeah, Chloe has some sort of virus. I took her to the hospital in the middle of the night when her fever hit a hundred and five."

"Jesus, is she okay?"

I want to tell him that I was worried and scared, but I don't do that either. "I think so. We're home now. Her fever is down, and she's sleeping. I think she's going to be all right."

"Wow," is all Jake can think to say.

"Actually, I don't think we could have made it to the ER any faster in an ambulance. Crazy Manhattan cabbies. Good thing, too, because she started convulsing on the way over. As soon as we got there they gave her an IV drip, you know, to rehydrate her." Who is this person casually tossing around big medical terms?

"Well, I'm here. Lunch is covered," Jake says.

I can't think of anything else to say, but I don't want to hang up yet. "What's up with Eddie?"

"Black bass," he says, after a pause. "Beautiful stuff."

"What are you going to do with it?" I ask, and for a minute we slip into our old ways. Talking food. He's animated as he tells me that he's thinking of roasting it on a bed of caramelized fennel and leeks.

"If there's any left you might think about a cioppino for lunch tomorrow," he finishes, embarrassed that he's let himself go like that. I am, he has just remembered, the enemy.

"Well, I have to see how Chloe's doing. Tell Tony to be on call for lunch tomorrow, too, just in case," I say coolly.

"Yeah, okay."

It isn't until after we hang up that I realize he didn't ask me about my meeting with Renata. Our conversation had taken approximately eight minutes, and I start to replay it in my mind, rehashing and recasting the nuances: what was said, what was implied.

Sustaining that calm and in-control tone I had adopted with Jake had been key in gaining the upper hand, but it sapped what little strength I had. I slump into the couch, maneuvering myself so that the loose spring isn't directly in the small of my back. Just another minute or two on the couch before I'll get up and get moving. Of course, I fall asleep.

Some time later a ringing wakes me from my doze. I click the phone on. "Hello?" Just a dial tone. I hear the ringing again and realize it's the doorbell.

It's Renata, and I've neither showered nor changed, much less made any biscotti.

When I open the door I can see my filthy sweat suit and greasy hair mirrored in Renata's shocked expression. I usually look much better than this, a fact that I'm counting on Renata remembering.

"You, *cara mia,* are a walking argument for birth control," Renata says, in her slightly accented English, putting down her briefcase and the two brown paper bags she has brought. I can see a large ciabatta protruding from one. A very good sign.

"Jake called right after we hung up. I was going to shower and change, but I must have fallen asleep after he called."

"I know he called you. I just talked to him."

"You did? When? Did you call him or did he call you?" I ask, instantly suspicious.

"He called me." Renata's voice is calm and patient, as if she is speaking to an unruly child. I want to tell her why this bothers me so much. To share my feeling that Jake is trying to take over the reins. That I'm feeling very threatened. I follow her into the kitchen where she begins unloading the two brown paper bags onto the butcher-block island. I stand there watching as she pulls out a huge, freshly smoked mozzarella, which, by the way she handles it, I can tell is still warm. She sets it down on the cutting board along with the loaf of ciabatta. While I'm considering my next line of questioning, Renata explains, "Jake called to tell me he forgot to show you the postcard I sent out last week listing some new specialty vinegars I'm offering. He asked me to tell you he's interested in sampling some of the blood orange." I stand there looking puzzled, having been only momentarily distracted by the salad possibilities afforded by the aforementioned specialty vinegars. Perhaps a mild goat cheese, encrusted in herbs, baked and drizzled with a fruity olive oil and blood orange vinaigrette. What else was on that postcard? And why hadn't I seen it?

"Mira?" Renata has stopped unloading the bag and is staring at me from across the kitchen table.

"What else do you have besides blood orange?" I ask. She answers by going over to her purse and pulling out a blue postcard. She hands me the card, tells me to go and take a shower, a nice hot one, and to change my clothes so that she doesn't have to look at that disgusting stain, the origin of which she does not care to know.

I make the shower as hot as I can stand and mull over the possibilities—salad and otherwise. I decide it's ridiculous to think Renata has been conspiring with Jake against me. In talking to her, Jake really hasn't committed any horrible crime, although there is the possibility he's been hiding mail from me, which might explain why I hadn't seen the postcard. I resolve to go in on Sunday to totally reorganize the office and make a concerted effort to get on top of everything.

After dressing I go to check on Chloe. She's not in her crib, but sitting at the kitchen table in Renata's lap. Renata has covered her expensive blouse with a large cotton dish towel, and Chloe is looking up at her, fascinated by the large, gold teardrop earrings swinging from Renata's ears. When Chloe sees me she smiles and reaches for me, and I scoop her up and kiss her forehead. Still warm.

"I heard her crying while you were in the shower. Poor baby," Renata coos in a high squeaky voice, which surprises me. I hadn't thought her the maternal sort.

I feed Chloe a bottle of the electrolyte solution the emergency room doctor gave us. She barely manages to finish it before she falls asleep again. I put her in her crib and, when I return, Renata has poured us each a glass of wine.

"Do you think it's normal for her to be sleeping so much?" I ask, plopping down at the table and taking a sip of the wine, a delicious full-bodied Valpolicella.

"She's sick, isn't she? What do you do when you're sick? You sleep, no?" Renata gives me a helpless shrug. "I don't know much about babies, Mira. I'm only guessing. What did the doctor say?"

I fill her in on the details of our midnight dash to the ER while Renata finishes setting out our lunch. Roasted red and yellow peppers, long-stemmed baby artichokes marinated in olive oil and herbs, several different kinds of olives, marinated white beans, and a salad of cold broccoli rabe, heavy on the garlic and hot pepper. I know she's been to Arthur Avenue in the Bronx to buy all of our favorite things, a true labor of love. I instantly regret every single paranoid thought I had about her being in cahoots with Jake.

"You know," Renata says, "I'm now also a mama." She smiles, enjoying my surprise. "Well, a stepmama anyway. Michael has a daughter."

"I didn't know. How old? Does she live with you?" It is hard to imagine a child living in Renata's loft, which is pristinely neat and minimalist.

"Oh, no," Renata says too quickly; the same thought has also apparently crossed her mind. "She's thirteen. The worst possible age for a girl. She lives with her mother on the Upper West Side. She goes to Miss Porter's." She pauses, taking a hefty gulp of her wine. "Of course, she hates me."

I'm about to say something comforting, how it takes a while in stepfamilies for everyone to settle in, but Renata holds up her hand to stop me.

"It's okay. I'm planning to buy my way into her heart. One thing about thirteen-year-old girls," she says, waving the heel of the ciabatta in my face, "is they all have their price. In Melissa's case, the price is a Prada backpack. All she wants for Christmas, the little dear. Can you believe it? A Prada backpack! I didn't have a Prada until I was thirty."

We schmooze a while longer, long enough to finish off the wine, and almost all of the cheese. I wipe up the last of the broccoli rabe with the remaining crust of bread and tell Renata about the hazelnut biscotti, which would have been the perfect finale.

"Well, it's a good thing you didn't make them, because I don't have time for coffee and I've eaten far too much anyway." Renata unties the dishcloth from around her neck and pushes her chair away from the table. It's almost one. She probably has six or seven other calls to make before the end of her day, and I feel guilty about having taken so much of her time.

"Thanks, Renata," I tell her, handing her my order, to which I have added a case each of the blood orange and black cherry vinegars. "Thanks for everything. Lunch was great." I want to say more, to tell her how much I'd needed this lunch, someone taking care of me, even in this small way. But I suspect that if I do, the conversation will quickly become maudlin and probably end in tears. Since neither of us is the mushy, sentimental type, I'm glad when she grabs me by the shoulders and gives me a shake.

"Mira," she says slowly, looking me in the eye, "just because Jake is a shit, doesn't mean you have to keep punishing yourself."

"I know," I say unconvincingly. Renata looks around the room, appraising the clutter, the busy box and ExerSaucer, Chloe's empty bottles, the papers everywhere. "First thing you should do is get yourself a cleaning lady. You're a working single mother. You can afford someone once or twice a week! Then, you've got to get out and be with people. When was the last time you went out to dinner, or lunch for that matter? When was the last time you had an adult conversation that didn't involve work? Ha! Don't answer that— I'm sure you can't remember, anyway. Get yourself a babysitter for Saturday night because I'm making reservations for us somewhere fabulous. It's about time you met Michael, and you ought to meet Arthur as well."

Arthur? But before I can even ask, Renata swings her wool merino wrap over her suit, deposits a peck on my cheek, and disappears down the hall.

chapter 4

Everyone loves New York at Christmas time, which is why I always feel funny confessing that I find it incredibly depressing. People are too full of Christmas cheer to be believable, never seeming to weary of the Musak renditions of Christmas carols played incessantly in every store and on every street corner, or the tourists clogging the streets oohing and ahhing over the hokey displays in the store windows. From October to January, the entire city appears to have undergone a collective lobotomy.

It will be Chloe's first Christmas, and this should thrill me. But the thought of putting up a tree and wrapping Chloe's gifts, which I would then have to open alone on Christmas morning, makes me ache. I'd briefly entertained the idea of going home to Pittsburgh for the holiday, but that plan was fraught with issues too exhausting to think about for very long. Besides, the holiday season is a busy one for restaurants, and it's too hard to take the time off. In the meantime, I haven't made any plans for Thanksgiving either, which might be even harder than Christmas this year. Jake and I always made a big deal about Thanksgiving, inviting several of our foodie friends over for a daylong cooking and eating extravaganza.

Renata calls to tell me we have a reservation at Le Bernadin for eight o'clock Saturday night. Prime time. She's also taken the liberty of lining up a babysitter for Chloe. Gabriella, a friend of her stepdaughter, is only fourteen but has a certificate in infant CPR and charges fifteen dollars an hour.

Renata had the audacity to suspect I was lying when I told her that Hope, my regular sitter, was sick, suffering an infection from her most recent tattoo. "Mira, I don't believe you. You just don't want to go."

She was right, of course. I was making this up, and we both knew it. I smile at the thought of Hope with a skull and crossbones emblazoned across one of her pudgy, middle-aged arms. "Well," Renata says, "I've taken care of the babysitter for you. Now, do I have to come over to help you pick out an outfit, or are you capable of dressing yourself?"

I groan into the phone.

"Just promise me that you'll wear something nice and try to plaster a smile on your face. Arthur has gone to a lot of trouble to get this reservation," Renata says peevishly.

"Who is this Arthur anyway?" I'm becoming increasingly concerned that Arthur is an eighty-year-old man, the only guy Renata has been able to come up with as a plausible date for me. No one under fifty is named Arthur.

"He's someone Michael knows. He's writing a book on the history of culinary science that Michael's editing. He writes for *Chef's Technique*. You've probably read his stuff."

"And your husband, Michael, a man whom I have never met, thinks he would be perfect for me why? Because we both know how to use a mezzaluna?"

"Look, Mira—"

"Wait a minute, is his name Arthur Cole?" I ask.

"Yes, it is. Do you know him?"

As a matter of fact, I do. I'm a regular reader of his column in *Chef's*. He's a detail freak, writing exhaustive treatises on his search for the quintessential recipe for tuna casserole, which involves trying about fifteen different versions.

"See, you do have something in common," Renata says when I tell her. "Come on, this will be fun."

"Renata, I don't know. I'm not really ready—"

"Funny, Jake didn't seem to wait too long. In fact, he didn't wait at all." I'm stunned into silence. "Mira, I had such high hopes for you. You started this divorce magnificently—just like an Italian woman. What has happened to you?"

I want to tell her that I don't feel pretty, or interesting, and that loving and hating Jake has taken up all of my available time and energy. When I don't answer her, Renata tells me what I need to hear, but don't for a minute believe.

"Mira, Jake is a consummate shit, and you are a beautiful woman in the prime of your life. Come on; buy yourself something pretty to wear. And let your hair down. Men like long hair. It's sexy."

I groan. "What Arthur Cole would find sexy is a really good recipe for short ribs."

Renata laughs. "Okay, so what's the worst thing that could happen? We have a sublime dinner, some fabulous wine, he's boring, and you go home. Right? Then we go to Plan B."

"Plan B?"

"Eddie Macarelli."

"Eddie the fish guy? Eddie Macarelli is Plan B?" I'm horrified. Eddie, while an excellent fish supplier—he handles the fish for most of the high-end restaurants in the city, doubtless including Le Bernadin—is a flamboyant guy. The kind of guy who likes to make a splash (one of Eddie's own unfortunate puns). He wears a diamond pinkie ring and talks like Tony Soprano. What possessed Renata to think we would have the slightest interest in each other?

"Renata, I can't go out with Eddie. We have a business relationship. I buy fish from him."

"So what? He likes you. I ran into him at Esca last week, and he asked about you, said he's seen more of Jake lately. He heard about the divorce and asked if you were seeing anyone. He told me he's always kind of liked you."

"I'm not divorced yet," I tell her. What I really want to say is that I have no desire to date anyone, never mind Arthur Cole or Eddie Macarelli, and I can't be forced. Suddenly I wish I'd had the foresight to come up with a more believable excuse. Ebola maybe, or a touch of bubonic plague.

"Okay, okay, forget Plan B. Let's stick with Plan A," says Renata. "Let's just go and have a wonderful dinner. Michael and I will bring Gabriella over to your place at seven. You can show her around and get Chloe settled. I'll tell Arthur we will meet him at the bar at eight."

I'm relieved when Renata hangs up, telling myself that I'm only going because no one passes up dinner at Le Bernadin.

When I arrive at Grappa the next morning, Jake is there, even though it's only a little after seven in the morning. Gesturing with the knife he's using to score the ends of cipolline, he tells me that there's some mail on the desk in the office I need to attend to. He then turns to me and says with a mysterious little smile that I also should take a look in the refrigerator where there's a small package with my name on it. Not only is Jake here uncharacteristically early, but scoring cipolline isn't the sort of work he usually does. That's the work of the sous-chefs. He looks slightly rumpled, and I again wonder what possibly could have gotten him out of bed this early.

On top of the stack of mail there's a phone message from my lawyer, in Jake's handwriting, confirming our meeting with opposing counsel on the disposition of the marital assets set for the week after Thanksgiving. Then, I open the refrigerator door, and my stomach lurches. Inside is a package wrapped in brown butcher paper and tied with string. On the package is a crude drawing of a fish with huge caricature-style cheeks. Underneath the drawing is a message scrawled in an uneven hand. "Cheeks for the sweet! Dinner for two, sometime?" I'm mortified that Jake knows old "Make a Splash" Eddie wants to date me and by this bizarre courting ritual that involves leaving halibut cheeks wrapped in butcher paper in my refrigerator.

I make myself an espresso and bring it over to the pastry station where I begin the pasta. I can hear Tony whistling in the large walk-in refrigerator as he unloads the day's shipment of meat and eggs. I measure out the semolina and deposit it into several piles of approximately equal size on the marble station. Tony has set out a large bowl of fresh eggs and several containers of pasta flavorings, two kinds of pepper (red and coarsely ground black), lemon zest, and anchovy paste. Over the years, I've trained all the sous-chefs to make pasta, but I really prefer to do it myself. It's a quiet and intense activity, a muscular workout, and relaxing, all at once. My favorite time to make pasta is in the early morning, before the full staff arrives, and before the kitchen really comes to life.

Evening is the time Jake loves best, when, at the height of the dinner service, he screams orders and brandishes kitchen knives like a frenzied maestro. During those times there's only room for one chef in the kitchen, no matter how large. When Jake and I first met, I thought we were perfectly complementary, my yin to his yang. That our relationship was better suited to a business partnership than a marriage is something I've only lately begun to realize. In a marriage, it's the little similarities that bring you closer. Nicola is more like Jake; they are both passionate people who take up the room, who burn up the space around them, who consume you, if you let them, and then toss you aside.

Jake approaches, sits down on the stool near the pastry station, and watches, silently, intently, as I knead the pasta dough. It's still in the early stage, before the gluten has developed, and I can feel the fine grains of the semolina scrape at the skin of my palms.

He doesn't say anything, and I don't look up. My hands have begun to tremble ever so slightly, and I don't know if it's because I'm working hard at suppressing an urge to strangle him or worse, grab him and kiss him. Because I'm not sure what they will do, it seems safer to keep my hands in the dough, which I know I won't be able to stop kneading as long as he's sitting there watching me.

"How's the baby?" he finally asks.

"*Chloe* is fine," I say, curtly, noticing again that Jake never calls Chloe by her name. "Totally recovered."

"Good. That's good," Jake says.

I continue working the dough. Jake continues watching me. I sense there's something more he wants to say, but I have no idea what it might be. Suddenly, I know there's not much more of this I can stand. I can't stand being here making pasta with Jake watching me, pretending that we are merely business partners.

"I'd like to come over and see her," Jake finally says. "See Chloe."

I keep kneading, unsure of what I've just heard. When I don't respond, Jake says, "I know that I haven't, ah," he pauses, "that *we* haven't worked out the details about Chloe and everything, but I won't leave the apartment with her if you don't want me to. I can just, you know, visit her. You can be there, or not."

It's unlike Jake to be so compromising, and his tone is vaguely deferential. Could it be that Chloe's near brush with death has caused him to reconsider his relationship with her?

"Sure, you can visit her. She's your daughter, after all." I look up at him for a split second. My subtle dig has had no visible effect on him.

"It would have to be a Sunday," Jake says, after a pause. We're closed on Sundays. God forbid Jake miss work to spend time with his child. So much for compromising. "Maybe in the early afternoon?"

"Sure," is all I trust myself to say.

"Well, I'll see you guys on Sunday afternoon, then," he says, standing. By the time I look up again, he has crossed the kitchen and returned to scoring the cipolline. I listen to him whistle the theme from "Musetta's Waltz," wondering what all this could possibly mean.

chapter 5

That evening after Chloe falls asleep, I dig out the last two years' worth of *Chef's Technique.* Comfortably ensconced on the couch with a glass of Barolo, I pore over Arthur Cole's articles, trying to get the measure of a man who makes eleven different attempts in search of the perfect spinach salad and writes, in excruciating detail, about each one.

As a person who eschews written recipes, I don't dwell on the obvious irony that I have at least five years' worth of back issues of *Gourmet, Bon Appétit, Saveur,* and, of course, *Chef's.* The more recent issues I keep on shelves in the kitchen; the rest are in carefully marked boxes, with the index of each issue taped to the box top. I don't attempt to analyze this behavior. All I know is that it is somehow comforting to know that if I ever have to whip up some bibimbap (*Gourmet,* August 2004) on short notice for visiting Korean dignitaries, I can. I also know that I probably shouldn't begrudge Mr. Cole his obsessions.

On Saturday afternoon, during Chloe's afternoon nap, I finally get around to thinking about what I will wear on my date and find that my wardrobe is a complete disaster. I haven't been shopping in months, practically since Chloe was born. Jake's drawstring chef's pants and either a chef's tunic or a big white shirt had gotten me through most of my pregnancy, and I had borrowed the rest, a party dress, a winter coat, and a couple of jumpers (which I hated). It wasn't the pregnancy, though, that kept me out of the stores. In the restaurant business you learn very quickly the value and comfort of the uniform. And pretty soon it becomes a way of life.

I finally choose a pair of black crepe pants and a black cashmere sweater. I consider heeding Renata's advice about leaving my hair down, but somehow I don't think long hair will be a turn on for Arthur. Someone that compulsive would surely be made uncomfortable by untamed hair. I settle for a simple chignon.

Gabriella, with Michael and Renata in tow, arrives precisely at seven, and from the instant they step into the room, Chloe begins to cry. Her whole body stiffens as she locks me in a death grip. Michael is the one who finally takes charge, removing Chloe from me and placing her in Gabriella's waiting arms. Then, Michael, to whom I've barely been introduced, gently but firmly maneuvers me out of the door and into the elevator. Once we are settled in the cab, he gives my shoulder a reassuring squeeze.

"She stopped crying before we even made it into the lobby, you know. They do that just to torture us, a conspiracy among babies everywhere."

"I feel like a wretch for leaving her. She doesn't know Gabriella and she's not used to being left with a babysitter at night."

"It's your own fault, Mira," says Renata. "You should have been doing this months ago. She'd be used to it by now."

"Ha," laughs Michael, giving me a knowing look. "They never get used to it."

Renata quickly steers the conversation clear of children, and we chat about what we're planning to eat, and laugh over the fact that none of us has eaten all day in preparation for tonight. This allows me an opportunity to sneak a look at Renata's husband who, I decide, isn't at all what I expected. For starters, he's much older than I imagined. He looks to be somewhere in his mid-fifties, making him roughly a decade older than Renata. He isn't a handsome man; his nose is too large and his eyes too small, but they're a lovely blue, soft and friendly. He's got a nice full head of dark hair, going silvery at the temples, and a small, neatly trimmed beard, black and flecked with gray. But what makes him not seem Renata's type is that he's a comfortable man, rumpled and slightly squishy around the edges, the sort whose preference might run toward flannel and gabardine instead of silk and cashmere. The kind of man who might own, and occasionally even wear, a sweat suit.

Compared to the few male friends of Renata's I've met on previous occasions, all of whom were younger than she, handsome, and impeccably groomed, Michael seems less sophisticated. But Renata seems different, too, softer than usual and more relaxed. She's taller than Michael, and the way he drapes his arm around her shoulders is awkward, yet occasionally he gives her an affectionate squeeze. A trace of a giggle escapes her as he whispers something inaudible, something, I imagine, so silly and tender that I glimpse, for an instant, the girl she'd once been. Already I like Michael and think Renata's lucky. There simply aren't enough men who can make women giggle, or who even care to try.

Le Bernadin is one of only a handful of Manhattan restaurants—including La Grenouille, the Four Seasons, and Café des Artistes—that has endured, almost unaltered, since its opening. Within months of its New York debut in January 1986, *Gourmet* magazine bestowed upon Le Bernadin and its chefs/owners, Gilbert and Maguy Le Coze, an unprecedented four-star rating, a historic event in the restaurant world. Now, a quarter of a century later, it has become one of New York's grande dames. If Le Bernadin were a woman, as I think most restaurants are, she would be Grace Kelly—beautiful, elegant, and understated.

The bar is crowded, and at first I don't see Arthur Cole, whom I think I'll recognize from the miniscule photograph that appears above his byline in *Chef's*. Michael spots him instantly. He's sitting with his back to the door, engaged in conversation with the bartender, probably interviewing him about how to make the perfect mai tai. When Michael taps him on the shoulder, he turns and, with one fluid movement, flips his notebook closed. "Now, Arthur, you are officially off duty tonight. You'll make me look bad," Michael says with a trace of a smile, gesturing to the notebook that Arthur is in the process of thrusting into his breast pocket. They shake hands, and Michael gives him a small pat on the arm. Arthur's hair is longer than in his picture in *Chef's,* and he's not wearing glasses, which in the picture are small and round.

"Mira, is it?" he says, turning to me and offering his hand. "It's lovely to meet you."

His smile is automatic, revealing a set of even, white teeth. He's immaculately groomed, and his hands look as if they are regularly manicured, making me instantly conscious of my own short, trimmed nails and workman's hands, ruddy and rough-skinned, which I have no choice but to offer in return.

Renata, who had been waylaid by a friend on the way to the bar, joins us, and Michael completes the introductions. Arthur quickly summons the bartender, and we order our drinks. I order myself a glass of Prosecco.

"Ah, Prosecco, a wonderful choice! It's great to see this previously little known aperitif is finally getting its due," Arthur says excitedly. "Of course, I mean outside of Italy," he adds, nodding in deference to Renata. "Are you familiar with this vineyard?" Arthur asks. As it turns out, I am, but Arthur doesn't wait for me to answer. Instead, he turns to Renata and Michael and says, "Do you mind? Why don't we order a bottle? Mira here has made a wonderful suggestion."

"I think you'll like it," I say. "It's a wonderful vintage from a small winery in the north of Italy. In Fruili." Why do I feel as if I'm in the midst of a job interview? "We stock it in the cellar at Grappa."

"Grappa?"

"Yes, our—my restaurant," I tell him, my tone a little more proprietary than I'd intended.

A flicker of recognition passes across Arthur's well-mannered face. I wonder if he's heard something and is only now putting two and two together. "Ah, yes, of course," he says. I can only hope that he has heard the short version of my sordid story and not the longer, assault and battery one. But, judging from his embarrassed look, and the way his eyes flit quickly toward the door, I suspect the latter. He has already decided that I'm an incalculable risk and is wondering just how quickly he can make an exit.

"Mira, my apologies," says Michael. "Renata has so many customers, and I couldn't recall the name of your restaurant when I told Arthur about you."

"I'm afraid I've never eaten there," Arthur says, with no trace of apology.

"Well, then you must come sometime."

"It's really a wonderful restaurant, Arthur," Renata pipes in. "Mira and her ex-husband started it on a shoestring, not unlike Le Bernadin. It's quite a success story." I chafe at the mention of Jake, my "ex-husband," and my leg accidentally bumps Renata's under the table.

I'm relieved when the Prosecco arrives and even more relieved when the maître d' approaches us with the news that our table is ready. Arthur balances his glass of Prosecco with one hand, and rests his other hand on my elbow as we make our way to the dining room. He leans into me, veering me slightly off course and, as I struggle to realign myself, I catch him sneaking a peek down my sweater. "So, what started you cooking, Mira?"

"My mother, actually. She was a chef."

"Oh? How interesting! Where did she train?"

"In Paris," I tell him, "at the Cordon Bleu."

"Really? Impressive for a woman of your mother's generation. Where did she cook?"

"Well, when I knew her, she cooked at home. Just for our family." The truth was my mother had never really made use of her impressive French pedigree, something she'd always regretted. While studying there she met my father, who was in the army and on leave in Paris. She was just finishing up her two-year course in French gastronomy; they married as soon as his tour of duty was up.

"In Manhattan?"

"No, in Pittsburgh. I grew up in Pittsburgh."

"In Pittsburgh?" Arthur says, a small snort escaping him. "An unlikely place for a classically trained chef."

"People have been known to eat in Pittsburgh, you know," I tell him, with a backwards glance as he pulls out my chair. The man is a snob.

"Well, of course they do. I just meant that, well, even today, it's not exactly the bastion of haute cuisine. Twenty, thirty years ago, forget it. In fact, can you remember the last time a Pittsburgh restaurant was featured in *Bon Appétit?*"

Touché. In fact, the only time I can remember a Pittsburgh restaurant being mentioned in a national magazine was several years ago when *Gourmet* mentioned Primanti Brothers in an interview with Mario Batali (who'd eaten there on a recent trip and enjoyed it). For the uninitiated, the Primanti sandwich is a cheesesteak sub, served on thick slabs of crusty Italian bread and topped with very well-done grease-still-glistening French fries, coleslaw, and, if you're really a traditionalist, a fried egg. Apparently, it has become the signature food of Pittsburgh. I do not remind Arthur Cole of this fact.

The bread basket is presented to us—warm, crusty, French farmhouse rolls with an herb and goat cheese spread. We study our menus, considering the delights within. I look over at Renata, who I can see is already mapping out how we can best cover the most ground. This, of course, involves sharing.

Some people are funny about that, and I'm betting Arthur Cole is one of them. You can tell a lot about a person by how liberal he is about sharing his food. That was one of the first things that had attracted me to Jake. I first met him when we were both waiting for a table at a little roadside trattoria in Piacenza. We were each overjoyed to find someone who could speak English and decided to share a table. During that first meal together he casually reached over and speared a piece of my calamari, delicately grabbing it by the ring with a single tine of his fork. It was an intimate gesture, and one that might have shocked me had I not already decided to sleep with him—which I did, immediately following dessert and espresso.

"Oh, look," says Michael, "fresh sardines."

"I'm looking at the spiny lobster with cepes risotto," says Renata, her nose buried in the menu.

"Imagine, pairing the most delicate of shellfish with such a strong fungal flavor," offers Arthur, wrinkling his nose. "Interesting, if he can pull it off." He sounds doubtful.

The subject of our dinner conversation is the demise of the

American restaurant, a not-quite-open forum conducted in sotto voce by Arthur, who has emerged from his research on culinary history finding America's traditions wanting.

"There simply are no traditions. Everything has been imported. There's nothing originally American, except perhaps corn." He waves a hand dismissively. "Not even the hamburger can we claim as our own!" he says with a sneer, as if anyone would want to.

When no one picks up the gauntlet Arthur has so conspicuously thrown, he continues unabashed. "Why then," he says, suddenly turning to me and folding his arms across his chest, "did your mother study in France? Why did you study in Italy? Which I presume you did because you know as well as I do that no culinary education is considered complete without an international apprenticeship." His voice is smug, his mouth curled in a half smile.

"Wait a minute," I say, feeling suddenly compelled to defend American culinary tradition (not to mention my own expensive and, in my opinion, extremely comprehensive education at the Culinary Institute of America). "I studied in Italy because I cook Italian food. My mother studied in France because in the late 1960s there was no other option. But that certainly doesn't mean that there isn't a rich and varied culinary tradition in America today. Stop at a roadside barbeque in Texas, eat a lobster roll in Bangor, Maine, order a fried egg on your Primanti sandwich in Pittsburgh, for heaven's sake!" I look over at Michael, who is humming the national anthem, his right hand on his heart, his left raised in mock salute. The moment dissolves into laughter, all of us, except perhaps Arthur, slightly embarrassed to have taken ourselves so seriously.

Arthur, I'm uncharitably pleased to note, is sporting a stray kernel of cepes risotto on his Fendi tie. Despite expressing his initial doubts about the dish, he ended up ordering it, anyway, and then—suspicions confirmed—was loath to share all but the tiniest taste.

We are all so full by dessert that we only order two, a tarte tatin and a cheese and fruit plate. When Arthur makes as if to summon the sommelier, Renata wrestles his arm to the table.

"Arthur, if you order another bottle of wine, I will fall into my cheese."

"Yes, she gets sloppy when she's drunk, to that I will attest," says Michael, a small belch escaping him.

"Are you sure? A small digestif, Michael, might be just the ticket."

I'm feeling slightly woozy myself, which I attribute to the wine, the rich food, and the lateness of the hour. I wonder fleetingly if Arthur Cole could be trying to get me drunk. His perfectly manicured hand is now lying mere inches from my own, his fingers slightly greasy from the shellfish. For some reason, I find this small and insignificant departure from perfection endearing. For several moments I can't stop thinking about his hands, which I imagine on my body. Not that I want them to be—in fact, I'm quite sure I don't. I look over at Renata, who has taken Michael's hand and is softly running her fingers across his knuckles. This gets me thinking about Michael's hands, which disturbs me even further. What's the matter with me? I must be drunk.

Arthur doesn't join us on the way home. He lives on the Upper East Side (where else?), and we are headed to the Village. Outside the restaurant he shakes my hand. "Lovely meal. Lovely," he says, planting a disinterested peck on my cheek. And then he's gone.

In the cab on the way home, Renata lays her head on Michael's shoulder and within seconds begins to snore. "You want to know the worst thing about foodies?" Michael asks, resting his head on the back of the cab and yawning. "I mean the diehards like Arthur Cole? They have no sense of humor. My God—it's only food!"

Michael may be right, but that still doesn't stop me from wondering why Arthur Cole, insufferable bore, found me so unappealing that he could barely muster a decent good night. Suddenly there's a lump in my throat and a tingling behind my eyes. Why should this upset me? This date I hadn't even wanted, with a guy I didn't even like.

"At least the food was exceptional," Michael says, and I can feel him turning to look at me. I'm not sure I trust myself to speak. "I'm sorry, Mira," he says softly. "But at least it's over."

"Yes, I don't think I'll be hearing from Arthur Cole." This I manage through tightened lips.

"No, I didn't mean that. If I know Arthur, he'll probably give you a call. He can sometimes be a little slow on the uptake socially, if you know what I mean. What I meant was the date. Your first post-separation date. It's over. That's a milestone. Welcome to the rest of your life, Mira," he says solemnly, offering me his hand. Suddenly, it's as if someone has loosened the plug in my throat, and I'm crying.

Michael pulls a wad of tissues from his pocket and hands them to me. "I know just how you feel," he says softly, wrapping his arm around me and patting my back. I bury my face in his jacket, which smells of the evening, of shellfish, and wine, and the subtle underlying scent of tobacco. The comfort of it sucks the breath from my body. When the cab pulls up in front of my building, Michael gently disengages me.

"Good night and thank you," I tell him, more formally than I intended, embarrassed at having sobbed for the last twenty blocks on the shoulder of my friend's husband, a man I hadn't met before tonight. "I'll send Gabriella down," I say, offering my hand. Michael gives it a reassuring squeeze. "It will get better, I promise, Mira," he says, gesturing to the still sleeping Renata. "Just be thankful this was only a date. At least you don't have to read his three hundred and fifty-page treatise on the germination of corn."

chapter 6

I'm out of practice. The rich food and the wine catch up with me, and I awaken at the uncharacteristically late hour of seven thirty with a touch of a hangover. This is the first time in the almost eight months since Chloe's birth that I can remember sleeping so late. I can hear her cooing and talking in her crib, making little raspberry noises and laughing to herself. She doesn't cry, blessed child, and I hold off getting up because once she hears me she will no longer be content to lie in her crib and amuse herself. She will want me to come in and sing her morning song, which she has lately begun to imitate, mimicking the cadence of the melody with her own little coos and squeals.

It's Sunday and an overcast one by the look of it, my favorite kind. I know few people who love rain like I do. Usually, rain makes me want to make soup and bake bread, to settle in and snuggle up. Maybe it's an adaptive response to having grown up in Pittsburgh, not a particularly sunny city. I settle back into the pillows and listen to Chloe's sweet voice and the pleasant patter of rain on the bedroom window. But there's a knot in the pit of my stomach, which at first I attribute to the hangover. It takes me a couple of minutes to realize that today is Sunday, and this afternoon Jake is coming by to see Chloe. Suddenly alert, I sit up in bed where I can see the message light on the bedside phone blinking at me. Gabriella said there had been a couple of calls, which she let the machine pick up while she was putting Chloe to sleep. I hit the Play button.

"Hi, Mira. It's Jake. Just calling to confirm my visit with Chloe." Pause. "Remember we talked about my coming over tomorrow afternoon?" There's another awkward pause as if Jake is expecting me to answer him. I can only hope he was wondering where I would be at ten thirty on a Saturday night. "Well, I was thinking about three o'clock. I have a couple of things to do earlier in the day, but I thought after her . . . Well, I don't know if she takes a nap or anything, but, if that time isn't good, just, I don't know, call me."

I'm still ruminating over Jake's message—of course she takes a nap and three is prime napping time—when I realize another message is still playing.

". . . never call me. Where are you? Have you been carted off to jail again—which is, by the way, about the only decent excuse you'd have for not getting back to me. Your father hasn't even heard from you. You should call him, too, you know. Anyway, what are you doing for Thanksgiving? Feel like some company?? The Steelers are playing the Jets in New York next Sunday. I can get a flight out on Wednesday, and, if you can get me a ticket to the game, I'll love you forever. Call me, you little shit, okay?" The message ends with an abrupt click. Richard, I think, with a smile. In fact, the last time I'd talked to him *had* been practically from jail—it was the day of the court hearing, and I ended up crying into the phone, spilling the whole sordid story, sparing nothing. That had been over two months ago. No wonder he was miffed.

I've known Richard Kistler more than half my life; in fact, he likes to tell people we grew up together, although he's sixteen years my senior. I met him at an AA meeting I attended when I was fifteen years old. By the time I was a sophomore in high school, several stints in treatment hadn't been able to cure my mother of a serious drinking problem, and her condition had escalated to the point of medical emergency. The transition from the sophisticated world of Parisian haute cuisine to Pittsburgh, land of pierogies, Jello molds, and Miracle Whip dips, had been an especially difficult one for my mother—one apparently made much more so by one significant complication: me. Motherhood, she often reflected in her more lucid moments, had been her downfall, sending her careening down the road to ruin, a fifth of Seagram's neatly concealed in the diaper bag.

Our next-door neighbor, Mrs. Favish, who, along with her posse of neighborhood Jewish grandmothers, was closely monitoring the goings-on in my family, had been the one to suggest Al-Anon to me. She'd told me in her heavily accented English that, although it was not a disease common to her people, her sister's husband also fought the same demons as my mother. That was the way she liked to put it, as if alcoholism was an evil spirit, rash and unaccountable, who snuck up on you and took you unawares while you were minding your own business.

Mrs. Favish dropped me off outside the Wightman School one Tuesday night in December. She'd wanted to accompany me in, but I hadn't let her. After watching her drive away, I stood under the streetlamp smoking cigarettes purloined from my mother's purse, trying to get up the nerve to go inside. Richard found me there, shivering in my jean jacket, and, guessing where I needed to go, delivered me to the classroom on the second floor. The real alcoholics met in the basement, and there had been a light turnout for his meeting, which, apparently, was the norm during the holiday months. Many alcoholics relapse during the weeks between Thanksgiving and New Year's, Richard later told me. Something about the holidays made it easier to recall, and harder to resist, all the pretty good reasons they have for drinking.

Even though I was the only kid in my Al-Anon meeting, I kept going back faithfully, week after week. Maybe it was the sympathetic faces of the members, mostly women, sweet maternal types, careful, indulgent listeners—who, just for the record, weren't listening to me; I was a silent fixture in the meetings, an angry kid, reeking of stale smoke and cheap Jovan musk oil. Perhaps it was the idea of having a secret—I hadn't told my parents I was going. No one knew—except Mrs. Favish.

Probably what kept me going was Richard. Eventually we became friends. Often when my meeting got out, Richard would be waiting for me. I soon learned he'd been attending the twice-weekly AA meetings for about a year and a half. He had gone at the insistence of his lover. Although the relationship didn't survive, by the time they were ready to throw in the towel Richard had totally quit drinking and had formed a surprisingly supportive network of friends at AA, most of them middle-aged ex-steelworkers who had, over the years, consumed a few too many Iron Cities. He claimed they put up with him because Richard's failed love affair now left one of his Steelers season tickets unused. Still, it was a pretty amazing trick for a thirty-something, gay antiques dealer with a former taste for expensive, single malt whiskey.

It was sweet of him to ask about Thanksgiving. It would be nice to have some company. I'd invited Renata and Michael, but they were going to be in Bermuda. Hope has been hinting around for an invitation, but the thought of two single, middle-aged women alone with a turkey breast had been simply too depressing to contemplate, so I hadn't picked up the bait. It would be nice to have Richard, though. He'd liven things up, and I'd invite Hope, too—a good deed, I tell myself.

By the time I finally put Chloe down for a nap, it's already two o'clock, and I've yet to call Jake back. I reach his voice mail and leave a message for him to call me. I also call Richard, who is probably at today's Steelers game, and leave him a message as well. "Hi, it's Mira. I'm still on the streets, temporarily at least, but I'm resisting all attempts at rehabilitation. If I can't manage to graduate from anger management, they will lock me up and throw away the key. Help! We would love to see you for Thanksgiving, and yes, I promise I *will* call my father."

But I don't, not yet at least.

It's the sort of rainy day in mid-November when the lamps need to be lit in the middle of the afternoon and you find yourself wishing you owned a cardigan. While Chloe sleeps, I change my clothes. No reason to greet Jake in a flour-covered sweat suit. I put on a blue V-necked sweater and, almost as an afterthought, loosen and brush my hair. The apartment, which I take some pains to tidy up, is suffused with a cozy, apricot glow, the rich woodsy smell of a long-simmering soup, and the heady aroma of freshly baked bread.

I turn on the gas fireplace, put on a Diana Krall CD, and settle into the sofa with the Sunday *Times*. The doorbell rings a little after three, and when I open the door, Jake is standing there in the doorway, holding a small stuffed gorilla.

"Hi."

"Hey," he says, gesturing sheepishly with the gorilla and looking around me into the apartment.

"Sorry, ah, come in. Chloe's still sleeping. I tried to call you. Did you get my message?"

"Yeah, I did. You didn't say what you were calling about, and I was in the neighborhood anyway, so I just came." There's an edge to his voice, as if he thinks I'm trying to get away with something. He takes off his windbreaker, which is slightly damp and smells of cigarette smoke. You wouldn't think it, but quite a few chefs smoke. I'd quit years ago, long before I'd even met Jake, but he still occasionally smoked, usually when he'd had a few too many. Or when he was nervous.

For reasons I can't fathom, Jake seems desperate to see Chloe. He was probably afraid that I was going to cancel on him, when actually nothing could have been farther from the truth. I *want* Jake to see Chloe.

He hangs his coat on the hook by the door. Like he still lives here. Then, he makes for the sofa, sits down in the spot I've just vacated, and begins flipping absently through the *Times,* the gorilla in his lap.

"Nice gorilla." My voice is teasing and, if I'm not mistaken, a tad flirtatious.

I've gotten him to smile at least.

"She ought to be getting up any time now. It's late for her to be sleeping," I tell him, even though it isn't. I don't offer to wake her, which I'm sure Jake would prefer so as not to have to sit in awkward silence in a living room that used to be his. "Want some minestra? I think I got the last spollichini of the season."

Jake follows me into the kitchen, lured presumably by the promise of the luscious legume, and grateful, I'm sure, for something to do. He lifts the lid and gives the soup a stir, closing his eyes and allowing the steam to waft up and moisten his face.

"Buono," he says, giving it a taste. Standing beside him I'm filled with longing, a jolt so piercing that I have to grab the counter to keep from doubling over. I can't believe he's no longer mine to touch, to hold, that we can't just take advantage of the fact that Chloe is napping and tumble into bed together. Jake looks up from the soup and meets my eye, a brief look, but I can tell he knows what I'm feeling.

"I'll have some," he says, looking quickly away.

I reach into the cupboard behind the stove for a bowl, which I hand to Jake without looking at him. He ladles himself some soup and picks up a bottle of wine on the counter.

"Okay?" he asks.

"Sure, it's already open," I say, handing him two glasses. While I get myself some soup, Jake pours the wine, and we eat in silence at the kitchen table where we have probably sat no less than a thousand times.

"Marvin's family is producing some really great pork," Jake says, out of nowhere, his mouth half full. Marvin Castelli is a farmer we know in Bucks County, whose family produces some of the best goat's milk cheese in the country.

"Really?"

"Yeah. We were out there last weekend. He's just back from San Daniele. Spent three months there studying their curing methods. His prosciutto is not quite there, but give him time. The pork was good, though. No, better than good. I'm thinking of placing an order."

The "we," I'm sure, includes Nicola.

Jake helps himself to more wine and reaches over to refill my glass. "At some point we should talk about making some seasonal changes to the menu. The holidays are almost here."

"Sure," I tell him, "maybe after our meeting."

"Meeting?"

I'm tempted to remind him none too gently about the meeting we have scheduled with our lawyers the Thursday after Thanksgiving to dispose of the remaining marital assets. It was the thinly veiled reference to Nicola that made me want to remind him that all this companionable eating together really hasn't changed the fact that we are about to be divorced.

"Oh, that meeting." Jake takes another bite of soup and chews thoughtfully.

We stare into our empty soup bowls. Jake looks across the table at me as if he's about to say something. I'm feeling hot and muddled, and the wine has caused an unpleasant flush to spread across my neck. Suddenly, I'm confused about everything, about why Jake is here, about why I didn't tell him this was Chloe's nap time, about whether we could ever exist like this, two parents who aren't together showing up at school functions, chatting amiably over punch and cookies at the PTA Fun Fair.

I gather up the bowls and take them to the sink, glad to have my back to him. I can tell without turning around that he's standing behind me. Suddenly, Jake reaches around me and puts his hand on my arm. He is standing so close that I can feel his breath on my hair.

"I'm sorry, Mira," he whispers, his voice so soft and low I think I've imagined it. Because he is standing so close to me, I brush against him as I turn around and suddenly we are kissing. It is strange and thrilling to be in his arms. Jake's hand cradles my head, his fingers entangled in my hair. With his other hand he grabs my arm and pulls me closer to him. His movements are rough, angry even, which I easily mistake for passion, because it's what I want. I feel the tears on my face, and I'm trembling and crying and gulping for air but all I can do is breathe in Jake, his mouth and tongue. His body is pressed close, his arm encircling my waist. It's several seconds before I realize that it's he who is crying, not me. Jake pushes me from him and I stumble, hitting the small of my back against the counter. My legs are weak, and I'm shaking. He puts both arms on the counter and hangs his head. I have never seen him cry before.

For several seconds I stand there with my back pressed against the counter. Then, I reach for Jake and put my hand consolingly on his arm. He shakes it off, not violently, but firmly, and stalks off in the direction of Chloe's room.

I don't know what he means to do and, terrified, I follow him.

The blinds in Chloe's room are partially drawn, and the murky afternoon light is filtering in, casting violet shadows on the walls, the bed, on Chloe's face. Jake stands by her crib looking down at her. His back is to me, so I cannot see his face, cannot tell what he is thinking, or if he's still crying. The opening of the door has disturbed Chloe. It begins as a gurgle, a whimper, followed by a tetchy, disgruntled half cry. Jake doesn't move, and because Chloe isn't used to the inactivity of adults whom she has summoned with her cries, she becomes more insistent, kicking her feet, attempting to rid herself of the blanket in which she's become entangled. And because I don't know what is best, best for Jake I mean—Chloe can survive a few minutes' cry—I don't do anything. I let her cry, hoping she can't see me standing in the doorway. He reaches into the crib and draws his hand gently across her cheek. She rolls away from him and onto her stomach, bent on escape. I lurch as Jake reaches into the crib to pick her up because I can't remember him ever picking her up and I'm not sure he knows how.

She's heavy and awkward in his arms, and he turns helplessly toward me. When Chloe catches sight of me, her cries become more piercing, and her little body grows rigid with indignation. I take her from him, pulling her close to my chest, and I move closer to Jake, so she can see him. She tugs at my shirt, and I know she wants to nurse. I take her chubby little fingers in my own and kiss them. "She's hungry and wet, poor thing, that's all." My voice is hushed, meant to soothe them both. "Jake, there's a bottle of juice in the fridge. Why don't you get it? I'll change her diaper, and then you can feed her." Jake leaves the room wordlessly, and I turn on Chloe's lamp and get her a clean diaper. She's calmer now, soothed by the low sound of my voice and by my familiar touch. "Daddy's coming with your juice. Be nice," I whisper. Don't scare him. Make him love you. It isn't until I hear the front door catch, as it only does when you shut it very slowly and quietly, that I realize Chloe and I are alone.

chapter 7

Before we opened Grappa, Jake and I would often walk down to J.J. Walker Park on our summer evenings off to cheer for whichever Little League teams were playing that night. We'd sit in the bleachers and watch the sweaty little boys spitting, swinging their bats, chalking their hands, and chewing big wads of bubble gum we knew they were pretending was tobacco. Surrounded by their grubby, ice cream–smeared siblings and their tired, happy parents, we would cheer loudly and zealously for the losing team.

I can remember thinking back then that Jake was the sort of person I could imagine one day coaching our child's team. And from there it wasn't too much of a stretch to picture him in a tie and jacket, kneeling close to the stage in order to snap a photo of our budding little Mozart knocking out "Twinkle Twinkle" at her first piano recital. Seeing the naked pleasure on his face as the chubby shortstop finally managed to catch the ball, watching him cheer with such utter abandon for a bunch of sweaty little kids he didn't even know, it had been easy, I suppose, to mistake his zeal for reserves of untapped paternal warmth. It never occurred to me that he could cheer with such abandon precisely because they *weren't* his children.

Could I somehow have foreseen Jake's reaction to parenthood?

Surely there must have been some clues, some evidence that Jake would have behaved as he has, but no matter how many times I replay scenes from our pre-Chloe marriage, I cannot find them. Was there some terror lurking in his past, some way in which his own parents had failed him that could explain his reluctance to connect, even in some small way, to his daughter? If there was, he hadn't shared it with me, and I could not divine it.

Jake's father is a distant man, but not an unfeeling one. Jake's mother is a sweet, pleasant woman. But we didn't see them much. I really don't know Jake's parents particularly well and, in fact, have only spoken to them once since the split. They have never shown much interest in Chloe, which of course irritates me, but I suppose not all grandparents are kid people, especially those who fancy themselves too young, too fit, and too much on the go to be saddled with such an elderly moniker and all of its encumbrances.

But, if I thought I could look for clues in Jake's past, then I also had my own to contend with. If something in Jake's past was keeping him from being a father to Chloe, then what of mine? I had loved being pregnant, relished every ache and kick. I gave up wine with dinner and drank milk by the gallon. I endured the discomfort of long days on my feet in the kitchen, not to mention an aching back, so consumed had I been with wanting Chloe. But where had that come from?

Certainly not from my own mother, a woman who could count among her many accomplishments speaking fluent French, making a perfect soufflé, and drinking a fifth of Seagram's daily. No, credit for my being any kind of a decent mother goes to my father, who did his best, who braided and brushed my hair at night, who read to me and coached my softball team, who made sure I practiced the piano and that my homework was done. Parenthood isn't something you can force on a person. Had my father realized this too? Had he wanted me enough for the two of them? Had I wanted Chloe that much?

I feel a pang of guilt at the thought of my dad, whom I haven't called in over a month. He has left me two messages in the interim, short ones, to the point and without one whit of guilt-inducing rhetoric embedded in them. He isn't the type to call often, but I know he's been worried about me lately. He is, by nature, a solitary guy, a widower and a professor of theoretical physics at Carnegie Mellon University, one who would rather contemplate the mathematical irregularities of the universe than hold a conversation with a fellow human being. Yet, he's solid and stoic, ready to be helpful so long as it doesn't involve an overly emotional response.

I've done my best to spare him the details of my separation. My humiliation would have embarrassed him, and, as for the sordid details, I've never really progressed psychologically to the point of being able to talk about sex in front of my dad. I'd even put off telling him about the separation for several weeks, thinking that it might blow over and Jake and I would be back together and he would be none the wiser. That I've been too immersed in my own personal funk to even return his calls is wretched.

Later in the evening, I call him, intending to invite him for Thanksgiving, along with Richard. I'm startled to get his machine at nine thirty on a Sunday evening, when he is always at home watching PBS. Not only that, he has recorded a new message, one that actually lets the caller know he or she is talking to a person with a name and not just some phone number. "Hi, this is Joe. I'm not here, so leave a message at the beep, and I'll get back to you." His voice sounds peppy and cheerful. Usually his message is something like "Hello. You have reached six-zero-nine-four-five-zero-seven." My father does not say "oh" for zero, this being one of his pet peeves—"oh," he will tell you, "is *not* a number!"

"Dad? Hi, it's Mira. Just calling to see how you are. Oh, and to invite you for Thanksgiving. I know it's last minute, but Richard called and said he's coming, and Chloe and I would love it if you can come too. Talk to you soon." At the last second, my throat begins to close, and I'm suddenly overcome with missing my father, his comforting, calm, and logical approach to any of life's conundrums. I whisper a throaty "Love you, Dad," just as the machine beeps.

The next morning, after dropping Chloe off at day care, I stop at the Beanery for a cappuccino, something I almost never do. Usually, I prefer to get into work early and have coffee there, but this morning I'm avoiding the restaurant, not certain whether Jake will be there, and dreading the inevitable awkwardness of our next meeting. Just in case he is at the restaurant when I get there, I decide to make some notes about the seasonal menu changes. That way we will have something to discuss apart from what did and didn't happen yesterday. I'm intrigued by Jake's mention of the Castelli Farms pork. And anything made with wild boar. Perhaps a wild boar ragout with braised carrots and fennel. Sausages are a must, lamb and spicy pork, served with black pepper flecked polenta. Mussels steamed in sweet vermouth, a salad of chicory and fresh anchovies with a warm caper vinaigrette. Finally, armed with enough ideas to ensure that we need never mention yesterday, I'm ready to take on Jake.

Only when I arrive at Grappa, it's not Jake who is waiting for me, but Nicola. I haven't seen her in months—I figured she was staying out of my way. I'm so surprised to see her sitting on a stool at the pastry station that I stop dead in my tracks at the kitchen door. She's wearing a pair of faded black, drawstring pants and an oversized chef's tunic, probably Jake's. She's cut her hair short in a pixieish bob (probably to better hide the bald spot, I think with satisfaction), and if the look is slightly less sultry, she makes up for it by looking utterly, charmingly, the gamine.

She swivels on her stool at the sound of the door, tucks her short hair behind her ears, and flashes me a saccharine smile. Of all the things I could be thinking, I'm struck by the fact that I can't ever recall seeing her in the strong morning light. When I was working full-time and she was maîtress, she typically didn't come in until the dinner shift. She appears out of her element here, in the morning in her outsized clothes, making me think, as I so often have, that she is a woman suited to the night.

I'm tempted to hint darkly that I think her brave, or to wonder aloud if we are alone, when I hear Tony whistling in the walk-in where he's probably hiding, so as to observe the fireworks from a place of relative safety.

"Relax, Mira, I won't report you for violating the restraining order," she says coolly. "Jake is sick. He has food poisoning. Hasn't moved since he got back from your place yesterday." She flashes me an accusatory look. "You'll have to fill in tonight."

Ignoring the dig at my culinary prowess, I reply just as coolly, "That's impossible, I'm afraid. And even if it were possible, I don't take orders from you, Nicola. You work for me, remember?"

"Yes, well. Would you like me to call Jake so he can tell you himself?" Her tone is proprietary and condescending.

Concealing from her the horror that particular suggestion evokes, I begin to consider the odd fact of Nicola's presence here this morning, which cannot be explained solely by Jake's specious case of food poisoning.

Jake would not have told her what happened at the apartment yesterday. That would have been a mistake of gargantuan proportions and one that an experienced adulterer like Jake would never make. There's a strange glimmer in Nicola's eyes as she fixes me with her intense gaze, and suddenly it dawns on me that she's worried. Worried that something happened yesterday between Jake and me, and she's here looking for clues she thinks I will reveal. And so I smile at her, an utterly false smile, one that hints of secrets and clandestine meetings, of *satisfaction*.

"Don't disturb him," I say casually, taking off my raincoat and depositing my bag next to her on the pastry station. "I'll take care of it." Without giving her a chance to respond, I set off in the direction of the walk-in. Tony is there, crouching in the corner, riffling through a basket of wild mushrooms.

"Good morning, Tony," I call, my voice louder than it needs to be. "Do we have any pumpkin pasta sheets left, or do we need to make some more? How are we on sage?" Tony and I have worked together long enough for him to know that this let's-get-down-to-business tone is all for Nicola's benefit, and he has the good grace to play along.

"Plenty," he says, tossing me a bunch of sage and gesturing over his shoulder to the pasta. "How about we do some fried sage leaves?" He lowers his voice. "Don't worry. The crew will be here in a few, and we can figure out what to do about tonight. About Jake."

I nod, and he gives me a wink as he squeezes past me with the basket of mushrooms. Nicola is on the phone when I come out, probably with Jake, because she turns away and lowers her voice as I pass.

I set out my supplies for the pasta and head into the office, where I write Jake a note, including a draft of my proposed winter menu and suggesting that he go ahead and place an order for the Castelli Farms pork. I also attach the meat and fish orders for the week after Thanksgiving, which need to be put in today. Normally I would leave them for him in the office, but since he won't be in, I'll send them home with Nicola, figuring that he can take care of them from there.

When I see that she is off the phone, I hand her a large, brown envelope containing the orders and tell her that Jake needs to see this ASAP, and if he is not up to taking care of this, he's to call me this afternoon. Nicola eyes me speculatively as she takes the envelope. She doesn't stay long and leaves without saying good-bye, a fact I barely notice because by then I'm deep into the pappardelle. Tony appears a few minutes later with two espressos, into which he pours hefty shots of anisette.

"It's still morning, so I thought we needed the coffee to be legit. It's not tippling if you have it in coffee, you know. Besides, you look like you need it." He hooks the stool from the pastry station with his foot, drags it over and sits. "What was *she* doing here this morning?"

"I have no idea. I thought her kind only came out at night."

Tony smiles as he raises his cup. *"Salute!"* he says, knocking his back and standing up. "I'm on for tonight, if you need me."

"Thanks, I might be able to stay, too, if I can get Hope to watch Chloe."

"Don't worry; it won't be a problem," he says. I'm not really worried, but wonder if I look it, because Tony has now mentioned it twice. It is, after all, a Monday night, and Mondays are notoriously slow in the restaurant world. People have eaten out all weekend and are more inclined to eat at home on Mondays than any other night of the week.

After eight, the lunch crew gradually filters in, and Tony and I put together a lineup for the evening. We tag an extra two for the kitchen tonight, neither of whom is thrilled at the prospect of working a double shift. Not that we are giving them a choice, especially because Tony informs me that we are booked solid, including two large corporate parties. So much for the usual slow Mondays.

Hope returns my call at the height of the lunch rush and I can't take it, but she leaves a message that she will be available tonight. All I need to do is get Chloe to her, which means that I will have to leave temporarily around four to pick Chloe up from day care and get her to Hope.

While I'm gone, Jake calls in to leave a few instructions. Tony takes the message, which includes the fascinating tidbit that Nicola won't be in either, as she is also feeling unwell. Tony and I scramble around for a few minutes looking for someone to fill in out front and decide that we can do with one less in the kitchen and send Ellen home to change. This latest wrinkle is a nuisance because Ellen, while a competent prep cook, hasn't worked the front before, and it is particularly important to make a good impression on the corporate parties.

Stuff like this happens all the time in restaurants. People get sick or don't show up. You get used to working shorthanded. Successful chefs go with the flow, learn to improvise, but not before taking out their frustrations on the staff, the line cooks, prep cooks, bus boys—anyone who has the misfortune to be in their paths. Most cooks I know have foul tempers, and I'm no exception. Most outbursts that happen during service can be forgiven. You can apologize later, and you do. And if you're on the receiving end, you get so used to being yelled at that pretty soon you don't hear it. I've been there, too.

Tonight the kitchen is so busy I hardly have time to breathe. My body is in constant motion, and I can feel it in my muscles as I reach up to pluck another head of garlic off the braid above the stove. I inspect every plate as it leaves the kitchen, making alterations in garnish, while continuing to cook and plate orders myself. When three orders of sea bass are overcooked and have to be chucked, I break my rhythm long enough to yell at the poor line cook, whose name I don't even know but who is responsible for ruining fifty dollars worth of fish. I don't stop until my throat hurts and she's crying, although she tries not to let me see.

By eleven thirty we're winding down. I ask one of the sous-chefs to put together a tray of biscotti and some limoncello for the members of the remaining corporate party, who are still lingering over coffee. They've ordered several bottles of expensive wine, in addition to appetizers and desserts, so the biscotti and digestif are a small, but important, gesture. I put on a fresh tunic and take them out myself. Making personal appearances is also part of the job, though one I've never relished. I've been on my feet for sixteen hours straight, and I can barely stand. So, I sit and schmooze for a few minutes, answer questions about what they've eaten and enjoyed, and, by the time they leave, Ellen informs me that they've taken an available date in early December for their office Christmas party.

It's well after midnight by the time the cooking staff has cleared away their stations and prepped for the next day. Tony pours some house wine for everyone, while Ellen, an apron over her elegant, black dress, serves leftover pasta from a big serving bowl. We sit around the table eating, drinking, and relaxing for the first time all evening, enjoying the camaraderie that follows the sharing of difficult experiences. Around this table, we are equals. I make a point of sitting next to Kristin, the young woman whose name I've learned from Tony. She avoids meeting my eye at first, and I know she's still embarrassed about the fish and angry at me for humiliating her in front of everyone. But we've had a good night, and the loss of the fish is no big deal. I tell her so, and thank her for all her hard work. I mean it, and she knows it. She gives me a shy smile before she leaves, and I know that she will come back tomorrow, that I haven't managed to kill the spirit that has motivated her to believe she could be a professional chef, though she seems hardly old enough to be out of high school.

I slip my feet out of my clogs and pour myself another glass of wine. I've long missed Chloe's bedtime, and Hope doesn't expect me until at least one. Besides, I'm so tired I can barely move. Tony moves over to the spot Kristin has just vacated. He unties his apron and uses it to wipe his meticulously shaved head, which glistens with sweat that drips in ripples down his smooth brown face, before tossing it in the general direction of the laundry bin. Helping himself to some more of the pasta, Tony offers, "We had a good night, eh?"

"I think so. It felt like a good night. I don't think I stopped moving—I must have plated over two hundred dinners. This makes lunch look like a breeze."

"You worked both, remember?"

"As did you," I tell him, raising my glass in salute.

"It felt good having you back for dinner. There's a, I don't know, a different feel to the kitchen."

"That's for sure," I snort. "Just ask Kristin."

"Who?" Tony asks with a puzzled look, apparently having already forgotten her name.

"The girl with the fish."

He grimaces at me and waves his hand as if swatting a fly. I suspect he's thinking I've gone soft. Maybe I have.

I want to ask him what he meant by his remark about the kitchen's having a different feel, but I'm suddenly too tired, exhausted by the realization that I will have to be back here in a mere seven hours. And that Chloe will be up in about four hours.

"Mira, go home. We're okay here for tonight. I'll hang around and wait for the cleanup crew to finish, and then I'll lock up."

I don't argue with him, and as I stand up I put my hand on his shoulder and give it a squeeze. "Thanks, Tony, are you sure?" He makes that fly-swatting gesture again, and I can tell my small suggestion of intimacy has embarrassed him.

The night is cold, but I walk home with my coat open. The heat in the kitchen was intense, and the cold air feels good on my flushed skin. For the first time today I have a moment to think about Jake's not showing up tonight. Jake hasn't missed a day at the restaurant since we opened, and I know he is not in bed with food poisoning or the flu or anything remotely medical. Something happened to him yesterday. I wasn't exactly sure what, but it's something Jake isn't ready to let me see.

chapter 8

Last week, when I dropped Chloe off at day care, her teacher handed me a flyer announcing the Christopher Street Kids Annual Thanksgiving Luncheon. On the flyer there was a space in the middle of the page where someone had filled in Chloe's name, followed by "has volunteered to bring," and then another space, where she has handwritten *three dozen corn muffins, individually wrapped!* This morning when I arrive at the day care, I find a printed reminder about the party, along with the news written in very small type at the bottom of the flyer, which I'd missed the first time, that the center will be closing early tomorrow, directly following the luncheon.

Standing next to me at the row of cubbies where we stow our children's things is Isaac's mother, Laura, whose reminder flyer I glimpse just before she shoves it into her briefcase. Isaac, who stands by his mother's side discreetly picking his nose while his mother unloads his backpack, has apparently volunteered to bring in two bags of miniature marshmallows, reminding me that it's probably not too early to talk with Chloe about volunteering her mother for school activities, as Isaac's mother clearly already has done.

I wonder how I'll even be able to make it to the lunch, and

whether, at eight months, Chloe is old enough to miss my being there. Everyone eats out the day before Thanksgiving, and we are booked solid for both lunch and dinner, so there's no question I'll have to work all day. In addition to shopping and cooking for Thanksgiving dinner, it now seems I'll have to deal with baking and wrapping three dozen corn muffins *and* finding someone to watch Chloe on Wednesday afternoon. Life, I reflect morosely, would be infinitely simpler if I weren't a professional chef. I could take the afternoon off like all the other corporate moms, don my construction paper Indian headdress, and take my rightful place at the Thanksgiving table. More important, I could buy the muffins. No busy corporate executive mother can be expected to bake muffins. But everybody at day care knows I cook for a living and will probably be expecting muffins in the shape of ears of corn, warm and buttery, wrapped in colored cellophane and tied with raffia. I'm instantly depressed at the thought of delivering a case of individually wrapped Otis Spunkmeyers and allowing Chloe to sit unaccompanied at her first Thanksgiving feast. It reeks, not only of bad mothering, but of bad cooking as well.

As soon as I get to Grappa I call my father. I haven't heard back from him about Thanksgiving, which is unusual. When Richard called me back to let me know that he was still planning on coming, even though I hadn't been able to scare up a ticket to the Steelers-Jets game, he mentioned that my dad hadn't returned his call either—stranger still. Although it would be impossible to get a flight out now, the drive isn't too bad. Even though it's only a little after seven in the morning, I get my father's machine. Since when does my father leave for work before seven? I also try him at the university, but he isn't there either. I leave messages at his home and office, all the while trying to fight the rising panic at the idea that something terrible has happened. He could be lying dead in the bathroom, felled by a dropped bar of soap. He *is* getting older. Maybe he shouldn't be living alone. Around nine, I finally reach his secretary, who tells me that he just got in and has gone straight to a meeting. Well, at least he isn't dead. I tell her to have him call me when he breaks free.

I offer to sell my soul to Tony in exchange for an hour during lunch service on Wednesday so that I can deliver the muffins and attend the day care party. While kneading the pasta dough I make a mental list of all the things I still need for Thanksgiving dinner. Richard has promised to make the stuffing, which he insists has to be made with Pepperidge Farm stuffing mix, because that is how his mother made it and if he doesn't eat it on Thanksgiving he will die. Hope is making "ambrosia," a concoction involving Cool Whip, sweetened coconut, and canned fruit. It's her mother's recipe, and apparently another holiday essential. I try not to cringe, particularly since she has volunteered to watch Chloe tomorrow afternoon so that I can finish up at work and do some last-minute grocery shopping. In addition to the free range bird that I have reserved at the Union Square Farmers Market, I add a few other necessities to the list: fresh Brussels sprouts, red and white pearl onions that I will serve creamed, and chestnuts for roasting, as that is what *my* mother used to serve on Thanksgiving.

Several hours and thirty-six muffins later, when I'm giving Chloe her bath, my dad calls back. Since we are both in the bathtub, I let the machine pick up, but as soon as I hear his voice, I wrap Chloe in a towel and we sprint, dripping, into the living room to pick up the phone.

"Dad—I'm here," I say, picking up the receiver, causing the answering machine to emit a high-pitched squeal. "Chloe was just in the bath," I tell him, reaching over to turn off the machine.

"Oh, okay. I'll call you ba—"

"No, no, it's okay. Hey, listen, I've been trying to reach you. Where were you this morning?"

My father doesn't say anything for a moment, and when he speaks his voice sounds unusually clear and crisp, as if he is taking special pains to enunciate each syllable. "I had a breakfast appointment, and I left the house early this morning," he replies.

"Well, I talked to Richard earlier, and he's arriving on the six fifteen flight tomorrow evening. I've been trying to call you to see if you'd like to come out for Thanksgiving too. You know, see Chloe. Spend some time?"

There is a long pause. I wonder if he's forgotten about the invitation. That wouldn't be surprising. My father has always been a bit absentminded. It also fit with the picture I was beginning to develop that my father, at the ripe old age of sixty-four, was suffering the earliest signs of dementia.

"You know, Thanksgiving?"

"Oh, Thanksgiving! Well, Mira, I don't think I'm going to be able to make it, honey. I'm having dinner with some friends."

Friends? Friends are where you go when your children couldn't have you over. Doesn't he know that any self-respecting father drops whatever he is doing to be with his daughter and granddaughter? And besides, since when does my father have friends?

"Oh," is all I can think of to say.

"That, and I also have to work on Friday. A big grant proposal is due in Washington on Monday. No rest for the weary," he says with a chuckle. "You know," he continues, nonplussed, "I think I'm getting too old for this nonsense. I have a good mind to retire," he says with a laugh, and we both know that nothing could be further from the truth. Suddenly my father is talking about RFPs and government contracts and his voice is chipper and peppy, which doesn't exactly fit with my picture of a partially demented senior citizen.

"Sounds like you've been busy. Are you sure everything is okay, Dad?"

He hesitates before continuing. "Well, I have a bit of bad news, actually. You remember Debbie Silverman?"

I'd gone to high school with Debbie's brother, Ronnie, and Debbie had been a few years ahead of me in school.

"Her husband—an orthopedic surgeon, I think—died unexpectedly. A heart attack at forty-eight. Dropped dead right in the operating room. Well, anyway, I don't mean to upset you, but I thought you should know. You might want to send her a card."

"Thanks, Dad, I will. Poor Debbie."

But what I really want to say is, "What about me?"

One of the many differences between being divorced and being widowed is that when you are a widow, everyone sympathizes with you. You get condolence cards by the bushel; people send you flowers and make you casseroles. But, if you've been jilted, and particularly when you have been spurned in favor of another woman, the underlying assumption is that *you* are somehow lacking. It makes me wonder, if Jake died now, would I be entitled to call myself a widow? And to all the rights and privileges thereof?

Not if the death looks too suspicious, I suppose.

By Wednesday evening, I've convinced Chloe's peers and their parents of my cooking prowess and dutifully eaten my sweet potato and marshmallow casserole while wearing a Pilgrim's collar and cuffs. I've also taken an entire roll of pictures of Chloe eating her first pumpkin pie, supervised the service of over two hundred lunches, finalized the winter menu, shopped, cooked, and cleaned the apartment. The complicated machinations that have allowed me to achieve this delicate balance between family and work have left me looking and feeling like a stale Krispy Kreme donut, glazed and pasty on the outside and filled with jelly. I'm in the midst of setting the table when Richard calls to tell me that his flight has been delayed. Instead of taking advantage of the extra time I have to sit down and relax before he arrives, I put Chloe to bed and start baking biscotti, because I think it's a nice hostessy thing to do.

Even though my mother had been a Cordon Bleu–trained chef, it was not she who taught me to cook—that I learned from Mrs. Favish, our next-door neighbor. It was during the first spring my mother was away, drying out at the expensive retreat center in New Hampshire. I was ten years old. Some people might have found it intimidating teaching the daughter of a professional chef to cook, but it hadn't seemed to bother Mrs. Favish. In fact, she undertook my culinary education with extraordinary zeal, teaching me first to bake because she believed that one must learn to follow the rules, culinarily speaking, before one could break them.

Chefs, I've found, can generally be divided into two groups: those who bake and those who do not. Baking is for the rule bound, the people who sat up front in cooking class and paid attention, who wrote things down, rather than relying on the *feel* of a recipe. I did none of those things, which was why it was unusual that I initially found my niche in the cooking world as a pastry chef. I think it was because Mrs. Favish taught me to bake first, and at a time in my life when I was craving predictability, looking for rules, for reasons why things should work.

I bake biscotti, dozens of them. Hazelnut, pistachio, cornmeal, anise, and black pepper. Before long the soothing aroma of anise and toasting nuts fills the kitchen. While I'm waiting for Richard, I sample one of each, along with a pot of tea, strong and very sweet, because that is how Mrs. Favish taught me to drink it. Sometimes I think my only chance for happiness is in a kitchen, that any life I live outside is destined to be a shadowy, half-lived sort of life. It is, after all, where I've spent the better part of my adult existence, and a decent chunk of my childhood as well, a place where things both tragic and wonderful have taken place. Maybe the only place I really know how to be me.

I'm shaping the last of the biscotti logs when the doorbell rings. Wiping my floury hands on my jeans, I run to answer it. I open the door and fling myself into Richard's arms.

"Sweetheart, watch the coat. Is that dough on your hands?" His words are light and teasing, but he holds me tightly.

"Yes, and I'm going to get it all over your expensive cashmere coat."

"This old thing? So, where is she, the divine Chloe? It's her I came to see," he says, ruffling my hair. I can smell his cologne. Bay Rum. A smell so comforting it makes me want to bury my face into his shirt and weep.

I take his coat and hang it on the coat rack while Richard meticulously folds his Burberry scarf and places it in the inside breast pocket of his jacket. At fifty-four years old Richard is still a good-looking man, due in part to two decades of near obsessive devotion to exercise and healthy eating, made necessary by a reckless and degenerate youth. In fact, the only clues to his age are a hint of silver in his golden hair and a few extra lines around his mouth and eyes.

We tiptoe into Chloe's room so that Richard can sneak a peek at her. She's sleeping on her back with her arms flung over her head in a gesture of complete surrender. Richard leans in, his palms to his cheeks in an exaggerated gesture of delight.

"She's gorgeous," he whispers, taking my hand.

She stirs, and I shush him. "Come on, you'll wake her," I tell him.

"Pleasant dreams, sweetie," he says, gently brushing a wisp of hair from her forehead.

"Come on, I've made biscotti," I tell him, hustling him out of the room. "And a pot of tea."

"I just survived the flight from hell. I think we're going to need something stronger than tea!"

In the kitchen, I watch as he opens the antique china cupboard and helps himself to two delicate demitasse cups and saucers. He opens another door and takes out the old-fashioned stove-top Italian coffee maker, for Richard's idea of something stronger—espresso. He does these things with a minimum of looking around. Although he has been here only a handful of times, somehow Richard knows his way around my kitchen.

We work side by side, in companionable silence. It doesn't seem to matter how seldom I see Richard, because no matter how long it's been, we are somehow in sync. He rolls up the sleeves of his expensive shirt, revealing two strong, tanned arms and a Rolex watch. The antique business was obviously doing well.

"Nice watch," I tell him.

"Thanks, it was a gift," he says, smiling at my raised eyebrows. "No, it's not what you think. I agreed to do the apartment of a little old matron who's been coming into the shop for years. She bought one of those hideous-looking condos on Mount Washington. I did a fabulous job. She was just trying to show her appreciation. Anyway, it's probably a fake, but it's a good one, so what do I care?"

We sit down at the kitchen table and sip our espresso. It is good, strong and hot. Neither of us says anything for a minute or so.

"Chloe's beautiful," Richard says finally. "Your father must be over the moon."

"He thinks she's great. Not that we've seen much of him. He came out when she was first born, and I was hoping that he'd be here for Thanksgiving, but . . ." I let this last bit hang in the air, trying to keep the resentment out of my voice.

"What about Jake? Does he see her?"

This is a dangerous question, one most people I know avoid.

Probably the reason most people don't ask is they assume that when a marriage breaks up so soon after the birth of a child, that somehow the child is at the heart of it. But Richard isn't most people. And, because it's Richard, I tell him everything—about Jake's doomed visit, how he had to feign food poisoning the next day, how Nicola showed up sniffing around for clues, and how Jake has been avoiding me ever since.

One of the great things about Richard is that you could tell him you just ax murdered your best friend, chopped her up, and fed her to the dog, and he would flick a piece of lint from his lapel and raise an eyebrow as if to say, "And then?" This is why I know I can tell him the truth. What actually happened matters less than what I know lurked menacingly beneath the surface. Seduction was in my heart, and I know that had Jake shown even the slightest interest, I would have taken him back. Not just back into my bed, but back into my life, and for that I hate myself. For being weak and needy and for being ready to resign Chloe to a father who doesn't want her.

Up until now I haven't verbalized any of this. I've told no one about Jake's visit. I can feel the tightness behind my eyes, and I know that I'm going to cry. Richard knows it, too, because he leans across the table and covers my folded hands with both of his and squeezes, hard.

"Come on now. Enough about Jake." Kind of him to say so when we really hadn't been talking about Jake. "It's definitely over and better for Chloe, if you ask me, that she doesn't see him." He leans in conspiratorially. "Now, what I really want are the gory details. Spare nothing!" he whispers, his voice husky with anticipation. "Did you really claw her eyes out?" This is Richard's modus operandi. When the going gets tough, distract them. Make 'em laugh. It's a pretty good strategy.

"No, of course not," I say, my sniffling turning quickly into a giggle. "It was her hair. I pulled some out." It is still a satisfying memory. Richard lifts the corner of his mouth in a half smile, but doesn't say anything.

"I know, I know," I tell him. "I went nuts."

"No, you didn't," he finally says, waving his hand dismissively and walking back over to the stove for more coffee. "You did what any sane jilted wife with an infant daughter would have done. *He's* the nut. An asshole, really. Never liked him. And *her,* the worst kind of slut."

I know Richard is not just saying this to make me feel good. He'd never liked Jake, and the feeling had been quite mutual. In the early days of our marriage, Richard had come to New York fairly frequently to visit us, me really. Although Richard was always perfectly pleasant, he'd made Jake uncomfortable. After the first couple of visits, Jake usually found some excuse to make himself scarce when Richard was here.

By the time the last of the biscotti are out of the oven, we have established that just about every single base impulse I've acted upon over the last several months has been completely justified, including the debacle at the anger-management class, that particular anecdote nearly causing Richard to choke on his espresso.

Richard is still asleep on the pullout couch in the living room when the doorbell rings early the next morning. It's Hope, bearing a large Tupperware container and a plastic plate covered with a paper napkin decorated with a cartoon turkey.

"Good morning!" she chirps. She's wearing a festive green velvet robe with puffed sleeves and, for once, isn't sporting large Velcro rollers in her hair.

"Now, Mira, I thought I'd bring over the ambrosia. Oh, and I went ahead and baked up a tin of those nice crescent rolls. I thought that your friend—Richard, is it?—might enjoy some for breakfast. And I know how busy you are this morning." She smiles in the direction of the sleeping Richard, her voice dropping to a whisper. "I hope I haven't woken him." Of course, what she has really come to do is spy on Richard, who I suspect is awake, because his snoring has suddenly stopped.

My suspicions are confirmed when Richard gets up mere seconds after Hope's departure. "Did I hear someone say there are warm crescent rolls?" he says, rolling over and clicking on the TV. I pour us steaming bowls of caffè latte, load up a tray with the rolls and some biscotti, and bring it into the living room, where Richard is watching the Macy's Thanksgiving Day Parade from the sofa bed. Now that he's awake, I give Chloe her busy box to play with. I climb across Richard and sit on the foot of the bed where I can keep an eye on Chloe who, intermittently, is distracted by the large floats on TV, as is Richard. Nonetheless, I decide the time is right for me to begin my interrogation. Besides, I might even get more information from Richard this way.

"So what is up with my dad?'

"What do you mean?"

"Is he okay? He seems just, I don't know, a little distant and distracted lately, and I was wondering if everything is all right."

Richard doesn't say anything. He and Chloe are mesmerized by a giant SpongeBob SquarePants balloon floating down Thirty-fourth Street.

"I'm worried. Do you think he is all right physically? Do you think he could be sick?"

"What makes you think he's sick?"

"I don't know, nothing really," I tell him, remembering my father's deliberate speech and his forgetfulness. "It's just that I get the feeling that he is keeping something from me, that's all. And it would be just like him to not want to share bad news like that."

Again, nothing from Richard. He helps himself to another roll, his third.

"Has he said anything to you? Because if he has, I think you should tell me. As his only child, I think I have a right to know. He is not a young man anymore, and any time now I might have to start, you know, making arrangements for his care."

"No, he hasn't said anything, and he doesn't look sick. Not that I have seen too much of him lately, but when I have, he seems the picture of health."

I slump against the pillows, unsatisfied. I suspect he's lying.

Rather improbably, Richard and my father had become friends over the years. Even though I'd done my best to keep him a secret, a few weeks after we met, Richard, tired of my begging to be left off at the top of my street when he dropped me off after the Al-Anon meeting, insisted on taking me home and meeting my parents. (He's a bit of a prude and wanted to dispel any notion of impropriety should I be seen getting out of his sports car late at night by one of our well-meaning but meddlesome neighbors.) And there was a time when my mother had tried to quit drinking in earnest and Richard had actually moved in with us briefly, acting in equal parts as an older brother, AA sponsor, and friend. Richard and my dad still occasionally meet for dinner, or take in a movie, or get together on a Sunday afternoon to watch the Steelers.

Richard takes a long draft of his coffee and helps himself to another biscotti. He knows me well enough to know that I haven't given up; I'm merely considering my next line of questioning.

Richard puts his coffee mug down on the breakfast tray, folds his hands across his stomach, and gives me his full attention. "Well, have you asked him if anything is wrong?"

"Of course I have."

"Well?"

"He said everything is fine, he's just been busy."

He pauses a minute, then continues, "Well, then, I think he's just been busy." There is something about the way he says *busy*. I look up sharply, and Richard quickly looks away.

"Really, Mira, if your father chooses not to tell you something, if, in fact, there is a glimmer of truth to your paranoid delusions, then he must have his reasons. It certainly isn't my place to . . ."

Sensing an opportunity, I move quickly to seize the advantage. "You obviously know something, Richard."

"The thing is, I really don't—not for sure anyway. He hasn't told me anything, either. Your father, in case it has escaped your notice, Mira, is an extremely private person. He tells nobody anything if he can help it. I've long since stopped taking it personally, and I suggest you do the same. Do you know," he says, looking over his half-moon glasses at me, "I've known him for almost twenty years, and I couldn't tell you his political party, his favorite restaurant, or his views on capital punishment, although I could probably guess. It also appears that I may have been wrong."

Bingo. "What do you mean, you may have been wrong?"

"Nothing, really. Just a conversation I had with your dad a while back."

"What kind of conversation?"

"Really, Mira, your father is a big boy. But, if you must know, it was a conversation about women."

"Women? Why would my father, who talks to no one, talk to you, of all people, about women? Do you think he's dating someone? Why wouldn't he want to tell me that?"

"I don't know. Maybe he feels disloyal. Guilty. I don't know."

"Guilty? Why should he feel guilty? My mother has been dead eighteen years, for goodness' sake!"

Richard ignores me. "I think I've met her," he says, sitting up in bed. "About a month ago a woman came into the shop, said she was a friend of your father's. Browsed around, inquired about a little religious figurine, a nothing item. A little della Robbia knockoff that's been hanging around the shop forever. When I told her the price, she smiled very politely and said she'd think about it. About a week later your father came into the shop and bought it. When I told him about the woman who had been in, saying that she was a friend of his, he got funny, embarrassed, I don't know. I offered just to give it to him, but he insisted on paying. Got all stiff and formal about it."

"Well, what was she like?"

"That's the thing. She looked young, much younger than your father, that's for sure. My age, or even younger, maybe. Very tan, lots of makeup, blond, tightly permed hair. Enormous breasts, probably fake. And she was wearing leopard pants. Can you believe it, leopard pants? Not exactly the kind of woman I'd picture your father with, which is why I didn't make anything of it. I figured maybe it was his secretary, and he wanted to buy her a gift or something."

My father has had the same secretary for the last twenty-five years, and she is neither young nor blond. Her name is Mrs. Hudson, and although she does have enormous breasts, she also has enormous everything else—hips, thighs, stomach, not to mention chins.

"I'm sure it's not his secretary. You've met Mrs. Hudson."

"Don't remember."

I'm instantly bombarded by obscene thoughts of my father and this woman Richard has described, and I give my head a violent shake. This amuses Richard, who knows exactly what I'm thinking.

"What do you say," he says, clapping his hands and putting himself in Chloe's line of vision, "that we get dressed and hustle over to Herald Square and catch part of the parade? I've never actually been to the Macy's Parade, and what better time to go than Chloe's first Thanksgiving?"

Later, on the subway home, Richard says, "I hope we're right about your dad. It is about time he had some fun. No one should be alone." I put my head on his shoulder and sigh. Richard and I are both alone. No partners. No prospects. "Don't worry," he whispers. "You won't be alone for long. You are much too beautiful and much too good a cook not to get married again, if that is what you decide you want. If I have to, I'll marry you myself—we could be the ultimate marriage of convenience. All you need to do is get ahold of that recipe for crescent rolls from your friend Hope, and I'll be a happy man."

As soon as we open the apartment door, we can smell the turkey roasting. I've cooked it in a paper bag (a neat trick that ensures an incredibly moist bird without basting). The smell is a heady combination of roasting turkey, and apple brandy, butter, and wild mushrooms that I've combined and rubbed on the inside of the bird and under the skin of the breast and legs. It will be delicious.

I refuse to think about what Jake is doing this year and wonder instead about my father, who is presumably eating his turkey with a woman I have never met, a woman with enormous fake breasts who owns a pair of leopard pants and who might not be much older than me. I'm suddenly sure it's a serious relationship, because you don't just have Thanksgiving with anybody. It implies a certain level of commitment.

My relationship with my father, I realize, is a disaster. It must be, because otherwise he would have told me about her. The doorbell rings, and I hear Richard greeting Hope and waxing enthusiastic about the delicious rolls he had for breakfast this morning. The turkey will be ready soon, and I still need to cream the onions. No time now to think about how I've managed to screw up my relationships with the two most important men in my life.

chapter 9

On Friday after Thanksgiving, when the rest of the civilized world is out beginning their Christmas shopping, I'm at the restaurant preparing lunch for what is sure to be a good-sized crowd. Spending money always makes people hungry. Hope and Richard have taken Chloe to the Bronx Zoo while I'm working. I linger a bit after lunch, hoping to run into Jake so that I can touch base on a few things, but Tony tells me he called to say he won't be in until after five. Too late to hang around, so I call his cell, but he doesn't pick up and his mailbox is full. I'm hoping to follow up on the items I had sent home with Nicola earlier in the week, including making sure he had phoned in the meat and fish orders for next week. Finally, I call him at Nicola's. No one is there either, so I leave him a message.

On Sunday morning Richard lets me sleep in. When I awake, it's well after nine, and I can hear Richard and Chloe in the kitchen. I tiptoe down the hall to find them sitting at the kitchen table eating breakfast. Richard is calling out clues to Chloe from the *Times* crossword puzzle in a high squeaky voice, while Chloe painstakingly picks up Cheerios between her thumb and forefinger. I've seldom seen Richard around children, but he genuinely seems to be enjoying Chloe, who, in my totally unbiased opinion, is an exceptionally likable child.

"What's a seven letter word for 'foundation garment'? Righto, Chloe, *bustier,* it is!"

I stand there quietly for a moment, taking advantage of the opportunity to observe them: Richard in his paisley bathrobe and Chloe, her delighted gaze fixed on Richard. She's clearly over her stranger anxiety, smiling and cooing at Richard and occasionally even offering him a soggy Cheerio, which he gobbles down to her delight. I sneak up behind Richard and put my arms around his neck. "You can't leave. Do you realize that I have not slept this late since Chloe was born? Thank you," I whisper in his ear, planting a kiss on the top of his head.

He pats my arm and gives it a squeeze. Then, extricating himself, he gestures for me to sit down. He brings me fresh coffee, French roast by the smell of it, along with a pitcher of warm milk. "Coffee, madame?"

There are warm rolls with marmalade and mascarpone cheese. Chloe clamors for my attention, and Richard brings her over and then sits down next to me.

"Why don't you come home?" he says, pouring milk into my coffee.

"Home? I am home."

"To Pittsburgh."

I don't say anything for a minute. "I can't, Richard. I have a life here. Chloe is in a great day care. I have the restaurant to run. There are a million reasons I have to stay."

"I'm sure there are, but probably not a single good one. You know, it wouldn't be a bad idea to pull back a bit. You're running yourself ragged, not to mention that you're subjecting yourself to a very unhealthy situation. No wonder you're having a hard time getting over Jake. You have to deal with him and his betrayal every single day. Sell your share to someone else. Let Jake buy you out, whatever. And besides," he says, buttering a piece of toast, "your money would go a lot further in Pittsburgh. You could take some time and figure out what you want to do. Be with Chloe, your dad, me."

I'm not sure what to say. It isn't that simple.

"My dad is apparently living the life of a swinging bachelor. The last thing he needs is his dumped daughter and granddaughter skulking back to him. We would cramp his style."

"Mira, that is not fair. You don't even know for sure he's dating anyone."

I straighten up and turn away. I'm disappointed that Richard doesn't seem to understand that my life is in New York now. I hate it when he treats me like the fifteen-year-old girl he once knew.

"Sorry, love, don't mean to end things on a bad note. It's just that you always seem to take the most difficult route and, for once, I'd like to see you take it easy."

Take it easy? How could Richard possibly think that going home to Pittsburgh would be taking it easy? That would be an admission of failure, not to mention a complete dead end. I'll take the Big Apple—twelve-hour days, the stress of running a restaurant, exorbitant rent, skyrocketing day care expenses, and terror alerts— any day of the week.

"Well, it's something to think about," he says, ruffling Chloe's curls and disappearing in the direction of the bathroom. We both watch him walk down the hall, striped towel swung over his shoulder, his spicy aftershave lingering in his wake. Chloe holds out a dimpled arm, her little body straining after Richard, her eyes following him all the way down the hallway. If she could talk, I know she would say, "take me with you," although as soon as the bathroom door shuts behind him, Chloe turns her attention back to me, with no trace of want or abandonment, almost as if he'd never been there. With an impish smile she places her fingers, sticky with marmalade, in my hair, pulling me closer in order to nuzzle my face. I once read in a parenting magazine that babies under the age of eight months or so have a hard time holding pictures of people in their minds, hence the saying "out of sight, out of mind." It is, I think, a convenient mechanism; it keeps children from missing people, from being disappointed too early in life.

Richard's visit has dredged up all sorts of complicated feelings, which, owing to the busy week I have coming up, I'm hoping to be able to avoid thinking about. Not only are we previewing the new winter lunch menu at Grappa, but Thursday is also our meeting with the lawyers about final disposition of the marital assets and my next anger-management session.

As of the day after Thanksgiving, Jake still hasn't shown his face at the restaurant when I've been there and isn't returning my telephone calls. When Jake fails to respond to my message asking him to approve the proofs for the winter dinner menu, I go ahead and send only the luncheon menu to the printer. It's starting to seem like we're running two parallel restaurants here, a dangerous situation, particularly in the notoriously fickle Manhattan dining world. People want consistency; they want to know that if they wander in on a Thursday evening, they can get the arugula salad they had at lunch last week. At the moment, Jake doesn't even know what's *in* the arugula salad, besides arugula.

Just how dangerous things have become doesn't become clear until the Monday after Thanksgiving. Arriving at the restaurant, I expect, as usual, to spend the morning taking inventory of the walk-in and unloading and stocking the week's shipment of meat and fish. But this morning something doesn't feel right. My vague feelings of discomfort about the management of the restaurant become all too concrete when, by eight o'clock, our deliveries still have not arrived. By five after, I'm on the phone. Clearly, something is wrong. The meat and fish are coming from different suppliers, and it's too unlikely a coincidence that both of them would be late. Meanwhile, the prep cooks are standing around with nothing to prep, and we open for lunch in three and a half hours.

"Hey, Mira, sweetheart, did you enjoy those halibut cheeks?" Eddie says, when I finally manage to get him on the phone. "I'm not used to having my gifts go unacknowledged."

I have no time for social graces, however.

"Eddie, where the hell is my fish?"

"What do you mean?"

"It's after eight, and I don't have the shipment I ordered. We open for lunch in three and a half hours, and all I have are a couple of pounds of tuna left from Friday's delivery. What's going on?"

"Deliveries went out already. Shoulda been there. Hang on a minute, and I'll check to see who had the Grappa drop this morning." He puts me on hold, and suddenly I'm listening to "Under the Sea" from the *Little Mermaid,* another of Eddie's little jokes. In a couple of minutes he's back on the line.

"Mira, I checked backwards and forwards, and I don't see no order from you guys. That's why you didn't get anything. No order, no fish."

"What? I put an order in, I have a copy of it right here," I say, rummaging through the files on the office desk for a copy. And then, I remember. I gave Nicola the orders for this week last Monday when Jake was "out sick." She was supposed to give it to Jake. Shit. Obviously, she hadn't done it, and that meant no fish and no meat.

"I gave that order to Jake, Eddie! I can't believe he didn't phone it in. Oh, my God. That bastard!"

"Listen, Mira, tell me what you need. I can't promise I'll have everything you want, but I'll take a look, see what we got left, then put together an order, something at least that will get you through lunch. I will deliver it personally within the hour. And you can repay my saving your behind by agreeing to have dinner with me, okay?"

I ignore Eddie's unconcealed attempt to blackmail me into a date and barrel ahead with my order. "Give me thirty pounds of mussels, twenty-five of scampi, as much squid as you can get me, some whitefish, snapper, sea bass, and sardines—whatever you've got. That will get me through today, and when you get here I'll give you an order for the rest of the week."

I'm too spent to repeat my outraged performance for Rob, the meat guy, because by now I know that neither he nor Eddie is to blame. But because we're great customers, Rob agrees to rush me over some sausage, a dozen pork tenderloins, and some flank steak, which I can cook quickly, for braciole.

I instruct the prep cooks to roll out some lasagna noodles and to start preparing béchamel in large quantities. We will resort to a couple of baked pasta entrees, flavored with meat and sausage and, depending on what Eddie sends over, a cioppino. It's now almost nine, and my adrenaline level remains high, although a plan, of sorts, is slowly coming together. Whether it will be sufficient to stave off the pending lunch disaster remains to be seen, but for the moment, at least, the prep staff is well occupied, and I have a moment to breathe. Instead, I lock myself in the office and call Jake. He picks up on the third ring, and I can tell right away from the background noise that he's at the gym.

"Jake, what the hell is going on? How could you have forgotten to order the fish and meat?" It's the first time we've actually spoken since that day in the apartment, but I don't have the time or the patience to feel weird about it.

"Mira? What are you talking about?"

"Last week, when you were out sick, I gave *her* some stuff to give to you, including the meat and fish orders, and told her to have you add what you needed and phone them in."

"Mira, *Nicola* gave me the package, the menu changes and the note about Castelli Farms pork, which I did order, by the way, but there were no meat or fish orders in there. I assumed that you'd taken care of the orders like you always do."

"What do you mean the orders weren't in there? Of course they were!" I scream into the phone.

"Look, I told you they weren't in the package. You must have forgotten to put them in."

"I did not forget! She must have taken them out! And I called you last week on Friday and left a message on your machine. What about that? Are you trying to tell me you didn't get my message either? Jesus, Jake, don't you see what she is doing?"

"Mira, stop screaming at me. I didn't get the orders, and I didn't get any message. And don't go accusing Nicola—get a grip, Mira. Why would she have taken them out? Call Eddie and Rob and get them to send over an emergency delivery. Just deal with it, okay?"

"I've already called them and made arrangements to make sure that we have food here today, but Jake, this is something we have to deal with now. We can't go on like this. If nothing else, we have to think of Grappa which, I might remind you, is our livelihood."

"You're right. We are going to have to make some changes. Listen, I can't talk about this right now." He lowers his voice, and I'm having trouble hearing him over the piped music at the gym.

"Jake, can't you get down here and help me sort out this mess? I'm going to be at least an hour behind in prep, and God knows what Rob and Eddie are sending over. I could really use the help."

Jake doesn't say anything, and if it wasn't for the iron-pumping music in the background I might have thought he hung up. Finally, he says, "No, Mira, I cannot come down there right now. I'm busy."

"Busy! You're at the fucking gym, Jake! And this is your fault. Nicola—"

"I'm not going to sit here and have you insult Nicola. Nicola had no reason to remove those orders. *You're* the one who screwed up, Mira. I'm done." And suddenly he *has* hung up on me.

No reason for Nicola to remove the orders? Without even trying I can think of several. For starters, it's a quick and easy way to make me look bad. Also, she's been around long enough to know that I'm the one who's on when the deliveries come in and that I'm the one who'll be sweating to organize emergency deliveries and scrambling to put together a menu on the fly. And perhaps more significantly, it forces Jake into the position of having to choose whom to believe—Nicola or me. If Nicola was feeling slightly uncertain about which way Jake was leaning, then this little tactic might just be a good barometer. What was beginning to be absolutely clear was that Nicola was willing to sacrifice the restaurant to get to me.

When news of their affair had first spread, everyone told me it wouldn't last. It was just a fling, not uncommon, especially for men of a certain age who are trying to adjust to fatherhood. I'd done my best to believe them, despite mounting evidence to the contrary and, until as recently as that afternoon in the apartment, had even entertained the possibility, albeit a slim one, that Jake might want to come back. But lately, I'd begun to seriously doubt that she and Jake were just a fling. She was, I feared, going to be around for the long haul. That meant only one thing. I would have to buy Jake out.

For the next five hours I do not have another thought in my head that does not involve managing this crisis. When Eddie calls to deliver the bad news—no squid to be found anywhere in the city—I send one of the prep cooks to Dean and Deluca to check the price of squid and to make some discreet inquiries as to how much they have on hand. I throw a twenty at her and tell her to buy me half a pound so I can check the quality. The grilled calamari and spinach antipasto has been a mainstay since we opened, so paying a premium to keep it on the menu is a no-brainer, providing the quality is sufficiently high. I get one of the line guys to pull the lunch menus and type a new one that I dictate while pulling stuff from the walk-in and freezer. Today, our prix fixe menu will feature *cucina poverta:* polpettone alla napoletana, an Italian meat loaf; pappa al pomodoro; a ragout with sausages and peppers; and braciole (providing Rob, the meat guy, comes through in time).

When the meat still has not shown up by ten I'm on the phone yelling at some hapless office person, although it's just about hopeless, because, unless the meat shows up in the next five minutes, there will not be enough time to make the braciole. To cover for the fact that we were only able to buy fifteen pounds of calamari from Dean and Deluca (at an exorbitant price), Tony and I devise an additional antipasto, a ricotta and Pecorino torta flavored with hot pepper and prosciutto.

By eleven the kitchen is a mess, and should a health inspector walk in at this moment, there's a good chance we'd be shut down. I patrol the various stations shouting orders to clean up and wipe down, to get it together. When it seems inconceivable that we can pull things together in half an hour, Tony jokes that we should flip a fuse or two and post a sign on the door reading, "Closed due to power failure." For his attempt at levity, he gets jabbed in the ribs with a whisk, and I tell him he's lucky I'm not holding a knife. I tell the staff that no dish is to leave the kitchen unless it goes by me. It is essential that I taste everything, since the majority of the food we are serving today is from recipes developed for the restaurant kitchen in the last two hours. In preparation, I chew a handful of Tums to quell the churning acid in my stomach.

As the first entrees go out, there's a collective holding of breath in the kitchen. It isn't that the food we are serving is bad. I would have taken Tony's suggestion and induced a power failure long before I served food that was seriously compromised. The issue isn't the *quality,* but the fact that we are serving *different* food. Grappa's signature dishes feature simple food, perfectly grilled meats, poultry, and fish, straightforward braises, and earthy flavors—a branzino delicately grilled on the bone and adorned by little besides some excellent quality olive oil and fresh herbs. Today, however, constrained by the small amount of meat and fish available, our menu is more reminiscent of Nonna's kitchen than what our well-heeled regulars are used to.

I'm in the midst of preparing a pesto for the fish stew when Eddie jogs through the back door and does a victory lap around the kitchen, while hefting a large bag of something over his head.

"Yo, I got the last in the city," he booms. "The last calamari on the island! Don't ask me whose ass I had to kiss to get it, Mira, but baby, you owe me." He grabs me by the waist and gives me a hug that I can't return, even if I wanted to. Still, the calamari is a nice gesture from Eddie, who has gone to considerable trouble just to please me.

"Thanks, Eddie," I say, turning and giving him a tight smile. "That's great."

"You'll have plenty of time to thank me later," he says with a leer, inducing a few snickers from the line. I turn around, brandishing my pestle, and deliver a murderous look.

"Okay, I get the picture, you're busy."

As nice as Eddie's gesture is, it does me little good right now. I've just shelled out close to three hundred bucks for a measly fifteen pounds of squid from Dean and Deluca that I'm now selling at a loss. Also, if Eddie has had as much trouble getting his hands on the squid as he says he has, then I know that I'm going to be paying for it through the nose. Maybe I *should* sleep with him.

Terry comes flying through the kitchen at a quarter to two announcing that she thinks she has spotted Frank Bruni in the dining room, causing me to burn myself on an open flame at the grill station. Tony locates some gauze, which he affixes to my burned hand with duct tape. I'm tempted to tell him not to bother. If Frank Bruni really is in the dining room, I might just as well throw myself into the pizza oven. When Tony is finished ministering to me, I allow myself a quick and surreptitious look, just to make sure. I decide, with relief, that Terry is probably wrong. The man in the toupee and tinted glasses is just as likely to be a movie star or a cheating husband as Frank Bruni.

By two thirty we're limping and hobbling toward the finish line. We are out of most things on the menu, and I have had to call back both Eddie and Rob and place additional rush orders for dinner. When I finally get around to opening the City Meats bill, I'm horrified at the substantial "rush delivery" fee they've charged, which I now have just doubled.

Usually I take a few minutes to look at the receipts, but I know without looking that we've taken a big hit financially today. My feet and back are aching, and my burned hand is throbbing. The thought of having to remove the duct tape bandage, not to mention the approximately six thousand calories worth of food I've tasted on its way out of the kitchen, make me feel like throwing up.

Finally, at three o'clock the last of the orders have gone out, and there's time to breathe. The kitchen staff is beat, and the waitstaff has had to put up with unhappy customers and bad tips; the kitchen is a mess, and we open for dinner in three hours. I can only hope that the meat will make it here in time. It suddenly seems so much easier to think of that as Jake's problem.

There isn't much in the way of leftovers, so I throw a few pounds of pasta in the pasta vats and prepare a simple aglio e olio for the troops. We open a couple of extra bottles of house wine, and the staff, at least the ones who are on for a double shift, gather to eat a well-deserved meal. I raise my glass and thank them, acknowledging that this was hell, but that today in my kitchen everybody is a chef. I'm tempted to stick around until Jake arrives, so that I can at least watch him suffer, but I'm still too angry. We'd probably just end up screaming at each other, and that might throw the dinner staff off their game. I clean up quickly and leave without even bothering to remove my tunic and clogs.

chapter 10

On Wednesday morning I buy the paper on the way to work, something I almost never do, because usually by the time I get around to reading it, everything is old news. I quickly check the Food section, just to make sure that the nightmare of Frank Bruni's being in the restaurant Monday was the result of Terry's stress-induced paranoia. Good, I note with relief, no scathing review. Nevertheless, I'll probably continue to check for the next several weeks, just to be sure. When I turn on my cell phone after dropping Chloe off, I see that I have two new messages. The first is from Eddie, who was just following up on how things went Monday, glad he could help, and wondering whether I was free for dinner on Saturday night. How did he get my cell phone number? Of course, in my panic Monday, I probably made the call from my cell phone. I delete the rest of the message before I even finish listening to it.

The second message is from my lawyer. "Mira, Jerry Fox returning your call. I just received Jake's settlement offer, and we need to sit down and go over it before our meeting with Jake and his lawyer tomorrow morning. Give me a call at your earliest convenience. Thanks." I call him back immediately but, as I expected, he's not there—lawyers are never there—so I leave him another message.

In typical fashion, Jerry doesn't return my call until later that evening while I'm trying to get Chloe to bed. I'm tempted to make a sarcastic comment about his returning my call at *his* earliest convenience, but he says, "Sorry, but I hope you don't mind if I finish my dinner while we talk. I'll try not to chew in your ear." Seeing as it is nearly eight, how can I say I mind?

I've watched enough episodes of *Boston Legal* and *The Practice* to know that lawyers do this stuff all the time. They rehearse arguments on their way to court, have conference calls on their cell phones during lunch at my restaurant, and scream instructions at their secretaries while clients are talking to them on the phone. They are the consummate multitaskers whom, for the record, I do not begrudge a penny of their six-figure salaries. In the kitchen I'm a multitasker, too, but now I need to talk to Jerry about my life. I need time to digest things. I need to be brought along slowly, particularly on issues of such immense personal importance. Jerry Fox, unfortunately, is a man willing to pander to my needs only so far. Time to digest? Don't be silly, he'd say. If you don't sleep, you'll have fourteen hours.

"Okay, where are we?" he says, all business with no hint of apology as to why it has taken so long to get back to me.

"Jake's settlement offer? Settlement meeting tomorrow?" I'm trying to be helpful without sounding snide.

"Yes, yes," he says, focusing. "I got their proposal, and it seems they want to wrap this up as quickly as possible, which we can use, by the way. Yup. They are in a big hurry. Okay, let's see . . ." I can hear him flipping through pages. "Well, the biggest development is that they've made us an offer, and a serious one, I think, to buy your share of Grappa: $950,000, with $250,000 up front and the rest over four years."

"The nerve of him! He won't buy me out—I'll buy him out! And anyway, Jake doesn't have that kind of money. What kind of game is he playing?"

"Mira, you own a successful restaurant in the heart of Manhattan that is grossing over three million per year. Even allowing reasonable salaries for you and Jake, at least ten percent of that is pure profit. We have a consultant, a CPA, on retainer in the office. I showed him Grappa's financials, and he's sure Jake can borrow that much, even more, based on the restaurant receipts alone. The offer is too low, but at least it's a serious opening. Anyway, there's more. They propose you take over the lease on the apartment; all outstanding credit card debt is to be split jointly; you get the Italian poster collection; he wants the season tickets to the Met. Add the price from the buyout, plus child support, and you are sitting pretty. In terms of a counteroffer, here's what I propose—"

"Hold on a minute, Jerry. I'm not selling the restaurant. I don't want to be bought out. And even if I did consider selling my share, I wouldn't sell it to Jake. No way. Selling out, particularly to Jake, means the end of everything. No, I want Grappa, Jerry. Make it happen."

Jerry doesn't say anything right away. After a pause, he says, "Look, Mira, I'll do whatever you want, but have you really thought about what this means? After all, you've got a baby to raise, and the money from a buyout could give you time to be at home with her. You could take a breather, figure out what you want to do, and still have capital to invest in a new venture if you want. I don't know, but if I were you, I'd at least consider it."

A new venture? Starting up a new restaurant? "No way, Jerry. I can't do another restaurant. It is a tough market; the start-up costs are prohibitive, not to mention the hours, the personal investment. Not while Chloe is a child. Grappa is well established, is operating in the black, and unless we keep screwing it up, we've got a loyal following. I'd be a fool to let it go."

"Jake will never agree to work for you. You'd lose him as chef."

"Just like he'd lose me if I sold to him. And with the extra hundred thousand or so Jake won't be taking out of the profits, I can look for someone really great. Or, better yet, promote Tony. He's been practically running the place as it is."

Quite frankly, I am offended by Jerry's attitude. *I'm* Grappa, not Jake. Why doesn't he see this? Sure, Jake can cook; sure, he's great under pressure in the kitchen, but great chefs do not necessarily make great business people. From the first, I've been the one to attend to the thousands of details, to run the business, to make sure we got some publicity, to schmooze with regular clients, and to add, I think, my own innovative approach to the preparation and delivery of the food.

Could it be because I'm a woman? I should be willing to cut Jerry some slack—he doesn't know much about the industry, and his comments may just be a knee-jerk reaction from a lawyer accustomed to representing the wives of wealthy executives. But this is my future we're talking about. I'm impatient and in no mood to walk him, a relative outsider, through the complicated inner workings of the restaurant world.

"Look, Jerry, this isn't just a whim of mine. I've been thinking about it for a while. I had just hoped that Jake and I would be able to work it out . . ." I say, suddenly embarrassed, "with Grappa."

I can hear him exhale into the phone. "That would be tough, Mira. I've seen many successful businesses fail because ex-partners just can't work together, particularly when the business involves as much day-to-day decision making as yours does. Divorce is war, most of the time anyway. Throw a business into the mix, and you've got the potential for some scorched earth. Okay, Mira, you want the restaurant. What do you think it is worth?"

What is Grappa worth? Of course, Jerry is asking me for a dollar figure, but that's only a small piece of what Grappa is worth to me.

"Jerry, you said this consultant has taken a look at the books? What does he think it is worth?"

"Well, he said Jake's offer was a bit low, but he did not mention a precise number. These accountants can be tough to nail down. Let me see if I can reach him and at least get a range of values."

Jerry calls me back half an hour later. "Well, it took some doing, but I got him to a pretty narrow range for an accountant: considering the existing debt and mortgage, the equity value of the restaurant is in the range of $2.1 to $2.2 million. . . ." Wow—we owned something worth over two million dollars, had been multimillionaires really, without ever even knowing it.

Fifteen minutes later Jerry has explained to me (for the second time) what is, in his opinion, a brilliant strategy. Our opening move will be to counteroffer Jake exactly the terms he offered me—

$950,000, with $250,000 up front and the rest over four years. When they reject it, as they are guaranteed to do, that puts us in the driver's seat. We will have established that they tried to lowball us. Then, we counter by proposing—and this Jerry assures me is the brilliant part—that I set the amount that I think Grappa is worth, and Jake gets to decide who buys out whom. Since Jake will have to pay me child support over the buyout period, we can set the buyout at a number that I can afford to pay, but Jake cannot, virtually guaranteeing that I end up with Grappa. Of course, the higher we set the number, the more I'm cheating myself, but the more I raise the odds of getting Grappa.

"Are you sure you're okay with a highball offer?" Jerry asks me, for the third time.

"Jerry, Grappa is like my child. How much would you pay to keep your child?"

In that case, Jerry assures me, there's no downside to this strategy. I either win Grappa or I get paid considerably more than my share is worth.

The meeting is scheduled for ten the following morning, and I agree to show up at Jerry's office by nine thirty for final strategizing. He tells me that I should be prepared for Nicola to be there, too. "What! Why would she have a right to be there? This is between me and Jake!" Jerry instructs me that, although Jake and I are the actual "parties," it would be bad form to try to exclude Nicola, and if I want to, I can bring a friend for moral support as well. Who would I bring? Hope? Renata? And why would I subject anyone to this, let alone someone I call a friend? Finally, Jerry further instructs me that if I'm worried about controlling myself, I should try to avoid looking at them. Nor should I talk directly to Jake. All communication will be handled through the lawyers.

Predictably, I don't sleep, my angst extending well beyond the ministrations of the lone Valium I manage to scrounge from the bottom of my travel bag at three fifteen in the morning. I'm a nervous flyer; it's left over from the trip we took to Italy for our anniversary three years ago and has probably long since expired, but I wipe off the lint and swallow it nonetheless, washing it down with the dregs from the wine bottle that I opened after Jerry's initial phone call.

Despite the confidence with which I've stated my intentions to Jerry, I have some lingering doubts about running the restaurant on my own. There's a niggling suspicion that perhaps I haven't been completely fair to Jake. After all, he had helped get Grappa off the ground. It had been his idea to expand, a risky move and one that originally I was against. But Jake sensed that the market was right, that there was room for at least one more good, midsized Italian restaurant in the Village. And so we had expanded from fifteen to twenty-six tables after our first year in business, a move that ultimately more than doubled our profits. Also, like it or not, Jake is a good chef, and I've learned more than a few things about cooking from him.

Finally, I give up trying to sleep and turn on TV Land, which, as luck would have it, is playing an *I Love Lucy* marathon. Fading in and out of consciousness I listen to Lucy and Ricky argue, tease, and deceive each other and then make up. All is forgiven at the end of each episode. I try not to think about Lucy and Desi's real life together, which I understand was plagued by domestic strife, conniving, and betrayal. Yet another married couple whose business and romantic relationships had gone sour. Not that the TV Land version of marriage was a picnic, but wouldn't it be nice if every twenty-four minutes you could start over, take a marital mulligan, wipe the domestic slate clean?

Who was I kidding? Jake and I hadn't been married long enough to make it to syndication.

The offices of Tyler, Fox, and Rosenberg are on the thirty-fifth floor of the Seagram Building. Perhaps because Jerry is anticipating that we may have to be rushed off to separate corners for pep talks, cool downs, or time-outs, he's provided us with a large conference room. Jake and I, along with our respective lawyers, sit across from each other at a table that could easily accommodate twenty people. To my immense relief, there's no sign of Nicola.

On the rosewood table between us is a tray with a coffee pot, some cups, and a plate of donuts. In case anyone feels like eating. Across the table Jake looks small and boyish, out of place in his khakis and blazer when I'm so used to seeing him in his chef's whites or a tee shirt and jeans. He looks like he's borrowed his older brother's clothes for some big date. He gives me a curt smile and a brief nod, then immediately looks away. His lawyer has probably given him the same instruction mine has given me. Jake's lawyer, whose name is Ethan Bowman, greets Jerry enthusiastically, shaking hands and patting him on the shoulder. They know each other well enough to ask after their respective wives, which I think is rather tactless given the fact that they are charged this morning with the severing of certain matrimonial ties, and ought not to be broadcasting their successful marriages under the noses of clients whose relationship failures, so obvious and recent, are paying their bills.

As Jerry advised, I don't look at Jake except once, when the conversation turns to the disposition of the season tickets to the Met. At that point, I dare to meet his gaze. I'd gotten Jake a three-opera subscription package for his birthday the year after Grappa opened. For the first time in our professional lives, we were calling the shots and could count on taking the occasional Monday evening off. I splurged on Dress Circle seats, hoping that one day I'd learn to share Jake's enthusiasm for opera, although I never had. I remove a medium-sized manila envelope from my purse and slide the package containing the tickets across the table to Jake.

"Here. You've missed the first one, but all the others are there. I didn't use the tickets to *Turandot,* so maybe you can exchange them for credit. The subscription is in my name, but you can renew it in yours and still keep the same seats next year, if you want. I checked."

Jerry gives me an annoyed look. We hadn't discussed this in advance, and I can tell that he thinks it's a bad move to just fork over the tickets when perhaps he could have used them to extract some other concession from Jake, but I don't care.

"I don't want them," I say, with a shrug of my shoulders, to Jake, to Jerry, to Ethan, if he cares. Then, turning to look at Jake, I say, "I hate opera."

"Thanks," Jake says very quietly, not meeting my eye and making no move to claim the tickets.

"While we're dealing with the disposition of the minor assets, my client, Ms. Rinaldi, requests that you reimburse her for the value of the subscription, the cost of which we will let you know, but which we estimate to be worth approximately a thousand dollars." Jerry delivers this bit of news without missing a beat, while giving me a look that seems to say, "Wipe that incredulous look off your face. You screwed up with the tickets, and now I'm backpedaling in order to save you from yourself." It's clear that if I open my mouth at this moment, Jerry will stab me with his Pentel Rolling Writer pen.

"Well, then, that takes care of that," says Ethan. "I think we can move on. Have you given any consideration to my client's offer to buy out your client's share of the restaurant for $950,000? I think you'll agree $950,000 is a generous offer."

"Ethan," Jerry says, shaking his head and clucking at him like an admonishing parent. "Generous? Do you really think so?"

"We don't just think it, we know it."

"I'm curious, just how did you arrive at that number? Did you just pull it 'out of the air' or was that based on a careful economic review of the financials?" Jerry leans forward and furrows his brow, apparently enjoying himself.

"I can assure you that we did a thorough review of the financials, and that review confirms that this buyout price is more than fair. Quite generous, in fact," Ethan says, picking up confidence as he hears himself talk.

"Okay, great. Your word is good enough for me. In that case, my client will agree to the price. Only we will suggest just one change. Instead of Mr. Shaw buying Ms. Rinaldi out, Ms. Rinaldi will buy Mr. Shaw out—at this very generous price."

I cannot help feeling respect and admiration for Jerry's skill as the trap is sprung. Ethan's broad smile quickly changes to a surprised scowl as it visibly dawns on him that he has been hoisted on his own petard. Jake, who is slower on the uptake, just sits with his jaw hanging wide open.

This is why I'm paying Jerry five hundred dollars an hour.

Jerry finishes with a cavalier shake of his head and lifts his open palms as if to say, "Who knew?" Jake exhales forcibly, his mouth now set in a grim line. Despite what a "generous" offer it is, for some reason Ethan does not even have to consult with his client before responding: "No deal."

"What's the matter? Don't you like the number?" Jerry's voice is light, teasing even, a look of feigned surprise slowly spreading across his well-trained face.

I can detect a thin, almost imperceptible sheen of sweat on Jake's furrowed brow. I can feel his eyes on me, too. Determined not to meet his gaze, I busy myself with removing stray traces of dried pasta dough from beneath my fingernails. Jake scribbles a note and passes it to Ethan. Ignoring Jerry's challenge, Ethan uses the note as an excuse to regroup. "Please give me a moment to confer with my client," he says.

After a brief, whispered conference, Ethan turns to Jerry and says, a little too good-naturedly, "We are approaching year's end, and my client feels that the financials we have to date may not anticipate the profits realized by the last quarter, and that, as you know, will impact the value of the buyout. Somehow, despite the economy, all signs indicate the biggest year for Grappa yet. So it seems that the number we have previously given you, while more than generous based on historical statistics, in fact"—Ethan pauses to clear his throat—"may not have adequately valued Grappa's future potential."

"Okay, so give us a new number." Jerry leans back into his swivel chair, removes his glasses, and carefully chews the plastic-coated earpiece.

This time Ethan looks at Jake, who gives a slight shake of the head. "Before we get to throwing out numbers here, I think we need to clarify exactly whose offer is on the table. Who is buying out whom?"

Without realizing it, I've been holding my breath, and as this last, thinly concealed challenge is tossed our way by Ethan Bowman, I exhale deeply, audibly. Jerry glances at me and flashes me a cautionary look.

"Exactly," says Jerry, who begins to rock gently in his swivel chair, letting the single word he has spoken hang like an odor, crisp and pungent, in the air. The only noise in the room is the squeak of the ball bearing in Jerry's leather armchair. Jerry appears to be the only one not bothered by the silence. The rest of us shift uncomfortably in our seats.

After a minute Ethan continues in an oily voice. "Well, my client feels that his work, in large measure, is responsible for Grappa's success. Not only does he have an inspiring pedigree and an excellent reputation, he is the signature chef. He is the person whose food people come to eat. Without him, Grappa's continued success is, I'm afraid, a very open question."

"What! Jake, how can you let him—" Jerry quickly cuts me off.

"Mira, it's okay. I'll handle it," Jerry says, his hand resting firmly on my forearm.

Ethan Bowman, the beast, has the nerve to smile at me as he reaches across the table and plucks a cream-filled donut from the plate. It's a smirk really, filled with bravura. Having lost round one to Jerry, Ethan apparently is now taking great delight in dangling an appendage dangerously close to the lion's cage and emerging, thus far at least, covered only in powdered sugar. Jake, at whom I'm now glaring, has poured himself a cup of coffee and is now reading the Equal package like it was a best seller.

"Ethan, as you and Mr. Shaw are undoubtedly aware, Ms. Rinaldi has been in charge of running the restaurant, managing the personnel, handling the lion's share of contacts with outside purveyors, and overseeing the financial aspects of running a successful business. In fact, since the parties' separation, Ms. Rinaldi has completely taken over the management of the restaurant, as well as continuing to run the kitchen during lunch five days a week, without much input or cooperation from your client. This, as you know, is a massive undertaking and one that my client has demonstrated considerable talent for. In addition to being an excellent cook, Ms. Rinaldi is also a shrewd businesswoman. One who, frankly, has some concerns about the continued good health of the restaurant should Mr. Shaw take over. There are no assurances that, absent *her* excellent management skills, Grappa will continue to prosper."

I permit myself another breath, satisfied that, at least for the time being, Jerry has managed to hold his own against Bowman's spurious assertions.

Ethan takes a bite out of the donut as he considers his next move. Wiping his mouth, and all traces of the smile, he turns to look from me to Jerry. "Of course, I'm by no means suggesting that in the past Ms. Rinaldi has made anything but a valuable contribution toward Grappa's success. One must consider, however, that lately your client has been known to have some, ah, difficulty controlling her emotions, which has, regrettably, hampered productive communication between the parties." Ethan pauses for effect, following the delivery of this last, fascinating tidbit, no doubt to allow his none-too-subtle dig at my anger-management sentence to fully register. "Her taking over the management of the restaurant, as you contend," he continues, "is not the result of any failing on my client's part. She has not assumed these responsibilities because my client has been derelict in his duties. Quite the contrary, in fact. She has bulldozed her way onto my client's turf, making decisions, important decisions, without consulting him. Most recently, her inability to communicate resulted in a disastrous day for the restaurant, and more disastrous days like that could quickly lose the goodwill that Grappa has taken years to accumulate."

Unable to look at Ethan, I grip the armrests of the chair while keeping my gaze riveted on a crumb that has fallen from Ethan's pathetic maw to the table in front of him, wishing all the while that I had paid more attention in anger-management class. I loathe him. Hate him for representing Jake, for believing Jake enough to spout these lies.

I look up at Jake, who is in the process of adding a third packet of Equal to his coffee. It is clear to me that even Jake knows this isn't true. It's simply too much.

"Jake, how can you sit there and let him say this. I tried to talk to you. . . ."

Jerry's hand is on my arm again, but I shrug it off. I will not be reined in this time.

Ethan clears his throat uncomfortably as I continue, my eyes boring into Jake, my voice rising against my will, as I challenge

Ethan's ridiculous interpretation of the events and deliver my own unwavering version of the truth—that Nicola removed those orders in a direct move to sabotage the restaurant. However, it's obvious that Jake isn't going to acknowledge what even he must now suspect is true. He sinks into his chair, withdrawing into the too-big collar of his shirt. Jerry stands up and puts a hand on my shoulder. "May we have a minute, please?" he says to Ethan and Jake.

Ethan picks up his donut as Jerry propels me out into the hallway. He closes the door and leans against it, facing me with his arms folded. "Jesus, Mira. Get a grip. I know this is hard, but use your head. This is posturing, pure and simple. And you have just played into their hands. They make a comment about your emotional volatility and suddenly you turn into the Incredible Hulk." Jerry takes off his glasses and begins massaging his temples. "How about we listen to their next move and see where it leads. Do you think you can just let me do the talking? I promise not to agree to anything without talking with you about it, okay?" Tight-lipped and abashed, I nod.

Jerry gestures toward the door. "Are you ready, or do you want to take a couple more minutes?"

"He's a dreadful man, who is taking considerable pleasure in baiting me. I would like to ram that donut down his porcine throat." I'm muttering, through clenched teeth, to no one in particular, and my breath is coming in quick gusts.

Jerry puts his hand on my shoulder and gives me an incredulous look. "Ethan? Are you talking about Ethan? Mira, don't be silly. Don't let him get to you. He's baiting you because he can. Don't let him. I've seen him do much worse. Take a deep breath or something. Let it go." Wish it were that simple.

"And what about Nicola? She's the one who screwed up. That whole thing was her fault, not mine. She's the one who didn't deliver those orders." My voice is strained and rising to an uncomfortable pitch as I threaten Jerry with a pointed finger.

He raises his arms in mock surrender. "Mira, my suggestion is that we stay away from Nicola altogether. It doesn't matter whose fault it was, okay? Let it go. Do you think you can do that, at least for these negotiations?"

"Fine," I tell him. I will keep myself quiet and under control even if I have to superglue my lips shut.

Ethan and Jake are in the midst of their own powwow, heads bent together, while Ethan scribbles furiously on the yellow legal pad between them. The table is covered in powdered sugar. When we enter the room, Ethan flips the page to display a blank one, and Jake slides a couple of inches back over to his side of the table.

"Ready?" Ethan chirps innocently.

We are barely ensconced on our side of the table when Ethan continues. "It appears we may have inadvertently hit a hot button. Of course, both Mr. Shaw and Ms. Rinaldi are responsible for Grappa's success, and although it's certainly regrettable that the parties can no longer remain married, the fact remains that the present arrangement is not the best possible one for Grappa, on which both parties rely for their livelihood. Income is a significant concern to both our clients. There is, after all, a child concerned."

"Precisely," Jerry continues, his tone suddenly impatient. "Both parties apparently want the restaurant, and it's clear that continuing on as they have been is not good for them or Grappa's long-term financial health. Okay, one obvious option would be for Mr. Shaw and Ms. Rinaldi to both agree to sell the restaurant to an independent third party. Which does not," Jerry pauses for a second, looking from Jake to me and noting our stiffened postures at the mere suggestion, "appear to be the preferred option. Therefore, after our own careful review of the financials we have come up with what we think is a fair and equitable compromise."

"We're listening," Ethan says, rubbing his jaw with his hand, leaving a thin sheen of powdered sugar across one of his chins.

"No more quibbling about price. My client will set the present value of the restaurant and four-year payment terms. Mr. Shaw gets to decide whether he wants to buy her share or sell his share at half the total restaurant value. The purchasing party also assumes one hundred percent of the existing assets, mortgage, and other debt."

Jerry, who delivers this small missile with a "let's go" attitude, picks up his pen and leans forward. His expectant gaze this time is fixed on Jake, who, I note with pleasure, looks totally flummoxed by Jerry's suggestion. Jake swivels to look at Ethan, who ignores him. So focused is Ethan on Jerry that he slowly puts down his latest donut, which he had been about to take a bite of, and stares at Jerry with a furrowed brow. It takes him several seconds before the idea fully registers.

"An interesting idea." Ethan sounds genuinely surprised by Jerry's offer and cannot quite manage to keep the admiration out of his voice. At least he recognizes a creative offer when he hears one. "Ms. Rinaldi sets the price and payout terms, and Mr. Shaw decides to buy out or sell?" Ethan says this speculatively, weighing each word, moving slowly so that Jake might take it in. Jake, who has now leaned in toward Ethan, is gesturing with the yellow legal pad, on which he's scribbled something. Ethan turns toward Jake, and the two of them exchange a couple of words. "Okay, we're in," he says with a smile, before continuing. "And have you and Ms. Rinaldi, by chance, developed a price and a payout proposal we might consider?" It is clear from the way Ethan says this that he knows we have, and he now turns his gaze from Jerry to me. This time there's no trace of condescension, only a speculative gleam in his eyes. It's apparent in the attention with which he holds my gaze that he understands he has underestimated my resolve. I toss a small smile in his direction that I hope he finds unnerving.

"As a matter of fact, gentlemen, she has. After careful consideration, the value of Grappa is set at $2.5 million."

chapter 11

Whatever I would have expected to feel at this moment, excitement, sadness, anger, frustration, exhilaration, is suddenly obscured by a sudden and almost uncontrollable urge for a bowl of escarole soup. Rich chicken stock, bitter escarole, the freshly grated Parmigiano Reggiano. Lots of black pepper. Some crusty warm bread and a glass of red wine. A big one. I look over at Jake, wondering if this is a natural foodie reaction, but one look tells me that Jake isn't thinking about food. Unless, perhaps it's me, roasting on a spit. From across the table I can see the vein in his forehead pulsating, and he's rubbing it like it hurts. Rubbing it with his burned, scarred, and calloused hands. Hands I loved.

Following the dropping of this latest bomb, and Jerry's explanation of the payment timing, the meeting is over quickly. Ethan promises to be in touch once they have had time to fully digest our proposal. The four of us stand, and Ethan and Jerry shake hands. Ethan offers me his hand, and I shake it as well, though I don't want to. Jerry and Jake shake, leaving Jake and me to stand there, with our arms dangling awkwardly by our sides, looking like the emotionally stunted fools we undoubtedly are.

Jerry detains me on the way out. "It couldn't have gone better, Mira. We've got them squirming. Something tells me we'll be hearing from them soon." Jerry's secretary waylays him on the way out of the conference room and hands him a sheaf of pink message slips. As Jerry flips through them, she calls over her shoulder, "You're late for your eleven o'clock conference call." Jerry says a hasty good-bye and hurries off, promising to call me as soon as he hears from Ethan.

I glance at my watch. Lunch starts in less than an hour, barely enough time for me to make it back down to Lower Manhattan and change my clothes. I call Tony from my cell phone to tell him I'm on my way, asking before we hang up how much escarole we have in the walk-in. I'm in the mood to pamper myself, and today I've decided that the only thing that will satisfy me, apart, of course, from Jake's instant capitulation, is the crisp, bitter flavor of that soup. Also, lunch will likely be the only opportunity I have to eat today, because right after lunch I have to attend another anger-management class.

Because I don't want to run the risk of having to ride down in the elevator with Jake and Ethan, I make a stop in the ladies' room, hopefully allowing them time to vacate the building. I wash my hands, trying to avoid looking at myself in the mirror. I'm uncomfortable in this constricting power suit, a pre-pregnancy outfit I had unearthed in the wee hours of the morning, the jacket of which, unbuttoned, is tight across my back. As I bend over the sink, I can hear a small, ominous rip somewhere in the jacket's recesses. My hair has come loose, and there are dark circles under my eyes, courtesy of the TV Land, wine and Valium cocktail I'd subjected myself to in preparation for this morning's meeting.

On my way out of the building, I see Jake, Ethan, and Nicola standing smack in the middle of the path out of the revolving door. So, she *had* been here, lurking around somewhere. Even from this distance I can see Jake's grim expression; he is talking animatedly, and his energetic gesticulations are causing people exiting the revolving door to have to duck to avoid being taken out by an errant swipe. Nicola has one arm linked through Jake's, her other arm resting consolingly on his chest.

Obviously, I can't take the revolving door without running smack into them, so instead I walk around to the other door, meaning that, once out of the building, I'll have to walk past them. Shit. I wish my jacket fit better and that I'd taken a minute to fix my hair, particularly since Nicola, as usual, is dressed to the nines. She's wearing a long orange sweater and a faux Pucci scarf over black pants and boots with stiletto heels. On my way out of the building I reach into my bag, rummaging for a baseball cap or an umbrella, anything that might allow me to pass them unnoticed, but luckily the three of them are far too absorbed in their strategizing to notice me at all. On my way by, I can't resist sneaking a look at her. Just as I'm about to pass them, Jake reaches across and gives Nicola's stomach a gentle pat. It's an intimate gesture and an unusual one. It takes a couple of seconds for my brain to fully register its implication; my body, as usual, is one step ahead. It begins as a chill at the base of my spine, quickly spreading its icy tentacles through my arms and legs. Luckily, the crowd passing in front of the building jostles me along; otherwise I might have stood frozen and rooted to the spot. Could it be?

I make it to the corner of Fifty-fourth and Fifth before I stop to hail a taxi. I slump back into the lumpy vinyl seat. I haven't seen Nicola in months, except for that day at the restaurant, and then she had been wearing baggy pants and a chef's tunic. Perhaps no accident, but pregnant? That couldn't be. It simply couldn't be. Jake had made it absolutely clear, at least after the fact, that he didn't want children, that he had no desire to be a father. Hadn't he?

I'm so busy pondering the fundamental truths of my life that I don't immediately realize that the cab driver is trying to get my attention. He's babbling in some language that I don't immediately recognize as English.

"What?" I snap.

"Ees that you fun?"

"What, what are you saying? My fun?"

"Reenging, your fun?" He holds up his cell phone so I can see it. Even then, it takes me a few seconds to realize that my cell phone is ringing in my purse. I fumble to find it. "Hello, Mira, Jerry Fox here." My heart, which is already racing, seems suddenly to skip several beats, and I wonder, fleetingly, if this could be the beginning of cardiac arrest.

"What? Jerry, is that you?"

"Yep, listen Mira, I forgot to mention this to you, but Avi seemed to think we should start the ball rolling with financing the purchase of Grappa. It's a little premature, but the pre-approval is easy, and there's no downside to putting those wheels in motion. I just wanted to get your permission because I wouldn't be surprised if things start to move quickly. I've got a hunch they are in a hurry to get this done."

"You keep saying that, Jerry. What exactly makes you think they're in a hurry? What has Ethan told you?"

"Mira, Ethan didn't tell me anything, except that, well,"—he hesitates—"Jake and Nicola want to get married. Apparently they've already set a date."

"What? She's pregnant, isn't she?"

Jerry hesitates.

"Jerry? What do you know?" I demand.

"Nothing, I don't know if she's pregnant, but now that you mention it, I wouldn't be surprised. It would explain some things."

"Explain some things? Like what? I can't for the life of me imagine what it would explain!" Suddenly I'm yelling at Jerry, who is, once again, the blameless recipient of my uncontrollable ire. What exactly is Jerry talking about? What hasn't he told me? But I'm too wrapped up in venting to even give him a chance to answer.

"Jake has no interest in his daughter. *I* was the one who browbeat him into having a baby, which, it is clear from recent events, he didn't want. And now *she* is pregnant, and there he is stroking her stomach in the middle of fucking Park Avenue like some proud father." I let go of whatever control I'd been struggling to maintain, but when I open my mouth to speak, a choking sound, half sob, half growl, escapes me. It feels primal and guttural. The driver, who doesn't speak much English, has turned around and is looking at me with alarm as he slides the Plexiglas divider between the front and back seats closed, no doubt to protect himself from the transforming alien she-beast now occupying the backseat of his cab.

Jerry doesn't say anything. What can he say? The man is my lawyer, not my therapist. But when, after a moment, he speaks, his voice is gentle. "Mira, hold on here. You're reacting emotionally. You don't know that Nicola is preg—"

"What do you mean I'm reacting emotionally? How the hell else am I supposed to react? How can Jake do these things? How can he destroy everything, our marriage, Chloe's chance for a father, Grappa? How can he sleep at night? The deal is off. I won't settle. I won't give him a divorce. Let them wait!" I'm crying in earnest now, and I can tell from the sound of his voice that Jerry has picked up the receiver, lest the sound of a sobbing, hysterical woman on his speakerphone intrude on the sanctity of his well-appointed law firm.

"Mira," Jerry says quietly. "I know this is hard for you, but breaking off all negotiations is only going to make it harder in the long run. If you really want Grappa, let's take advantage of the situation. Why don't you take some time to calm down, and we can talk later when you're feeling better."

I nod mutely and mumble something about how we could all grow old waiting for that to happen and hang up without even saying good-bye. I sit there crying in the cab, which, it takes a minute for me to realize, is already stopped in front of the restaurant. The driver is looking at me expectantly from behind the Plexiglas screen.

"Ees this it, lady?"

As I pay the cabbie, I ask if he has any children and if he could ever imagine turning his back on them. What would make a man do such a thing, I ask? He considers my question, perhaps only pretending to have understood me. Then, after a moment, he says, "I dunnot know, lady. Maybe he is scared, or maybe he just don't love the mother enay more." Another sob escapes me, and he turns away to reset the meter. "But what do I know? I'm no Dr. Phil." And with a shrug of his shoulders he is gone.

At Grappa the final preparations are under way for lunch; the kitchen is tidy and well prepped. A vat of chicken stock is simmering, the fresh pasta is already drying on the racks, and Tony, bless him, has the prep cooks washing and chopping mountains of escarole. Ellen gestures to the bulletin board where she has pinned a couple of phone messages for me. There's just enough time before lunch orders start coming through to slip into the office and change. I studiously avoid looking at or sitting on the black leather couch, hideous talisman, the scene of the crime, as it were, the beginning of the end of life as I'd known it. As I lean against the desk, struggling to maintain my balance, trying to get both feet out of my pantyhose and into my pants, I feel the ire beginning to build. It is, by now, an uncomfortably familiar feeling, the seeds of which were planted here in this room, nurtured and sown on that very couch.

Suddenly, I'm straddling the couch cushion, a letter opener I've picked up off the desk poised dagger style in my hand. I plunge the opener in again and again, until the stuffing begins to fly and my chest is heaving. Finally, weakened and dizzy from the effort, I flip the cushion over and restuff and replace the pillows I've disturbed in my frenzy. I pull on my drawstring pants and tunic and wrap my apron, meticulously folding down the edge. I run my hand over it, appreciating its cool crispness against my flushed skin. Attacking the defenseless seat cushion was a childish, vindictive move, but it has given me a rush of satisfaction that only an act of pure and naked aggression can engender. Even Dr. Phil might understand.

Paolo, the guy who runs the security scanner at the Manhattan County Courthouse, and I have become sort of friends. Our friendship has evolved over the several weeks I've been attending anger-management classes, helped along by my chronic lateness and natural absentmindedness. The class meets at two thirty, which means that I have to leave Grappa before lunch is really over, often when things are most chaotic. In my haste, I invariably forget to remove from my knapsack or pockets items considered dangerous by the powers that be in Manhattan County. Things like a pepper mill, a whisk, assorted spoons, and once, an antique French fish-boning knife that I'd thrust into my belt during lunch and forgotten to remove. Okay, even I can see that the French boning knife, wonderful for filleting, represents a justifiable threat, but the pepper mill, at best, is questionable, and the only things at risk for being beaten senseless with the wire whisk are some unruly egg whites.

Usually confiscated items are not returned. Paolo, however, has been intrigued by my interesting and exotic contraband. It has been the subject of several conversations between us, usually as he summons the female matron to direct the hand search of my person. He knows and understands the attachment chefs have to the tools of our trade, having a brother who's a line cook at the Mesa Grill, who (you never know) might need a job someday. I'm sure Paolo sees our friendship as a potentially reciprocal one, which is fine with me. He's been gracious enough to hold my tools until class is over, sans the paperwork. Today, I've forgotten to remove my meat thermometer from my tunic pocket, a long, needle-like skewer with a sharp, pointed tip. He stows it in the top front pocket of his uniform and gives it a surreptitious little pat.

Class has already begun. The other five members are seated in a circle on the floor, eyes closed, practicing their breathing exercises. Mary Ann gives me a disapproving look as she gestures to a spot near her on the floor. I've learned from Mary Ann that my chronic lateness is a "passive-aggressive act," and that, for my optimal growth and development, I should at least attempt to "master" this unhealthy impulse. She's probably right about my lateness being passive-aggressive, but I personally prefer to think of this move from active to passive aggression as progress in the right direction, something to be lauded, not criticized.

Today I'm so mentally and physically depleted that I'm actually glad to be sitting on the filthy linoleum, breathing quietly in and out in the close company of the other unfortunate victims of their own impulses, with whom I have lately begun to feel a deeper kinship. I take my seat on the floor, positioning myself so I can stare into the laces of Mary Ann's brown Easy Spirit shoes and try to think quieting thoughts.

The only bright spot has been the catharsis afforded by the mutilated cushion, although even that has left me feeling exhausted. I know I'm being morose. Jerry's confidence ought to be infectious and probably would be, if it hadn't been for my suspicions, now rampant and unbridled, that Nicola is pregnant. And why should this matter so? I tell myself that I'm upset on Chloe's behalf. She has done nothing to warrant her father's rejection. I forced Jake into fatherhood when I should have known better. In truth, I viewed Jake's rejection of her as temporary, maybe because I still held out hope that our separation was temporary. I nursed a secret fantasy that perhaps it was her baby-ness that troubled Jake and once she began to walk and talk, as soon as she became a real person, Jake would come around. Only now, with the specter of Nicola's pregnancy, can I see how foolish I've been.

We're in the midst of our deep, cleansing breaths when my cell phone begins ringing. This is very bad. Not only was I late to class, but I've violated one of Mary Ann's other cardinal rules: Thou Shalt Not Forget to Turn Off Thy Cell Phone. I'm sure this particular instruction was repeated to everyone, as usual, at the beginning of class. Mary Ann is bristling, clearly prepared to excoriate the offender, so I follow my instincts and lie.

"It's me. I'm so sorry. My daughter has been quite ill, and I just didn't feel comfortable not being accessible. I'll just be a minute, I hope." I grab my purse and head for the door.

"Jerry?" I whisper, as soon as I'm safely in the hall outside the room.

"Mira, is that you? It's Jerry Fox."

At the sound of his voice I have a premonition that I should hang up instantly, let him think he got my voice mail. "I'm in anger-management class," I whisper into the phone.

"Oh." No apology. "Listen, I just got off the phone with Ethan Bowman. We need to talk."

There's something in Jerry's voice that I can hear quite clearly now.

"What, what is it?" I can feel panic rising, a fluttering that begins tremor-like at the base of my spine. I slide down the wall so that I'm sitting on the floor.

"Don't panic, Mira. Just an unexpected development that could turn out to be to your advantage," Jerry says, his voice intended to be soothing, but not in the least believable.

I hear him take a deep breath. "Jake's taken the option of buying Grappa. I know this isn't something we expected, but remember that we set the price for Grappa way above its fair market value. This can be a real windfall for you. . . ."

"Jerry," I say, my voice rising, "I thought you said this wouldn't happen!"

"Look, we did our best to minimize the likelihood that something like this would happen, but apparently they found some other way to finance the deal—not something we counted on. Listen, Mira, you can stay in the restaurant business if you want. In fact, with the money you receive from this deal, you could even buy into a bigger restaurant. . . ."

"Jerry," I interrupt, my voice steely, "I don't want another restaurant. I want this one. I want Grappa! *Your* job is to get me out of this deal. I don't care how you do it, but get me out of it. I will kill that fucking bastard and his whore before I see them take over MY restaurant!"

So absorbed and devastated am I by this news, I don't notice the door has opened. In fact, it's not until I find myself once again staring into a pair of brown lace-up shoes that I realize Mary Ann is standing right above me. I don't know how long she's been listening, but one look at her horrified face and I know that there's no way she has missed my last statement.

"Oh, Mira," she says, her eyes tired, her shoulders slumped. And then, turning noiselessly on her rubber-soled shoes, she returns to the classroom, shutting the door quietly and carefully behind her.

chapter 12

Of course, I try my best to salvage the situation. Once I realize Mary Ann has overheard my conversation with Jerry, I hang up immediately, thinking that if I can pull myself together, maybe I can turn this around. I dutifully turn off my cell phone and reclaim my place in the circle, doing my best to make helpful and encouraging comments to my fellow classmates. When, in response to one of Mary Ann's bland inquiries, an uncomfortable silence hangs in the room, I even jump to her aid, offering up a rare nugget from my own childhood, which necessitates an uncharacteristic foray into the uncharted land of self-disclosure.

Apart from her pitying gaze and the soft and defeated way in which she'd uttered my name, Mary Ann gives me no indication that she is inclined to view my unfortunate outburst as anything other than what it really is—emotional, careless in the extreme, but perhaps forgivable for having been uttered in the heat of anger and born of overwhelming disappointment. When the class is dismissed, Mary Ann doesn't meet my eye or make any attempt to detain me, a response, at the time, that I choose to interpret as empathic and merciful.

Perhaps I should have stayed behind, offering some explanation, but I didn't want to risk changing her mind. I am worried that in my frazzled emotional state I might say something to make things worse. I am so bent on escape that I don't even stop to retrieve my thermometer from Paolo on the way out, the loss of which, at the time, seems a small thing.

In addition to the disastrous Grappa negotiations, the incident in class gives me one more thing to worry about. I decide to give myself twenty-four hours to properly digest the news before calling Jerry back. So, the next day, when Ellen comes back into the kitchen to tell me that Jerry is in the restaurant and asking for me, I'm only a little surprised. I assume he's annoyed that I haven't returned his phone call, although I tell myself he might just as easily be meeting a client for lunch and wanting to make sure he got a good table. But, one look at his face, exhausted and lined, and the way his body seems to deflate once he catches sight of me, and I know the news isn't good.

"You should have at least told me," Jerry says, sneaking a glance toward the front door of the restaurant. He then slides a legal-sized manila folder onto the empty plate in front of me.

It seems that Ethan Bowman has filed a contempt petition against me and a warrant has been issued for my arrest. I'm charged with violating the Order of Protection—the evidence of which, Jerry tells me with a small and very tired smile, is two death threats made on the lives of Jake and Nicola, one verbal and the other involving the "willful destruction and mutilation of a black leather couch in the victims' private office, constituting an obvious threat to the health and well-being of said victims."

Jerry hands me the papers. *The State of New York v. Mirabella Rinaldi.* Attached as Exhibit A to the Emergency Contempt Petition is a typed letter from Mary Ann Chambers, MSW, describing, complete with an unfortunately accurate quote, my overheard statement in the hallway. In addition, she notes that in her considered professional opinion I have not demonstrated sufficient effort in the class, as evidenced by my chronic lateness and my previous lack of control.

And that was even before Ethan Bowman had gotten to her.

Ethan received a copy of the letter by messenger early this morning, conveniently timed to coincide with a phone call from

Jake and Nicola reporting their discovery of the couch cushion late last night. The substance of Ethan's follow-up phone conversation with Mary Ann is attached in Ethan's affirmation (Exhibit B of the petition), wherein she allegedly responds to Ethan's allegation that I had been stalking Nicola as "consistent with my prior behavior." She also claims that my behavior and psychological state creates "a significant risk of further injury to said victims." I wonder whether these are really Mary Ann's statements or, like Ethan's tactics in our negotiation session, rococo-style elaborations of the truth.

The letter opener, the alleged weapon, has been removed from the premises as evidence, along with my confiscated meat thermometer, relinquished by Paolo when it had gone unclaimed. The petition seeks my immediate arrest for violation of my parole.

And so, Jerry has arrived at Grappa one step ahead of the sheriff, in an attempt to spare me the ignominy of another public arrest. "In situations like this, where potential for imminent harm is alleged, they arrest first and hold the hearing after. When I received service of the petition this morning, I called a friend at the sheriff's office and asked them to let you turn yourself in voluntarily. We have until two this afternoon to get you down there. If you do this voluntarily, it will also help us get lower bail."

"Jerry, how could this be happening? What am I supposed to do about Chloe?"

"My partner Martin is meeting us at the courthouse. He's already working on an answer to the petition. If you come voluntarily, and things go as I expect, we can post bail and get you back home by dinnertime."

Once we are both safely seated in the back of the Lincoln Town Car Jerry's firm sent, Jerry pours two scotches.

"Drink this. It'll take the edge off," he tells me, handing me one of the cut crystal tumblers, then taking a hefty swig himself.

Nothing short of a lobotomy, however, could have taken the edge off arriving at the courthouse, where, for the second time in three months, I'm fingerprinted, photographed, and asked to post bail, which I'm granted, but only on the condition that I not come within two hundred yards of Jake, Nicola, their residence, or their place of work. I'm banished from my own restaurant, at least until the parole revocation hearing, scheduled for December the twenty-third.

In the two weeks since the bail hearing, Jerry's partner, Martin, the criminal attorney who will take the lead in defending me, has been calling me regularly with lists of things I should do to help prepare my case. One of my primary assignments has been to round up character witnesses, people who are willing to testify that I am, in fact, a reasonable woman, kind, friendly, a good mother. I've asked Renata and Hope and, to my surprise and gratitude, Tony has also volunteered to testify on my behalf, a risky move given the fact that allegiance to Jake, or at least not offending him, would be a much safer bet for his future livelihood. Although touched, I tell Tony that I can't accept his offer and that he best keep his head down in this conflict.

Yesterday's "to do" list, which I'm just getting around to fulfilling, was to find a witness from Chloe's day care to testify about my good parenting skills. I spent the better part of yesterday blanching at the idea, but because my legal team has managed to convince me of the seriousness of the charges I'm facing, I've agreed to do it. It is the thought of this loathsome task that has me awake and crying in the predawn gloom, waiting until a little bit before seven when I know that Chloe's teacher, Lucy, will arrive at the day care. I'm steeling myself to disclose the entire sordid story and convince her that she should help me. I should be embarrassed, but at this point embarrassment seems a strange and distant emotion, a luxury I can no longer afford.

Martin has told me that we have no defense to the charges that I'm technically in contempt— I cannot deny making the statement I made, and my fingerprints are all over the letter opener. We will plead nolo contendere to the charges and focus on the fact that, while perhaps a technical violation, there was never any serious threat to Jake or Nicola. In addition, we must develop a proposal to convince the court that I'm in no position to cause them any further harm. Martin and Jerry want me to agree to exile myself—to voluntarily leave the city for at least the next six months. They assure me that given a choice between jail and Pittsburgh, I should choose the latter.

I don't like Martin, and I'm not sure how much I should trust him. The best assurance he can give me is that even if the judge fails to suspend the sentence, it will definitely be a "short term in a minimum security facility." No sweat. It may not seem like much to Martin, who represents clients who go to the "Big House" to spend decades of their lives wearing orange jumpsuits and rubber-soled shoes, but to me it is precious little comfort. Jerry, on the other hand, has been more optimistic, saying that he thinks it likely that the judge will give me a suspended sentence, particularly in light of our voluntary exile offer. But, after his miscalculation on Grappa, I'm not much inclined to trust his judgment either.

Perhaps I've already begun to anticipate the inevitable. If I'm fortunate enough to escape jail time, I'm prepared to flee, and Pittsburgh now has more to recommend it than it did a few short weeks ago. For starters, I have at least two people there who love me, two more than this city of six million can claim. And even if Jerry and Martin hadn't convinced me to offer to exile myself, I couldn't have stayed here, in this apartment, a mere three blocks from Grappa, and where I can no longer buy an espresso and a *Times* at my favorite coffee bar without danger of arrest.

Of course, there are other possibilities, other cities, other countries even. I could go back to Italy, where for years I'd been happy. While there's something to be said for seeking anonymity, it, like embarrassment, might be a luxury I can no longer afford. There's Chloe to think of.

A child needs family, and I doubt that, on my own, I'm strong enough or competent enough to give her all she needs. Sure, I can feed and nourish her body, because that's what I know how to do, but what about nourishing her tiny soul? How can I do that when all reason, all capacity for self-control is seeping out of me, a slow and steady leak that began when Jake left? When will I stop leaking, and what will happen then, when there's nothing left? Could love and betrayal really have transformed me into this rash, vengeful person?

With a sigh I fling back the coverlet in which I've cocooned myself, make my way to the kitchen, and put on some coffee. It's another misty day, cold and overcast from the look of it. I sit at the table, sipping an espresso and looking out the window below me onto Perry Street. It's only after I've been looking steadily, staring really, because I've been up for so long and am tired in a dazed kind of way, that I notice a person standing in the alleyway across the street. There's a slight mist, and he, or she, is wearing a rain jacket with a hood, so I cannot see a face, but the drawstring chef's pants are unmistakable.

Seconds later the phone rings, and I answer it with trembling hands. It's Jake. Looking out the window I can see him holding the phone to his ear. He's crossed the street and is standing on the bottom step of the brownstone, leaning against the railing. He looks up at the apartment window, and when he sees me watching him, he raises his hand in a kind of half wave. He doesn't say anything for several seconds, and I think maybe he's trying to spook me.

"I need to talk to you," he finally says, his voice raspy and soft.

I don't ask him why. In fact, I don't say anything at all. I feel only a small shiver of apprehension as I cross the room and press the buzzer. I can hear his steps on the stairs, heavy and uneven. I open the door and watch his approach. I'm no longer afraid, not really anyway. Let him do his worst, whatever that may be.

"I didn't mean for this—" Jake begins, standing in the doorway, dripping onto the carpet. He can't seem to finish the sentence. I pull the door open wider and move aside. Even after everything that has happened between us, I'm unable to let Jake, the man who has cost me my beloved restaurant and everything I've struggled to build in the last decade of my life, stand there dripping on my front carpet. "Nicola doesn't know I'm here," he says, stepping into the apartment and taking off his raincoat. He runs his fingers through his damp hair, slicking it back against his head. "But this needs to be done, Mira." He doesn't look at me, hasn't from the moment he entered the apartment. Instead, he looks around the sparsely furnished room, at the empty boxes stacked in the middle of the living room.

"Where are you going?" he asks.

Where am I going?

"I don't know, Jake, but it looks like jail at the moment. I'll be sure to send you my forwarding address."

He flinches. "Listen, Mira, that's why I'm here. I never meant things to go this far. I don't want you to go to jail. It isn't fair to you or to Chloe."

"Well, Jake, exactly what part did you think was fair to us? Leaving me for Nicola? Abandoning your only child? Cutting me out of Grappa?" He looks stricken, as if I've slapped him.

"Cutting *you* out of Grappa? You had a fair shot, Mira! It was your prop—Wait, I'm not going to do this. I didn't come here to argue with you," he says, raising his hands to cover his eyes, as if he can't trust himself to look at me.

"So, why did you come here then? What more could you possibly want from us?"

"I came here to offer you a compromise. I want Grappa. But I can't afford to pay you what you want *and* continue to pay child support."

"But you agreed to the price!"

"I know. I know. But it isn't that simple, as I think you know." He raises one eyebrow and flashes me a disgusted look. "Ethan's plan to help finance the deal was to file a civil suit against you, on Nicola's behalf, seeking damages for your assault on her. She went through a very rough time and still isn't over it. I didn't want to go along with that, but I didn't know what else to do. Now Ethan is pressuring us to press these other charges partially for the leverage it will give us in the civil lawsuit."

I let Jake's words wash over me. A civil suit on top of everything else? The whole offer to pay me the extra money was part of a ploy? I'm so overwhelmed that, for once, my reliable temper has failed to ignite. I sink into the sofa.

"Look," Jake says. "Don't worry about it. I've found another alternative. The money is no longer as much of an issue. I just want this to be over. Ethan tells me you're offering to leave New York. If I can convince Nicola to drop all of the charges and claims against you, make this whole Order of Protection violation go away, will you just . . ." He lets the sentence hang there, as if I'll somehow understand the perversity of his suggestion without his having to sully himself by uttering the words.

But I refuse to spare him. I stare up at him, our eyes locked in a grim face-off until Jake is forced to turn away. I suppose I should find it encouraging, evidence that he has some remaining scruples, that he can't look me in the eye as he gathers the courage to sell his daughter.

"We will drop all charges and claims against you if you agree to leave New York for at least six months, grant an immediate divorce, and forego all child support." He says this quickly, as if he has rehearsed it many times, and exhales deeply once he's finished. "You still walk away with well over a million dollars, plenty of money to take care of you and Chloe until you decide what you want to do next. I'm not going to try to be an involved father, Mira. You're free to walk away. Go away. I'll relinquish my parental rights, if that's what you want. She doesn't need to be one of those messed up kids with two families who are constantly battling each other."

"Jesus Christ, Jake! Don't you pretend for one minute that what you're doing is good for her or for me. Just tell me one thing. Is it true? Is she pregnant?" He turns away and reaches for his raincoat. "I'm sorry," is all he has to say.

A couple of hours later I make one last call to Jake. By nine thirty I'm on the phone to Jerry, telling him I want to settle and filling him in on the substance of Jake's offer. I'm efficient and businesslike, and if Jerry is startled by my composure, by the way I have just been able to let go of everything I had fought so long and so hard to keep, he doesn't let on.

"Mira, I think this is the best thing for you to do under the circumstances," Jerry says. "You're going to be fine, you know."

"I know, Jerry. Thanks." When I hang up I'm numb, and I wonder if this is what it feels like to die, this feeling of letting go of almost everything you've ever cherished.

I spend Christmas Eve packing up the last remaining bits and pieces of my life into four large boxes, which I lug, one at a time, to the post office on Hudson Street, each time standing in a long line of procrastinating New Yorkers cheerfully waiting to mail their Christmas presents, none of which has any chance of arriving on time.

With the exception of my dining room set, which Hope has volunteered to keep for me, I've arranged to put most of my remaining furniture in storage. Hope has also enthusiastically agreed to sublet my apartment, and I can tell by her speculative gaze as she appraises the room that she's anxious to move in. Her apartment is small, a one bedroom, which she, in turn, has sublet to a newly married couple she met in her romance writers group. This is good news, because I'd rather sublet my apartment to Hope, who has promised to give it back to me when I return.

Renata and Michael insist that Chloe and I stay with them over Christmas. On Christmas Eve, Renata prepares the traditional Italian Feast of the Seven Fishes. We dine on fresh lobster, crab, and shrimp, clams casino, calamari, baccalà, and mussels—none of which I have any appetite for, but, touched by her thoughtfulness, do my best to eat. Michael fills up an entire memory card with photos of Chloe opening her presents and of me reading her "The Night Before Christmas."

The day after New Year's, Renata and Michael arrive at my empty apartment to drive Chloe and me to the airport. As we fight to make room for the suitcases in the trunk of Michael's Prius, Renata removes an insulated food carrier containing two freshly smoked mozzarella di buffalo and a small round of Pecorino Romano.

"A little comfort food," she says, handing it to me. "To remind you of home."

What is she thinking? That I'm going to the ends of the earth? Does she think I'm never coming back? When I remind her that some of the world's best cheeses come from the United States, actually west of the Hudson, she snorts. I tell her she should give Arthur Cole a call. I feign annoyance because I don't want Renata or Michael to see how touched I am that they will actually miss me. Michael holds Chloe while Renata and I reorganize the luggage.

"I give them six months, tops," Renata says, referring to Jake and Nicola. I'm not sure if she means the relationship or the restaurant. "I've taken them off the list of preferred customers. No more advance notice on special imports." It's a nice gesture on Renata's part, though I don't really believe her.

Later, on the way to the airport, Michael tells me that Arthur Cole has finished his tome (at close to a thousand pages) on the history of culinary science and is already busy planning his next project on American regional cooking, an idea, Michael reminds me, that I inspired.

"You're his editor, Michael. For God's sake, don't encourage him." I'm imagining at least three hundred pages devoted to the evolution of the breakfast cereal.

"He must really like you. Arthur is the kind of guy who doesn't change his mind very easily."

"Tell him that if he's ever in Pittsburgh, I'll take him out for a Primanti sandwich."

Michael laughs and shakes his head. "If only Arthur Cole had your sense of humor, Mira. A food writer *needs* a sense of humor. You, Mira, deserve someone with a sense of humor," Michael says definitively, giving my arm a squeeze.

I want to cry.

Standing in front of the Jet Blue terminal at JFK, Renata and I both dab away our tears. "You're going to be fine," Renata says, holding me at arm's length and giving me a searching look. "Yes," Michael echoes, "you will."

"Of course I will," I tell them, my voice bright and filled with false bravado, as I pull them both close into a final embrace. "Thanks for everything," I whisper in Renata's ear, my voice husky with unshed tears. "Take good care of Grappa for me, please. You will, won't you?" I know in my heart that Renata will do what she can, with what little influence she has, and this, in the end, is exactly how I want it.

Secondi

She who forgets the pasta is destined to reheat it.

—Anonymous

chapter 13

"Look," he says, "so thin you can see through it." The man behind the counter holds up the piece of prosciutto draped over the back of his hand, a gossamer wisp of meat for me to admire. "Melt in your mouth, this will," he says, curling his lips into a smile.

"Yes, it's beautiful," I agree.

"I'll put a paper in between each piece 'cause if I don't they'll all stick together. At twenty bucks a pound, I know yins don't want that." He speaks slowly, as if he means to teach me something, his accent pure Pittsburghese. He curls his hand into a fist and allows the wafer thin pieces of ham to drape over it.

Then, with a bravado-infused flick of his wrist, he delicately transfers the wisps of meat onto the sheet of butcher paper. With one fluid motion he wraps the package, ties it neatly with butcher's string, and hands it to me.

"A piece for the little one? I got something she gonna like. No prosciutto di Parma. Don't waste that when she got no teeth," he chuckles.

"How about this," he says, thrusting a large, fat-flecked sausage at me over the counter. "Mortadella, a good mild taste. Not spicy." He cuts Chloe a piece and removes the casing before putting it into her outstretched hands. She begins to gnaw.

"Look," he says, laughing. "She know what's good, that little girl." We both look at her admiringly.

Chloe and I have spent the first few days settling in, buying the various things I didn't own or hadn't packed, which, as it turned out, was a lot. In addition to things like shampoo and conditioner, which my father hasn't needed since roughly 1979, we also had to pick up safety gates for the stairways, little plugs for the electrical outlets, and corner protectors for the coffee and end tables, necessities now that Chloe is becoming mobile.

We've been here three days already, and I've yet to cook a single meal. The night we arrived, my dad ordered Chinese takeout from the old Cantonese restaurant around the corner, where they still serve the best egg foo yung, light and fluffy and swimming in rich, brown gravy. Then there had been Mineo's pizza and corned beef sandwiches from the kosher deli on Murray, all my childhood favorites. But last night I'd fallen asleep reading Arthur Schwartz's *Naples at Table* and had dreamed of pizza rustica, so when I awoke early on Saturday morning with a powerful craving for Italian peasant food, I decided to go shopping. Besides, I don't ever really feel at home anywhere until I've cooked a meal.

The Strip is down by the Allegheny River, a five- or six-block stretch filled with produce markets, old-fashioned butcher shops, fishmongers, cheese shops, flower stalls, and a shop that sells coffee that's been roasted on the premises. It used to be, and perhaps still is, where chefs pick up their produce and order cheeses, meats, and fish. The side streets and alleys are littered with moldering vegetables, fruits, and discarded lettuce leaves, and the smell in places is vaguely unpleasant. There are lots of beautiful, old warehouse buildings, brick with lovely arched windows, some of which are now, to my surprise, being converted into trendy loft apartments.

If you're a restaurateur you get here early, four or five in the morning. Around seven or eight o'clock, home cooks, tourists, and various passers-through begin to clog the Strip, aggressively vying for the precious few available parking spaces, not to mention tables at Pamela's, a retro diner that serves the best hotcakes in Pittsburgh.

On weekends, street vendors crowd the sidewalks, selling beaded necklaces, used CDs, bandanas in exotic colors, cheap, plastic running shoes, and Steelers paraphernalia by the ton. It's a loud, jostling, carnivalesque experience and one of the best things about Pittsburgh. There's even a bakery called Bruno's that sells only biscotti—at least fifteen different varieties daily. Bruno used to be an accountant until he retired from Mellon Bank at the age of sixty-five to bake biscotti full-time. There's a little hand-scrawled sign in the front window that says, GET IN HERE! You can't pass it without smiling.

It's a little after eight when Chloe and I finish up at the Pennsylvania Macaroni Company where, in addition to the prosciutto, soppressata, both hot and sweet sausages, fresh ricotta, mozzarella, and imported Parmigiano Reggiano, all essential ingredients for pizza rustica, I've also picked up a couple of cans of San Marzano tomatoes, which I happily note are thirty-nine cents cheaper here than in New York.

I'm planning a feast. Today my father and I will cook Italian peasant food, fried, heavy, greasy stuff. We will make Chloe a fried pizza with plain tomato sauce. She'll get it all over her face and love it. Kid food. It will take all day, and the smell of garlic, oil, and the fried dough will hang in the air for a week. I can already feel my spirits begin to lift.

There's already a line at Bruno's coming out the door and snaking its way along Penn Avenue. Chloe and I join the line, which, this particular Saturday morning, looks to be made up of mostly the well-heeled sipping their Starbucks lattes while waiting for the biscotti flavors of the day.

Bruno's opened years ago, when I was still in high school. I used to come here often then, mostly to do my homework on the worn wooden tables, sipping lattes and nibbling the biscotti ends, the burnt, crusty little bits that Bruno sold for a dollar a bag because they were too small and too well-done for most people to want them.

I'm sure Bruno won't remember me. After all, it's been over twenty years, and even if Bruno is still around, he'll be well over eighty. Chloe and I brave the long line anyway and are finally rewarded a good fifteen minutes later with a black pepper biscotti for me and a vanilla one for Chloe. We are waited on by a young woman who has a thick hoop running through her top lip and another at the top of her ear. No sign of Bruno. Although I'm tempted to ask about him, I don't.

When we arrive home, my father is sitting in the kitchen, the newspaper open in front of him, putting the finishing touches on the crossword. "Good morning, ladies," he says with a smile.

Chloe strains in her stroller, arching her back and reaching for me to release her. Seeing my hands are full of groceries, my father moves to free her. "Watch out, Dad, she's a mess. She'll spoil your sweater." Chloe's hands are greasy from the sausage and the biscotti, which she has managed to completely dissolve by gumming it into a glutinous paste, most of which is now smeared all over her face.

"Ah, I see you've been to Bruno's," my father says, dampening a paper towel and handing it to me.

"Yes," I tell him, wiping Chloe's face and hands. "We brought you some. Black pepper and cornmeal are still my favorites." I put the packages down. "We didn't see Bruno, though. Is he—"

"Retired. Or semi anyway. I see him there every once in a while. His family, a son and a couple of grandkids, run the business now."

"Hey," I say, fishing around in the groceries for the bag from Bruno's. "I got the fixings for pizza rustica. Want to help?"

"Well, okay, but I've got a few things to do this morning," he says, studying his watch. "If you start the dough, I'll help you when I get back."

Once my father leaves, I finish putting away the groceries, taking inventory, as I do, of the contents of his refrigerator. As a cook I generally believe that you can tell a lot about people by what they keep in their refrigerators. What comforts them, what they need to have on hand to sustain them. *Bon Appétit* magazine publishes an interview with a different famous person each month, and often the interviewer will ask the celebrity to name three things that can always be found in his or her refrigerator. The answers are generally too finely crafted to be believable. "A bottle of Stoli, fresh raspberries, and beluga caviar," or, "San Pellegrino, fresh figs, and key limes."

Doesn't anyone else in the world have the wizened carrots and limp celery, the perpetually moldering Tupperware container with last month's leftovers? The kind you finally throw away, unopened, because the contents are simply too disgusting to deal with? It has been a point of honor with me that every professional refrigerator I've been in charge of has always been scrupulously clean, but my home fridge, well, that's another story. It had been one of the bones of contention between Jake and me. I have trouble letting go of things. I hold on to them until they rot. Not a pleasant thing to admit about oneself and probably, in Jake's defense, not an easy thing to live with either. If I'm ever interviewed by *Bon Appétit* magazine, will I have the courage to admit to my own bulging Tupperware? Certainly not. "A bottle of Pouilly-Fuissé, Niçoise olives, and a wedge of camembert," I'll gamely respond.

My father, however, belies what I refer to as the Tao of the Fridge. He's a scientist, which, I suppose, explains the neatly stacked rows of Tupperware containers in the freezer, labeled with the contents and the date in clear, block printing. But he's also a cook, though you might not know it from examining the contents of his refrigerator: a carton of skim milk, two lemons, a container of low-fat cottage cheese, an unidentifiable cheese wrapped in several thicknesses of plastic wrap, a loaf of Jewish corn rye, a large bottle of kimchee hot sauce (for the Chinese takeout), and, in the door, a bottle of red nail polish.

He has lived alone for eighteen years and has gotten used to cooking for himself. From the many years of living with my mother he learned to shop the European way, going to the market every day. Buy only enough lettuce for the evening's salad, only enough bread for tonight and perhaps tomorrow's breakfast. Buy fresh herbs only when you need them. This explains everything currently in his refrigerator. Except the red nail polish.

I work for the next couple of hours while Chloe plays on the floor by my feet. I spread out a blanket and put out some toys. I talk to her as I cook, describing the ingredients and what I'm doing with them in that foolish, unnaturally high-pitched voice mothers use. When the dough for the pizza has risen, I retrieve Chloe from under the kitchen table where she has settled and sit her on my knee. Together we punch down the dough, burying our fists in its luxurious folds.

We stop for a snack, a couple of slices of prosciutto, some cheese, and the heel of a loaf of Italian bread. Because I'm training Chloe to have a sophisticated palate, I do not heed the butcher's maxim that prosciutto di Parma shouldn't be wasted on someone who has no teeth. Besides, she has four. Not that she needs them, anyway. The meat really does melt in your mouth.

Sometime later, there's a knock at the back door. It's Richard, holding a small potted palm and a little, stuffed teddy bear. I fling open the door and throw my arms around him.

"Welcome home, sweetie! Careful," he says into my neck, where I've imprisoned him in a hug, "or you will squish these expensive silk leaves. I knew better than to get you a live plant. And this," he says, holding out the teddy bear and stepping into the house, "is for *la diva*. I'm sure she has forgotten me by now, so I have decided to bribe my way back into her heart. Where is she?"

Richard follows me into the kitchen where Chloe is again playing under the table. He gestures for me to be quiet as he pulls out one of the chairs and sits down, dangling the teddy bear in between his knees. To Richard's delight, it takes Chloe about five seconds to crawl over and reach for the bear, and when she does, he leans down, puts his head under the table and smiles at her.

"Hello, you. Remember me?" Chloe gives him a tentative half smile and tugs gently on the bear's leg. It seems that the measure of her response will be dependent on how quickly Richard will release the bear into her custody. He lets go at once, and she gives him a smile showing all four of her new teeth.

"Settling in?"

"Yes, well enough. Dad set us up a nice little apartment on the third floor. Decorated it and everything. He hung some pictures and polished my old bedroom furniture. Really nice."

For as long as I could remember, the third floor had been my father's haven, filled with all his books, his drafting table, and other assorted tools of his trade. I was touched to find he'd converted my old bedroom on the second floor into his new office and taken great pains to set up a little apartment for Chloe and me on the third. There are two rooms, one a little sitting area with an old couch he dragged up from the basement and a couple of bookshelves which he emptied for me. He put my old bedroom furniture in the adjacent bedroom. Nice Danish Modern stuff that I'd thought hopelessly faddish when I was growing up, but which now had taken on a kind of chic mid-century patina. He'd also borrowed a crib from somewhere—he was vague about it when I asked where it had come from—complete with (used, but clean) Winnie the Pooh quilt and bumpers.

"But you know I won't really feel settled until I cook something. So," I say, gesturing to the dough into which I have just again sunk my hands, "pizza rustica."

"Mmm. Sounds great. I'm starving."

"Well, you better have a little snack or something, because this won't be ready for a while. Dad must have gone into the office. He left hours ago. I kind of thought he would enjoy helping me make it."

"Since when does your father decorate?" Richard says, standing up and brushing away a line of flour from his trousers. "This I'll have to see. And what does he think of his divine granddaughter?"

"He thinks she's great. You know, he's acting silly and talking to her in this cute little voice. And he bought her a ton of toys. She's going to get spoiled." I pause. I suddenly feel tired, and my eyes begin to sting. "Really, he's been wonderful."

Richard passes behind me and gives my arm a gentle squeeze. Then, he reaches around me and absently rattles the lid of the sugar bowl, trying to fit the cover back on. "What we really could use is something to nibble." He gets up and begins randomly opening cupboards, in search of a distraction. "I can't believe I'm sitting here with a chef so incredible that *Gourmet* has written about her and there's nothing to dip in my coffee." He opens the refrigerator door and turns to look at me with an expression of mock horror on his face. "Starvation rations in here! I don't know that I've ever seen this refrigerator so empty," he says, leaning in and pulling out one of the white, butcher-wrapped packages.

"Hey, go easy on that. It's for the pizza," I say, which earns me a scowl from Richard. "Take some biscotti from that bag on the counter. But while you're in there, check out that red nail polish in the door of the fridge."

"In the door, eh?" he repeats.

"Uh-huh. In the butter compartment." Richard opens the compartment, takes out the polish, and, reaching into the breast pocket of his shirt, pulls out his half-moon glasses in order to inspect the bottle more closely.

"Christian Dior, Flame. Expensive stuff." He unscrews the cap and pulls out the brush, holding it up to the light. "On the right person, a great color. Not for everyone, a red like this." When I don't say anything, he continues with his analysis. "She's neat, too. The bottle is half-empty, but there's no clumpy, dried gunk on the rim," he says, showing me. Richard screws the cap back on and looks over his glasses at me.

"A scintillating analysis, Richard. If the antique business ever goes bust, I think you could make a go of it in the field of nail polish forensics."

"This," he says, as if taking my comment seriously, "this is the choice of a confident woman. And one who has lots of experience with makeup. Only the most sophisticated of cosmetics consumers know that you extend the life of your polish by keeping it in the fridge." He sits down, takes off his glasses, and places the bottle on the table between us.

At that moment, as if on cue, we hear the front door open and seconds later voices in the front hall: my father's deep baritone and another—softer, higher. My father enters the kitchen, and on his heels is a small, neat woman with blond, tightly permed hair. She's wearing an aquamarine pantsuit with a plunging décolletage, revealing a large expanse of artificially tanned skin.

"Richard," my father exclaims, with an air of forced joviality, as if he had rehearsed a certain script but has suddenly found himself forced to ad-lib. "How nice to see you!" He strides a couple of steps toward him and offers his hand, which Richard takes and shakes. The woman, now standing behind him, softly clears her throat.

"Oh, forgive me. I've brought someone along, a fan of pizza rustica and well, in fact, of all things Italian. Mira, Richard, I'd like you to meet a friend of mine, Miss Fiona O'Hare."

Fiona smiles sweetly. "Richard, I've had the pleasure of shopping in your lovely store, but we've never been formally introduced." As she extends her hand, first to me and then to Richard, we can't help but notice that her two-inch nails are painted, what else? Flame.

chapter 14

Fiona, it turns out, is a picky eater, making my father's comment about her being a lover of things Italian either inaccurate or, given my father's Tuscan ancestry, vaguely creepy. Take your pick. She pokes around at the pizza rustica, saying that she thought we were having pizza. When I bring out the salad, she asks for more dressing and seems totally flummoxed when I bring out the oil and vinegar—surprised, I imagine, to find that it didn't come out of a prepackaged bottle made by Kraft and featuring the word *zesty*.

Richard, bless him, makes it easier.

"So," he asks, "how did you two meet?" Fiona looks to my father, who is busy pouring himself another glass of wine, leaving Fiona to field the question.

"Well," she says demurely, "we've known each other for years, but it wasn't until I signed up for an Italian conversation course that we actually got to know each other socially." She looks over and smiles at my father, whose lips twitch in response.

"Fiona's a secretary in the chemistry department," he says, without looking at her. "We have been passing each other in the Science Hall for years."

"Che bello! Che interessante! Ci sei mai andata?" I ask.

"What, dear?" she asks, leaning toward me and brushing aside a lacquered curl.

"To Italy," I repeat, this time in English. "Have you ever been there?"

"Me? Oh, my goodness, no." She laughs as if I've just said something incredibly amusing. "But last year for my birthday, my sons sent me to the Venetian Hotel in Las Vegas, and ever since then I've wanted to go and ride a real gondola. Came home and signed up for Italian lessons with the money I won playing keno. Have you ever been there?"

I look at her and then at my father. "Well, yes, as a matter of fact, I lived in Italy for several years," I say, thinking it funny that my father wouldn't have mentioned it.

"Oh, I know you lived in Italy, but have you ever been to Las Vegas?"

When I tell her no, she says, "Too bad. If you had you could tell me how the Grand Canal in the Venetian compares to the one in Italy. In case I never get there," she sighs.

After lunch, Fiona offers to help clean up. I make the espresso while I watch Fiona empty the dishwasher. I can't help but notice that she seems to know where everything goes. While we work, Fiona chatters on about the various trips she has taken. "Isn't it terrible what has happened to the airline industry since 9/11?" she asks, pausing before adjusting the Cling Wrap over the leftover salad. "When I flew to Las Vegas, they confiscated my knitting needles right out of my purse! What a nuisance. Speaking of knitting, maybe I'll knit that precious Chloe a little something. It will be fun to have someone to knit for. I have only one grandchild, who I hardly ever see," she says, her mouth set in a hard line. I'm about to ask her why, but perhaps anticipating my question she says, "Families are complicated." This strikes me as the most insightful thing anyone has said all afternoon.

Later, after Dad leaves to take Fiona home, Richard tells me I should be ashamed of myself.

"For what?" I ask him.

"For rolling your eyes when she mentioned her Vegas trip, for one thing. Your disdain was palpable."

Richard continues on, suggesting that I've underestimated Fiona's intelligence. "Not everyone is good at languages," he explains, and I think for a minute he's going to remind me of the *D* I got in high school French. "You," he says in a supercilious tone, "are a snob."

This, from a man who wears Prada sneakers and has his shirts hand tailored, facts I lose no time in pointing out. "Listen, what makes you sure she's so smart? What did you do, give her an IQ test while I was changing Chloe?"

Richard snorts.

"Well, maybe she's an idiot savant," I say, thinking about her insightful comment about families, which I don't mention to Richard, so as not to concede the point.

I really don't know what bothers me about Fiona. Yes, she's different from my own mother, but there was a time when that was the chief criterion necessary to secure my friendship. Chloe had warmed to Fiona right away, fascinated by her dangling plastic earrings and bangle bracelets, which Fiona quite generously allowed her to gnaw upon.

And why should I care who my father dates? I know it's selfish, but part of what bothers me is that I'd rather not have to deal with anyone else's relationship at the moment. Also, it's difficult when your father, who has been a widower for the last eighteen years, suddenly starts strutting his stuff like some randy peacock.

The real problem, I finally decide, is that I've come back to a place I thought I knew, only to find it different. I'd visited, of course, but I haven't lived here for almost twenty years, and the last time I did, my mother had been alive. I've felt her pull all these years, as if some vestige of the woman she was, a woman who had filled our lives for better or worse, still lingered in these walls, in the fabric of the curtains, or in the chipped china teacups in the kitchen cabinets. But now her presence has gone cold, just like that. And if I'm disconcerted to find that her ghost has dissipated, it's due as much as anything to the fact that it has been chased away by someone as banal and mild-mannered as Fiona O'Hare.

Fiona and my father spend most evenings together, but fewer nights. Sometimes he calls on his way home and invites Chloe and me to meet the two of them for dinner out, and sometimes they come here for dinner. When my father drives her home, he returns late. Once I saw him coming home early in the morning, just in time to shower, change, and go to work. It's nice that he seems to want to include us, but most of the time when he calls to invite us out, I decline. I feel guilty having disrupted the only social life I can ever remember my father having.

And what do I do to fill the hours and days? I cook. I cook until my father's entire refrigerator and downstairs freezer are stocked with restaurant-quality food. I've made several cheesecakes, some sweet, some savory, at least five different kinds of lasagna, and ten different types of soup, enough for a whole chapter in a cookbook. In fact, that's exactly what I tell my father and Fiona I'm doing—writing a cookbook—and that I need to try out the recipes.

"Well, then I think we should have a party," Fiona says when, while helping me clean up after dinner one night, she's forced to put the leftovers in the bin of the automatic ice maker because there's no room anywhere in the fridge. "We certainly have enough food!"

At which point I burst into tears.

"Mira," Fiona says, coming around to the table, where I've slumped, head in my hands. Teetering on her high-heeled sandals, Fiona bends over me and envelops me in a hug, pressing me so close to her that I can smell her perfume, a sweet, musky scent. This makes me cry even harder as now, on top of everything else, I feel guilty that I don't like her more.

"Bunko, next Thursday night," she whispers into my hair. "It's my turn to host, and I think you should come. Meet some of the girls. We could make it a dinner party. Put some of this wonderful food to good use. Come on, say you'll come." I have no idea what Bunko is, but somehow doubt that it's my cup of tea.

And then, pulling away slightly, Fiona prods my scalp with her fingernails. "Hmm, you've got a few little, gray nasties you might want to take care of. You're back on the market now. And you have such pretty hair. I have a great girl up the street on Murray Avenue who can take care of that in no time."

In the end, I'm not able to face it, either Bunko or, appealing as it sounded, having my nasties chemically treated. I call Fiona the following Thursday afternoon, pleading a headache, an excuse I know she doesn't buy. When she comes over to pick up the food for the party, she slips me a piece of paper with a name and a telephone number on it. With a knowing look, she tells me that everyone needs help now and again and that even she on occasion has found it helpful to seek advice and counsel. Notwithstanding the permed hair and surgically altered breasts, she instantly conjures the specter of Mary Ann. Not wanting to risk losing another chance at mental health, I tape the scrap of paper to my bathroom mirror where it remains, the edges curling from the damp and the numbers fading into an inky stream where I manage to splash it nearly every time I brush my teeth.

For so many years Grappa took up the better part of my life, and I'm now missing it like a severed appendage, the wound still fresh and deep. Often, I lie awake wondering what's on the menu or remembering how it felt to roll out the pasta dough on the marble surface of the workstation, or how it smelled to open an entire crate of fresh lemons that had been sitting in some warm delivery truck all morning, their skins sweating lemon oil.

Finally, in desperation, I register Chloe and myself for a mom and baby Gymboree class that meets weekly at the Jewish Community Center on Forbes Avenue. It's the kind of thing I'd always wished I had time to do when I was working. Maybe I could even make friends with some other mothers. Of course, most of the other mothers are still married to the fathers of their babies, and they all seem to know each other already. In New York, at least I could count on several single parents and a few same-sex couples, which might have made me not feel so different, but this is Pittsburgh, not New York. Chloe enjoys it, though. There are all sorts of slides and swings, things to feel and crawl upon, and I take delight in watching what she can now do. She's pulling herself up and, last week, reaching for a bubble, she even let go for a couple of seconds before falling.

The following week when we arrive, I notice an older woman with a Latino child. She probably is the grandmother or, judging from her graying hair and lack of Latino coloring, the nanny. Her charge, a little boy a bit older than Chloe, fusses and strains in her arms. I'm pushing Chloe on the pony swing when they sidle up to us. "How old?" she asks me with an anxious smile.

"Almost eleven months. And yours?" I ask her.

"Carlos is about fourteen months. We think, anyway. I found him in a private orphanage in Guatemala. They didn't keep particularly good records." She smiles and shrugs. "Obviously, he's adopted." She seems nervous. "I've only had him for two weeks." She tries to put him in the swing next to Chloe, but he seems to be glued to her hip, handfuls of her hair clenched in his tiny fists. She gives up quickly, then reaches up and swipes away a wisp of hair that Carlos has pulled loose from her ponytail. She looks exhausted.

"He doesn't seem to want to do anything. He clings to me, but I can't seem to soothe him." She's swaying rhythmically to the cheerful music, but Carlos is buying none of it. He reaches beyond her to the large, brightly colored yoga balls behind us on the gym mats and shrieks.

"Maybe we'll give those a try," she says with a sigh.

At the end of class we all assemble in a circle. Carlos and his mother look around, not really knowing what to do. I catch her eye and pat the gym mat next to us.

"It's 'The Bubble Song,'" I tell her, when she and Carlos settle in beside us. "At the end of the class we all sit in a circle and sing 'The Bubble Song.' The leaders make all these bubbles, and the kids try to catch them. It's cute," I tell her when she gives me a doubtful look. Carlos, however, is already enchanted and sits quietly on his mother's lap, eagerly reaching for the bubbles, which he takes great delight in popping.

"By the way, I'm Mira, and this is Chloe," I tell her later in the coatroom, as we are attempting to stuff our children into their respective snowsuits.

"I'm Ruth, and, well, you've already met Carlos." She gives us a fleeting look and a weak smile as she struggles to put Carlos's kicking feet into his snowsuit. "Jeez, it's like trying to hit a moving target! We'll be here all day." I sit down next to her on the bench and pull out the small jar of bubbles that we picked up on the way out.

I start blowing some in Carlos's direction. Almost immediately he relaxes, concentrating on the bubbles and allowing his mother to maneuver his feet into his snowsuit.

"Thanks. I've got to get some of those."

"Here, take these," I say, handing them to her. "We've got plenty more at home. They put them out each week. It's the least they can do for sixty dollars a month, put out some gym equipment and give us a couple of ounces of soapy water."

On the walk to our cars, Ruth and I exchange phone numbers and addresses. As it turns out, they live on Murray Hill Avenue, just a few blocks from us.

"I would suggest we go somewhere for coffee or something, but Carlos and I don't have the whole public place thing down quite yet and besides, he has a pediatrician appointment. Maybe next week?" Ruth asks eagerly, and I readily agree.

That afternoon, while Chloe is napping, I take inventory of the freezer and begin assembling a care package, thinking that Ruth and her husband might need a few frozen meals to help them through the next few weeks. When Chloe wakes up, I throw together a salad and call Ruth's number. Eventually, a machine picks up, with no personal greeting, just one of those automated voices telling me to leave a message.

"Ah, I hope this is Ruth. Ruth, this is Mira. We met today at the baby gym class?" I pause. "Listen, I was wondering if you could use a few extra prepared meals."

"Hello, hello—I'm here." The machine shuts off, but I can barely hear Ruth's voice because Carlos is screaming into the voice piece of the phone. Over the cacophony I manage to ascertain that she hasn't eaten anything but Lean Cuisine and Cheerios since Carlos's arrival two weeks ago, so yes, she'd be grateful for anything I had.

"Great, we'll be right over."

Ruth lives in one of the beautiful and expensive brick townhouses on Murray Hill Avenue. It's on the edge of the Chatham College campus, and the view out of the front of the house is of the bucolic rolling hills of the south campus.

Ruth meets me at the door. She's alone, and the house is quiet.

She holds a finger to her lips and whispers, "He's sleeping, thank God. I think he just wore himself out. Come in, come in."

She throws on a coat over her sweatshirt and together we finish unloading the food from the back of Chloe's stroller. "I hope you have room for it all," I tell her.

"Wow! Where did you get all this?"

"Well, I used to cook for a living, and I guess I'm suffering from withdrawal," I offer apologetically. "When you run out, let me know. There's plenty more where this came from."

Ruth's kitchen is small, like most townhouse kitchens, but state-of-the-art. Beautiful cherry cabinets, a six-burner Wolf range with a built-in warming oven, and a small Sub-Zero. "You must like to cook, too," I tell her, looking around.

Ruth laughs. "No, not me. The couple who sold it to me liked to cook, though. I've barely used this stuff since I bought the place three years ago. My appliance of choice is the microwave," she says, opening the freezer and gesturing to the stack of Lean Cuisines inside. "As you can see, I've got plenty of room."

Ruth hasn't mentioned a husband or a partner, and I find myself looking around for evidence that someone besides Ruth and Carlos lives here, although the Lean Cuisines ought to be a dead giveaway.

"Can I offer you a drink, a glass of wine or some juice?" she says, giving Chloe a smile. I've unzipped Chloe's snowsuit and taken off her hat, but she is getting antsy. "I mean, unless you, ah, have someone to get home for?" Ruth stammers.

"No, just my father, but not for a while. It's Chloe, though; she eats around five."

"Say no more; I'm now fully stocked in that department. Please say you'll stay and have dinner with me. It's been so long since I've eaten anything that doesn't come in a little, black plastic tray, never mind having an adult conversation while eating. I may just keel over!"

Ruth pulls Carlos's high chair over to the kitchen table and opens up her cupboard, where she has jars of Gerber baby food stacked three deep. "Okay, what will it be, chicken, beef, or lamb?"

Despite the fact that, up until now, all of Chloe's baby food has been organic and custom prepared, she loves Gerber's chicken and rice, and I try not to flinch each time she takes a bite. Ruth opens a bottle of wine, a yummy Saintsbury Pinot Noir. She may not know how to cook, but she does know a thing or two about wine. By the time we've finished the bottle and Chloe has polished off the last of her vanilla custard (another Gerber success), I've learned that Ruth has never been married, that she's on extended maternity leave from Bayer, where she was a senior financial analyst, and that she's forty-three years old.

"The last time I had a serious boyfriend, I was at Yale. From there, I went right on to B-school, and I really never had time for dating," she says, sipping her wine. "Then, I started working, and it took me a while to get my career going. The only people I met were at work, and most of them were already married. Once I figured out marriage wasn't in the cards for me, I tried to adopt, but I was traveling a lot and it wasn't so easy. So, I saved for a few years, got my name in with some private adoption agencies, cashed out some investments, and got out of the market just in time. I can afford to take at least a year off and when I do go back to work, it can be part-time, so I can be more involved in raising Carlos." She takes another gulp of wine. "The problem is I just didn't expect it would be this hard. A single parent—what was I thinking!" Ruth looks miserable. "I did research for three years, bought every baby book known to woman, and not one of them prepared me for this." She waves her hand in front of her face. "I'm sorry, it's just, I guess that even adoptive moms can suffer from postpartum blues, although, in my case it is far more likely to be perimenopause. I'm just too *old* for this!" She wipes her watery eyes, blows her nose in the used Kleenex she pulls from the sleeve of her sweatshirt, and laughs.

Encouraged by Ruth's candor, I launch into my own story. We've made a sizeable dent in the lasagna, and Ruth is uncorking the second bottle of wine by the time I get to the part about my arrest and Jake's early morning arrival and offer of reprieve. Her only response, apart from a gleeful laugh, is to bring out the cheesecake. No plates, two forks. She hands me one and, raising both her glass and her fork, she says, "To single motherhood!"

chapter 15

In the Squirrel Hill neighborhood of Pittsburgh where my father
lives, there are five synagogues within a four-block radius, four Orthodox and one Conservative. When I was growing up, the neighborhood had been almost exclusively Jewish. If the retail landscape
of the Murray Avenue shopping district is any indication, it still is.
Of the two bagel bakeries and three kosher restaurants I remember
from my childhood (two dairy, one fleishig), all remain in business,
albeit now peaceably coexisting alongside a French bistro, a Thai
noodle bar, and an Indian grocer.

   Growing up, many of our neighbors had been Orthodox Jews.
It wasn't until I moved back home to Pittsburgh that I thought
about how interesting it was that my parents decided to live there.
We weren't a religious family; in fact, we hardly ever went to
church. My father was a self-proclaimed agnostic, and the only
gods I could ever remember my mother worshipping were the
great gourmands of the world, people like Pellegrino Artusi, Jean
Anthelme Brillat-Savarin, Auguste Escoffier, and Phileas Gilbert,
followed in later years by Johnny Walker and Jack Daniels. (If our
neighbors considered us an oddity, perhaps it wasn't solely due to
our lack of religious affiliation.) For the most part, though, we'd
been accepted, more or less generously, into their fold and over the

years had been invited to our share of dinners in their sukkahs, Yom Kippur break fasts, and Passover seders.

Few of our old neighbors are left. Mrs. Favish sold her house and moved to a retirement community in Sarasota shortly after I left for culinary school. For years afterward I sent her a card and a box of homemade rugelach at Rosh Hashannah, but about ten years ago, I received a note from her granddaughter, thanking me for my thoughtfulness and informing me that she'd died. Only two of the families—the Friedmans and the Silvermans, both of whom had sons my age—still live in the neighborhood. Young Shlomo Friedman, who would've been in my grade except that he'd gone to yeshiva, wore Orthodox tzitzis and had side curls. The other boy, Ronnie Silverman, the brother of the recently widowed Debbie Silverman Levine, had been a year ahead of me in school. Ronnie and I had had a couple of sweaty adolescent encounters back then—several unsatisfying metal-on-metal kisses, along with some furtive groping. He was never without his Star of David, which he wore on a heavy gold chain that invariably got stuck in my long hair when we made out.

I've run into Mrs. Silverman a couple of times since I've been back, once while picking up Chinese takeout and then again when we were both unloading groceries. Both times she presented me with a whole wallet's worth of photos of Debbie and her children and Ronnie and his family, two daughters and a wife, a lovely Jewish girl, and a lawyer to boot. Rona Silverman had never liked me, mostly, I had assumed, because she didn't like her son being interested in a *shiksa*, even a fourteen-year-old one. But as I learned one muggy summer's evening when the Silvermans' windows were open and Ronnie and I were making out on the Silvermans' back porch, the real reason she didn't like me was because she thought my mother was damaged and it was her belief that those kinds of things run in families.

When she hauled out the photos of Ronnie and his family, she cross-examined me about why I was back home and didn't seem at all surprised to learn I was divorced. During our brief conversation, I caught her examining me for signs of alcoholism or other sorts of goyish afflictions. She was probably barely inside the front door before placing a call to Ronnie to tell him how lucky he was to have escaped me.

She also asked me about Grappa. A friend of hers had eaten there on a trip to New York a few weeks ago and had raved about the food. I didn't have the heart to tell her that I'd lost that, too, my only capital, the only stake I had in anything useful, meaningful, or worthwhile. Instead, I smiled and lied, telling her I was taking a sabbatical from the restaurant, but that Chloe and I were headed back there soon. And then I had to hurry into the house before, unable to resist the impulse, I'd wheedle the friend's phone number from Mrs. Silverman so that I might grill her about the meal she'd eaten, looking for a misstep: a broken sauce, lumps in the polenta, an inadequately braised piece of meat.

Afraid of running into her again, I've taken to scoping out her house from the upstairs window before venturing out, looking for her car in the driveway, or waiting until Saturday morning when she'll be at services. This particular Saturday morning, I've waited until the Silvermans left their house on foot for Shabbat services before setting off to buy some decongestant for Chloe. She's been sniffling for the last couple of days and woke up last night with a throaty cough.

While I'm standing in line at the drugstore, I notice that the Waterpik Dental Care System is a featured special, so at the last minute I throw that into the cart as well, thinking it's been a while since I've had my teeth cleaned. Chloe hasn't been to the pediatrician since before we left Manhattan either, and I'm hoping that these over the counter medicines will nip this cold in the bud because I'm not ready to transfer our medical and dental care to Pittsburgh. That would make it too much like we were living here, rather than just visiting.

When I get home, Chloe is sleeping in the playpen in the living room, and Dad and Fiona are playing Scrabble at the kitchen table. At least I think they are. The board is open in front of them, but Dad's reading a novel and Fiona is poring over the *Official Scrabble Player's Dictionary*. They both look up as I enter.

"How long has Chloe been sleeping?"

"Just a few minutes. She's tired, poor baby," Fiona says, studying the dictionary.

"She fussed for a bit," my father says, glancing up at me, "but Fi rocked her until she fell asleep."

"Don't forget, you read her a story, Grandpa," Fiona says, looking up from the dictionary as she places her letters on the board. "Here we go. C-L-A-M, and this blank is P. That will be sixteen points. That makes the score"—she consults the score sheet—"um, two hundred fifty-six to ninety-nine." She looks over her glasses at me. "Your father is winning. He even lets me use the dictionary, and he still wins." She sighs.

My father immediately leans over and puts XI under the AM in CLAMP to make ax, xi, and mi. "The X is on a triple letter, counted twice makes forty-eight, so that will be fifty-four points altogether."

He goes back to his book, a Robert B. Parker mystery.

Fiona lurches toward the dictionary, muttering under her breath.

"Xi is a Greek letter; mi is the third tone in the diatonic scale. And I presume you know what an ax is, Fi," my father says, giving Fiona a look over his half-moon glasses. Not even a trace of a smile. How could it have escaped my notice for the last thirty-eight years that my father is an insufferable snob?

"Well, I didn't know that, Mr. Smarty Pants. You use these silly two letter words all the time." She turns to me. "Who ever heard of E-S being a word?"

"It is the spelling for the letter s," my father says.

"I mean, really—you want to spell the letter, you just write it!"

They both sigh.

I take advantage of Chloe's being asleep and cart all of our stuff upstairs. I think about hanging the Waterpik on the wall beside the sink, but looking at the directions, I see that it requires anchors and a drill. I tell myself I just don't want to wake up Chloe, although she's sleeping downstairs and I'm on the third floor. I put the Waterpik back in its box, stow the box on the back of the toilet, and lie down on the bed. The mere thought of hanging it has suddenly taxed me to the point of complete exhaustion.

Anchors and a drill imply commitment. I've been a renter long enough to realize that you just don't go making holes in walls of places you won't be staying. We've been here almost six weeks and, outside of registering for Gymboree class, I've done almost nothing else to settle in. I haven't hung a single picture or unpacked a single box, and here I'm quaking at the thought of hanging a Waterpik in the bathroom. What am I waiting for? Some sign that our life here is about to begin?

Later, I make a halfhearted attempt to locate a drill and am surprised to find that someone, probably Fiona, has reorganized my father's tool area in the basement. My father used to throw his motley collection of tools (a rusty hammer, a few loose screws and washers, a bunch of screwdrivers, and a drill with a fraying cord and a partial collection of drill bits that never seem to be the right size for anything you want to drill) into an orange crate by the washer. The rotting orange crate has been replaced by a red Craftsman tool chest filled with a small but impressive arsenal of brand new tools. Now, not only does my father own a drill that can be used without danger of electrocution, but he also has anchors, picture hooks, and two different kinds of wrenches—in short, every implement necessary to hang my Waterpik set. Well then, I think, closing the lid on the tool chest and giving it a small but determined kick, now that I have all of the necessary tools at my disposal, I can do it whenever I want.

The next day I don't get out of bed. It's a chilly February morning, the sky the murky color of dishwater, and it looks as if it might snow. I'd gone to bed early the night before, just after Chloe, and had then awakened in the early hours of the morning to fiddle with the space heater to fight the chill in the room, only having to rouse myself later when the temperature felt too high, not quite understanding it was my own personal thermostat that needed the adjustment. Since then I've hardly slept, tossing and turning in a fitful, uneasy doze.

My father climbs the attic stairs when I'm unable to even drag myself from bed to attend to Chloe's cries. He's already dressed, which means it must be late. He comes in with Chloe, but after taking one look at me, immediately deposits her back into her bed. He returns a minute later with the thermometer, which he puts in my mouth, telling me that I need to keep it under my tongue, like I'm five years old. I can hear him in the next room dressing Chloe. The thermometer beeps, but I don't even have the energy to take it out. Instead, I let it slide out of my mouth, where it makes a little moist spot on the pillow. When I open my eyes, my father is picking up the thermometer, Chloe in his arms.

"Hmm," is all he says. He brings me a cool glass of water and a couple of Tylenol and tells me I need to rest.

I drift in and out of consciousness for most of the day, losing track of the time. When I next see my father hovering over me, the room is dark. When I ask for Chloe, he tells me that she is already asleep.

It is two days later, Tuesday, when I finally and fully awaken. Fiona has moved in downstairs, ostensibly to take care of Chloe, although I can't help but think she was just waiting for a convenient opportunity to tighten her grip on my father. Now, here she is, balancing a tray on one hand and wearing some sort of frilly apron over a pair of spandex pants.

"Don't be silly. I have a zillion vacation days I haven't used," Fiona says when I manage to thank her for helping take care of Chloe. "It's fun, kind of like a tag team," she says, looking at her watch. "Your father should be home in a few minutes to watch the baby, and then I'm off to my exercise class. Don't worry, dear, Chloe's just fine," she tells me. When I ask to see her, Fiona replies that she's happily playing downstairs in the playpen, and besides, she's worried that I might still be contagious. Then she pulls from her apron pocket the large, rectangular baby monitor, which she plugs in beside the bed. "Here you go. You can listen to her at least." After the initial burp of static I can hear Chloe's small voice. I resent Fiona's proprietary tone, but the thought of protesting seems infinitely more exhausting, and so I sink back into the pillows, my forehead damp with exertion.

"Look," she says, depositing a small stack of magazines onto the bed, along with a tray of soup and some ginger ale. "I brought you these, in case you feel like reading."

Along with *Pittsburgh Magazine,* Fiona has brought me the most recent issue of *Cosmo,* which features an article on the current sex toy craze, and a magazine called *Channel* that has as its lead article an interview with Genghis Khan as told to medium John Edward.

Fiona lays the back of her hand on my forehead. The gesture is at once maternal and self-conscious and speaks of a certain intimacy, the desire for which, at least on Fiona's part, I can only guess at. For some reason, I'm reminded all at once of my mother, who was not in the least the maternal sort. When I look up at Fiona, I see that her eyes are soft and kind and that she has meant the gesture to be comforting and is now looking to me for some sign that it was welcome. Instead, I shut my eyes and turn my face into the pillow, searching for a cool spot on which to rest my aching head.

Although my fever has been gone for twenty-four hours, I haven't been able to shake the malaise. A weariness has settled in and taken root, helped along by the gray and frigid weather and the aftermath of a headache, a blousy, bilious feeling, dense as pound cake. I actually planned on taking Chloe to Gymboree today, even went so far as to get myself and Chloe dressed—right down to Chloe's snowsuit—but it was her mittens that finally did me in. Bending low over Chloe, struggling to separate her fingers and coax her tiny thumbs into the pink woolen casings, I'd sunk to my knees, exhausted by the effort. The thought of having to undress her, only to have to redress her again an hour later, made me so tired I wept right there on the kitchen floor.

Later, Ruth leaves me a voice mail message on my cell phone. "Hi, Mira. Listen, I've been meaning to call you, to thank you for, wow, all this wonderful food. Everything's been great and, jeez, what a help! Anyway, Carlos and I missed you guys at class today. Oh, hey, big news. A guy showed up at Gymboree today. An actual dad—cute and no ring," Ruth whispers giddily into the phone. "Give me a call, and I'll fill you in. Better come back next week, or I'm staking claim."

Actually, I was right here when Ruth called but didn't answer the phone. I was back in bed, still feeling tired, despite the fact that I'd slept while Chloe napped. Immune to Ruth's enthusiasm over the sudden presence of a man at Gymboree, I lay there listening to her message and staring at the crack in the ceiling, all the while wondering what Jake was serving for lunch at Grappa.

Suddenly, I sit up in bed. I can't remember if I fed Chloe lunch. I look over where she's playing on the rug by the television, studying her for signs of malnutrition. Had I fed her? Or, was it breakfast I was remembering? I looked at the clock by the bedside table. Four fifteen. Had we been in this room all day?

That evening I'm in the kitchen heating up a can of soup for Chloe's dinner when Fiona breezes in. "Lookie, lookie, who's got a cookie?" she says, pulling a small, wax paper bag from her purse.

Chloe squeals delightedly as Fiona unwraps a large, iced cookie with a blue smiley face and hands it to her. Without asking me.

"Don't you think Eat'n Park makes the best cookies? When was the last time you had one, Mira?" Fiona asks, digging in her purse. "I got one for you, too," she says, handing me another small bag. Mine is red, a hastily iced cookie with a crooked gash of a grin.

"I had dinner there tonight with a girlfriend," Fiona tells me. "I just love their chicken potpie." Fiona sits down at the table, and Chloe brightens instantly; she even abandons her assault on the cookie to smile at her.

Fiona says that, as long as she's here, she might as well stick around to see my father, whose class should be over soon. She knows it's his night to teach, and I have the distinct feeling that she's come to spy on me, as if she thinks my recent bout of flu has rendered me permanently incapable of taking decent care of Chloe. When she volunteers to read Chloe a story while I finish cleaning up, I don't argue with her. "She fell right to sleep in my arms, sweet thing. I put her in the porta-crib in your father's bedroom," Fiona reports when she comes downstairs a while later. I want to protest that I wanted to put Chloe to bed myself, but it seems petty to complain to someone who's just done you a favor. So even though it's only eight thirty, I go to bed. What else is there to do?

I'm hardly surprised then, to find myself awake at three fifteen in the morning, alone in the attic bedroom. I lie there for quite a while thinking of Chloe, wondering if she misses me as much as I miss her, or if it's possible I've disappeared from her life unnoticed.

It's a morose thought, and deep down one I know is irrational, but over the last few weeks and months I've been working up to this notion that I could disappear and no one would spend very much time looking for me or missing me.

I throw on an oversized sweatshirt, pull on a pair of woolen socks, and pad over to the corner where weeks ago I had stacked some boxes under the eaves, remnants of my past life, evidence that I had at one time done something that mattered. The first box is filled with magazine clippings, recipes, multiple copies of the *Gourmet* article on Grappa, and a dozen or so journals filled with notes and menu ideas written in Italian. These are from my apprenticeship in Italy, where I had met Jake. I pick one up and leaf through it, stopping at a page where I'd written his name over and over, filling the entire page. I toss the journal back into the box and fold the lid closed, thinking that it would be an important step to throw the rest of the boxes away unopened, something I know I could never do. I won't be satisfied until I've opened each box, touched each scrap of paper, pored over every photograph. Even then I will not be done with them.

Lately, I've begun to doubt my past, my feelings and memories, to which I no longer feel entitled, and the result is a disconcerting mix of confusion, exhilaration, and ennui. Apart from several cartons containing my cookbook collection, the rest of the boxes are all filled with the same sorts of things, little things really, most of them neither important nor useful. The last box is shoved so deeply under the eaves that I almost don't see it. The packing tape is cracked and yellowed, which has made the seal loose. When I flip open the flaps, I'm bathed in a thin cloud of dust.

Inside is my mother's dog-eared copy of *Larousse Gastronomique*. This book had fascinated me as a child, mostly because it is written in French, a language I didn't understand. I can remember my mother poring over it, whispering the recipes like incantations in her beautiful, honeyed French. Thrust in between its pages, rendering its spine loose and broken in many places, was a catalogue of her life: wine labels, notes in French from friends, letters from my father, menus she had particularly enjoyed. As a child I often leafed through its pages searching for something of mine, a birth announcement, a picture, handwritten documentation of my first real meal, but the collection stopped the year she moved to Pittsburgh.

The sight of my mother's handwriting on the slips of paper and in the margins of the book causes me to inhale sharply, and for a moment I smell licorice, as if the mere sight of her heavily styled penmanship has produced an olfactory hallucination. It's a delicate smell, more like anise or fresh tarragon than the sugary smell of a licorice pastille.

Smell, I remember my mother once telling me, is the most powerful of the senses. Without it, there is no taste. Long ago I lost the memory of her face, the sound of her voice, the touch of her fingers. But I can still remember her smell, in the aroma of a sherry reduction, the perfume, delicate and faint, that lingers on your hands after you've run them through a hedge of rosemary, the pungent assault of a Gauloises cigarette. Any of a thousand smells are enough to conjure her memory.

I shut the box and return to bed, wondering why it had been so hard for two people who'd shared a love of cooking to connect. Over the years there had been so many opportunities lost or deliberately avoided, when we had so much in common. Even after all this time, I was surprised to find it still hurt.

The next morning when I open my eyes, Chloe has my cheeks sandwiched in between her chubby palms and is peering earnestly into my face. She grins at me, a full-fledged smile followed by a little giggle. Her breath is warm, sweet, and smells of banana. "She's already had her breakfast," my father says, a peevish note seeping into his voice. "Fiona fed her."

I know I've been a wretch, barely being civil to Fiona, and my father has every right to be annoyed.

"Don't wait dinner for me," my dad says, leaning over me to kiss Chloe good-bye. "Brian Greene is lecturing tonight. Fiona and I have tickets." Clearly, my father has assumed that I will be making dinner tonight, an only slightly less outlandish assumption than that Fiona will enjoy a lecture about the origin of the cosmos.

"Okay," I tell him, pushing myself up on one arm and encircling Chloe with the other, pulling her in close to me and waiting to see if my father will kiss me, too. He does, a perfunctory peck on the top of my head. I know I'm behaving like a petulant child, holding unreasonable and wholly unsupported opinions about the woman my father is dating, a woman who has been nothing but kind to me. And to my daughter. Which, of course, is part of the problem.

Throughout the morning I catch Chloe watching me, sneaking little sidelong glances and venturing closer to me whenever she senses she's lost my attention. It's amazing, the uncanny ability of babies to gauge the moods of adults, to monitor our every move, almost without seeming to. I suppose it's evidence of their capacity for adaptation, for survival, this vested interest in keeping close tabs on our mental states, taking stock of us, making sure we don't forget them—or, just as bad—forget ourselves. It might be my imagination, but Chloe plays with her toys listlessly, as if, having spent the morning watching my dull expression, she too has decided that there's nothing worth getting too excited about.

I've gotten as far as rereading my mother's recipes, desultorily thumbing through the pages of handwritten notes, and morosely reflecting on how much time the French have wasted over the centuries by uniformly dicing their vegetables and carefully fanning slices of potato and apple into complicated tarts. I've been hoping to summon up a little enthusiasm for a trip to the grocery store, but when I catch sight of myself in the bathroom mirror, I'm so shocked by my appearance that it dashes any hopes of venturing outside, at least until cover of darkness.

I draw a bath for myself and Chloe, gather up her rubber duckies and tub toys, and add several capfuls of bubble bath to the tub. Chloe giggles as I lower us both into the warm water and offer her a palm full of bubbles in the shape of a frosted cupcake. I put her on my lap facing me, and she delights in playing with the bubbles, dotting my hair with little fistfuls of them. I wet her hair and twist what little there is into an upward spiral and put the hand mirror in front of her so she can see. Then I do mine, fashioning myself several long, soapy dreadlocks.

I've left the door to the bathroom wide open, and suddenly the baby monitor jumps to life, picking up the static of a slammed door and the rumble of steps in the back hall. It must be my father, coming home at lunchtime to check on us. Sure enough, I hear his heavy step on the stairs, whistling a bluesy tune I don't know.

"Dad?" I call. "I'm in the tub with Chloe." No answer. I pull Chloe onto my lap and sink lower in the tub, hoping to avoid shocking my father. "Dad?"

But the man who rounds the corner isn't my father.

My scream startles him, and immediately Chloe begins to cry. I reach for the hand mirror, which I hurl at him. He barely manages to sidestep it as it crashes against the doorframe, scattering shards of glass and plastic all over the bathroom floor.

He yanks the earplugs from his ears. "Jeez! Oh, my God, I'm so sorry. I didn't think anyone was home," he says, covering his eyes and backing out the door.

"Who are you? How did you get in?" I scream.

I put an arm protectively around Chloe, who is still screaming, and sink lower into the tub, noticing with renewed horror that the bubbles seem to have totally dissipated.

"I'm sorry! I didn't mean to scare you. I'm Ben, Ben Stemple. Fi's nephew. See? I have a key," he says, still standing behind the door, but holding his key ring at arm's length so I can see it from the tub.

"Who?"

"Fiona? I'm her nephew—I'm a plumber. She called me about the leak under your sink."

"What leak?"

"You must be Mira, right? And that must be Chloe. Fiona's always talking about her. She's a cutie."

"Do you mind?" I ask, incredulous that this man who has just barged into my bathroom unannounced is now making clear that he got a good look at us in the tub. I yell at him, "The door. Do you mind shutting the door?"

"Wait a minute," he says. "There's glass all over the floor. If you get out of the tub, you'll step on it. I'll get a broom, okay?"

I crouch in the tub, Chloe still whimpering in my arms, and grab a towel, which I wrap around the two of us. A minute later, Ben is back with a broom. "I swear I'm not looking. I'll just clean up the

floor, okay?" he says, as he proceeds to sweep the glass into the
dustpan while Chloe and I huddle together in the too small towel.

While he sweeps, I study him, wondering if he really is Fiona's
nephew or if he's going to ax murder the two of us as soon as he's finished sweeping our floor. He appears to be in his thirties, with sandy
hair and a scraggly beard. He's wearing greasy coveralls, a heavy tool
belt slung low around his hips, and an iPod on an armband, from
which I can hear Warren Zevon playing. He's also got a cut across his
cheek, where a piece of flying glass must have caught him.

"You're bleeding," I tell him. Ben looks at me, then remembering the skimpy bath towel I'm wearing, looks quickly away. "There,
on your cheek," I say, pointing.

He reaches up to touch his face and then examines the blood on
his fingertips. "You got me," he says, with a trace of a smile. "I'll
just wait downstairs until you're ready for me to fix the leak,
okay?" he says. He waits a second for me to answer, but when I
don't, he leaves, shutting the bathroom door behind him.

As I pull Chloe and myself out of the tub, I catch sight of our reflection in the full-length mirror on the back of the bathroom door.
Both my hair and Chloe's are still encrusted in bubbles, twisted
into stiff strands sticking out like porcupine's thorns from our
heads. I stand there staring at our ridiculous reflection, dripping
tiny bubbles onto the freshly swept floor.

"You shouldn't let leaks go, even tiny ones like this one," Ben
says a while later, tightening something with his wrench. "Didn't
you notice the puddle of water under the sink cabinet?"

"Oh, that," I say. In New York, a leak like that would go unnoticed by any self-respecting landlord in the city. Renters are conditioned to follow suit.

"Come here and take a look," he calls, gesturing with the
wrench. "The bottom of this metal cabinet is starting to rust. When
you wash your hands or use the sink, you have to be careful to turn
the faucet all the way off." He has a heavy Pittsburgh accent, pro-
nouncing "wash" as "warsh." He pops up from underneath the
sink and demonstrates, giving the faucet an exaggerated turn.

"And this," he says, pointing accusingly at a stain at the back of the sink, waiting for the ominous nature of the offending stain to fully register. "Do you see this? It's rust. Caused by a drippy faucet. Really," he says, shaking his head, "this whole unit should be replaced. Good thing Aunt Fi noticed it. Hey, when I'm finished here, you want me to hang up your Waterpik for you? Might as well. You get it at Eckerd? I got one on sale last week, too. Works great."

"Thanks, but..." But what? I'm not sure I'm staying? I'm scared of commitment? "Sure, that'd be great."

"No problem. Which side do you want it on, right or left?"

"Right, I guess," I say, without even thinking about it.

"You sure?" he says from under the sink, his voice slightly muffled. "Might be better on the left. Dentists recommend keeping toothbrushes at least five feet from the toilet."

"That's a disgusting thought."

"Well, probably not as disgusting as actually hanging your toothbrush less than five feet from the toilet and *not* thinking about it. Know what I mean?" Ben says, emerging from under the sink to grab a wrench from his toolbox.

"Eew," I shudder. "Fine, whatever you think," I tell him. Ben looks at me and shrugs before replacing his earphones and disappearing back underneath the sink, where seconds later he begins howling to "Werewolves of London."

It's barely nine o'clock. Dad and Fiona are still at the Brian Greene lecture. Chloe is long asleep, and I'm already in my pajamas, teeth brushed and Waterpikked. But I'm unsettled and jumpy, so I pad down to the kitchen where I flip absently through a pile of junk mail on the counter. I sit down at the kitchen table and pour myself a glass of wine, even though I've just brushed my teeth. It's prime dinner service, and I allow myself to imagine Grappa, first the dining room, the deep golden walls, the exposed brick, the white tablecloths and candles; then the kitchen, frenzied, pots steaming, braziers glowing, the scrape of a well-worn copper pan sliding over a burner, its contents tossed effortlessly with one hand by a line cook. Jake reaching for a splash of olive oil to finish a dish; the intensity of his gaze as he meticulously wipes the rim of the din-

ner plate, the small movement of his mouth as he places his com-
position, perfect, steaming, on the line.

Renata and Michael aren't home when I call, and I don't bother
leaving a message. I'm not sure what I mean to say, but when I hear
Renata's softly lilting accent I'm reminded of home and of Italy and
I don't trust myself to speak. Hope, though, answers on the third
ring. "Mira, how *are* you, dear?" There is noise in the background,
the sound of people talking and laughing. Hope is having a party in
my apartment.

"Just a few friends over for a housewarming," she says. I try not
to imagine the spread of crescent rolls and deviled ham, the Cheese
Whiz dips and Ritz crackers arrayed on what once had been my
dining room table. I tell Hope I'm not calling about anything important and she should get back to her guests.

I finish the wine and pour myself a hefty shot from a bottle of
brandy I find in my father's liquor cabinet, a bottle that probably
has been in there since I was in high school. Fortified, I call Grappa
using my father's house phone, which has an unlisted number that
doesn't show up on caller ID.

I don't stop until the brandy is finished and I've booked two
Saturday night dinners on successive weekends and one banquet
for twenty, occupying the whole upstairs room. I've made up
names and given fake telephone numbers with which to confirm
the counterfeit reservations. I've even used different voices, my
repertoire increasing in direct proportion to the amount of brandy
I consume. The highlight: a tour de force impersonation of an Italian contessa Jake and I had met on a trip to Capri.

The next morning Richard shows up with a large cup of coffee,
a liter bottle of San Pellegrino, two Extra Strength Tylenol, and the
Post-Gazette.

"What, no *Times*?" I ask when he throws the paper at me.

"No, you're in Pittsburgh now. Pittsburghers read the *Post-
Gazette*," Richard says as he sits down on the side of my bed. Although he doesn't play, he's dressed as if he has just come from a
tennis match, a white cotton sweater knotted nattily around his
neck. "Here, take these," he says, opening the sparkling water and
handing me the Tylenol.

I groan when I try to move my head, which feels like someone has removed the top of my skull and replaced it with the chittering lid of a pressure cooker.

"Look, what you are doing here, it's not good. You've got to get out of this bed."

"I'm sick," I tell him. "Go away."

"No, you're hungover. Or maybe you're still drunk. It's a wonder you don't have alcohol poisoning. A disgusting display from what I heard of it."

Richard proceeds to outline in excruciating detail how my father and Fiona found me head down on the kitchen table, the phone still clutched in my hand. When they'd tried to rouse me, I'd insisted on speaking only in Italian, unleashing a torrent of epithets that, although my father understood them, were fortunately beyond Fiona's meager grasp of Italian conversation. It had taken the two of them to get me upstairs to bed, and I'd woken Chloe in the process.

What I can't explain to Richard, to my father, or heavens, to Fiona, is that there is something wrong with me.

"I'm dying," I tell him, hoping that he will hear the desperation in my voice.

Richard snorts. "Oh, please, you are not. You're depressed, and that makes you feel tired and sick. Mira, Chloe needs you. Do you expect Fiona to quit her job and take care of your daughter?"

"No, but . . ." I let the sentence hang there unfinished because there's a lump in my throat. I can't tell Richard that I think that Chloe is better off without me. If I say it, it might be true. "That's probably what she wants anyway," I snap at him, deciding that the best defense is a good offense. "They hardly even let me see her," I tell him, pulling the covers over my face. "Look, I'm reduced to listening to my own child on this damned baby monitor."

"You need to go and see someone, Mira. A therapist. You've been through a lot, and all of us can use some help every now and then." I sneak a look at him from under the covers. He's sitting on the edge of the bed. His voice is tight, and his head is in his hands, his fingers gently pulling at his hair. "One of the problems is that you're bored. You don't have enough to do."

I don't respond. I don't trust myself. Suddenly, I'm furious with Richard for not understanding. I feel him get up from the bed. He walks to the door, and I think maybe he'll leave me alone when he says, "You know, that was the root of her problem, too. You don't want to become like your mother." His tone is sad and, to make it worse, he lets his words hang there for a second, long enough to suck every ounce of air from the room. A moment later I hear his heavy step on the attic stairs.

You don't want to become like your mother. Richard, having exhausted all traditional means, has delivered this last blow in order to shock me into action. But what he has failed to realize is that he's just given voice to something I've long feared. Now that it's been said, I can do nothing but lie here, stunned and sapped. The baby monitor beside my bed suddenly kicks in, and I can hear him in the kitchen, talking to Fiona.

"Well, I suggested it, but she'll never go to therapy," Richard is saying. "Mira is too proud." My father doesn't say anything in my defense. I know he's there because I can hear him crunching his Grape-Nuts.

"I gave her a name," Fiona says. "But I guess she never called. I didn't want to ask."

"Look what happened when she was court-ordered to take anger-management classes!" says Richard.

"I worry about her poor little girl," Fiona continues. "There are some people who just never get over these sorts of things. My cousin's sister-in-law never got over her husband's leaving her. Her kids were running wild in the streets. They got into all kinds of trouble until finally she just couldn't take it anymore. Gave all three of them to her ex-husband and let them be raised by the woman he left her for. Now, how about that?"

Finally, Dad pipes in. "Well, Mira doesn't even have that luxury, Fiona." Gee, thanks, Dad.

"She'll get out of bed eventually. She'll have to, if you stop feeding her. I'd start marking the liquor bottles, though. That would be the next step." This from Richard, whose voice is suddenly louder, as if he is standing right next to the baby monitor speaking directly into it. I can almost see his tight-lipped grin.

chapter 16

As soon as the house is quiet, I venture downstairs and take out the phone book, intending to make a list of all the therapists within walking distance. As it turns out, there are quite a few, five by the time I'm finished with the *Ds*. I've stopped at the *Ds* because I'm intrigued by a small ad proclaiming in an elegant typeface: DEBRA DOBRANSKY-PULLMAN, PhD, CERTIFIED LIFE COACH. ARE YOU READY FOR THE REST OF YOUR LIFE?

I skim through the other ads and don't see any other psychologist in the book advertising as a "life coach." That she answers her own phone and has an opening this afternoon at two o'clock probably should make me a little uneasy, but, I tell myself, she has a legitimate office, a PhD, and is close by. Besides, one session certainly won't obligate me to continue. Even if she's a total flake, how much damage can she possibly do in an hour?

If "proud" was code for stubborn, then Richard was right. Which means I'm more than a little troubled by the thought that I have been so predictably vulnerable to his obvious use of reverse psychology. At least I can take some small comfort in the knowledge that Dr. Dobransky-Pullman isn't really a psychotherapist. She's a life coach. A life coach sounds to me like someone who might not focus too closely on past events, but who might be a sort of paid cheerleader, helping to get you back on the path you had somehow wandered away from. Less embarrassing somehow, like a personal trainer or a makeup artist.

I'm on my way out the back door when I see the note left on the kitchen table in Fiona's loopy hand. *Took Chloe to Gymboree. Back for nap time! Fi.* I know I should leave a note, but I don't because I'm still stinging from Richard's comments and my father's failure to muster even a pathetic defense of his only child. Let them wonder where I am.

Dr. Dobransky-Pullman's office is in the Highland Towers apartment complex. There is no receptionist to greet me when I arrive, just a large, windowless waiting room with a beige linen sofa, a brass and glass coffee table, and a couple of simple, but expensively framed, lithographs on the wall. There is a door at one end, which I presume leads to her office. I'm alone in the waiting room. I take a seat on the sofa, and nervously leaf through a copy of *People* magazine while silently rehearsing what I might say about my life and what has brought me here.

At precisely two o'clock, the door opens, and a tall, beautifully dressed woman emerges, carrying a clipboard and wafting some sort of expensive scent. "Mira? I'm Dr. Dobransky-Pullman. Before we get started, would you mind filling out a short questionnaire?"

It's technically a question, but she delivers it like a statement.

She hands me the clipboard, flashes me a saccharine smile, and, without waiting for me to answer, returns to her office, shutting the door behind her.

In addition to requiring the usual contact information, the form also includes several questions about my behavior and mental state over the last six months. "Six months" is written in italics, so for some reason this must be important.

Are you currently experiencing any sexual difficulties? It's been so long, how would I know? Mark that a "no."

Have you ever been a victim of domestic violence? Ha! Domestic violence, yes, but I hadn't exactly been the victim. "No" again.

Did you ever feel as if your emotions were out of control (e.g., do you ever have trouble managing your anger or do you ever find your-

self crying for no particular reason)? "Out of control," I decide after several minutes of deliberation, is a relative term. Sure, I've lost my temper a bunch of times in the last six months, who hasn't? But I don't necessarily think I was out of control. On the other hand, some might consider having to be handcuffed and hauled away in a police cruiser evidence of, if not a total loss of control, at least a significantly diminished capacity for it. However, when I mentally calculate how long it's been since the attack on Nicola I'm relieved to find it falls just outside the six-month window. "No" again.

Do you ever think of harming yourself or others? I haven't ever really considered doing myself any harm, and it has been a few weeks, practically months, since I harbored any serious violent feelings toward Jake or Nicola. Good enough. "No" again. Skimming the rest of the questions, I check off the rest of the "no" boxes and flip to the other side of the form. On the reverse side there are four questions, each separated by a large expanse of white paper.

1. Why did you choose a life coach?
2. What areas of your life do you feel most need to be improved?
3. What is the source of your greatest disappointment?
4. What is the single thing you want most in life?

In response to the first one I write: *I have recently made some significant changes in my life, and I would like some help in deciding where to go from here.* Good—short and to the point. For the second question, I briefly consider simply naming the areas of my life that are going well, since that would take up far less space. Instead, I settle on targeting two main areas for improvement: *I would like to improve the professional and social aspects of my life.* The third question is much more problematic. My initial inclination is to note my divorce, but it seems too whiny, and I don't want her to think I'm one of those pathetic women, like Fiona's friend, who is wallowing in self-pity, so I write *losing my restaurant.* But will she think I'm callous for putting business over a relationship? So, I go back and add *and my husband.*

Maybe she'll think Jake died in a horrible restaurant fire.

What is the single thing I want most in life? I sit there staring at the blank page with an uncomfortably empty feeling in the pit of my stomach, realizing that I have absolutely no idea. I once thought I knew exactly what I wanted in my life, but no longer. How could someone go from knowing, or thinking she knows, exactly what she wants in life, to having absolutely no idea? The door opens, and Dr. Dobransky-Pullman breezes in.

"Don't worry if you haven't finished all the questions, Mira. We can go ahead and get started anyway." She holds her hand out for the clipboard and then gestures ahead through the door. I lead the way down a short hallway into a large room. Inside there is a large desk and a couple of chairs. Against the opposite wall, a long cream-colored sofa and two leather armchairs surround a low, walnut coffee table. She gestures to the sofa. "Have a seat. Make yourself comfortable."

Yeah, right.

Dr. Dobransky-Pullman makes for one of the leather club chairs but, before sitting down, she unbuttons her blazer and smoothes the collar of her white silk shirt. She sits carefully, crossing her legs and balancing the clipboard on her knee. As she looks over the questionnaire, her face is expressionless. She's wearing sheer stockings, the expensive kind, and sharply pointed high-heeled shoes. I can see that her legs are tanned even though it's the middle of winter. I feel self-conscious in my jeans and pullover sweater and have the sudden urge to sit on my hands so she doesn't see my short, bitten nails.

It is hard to tell her age. She's wearing a lot of makeup and has the flawless clear skin of a model, but she has thin lines around her eyes and mouth. She could be anywhere between thirty-five and fifty, I suppose. One thing, however, is clear. This is a woman who is used to taking care of herself. What else would one expect from a life coach? After all, you're hardly going to put your life in the hands of someone slovenly, poorly dressed, or ill-kempt. Somebody who looks like me, I can't help but think, looking down at my sagging socks and scuffed clogs.

"So," she says, suddenly looking up from the questionnaire,

"you've recently made some changes in your life, I see. What sort of changes might they be?"

"Well, I just moved here from New York a few weeks ago. I mean back here, with my father. My daughter and I, that is."

She looks straight at me with her deep, penetrating brown eyes and nods. "What's your daughter's name?" she asks softly.

"Chloe, her name is Chloe."

"Pretty name. And how old is Chloe?" She is now looking down over the form again and appears to be studying my answers.

"Eleven months. Her birthday is next month."

"Well, that's a milestone, isn't it? So," she says, taking out a notepad and clicking open her pen. "Tell me, why is it that you and Chloe have made this move back to Pittsburgh?"

I give her the abbreviated version of the events leading up to our big move, including most of the Jake and Nicola saga, but deliberately omitting my anger-management fiasco. She listens carefully, not taking her eyes from my face except to make a note here and there.

When I'm finished, I take a deep breath and slump back into the pillows of the couch, exhausted. Dr. Dobransky-Pullman inclines her head and gives me a warm smile. "Well, that was tiring, wasn't it?" she says. I nod glumly.

She lets the silence hang in the air for a while, and I wonder if she just expects me to start talking. After a moment she flexes her foot, purses her lips, and says, without even a blink, "So do you think that your romantic feelings for other women might have played a role in the breakup of your marriage?"

For a minute I think I haven't heard her correctly. Of course *Jake's* feelings for another woman played a role in the breakup of our marriage. Hadn't she been listening?

"Well, of course, Jake's feelings had everything to do with it! The divorce and, ah, everything that happened afterward, it was all his idea."

"No, Mira, we are talking about your feelings here," she says, looking at me squarely and pointedly flexing her foot again.

"What do you mean, my feelings? I love—loved Jake!"

Dr. D-P leans in, puts the clipboard down on the table, then sits back in her chair. "Look, Mira, I realize that you may not have *acted* on these feelings, but recognizing them is an important step in dealing with them. Many women, and men for that matter, get to your age and realize that they've had feelings for members of their own sex. It's nothing to be embarrassed about. What may help you come to terms with all this is for you to acknowledge that these feelings did play a role, either consciously or not, in the breakup of your marriage. I'm sensing some unresolved feelings. An element of jealousy, perhaps?" She makes a note on her pad and continues. "Has it ever occurred to you that you may be jealous, not of *Jake,* but because of your feelings about *Nicola*—"

"Excuse me?" I've sunk into the recesses of the deep sofa and now, as she is speaking, I struggle unsuccessfully to regain my equilibrium and sit upright.

"Have you ever thought that it might be Nicola instead of Jake?"

My mind is going a mile a minute wondering what she could possibly be picking up on. Sure, I had looked at her legs, but what else was I supposed to look at? The sofa was so deep that they'd been about eye level. Has she somehow, within minutes of meeting me, identified some latent desire that has gone undetected for the last thirty-eight years? "No—wait a minute!" I cry, finally righting myself. "What makes you think that?"

She nods in the direction of the questionnaire that is now sitting on the table between us and continues speaking. "Many people are not exclusively heterosexual or homosexual. It's useful, I think, to regard one's sexual inclination on a continuum. We've learned that much from Kinsey's research." I snatch the clipboard from the table and scan the form.

"Of course, if you are not comfortable talking about this now, that's okay, too. Mira, I didn't mean to upset—"

Aha! There it is, number 22a: "Would you describe your sexual orientation as exclusively heterosexual?" to which I had carelessly checked the "no" box. "No, you don't understand," I interrupt.

She is silent now, leaning back in her chair, waiting.

"I didn't mean to answer this way," I tell her. "I wasn't paying enough attention. I just, you know, started checking all the 'no' boxes." She doesn't say anything for a minute, and I look back at the questionnaire and notice that there are also a couple of other things I had failed to notice. For instance, question 22 reads, "Do you feel comfortable with your sexual identity?" and to this I also had answered no. She holds out her hand, and I give her back the form, which she takes and re-checks.

"Okay, fair enough," she says with a brief smile.

Fair enough? What's that supposed to mean? Now she probably thinks that I'm either a severely repressed lesbian, or worse, a raving homophobe. Or both.

"Of course, I have no objection to being gay," I tell her, and she nods. "My best friend is gay." Even though this is true, it sounds like the weakest of lies, the sort of thing Pat Buchanan might say when pressed on the issue of gay marriage. Right before he says that "the gays," friends though they may be, are still an aberration in the sight of God. This isn't how I feel, of course, and I have no idea why I have reacted this way, but suddenly I'm momentarily overtaken by an image of Nicola and me locked in a steamy embrace and I begin to gag. Only when the doctor stops mid-sentence to look at me with concern do I realize that she has been talking. "Are you all right, Mira?"

I nod, and take a deep breath, silently damning Richard, my father, and Fiona.

"I didn't mean to upset you. It was an honest mistake, wasn't it?"

"Yes, of course," I say, taking another deep breath. Don't start hyperventilating, I tell myself.

"Now, what do you think?" she asks, glancing at her watch and giving me a tentative look.

I look at her blankly.

"Mira, I was asking you if you felt ready to begin another chapter in your life."

"Another chapter?" I stare at her, having no idea of what to say.

"Yes. Are you ready to begin another chapter in your life?"

Then, as if reading my mind she says, "Mira, I know that you may not feel particularly ready, but you've taken an important step in coming here today." She leans forward, resting her forearms on her knees, and looks directly at me. "Now, I'm going to suggest something pretty radical. Even if you don't feel ready, I'm going to ask you to pretend that you are. Sometimes feelings follow behavior. If you act a certain way, then very often you actually start to feel that way. We are going to jump-start your life."

With a final glance at her watch, she tells me, "We should probably explore why this was so hard for you, but unfortunately we are out of time for today." I leave the office with specific instructions as to what I need to do before next week. Dr. D-P, as it turns out, is big on lists. My first assignment is to buy a "Life Notebook," in which I'm to record my assignments, the first of which is to write down five things that would make me happy and to do at least two of them before next week. In addition to that, I'm to write down five professional goals and five personal goals and a description of where I see myself in five years. She also apparently is big on the number five. Dr. D-P says that it's not at all unusual for women in my position to feel lost and unsure of themselves. I'll figure out what I want eventually, she tells me. When I give her a dubious look, she laughs and tells me that she has seen far worse cases than mine. It makes me wish that I'd come clean about having basically failed at my court-ordered rehabilitation.

I want to believe Dr. D-P. I want to believe that doing the things she asks of me will make a difference. She seems so cool and confident, so in control of things. Would it be so wrong to believe that she might be right?

chapter 17

The following week, Ruth and I are sitting at the Coffee Tree on Walnut Street. When she heard I'd been sick, she'd brought me some matzo ball soup. After the last Gymboree class, I suggested meeting for coffee the next day, and she'd accepted. She made me swear not to tell her Jewish mother, whom I've never met and who doesn't even live in Pittsburgh, that she'd bought, rather than made, the matzo ball soup.

"No seriously, there's a mafia-like code of conduct among Jewish mothers everywhere governing the cooking and dispensing of matzo ball soup," Ruth says with a nervous backwards glance. "If it ever leaked out that I bought it," she says with a wry smile, "I could be excommunicated." Can Jewish people really be excommunicated?

"Okay, here's what you need to do," Ruth tells me. We are working on the second part of my assignment for Dr. D-P, the "where do I see myself in five years" part.

"You need to come up with a plan that allows you to do the thing you love—obviously cooking—while being able to balance and maintain a significant family commitment. That's easy," she says, pausing to take a sip of her double latte. "There are probably lots of things you could do. How about being a caterer or a personal chef? Hell, you're practically mine. Or maybe you could come up with one thing and make it and sell it mail order. There's probably a huge market for online foodstuffs. Fudge, fruitcake, things like that." Carlos toddles over to a neighboring table and proceeds to gnaw on the edge of one of the chairs. In one fluid movement, Ruth retrieves him, wipes down the section of the armrest Carlos has drooled upon, and apologizes to the annoyed woman sitting there. "Or how about gourmet teething biscuits?" she asks, reclaiming her seat.

"No way," I tell her. Apart from the fact that I cannot bear the thought of wasting my excellent culinary education hawking chocolate chip cookies or Rocky Road fudge from my home, one of the many problems with Ruth's plan is logistics. Where am I to do this catering and cooking? There are probably zoning laws or Board of Health constraints that prohibit cooking for wide distribution in one's home. Even if there aren't, my father's kitchen is too small and antiquated. When I tell this to Ruth, she just shrugs.

"Don't worry about that. The assignment is where you see yourself in five years. First think about where you want to end up, and then you can figure out how to get there. So, what do you think about getting bangs?"

"What? How is getting bangs going to help me get where I'm going?"

"Not you. Me. I'm thinking about changing my hair, something soft swept across the forehead. Look at this," Ruth says, pulling her hair severely back from her forehead and furrowing her brow. "Wrinkles. I read in *More* magazine that getting bangs is the poor girl's facelift. Cheaper than Botox, for sure."

I consider Ruth's face. She has curly, shoulder-length hair, dark and peppered with wisps of gray. It's soft and pretty. When I tell her so, she rolls her eyes. "You're no help," she says, bending to retrieve Carlos's pacifier, which has rolled under the table.

"I don't know," I tell her. "Maybe I'm not the best person to ask. I've had the same hairstyle since the seventh grade."

"That's because you have perfect hair. Long and thick and straight. I hate you." Ruth laughs. "But seriously, how am I going to get Gym-Dad to notice me looking like this?" she asks, pulling her hair in tight fists away from her face and groaning.

"You're fine," I repeat, "You've got great eyes, an intelligent face, and you probably don't have any stretch marks. I'd trade good hair for no stretch marks," I say, picking up a piece of hazelnut biscotti and dunking it in my latte.

Ruth considers this a minute and smiles. "Yeah? Well, maybe."

"All I know is that whoever this guy is, he can't possibly be worth all this fuss," I tell her, surprised that she's clearly given him so much thought.

"That's because you haven't seen him yet. He's adorable, boyish, you know? The kind of guy you look at and know exactly what he looked like in the third grade. But he's graying at the temples, which is good because that means he's in the right ballpark age-wise. Why is it that gray hair is sexy on men and on us it just looks old?"

"So where was this phantom Gym-Dad yesterday? For all you know, he's married and his wife was there yesterday. Maybe she just couldn't make it last week."

"No. For starters, the kid wasn't there. I'd have recognized him, a cute little redheaded boy a little older than Carlos. Besides, the buzz in the gym last week was that he's a widower." Ruth says this breathlessly, as if she's just found out the Dow had risen three hundred points, leaving me to ponder the particular brand of buzz that widowerhood engenders among the Gymboree set.

"Hello, we're supposed to be planning my life, remember?" I tell her, waving my Life Notebook in her face.

"Okay, okay. I'm on it," Ruth says, picking up the Food section of the *Post-Gazette*. "Hey, what about teaching a cooking class? Look," she says. "There are all kinds of cooking classes being offered. Low-Fat Indian Favorites, Guiltless Gourmet Party Stoppers, Ground Beef 101." Ruth looks at me over her newspaper and raises one eyebrow. When I shake my head, she goes back to her newspaper.

On the back page of the Food section is a restaurant review. Just looking at one, even for a restaurant I don't have anything to do with, is enough to give me a stomachache. The restaurant is being reviewed by the Nibbler, the anonymous Pittsburgh restaurant reviewer whose byline is a trademark picture of a person holding a knife and a fork and wearing a checkered napkin bandit-style, the rest of the face obscured by a fake nose and glasses. "Hey, look at this," Ruth says, waving the paper in front of me. "Do you have a pair of scissors? I want to cut out this recipe. It looks like something my mother used to make." The recipe is from a column entitled "Five Ingredient Recipe Wonders" and involves cream of mushroom soup, a package of Lipton's dry onion soup, and a chuck roast. The other two ingredients are carrots and potatoes.

"Hey, didn't you say your mother would kill you if she found out you bought matzo ball soup? Now you're telling me she made things with Campbell's Cream of Mushroom?"

"Of course. All the time. Lipton's onion soup mix, too, the powdered kind. The matzo ball soup is definitely an exception. That's because it's basically part of the religion. Seriously, I learned to make it in Hebrew School," she says, when I give her a doubtful look. "That's how my mother cooked. Her famous brisket recipe calls for dry onion soup mix and a bottle of Coke." She laughs when I shudder. "Snob. Actually, it's delicious."

She gives the recipe a surreptitious rip. The paper belongs to the Coffee Tree. "I think I'm going to make this," she says, pocketing the recipe.

That night, about ten, Ruth calls me in desperation. "Did you know that crock pots have two settings?" she asks me.

"Well, yeah," I tell her. "Why?"

"Because I didn't. I put it on low, and the meat still isn't done, and it's late and I'm starving. Besides, I'm not sure I want to eat it. Is the meat supposed to be gray?"

"No, gray meat isn't usually a good sign. But I don't know. I've never cooked with cream of mushroom soup. It's kind of gray, so maybe that's the way it's supposed to be," I tell her.

"Are you sure you're a real chef?" Ruth says, obviously cranky and hungry.

"Well, does it look like what your mother made?"

"No. Definitely not."

"Did you brown the meat first?"

"No, the recipe didn't say to."

"Okay, it's just that browning the meat first allows a nice crust to form on the meat, which lends a certain depth of flavor, not to mention color, to the dish. It's probably gray because you didn't brown it first." So much for not sounding like a chef.

"It didn't say to," Ruth stubbornly repeats.

"Well, I don't know, then. Call up your mother and ask her if she browned her meat. I'll bet she did."

"No, forget it. I'd just get a lecture on how I should have paid attention to her cooking and that if I had, I'd be married now. Who needs that?"

After hanging up with Ruth, I rummage around in the den for today's newspaper, looking for the recipe that Ruth has obviously mucked up. I find the Food section and, sure enough, Ruth was right—the recipe didn't call for browning the meat. I end up reading the entire section cover to cover, including the restaurant review that I had avoided reading at the Coffee Tree, which I could tell from the first sentence was going to be a bad one.

The restaurant being reviewed is Koko's Caribbean Bistro, which right away the reviewer had pounced upon as evoking an alarming image. Bistros were French, and the notion of a Caribbean bistro obviously troubled the reviewer, who had apparently forgotten that part of the Caribbean was, in fact, settled by the French. In addition, he griped that too many of the dishes served were overly sweet and used too many exotic ingredients. The sweet dishes might not have been to his taste, but the cuisine of the Caribbean is heavily dependent on sugar cane, as well as several indigenous starchy vegetables that, when cooked, release their latent sugars. Alligator was on the menu, as was conch, both of which the reviewer said he had tried (they both tasted like chicken), but I'm not sure I believe him.

In the hallway I hear Dad and Fiona saying good night. Their voices fall silent after a minute. Maybe they are kissing. A few minutes later, I hear my father climb the stairs to bed.

I always thought that restaurant reviewers had cushy jobs, but in New York I'd actually known one. She reviewed mostly sandwich shops and Chinese buffets, so it wasn't like she was eating out at three-star restaurants every night of the week, hobnobbing after hours with Joel Robuchon and Mario Batali, but still, how bad could it be?

Why hadn't I thought of it before? The hours would be great, and I could do the writing at home. An added bonus would be that, as a reviewer, I'd have the potential to influence the trends in Pittsburgh, a heady prospect. By the time I climb the stairs to bed, I've convinced myself I'm poised to become Pittsburgh's own Frank Bruni.

I peek in on Chloe and then tackle the boxes under the eaves, tiptoeing around so as not to wake her. I finally hunt down what I'm looking for: *Tastes of the Caribbean*. It's been a long day, and the cool sheets feel good against my skin. I open the book and leaf through it. I can't remember ever having read this particular book or having prepared any of the dishes in it. It probably had been Jake's. The author seems to know her stuff, displaying an academic interest in the food and the culture of the islands, while writing vividly, capturing the nuances of sight, smell, and taste. In the middle of the book there is a large color spread of photographs depicting some of the more ambitious dishes. I find myself looking at pictures of rich and beautiful food, sensually displayed against the lush and verdant backdrop of an island paradise. If nothing else, I'm hoping to dream of conch fritters and deep blue seas.

I need someone to watch Chloe during my weekly therapist appointment, and Ruth is also desperate for time alone—some relief from Carlos. Time, she says, where she can go and sip coffee or get her nails done, all the while wallowing in guilt about the craven need she has to escape her own child. And so, we have made a deal. One day each week, we will watch each other's children.

It's her turn on Tuesday so, after dropping Chloe at Ruth's, I'm able to spend the entire morning at the Squirrel Hill Library preparing for my life coach appointment at noon. First, I do some research on the Pittsburgh food scene (which takes about five minutes), then I spend the rest of the time updating my résumé and drafting a cover letter to the food editor, whose name is Enid Maxwell.

Dr. D-P is pleased with my progress and doles out another set of tasks for next week, mostly having to do with résumés and mass mailings.

On the way home I decide to stop and visit Richard, whom I haven't seen or spoken to since last week. He'd deliberately hurt me with his comments about my mother, which I now have to admit, may have been helpful. He's probably avoiding me, thinking I'm still angry.

Richard's shop is on Ellsworth Avenue, occupying the first floor of an old turn of the century row house, sandwiched in between an elegant ladies resale shop called Plan B and a used CD and record exchange called Astro and the Jetsons. The shop is empty, but I can see Richard look up in his office as the bell on the door gives a metallic tinkle. He's on the phone, which he places in the crook of his neck, as he beckons me back into his office. He reaches over his desk and removes a stack of fabric samples from the guest chair. He tries not to show that he is either surprised or pleased to see me, but I can tell by the flash of his eyes that he's glad, maybe even relieved, that I've come. I can also tell by the way he is doggedly biting the inside of his mouth that he is probably dealing with a difficult client, one who is refusing to bend to Richard's rather implacable decorating will.

"Okay, okay, we'll just cancel it and reorder the Parsons chairs. It will take an additional six weeks, but if you are in no hurry... Yes. Okay. Fine." I can tell by the way he says "fine" that it really isn't, that it really is anything but.

He hangs up the phone. "Zebra-striped Parsons chairs. Sometimes you just can't save people from themselves, no matter how hard you try."

How true.

"I'm glad to see that you're feeling better," he continues, after a moment. His voice is formal, as if he is still talking to the recalcitrant client, and I suspect he feels guilty about hurting me.

"I am better. I'm fine, really." My voice is only slightly less formal than his. "I'm seeing a therapist now. I've just come from her, in fact," I tell him. And then, unable to resist a gratuitous dig, I add softly, "See, I'm not too proud for that." Richard winces.

"Actually, she isn't really a therapist," I continue, my voice louder and just a bit smug. "She's a life coach, which, if you ever get sick of decorating people's houses, you might look into. As a life coach you get to hound people for a living, nag at them until they do what you want, until they do what *you* think is good for them. You'd be perfect at it." This, of course, isn't really true (at least the part about Dr. D-P hounding me to do what she wanted), but I can't resist teasing Richard. It's always been the best and quickest way to clear the air between us.

He finally smiles. "Good for you," he says quietly, and I can tell he really means it.

Richard makes us some chamomile tea in the little kitchenette beside his workroom. I sit on one of the high stools beside his drafting table and tell him about my plan to take over the Pittsburgh dining world.

"This life coach sounds worth her weight in gold. Maybe I should go and see her."

"What on earth would she do for you?" I ask him, surprised. "Your life has always been exactly as you like it. At least since I've known you," I add, tacitly acknowledging the time in his life long before I knew him, when Richard probably could have used a life coach. It's something we almost never talk about. "Besides, you are definitely not coachable," I tell him, taking a sip of tea.

"And you are?" He shoots me an amused look. "Anyway, let's not talk about it. I'm having a perfectly nice time right now and don't want to get depressed. And conversations concerning matters of the heart have a habit of doing just that."

Richard doesn't usually talk about his romantic entanglements, or if he does, he scrupulously avoids specifics. I don't know if he thinks it unseemly to tell me about his boyfriends; he can, at times, be rather prudish. I could understand his reluctance when I was younger, but now that we're both adults, I wonder at his reticence regarding discussing "matters of the heart," as he had called them.

"So, are you seeing someone?" I ask. Judging from the way he shakes his head and looks quickly away, I know that he is, or has been. Richard refills our cups and pulls out a stash of Carr's wheat-meal biscuits from the cupboard by the sink. He hands me the package to open and then, ducking out into the shop for a minute, grabs a delicate Limoges dish.

"Here," he says, handing me the plate. "Use this."

I arrange the cookies on the plate, glad to have something to do.

Richard changes the subject. "I like Fiona," he says, breaking a biscuit in half and dipping it delicately in his tea.

"That's nice," I say, adding another lump of sugar to my cup. Richard hands me a spoon.

"Mira—"

"Look, it isn't that I don't like her, it's just that she's not . . ."

"She's not what? Not smart enough? So what? Smart is over-rated."

"It isn't just that. They don't have any of the same interests. It was painful watching them try to play Scrabble."

"Well, good for her. At least she's trying to learn." Richard shrugs, as if this too is no big deal. I stare at him, incredulous. Richard's always maintained that he could never fall for anyone who hadn't read (and loved) *Gravity's Rainbow*, couldn't tell Lap-sang souchong from Darjeeling, and didn't worship the Pittsburgh Steelers. Which might just explain why his love life is suffering.

"She's just so—I don't know—different."

Richard takes a bite of his biscuit and chews noisily. "You mean from your mother?"

"You say that like it's a bad thing."

Richard frowns. He doesn't believe in speaking ill of the dead, even though he knows I'm half kidding.

"Let's face it, she was difficult," I tell him.

"She was temperamental. Like lots of creative people."

"Not all creative people drink a fifth of whiskey a day," I remind him.

"True," Richard says, pausing to sip his tea.

"Well, I guess if Fiona makes him happy, who am I to say?" I tell him, even though I don't really mean it.

"Creative temperament aside, even though your mother might

have been his intellectual match and shared his interests, Fiona's a much better choice. She's one for the distance," Richard says, shaking a biscuit in my direction.

I'm about to tell him that I find it difficult to believe that someone who wears spandex and plays Bunko has the staying power to satisfy my father in the long term, but Richard interrupts me.

"Besides, Fiona takes good care of your father. He's never looked better, and when a man gets to be his age, what he wants is to be taken care of." I look up, surprised by the sudden intensity in Richard's voice. He isn't looking at me, though. He's studying the other half of his biscuit like it's the Rosetta stone.

Neither one of us says anything for a moment. Richard and my father are pretty close in age, within ten or so years anyway, and I'm starting to get the feeling we haven't just been talking about my father. I also know better than to press him. Again, Richard changes the subject, and we talk about other things—his latest design project, whether Fiona's breasts have indeed been surgically altered, my new friend Ruth.

On the way home I think about what Richard said, what we both said, and, more important, didn't say. He's got a cagey, secretive side, not to mention a disarming smile and a well-developed capacity for changing the subject whenever it hits too close to home. Even after all these years, for someone I consider my best friend, there's still a lot I don't know about Richard.

chapter 18

I'm in the coatroom at Gymboree the following morning, wrestling Chloe out of her jacket, when Ruth breezes in. She's wearing eye makeup and lipstick, and her hair is swept up in a complicated chignon. Instead of her favorite Wharton B-School sweatshirt and faded Gap chinos, she's wearing designer jeans and a turquoise cowl-necked sweater. She looks around the coatroom furtively. "Well?"

"You look great," I tell her.

"Thanks," she says, plopping Carlos down on the bench next to Chloe. "Is he here? Did you see him yet?" she whispers, rummaging around in her diaper bag. I shake my head. Carlos has begun to squirm, so I start unzipping his coat while Ruth pulls a pair of wedge heels from the bag and holds them against her sweater. "Too much?" she asks. "I couldn't decide."

"Yup, definitely," I tell her, slipping Carlos out of his jacket.

"Okay, right," she says, stuffing them back into the diaper bag. I thrust the kids' jackets and bags into the cubbies while Ruth stands there hyperventilating.

"Wait a minute," she says, laying a hand on my arm. "Can you just check to see if he's out there?"

"Ruth, get a grip. What is the big deal? You've never even spoken to the guy. He might be a complete moron."

"You've been married, Mira. Do you have any idea of the stigma attached to someone my age who's never even been *asked?*" I look over at Ruth, whose face threatens to collapse in a mass of worry lines.

"Okay, okay, I'll check." I duck my head out into the gym and look around. "No. He's not even here. Come on, let's go," I say, propelling Ruth and Carlos into the JCC gym.

After a while, Ruth relaxes. I lift Chloe into the long tube, and Carlos toddles in after her. Ruth sinks down onto the brightly colored mat and blows a wisp of hair that has escaped her chignon out of her face. "I can't believe I let someone I don't even know unglue me like that. What a loser I am, huh?"

I sit down next to her and give her hand a squeeze. "Not at all," I tell her. Chloe emerges from the other side of the tube and makes her way at a fast crawl to join us on the mat. When Carlos fails to follow her, Ruth ducks her head inside the tube only to find that he's parked himself smack in the middle of it, causing a traffic jam of testy toddlers to build up from the other side. Ruth leans in and calls his name. "Come on out, buddy." Nothing. Ruth looks at me and rolls her eyes before climbing in after him. Because she's tall, she has to arch her back to fit inside the tube, which makes her rear end stick out at an unattractive angle.

I gather Chloe into my lap and think about what Ruth had said. She's right. No one would think it odd if a forty-three-year-old man had never been married, but a woman? Forget it.

Just then I look up and see him. Gym-Dad is standing in the doorway of the coatroom, looking nervously around the room. He's holding his son, a redheaded toddler. One of the other moms advances on him, offering a name tag and a pen.

"Hey, Ruth," I whisper.

"Hang on, I can't quite reach him," Ruth says, inching her way further into the tube, so that her backside is now fully encased. "Mira, can you go around and try to get him from the other side? I think he's closer." Gym-Dad makes his way into the room, pausing to release his son, who, of course, makes his way at a fast clip to the large huddle of toddlers surrounding the other side of the yellow tube.

"Ah, Ruth," I say, this time leaning in and tugging urgently at her foot.

"Damn, these things aren't exactly made to accommodate the middle-aged woman's anatomy. I think I'm stuck," Ruth says, her voice echoing hollowly in the yellow plastic tube.

Just then Carlos emerges from the other end, and the little red-headed boy joins the crush of kids scrambling back in. When I look up, Gym-Dad is crouching next to me, leaning down to look into the back end of the tube, expecting, I assume, to see his son, but instead gazing straight into Ruth's backside.

"Bit of a roadblock, I see," he says evenly, his eyes smiling. He's got a pleasant face, more youthful than boyish, at odds with the softly graying temples and small craggy lines around his eyes and mouth.

I can see Ruth's body tense at the sound of his voice. "Mira?" she says, hesitantly.

"I'm right here," I tell her as I watch Carlos, who has now escaped the tube, hurl himself toward a sea of yoga balls.

"Grab Carlos, will you? While I, um, try to get out of here," she mutters.

When I return with Carlos and Chloe, Gym-Dad is helping Ruth to her feet. Her hair's come loose, one of Carlos's tiny gym socks is stuck to her pant leg, and her face is the color of a late season persimmon.

"Thanks," Ruth says, bending low to dust off the knees of her pants and remove the stray sock. I bend down to put Carlos's sock back on, and when I catch Ruth's eye, she glares at me. The two of us stand up.

"Hi, I'm Mira," I say, extending my hand to Gym-Dad. "This is Chloe, and this is Carlos, who belongs to Ruth, whom you've already met."

"No, I haven't, but it's nice to meet you both," he says, taking my hand and shaking it. "I'm Neil, and this is Eli," he says, running his fingers through Eli's thick red curls as he stands with his head buried in his father's pant leg. "Those tubes can be tricky," Neil says sympathetically. Ruth nods mutely and looks down with concern at Eli.

"I'm sorry. I think I scared him," she says.

"He'll be all right. He's a bit of a nervous kid, that's all." The three of us stand there awkwardly until Carlos pokes Eli in the back. Eli begins to whimper.

"Carlos!" Ruth says.

"No, don't worry about it," Neil says, picking up Eli. "He was just being curious. Well, I guess we'll look around a bit," he says, wandering off in the direction of the rocking horses.

"How could you?" Ruth hisses, as soon as Neil is out of earshot.

"I tried to warn you—" I begin, but Ruth interrupts.

"Then his kid comes charging through the other end of the tube, takes one look at me, and begins to cry. Nice."

"Who cares? And besides, now at least he'll remember you," I tell her.

"My butt, more likely—not exactly my finest feature, in case you hadn't noticed."

I give Ruth's arm a nudge and incline my head in the direction of the rocking horses. "Come on, Carlos loves those. Let's go over and—"

"No!"

"Don't you want a chance to talk to him?" When I look over, Neil is looking at us. "Don't look now, but he's looking this way. Come on, let's just go over and—"

"NO!" Ruth says, grabbing my arm, panic in her eyes.

"Okay, okay. Never mind. It's almost time for 'The Bubble Song' anyway." Ruth, the kids, and I make our way over to where the instructors are setting up the parachute and filling the bubble trays.

Ruth is quiet during the rest of class and, for some reason I can't fathom, still seems annoyed with me. In the coatroom after class, I tell her I was just trying to help. "You spent the better part of the week talking about the guy; I figured you might want a chance to get to know him, that's all."

"I know. It's not your fault, really. I've always been this way. I get nervous and tongue-tied, and you're all 'Hi, I'm Mira,' and then

I feel like even more of a yutz," Ruth says miserably. "And p.s., I think he was looking at you, not me, anyway. And why wouldn't he? You didn't get your fat ass stuck in—"

We're on our way out the door of the coatroom and into the JCC lobby when I catch sight of Rona Silverman standing smack in the middle of the lobby, talking with an older woman with platinum hair. I groan.

"What's the matter?" Ruth asks.

At the last minute I try to steer Ruth out of the way, but it's too late. Rona's already spotted me. "Why, Mira dear," she calls to me, waving me over. "What are you doing still in town? I thought you'd left ages ago!"

"No, still here," I tell her.

Rona pats her frosted bob and smiles at Chloe. "How is that restaurant of yours surviving without you?" And then, turning to her companion, Rona says, "Leah, Mira's the one I was telling you about. She's a cook in New York. You ate at her restaurant when you were there a couple of months ago, remember?"

"Did I?" asks Leah. "Oh, yes, of course, delicious," she says absently, which makes me flinch. I feel like I've been punched. Ruth looks at me with concern.

"Forgive me, girls, this is my friend, Leah Hollander," Rona says, introducing her companion. "We're playing mah-jongg at eleven." She looks at her watch and clucks. "Supposed to anyway. Your class got out late," she says, frowning.

"I love mah-jongg," Ruth says. All three of us turn to look at her.

"Really, dear? Not many people your age know the game," Rona says, sizing Ruth up and exchanging a look with her friend. "And you are?" Rona says, turning to look from Ruth to me for the introduction.

"Oh, this is my friend, Ruth Bernstein," I tell the women.

"How lovely to meet you, Ruth," Leah says, taking Ruth's hand in hers. "We don't usually play here," she continues. "We usually play at one of our houses on Thursday afternoons, but our fourth recently broke her ankle and can't negotiate the steps, so until she's better, we're relegated to playing here. Have you girls just come from the baby exercise class? I was hoping to catch a glimpse of my grandson, but we must have missed him," says Leah, looking beyond us into the gym.

Just then, Rona Silverman begins waving. "Look, Leah, there they are." Ruth, Leah, and I all turn around, just as Neil and Eli make their way out of the men's room and head toward us.

"Neil dear, we thought we'd missed you," Leah calls to her son. "There's my darling boy," she says, reaching to take Eli from Neil.

"Mother, Mrs. Silverman," Neil says, smiling. "There's no changing table in the men's room. Posed a bit of a challenge, I'm afraid."

"Neil, come meet Mira and her friend Ruth *Bernstein,*" Rona Silverman says.

"We've already met. Ladies, nice to see you again," Neil says, pausing to pull his BlackBerry from his pocket.

Leah Hollander frowns at her son. "Put that thing away, Neil. It's rude, and besides you shouldn't be keeping it in your pocket. You could get testicular cancer, you know."

"Mother!" Neil exclaims, horrified. I can't help laughing. Ruth, Rona, and Leah all look at me askance while Neil shakes his head. "Apparently, nothing is sacred," he says, turning to me and smiling before slipping his BlackBerry back into his pocket and taking Eli from his mother's arms.

"Oh, don't be such a prude, Neil," his mother says, even though she's looking at me like she knows I'm the kid who laughed in fifth grade health class at the first mention of the word "penis," which, for the record, I was. "These are both married women. They know what testicles are. They've got babies for goodness—"

"We're not married," Ruth interrupts, breathlessly.

"Look, they're going to start without you," Neil says, gesturing beyond us into the gym, where a dozen women are now taking their places at the folding tables just set up by the custodian. "Don't you think you'd better start racking your tiles?"

"Yes, come on, Leah, let's go. I don't want to be stuck sitting with Heddy Markowicz again. She's too slow," Rona says.

"Don't forget you're coming for dinner tonight. Six thirty, sharp," Leah says, reaching up to kiss her son's cheek.

"Yes, Mother," Neil says, bending low to receive her kiss. "Mrs. Silverman, ladies," and with a nod he's gone.

We're almost to the door when Leah flags us down again. "Ruth dear, so glad I caught you. Rona and I were just talking. Perhaps you'd like to join us for mahj sometime? I don't suppose you have a card, do you?"

"Sure, I do," Ruth says, rummaging in her purse for a moment before handing Leah her card. "It's been ages since I've played, so I'm sure I'm rusty, but I'd love to, if you can tolerate me," she says, smiling like she's just won the lottery.

"What are you smiling at?" I ask her, as soon as Leah is out of sight.

"The game is afoot," Ruth says softly.

Enid Maxwell, the food editor at the *Post-Gazette*, has sent me a form letter, thanking me for my interest. There are no openings at this time, she writes, but my interest is appreciated. The letter looks odd, as if she is trying to fill up the expanse of white letterhead with three lousy lines. Enid even signed her name with a big, bold flourish, probably trying to take up more space. It seems as if a letter from a journalist should be more eloquent.

My first reaction is to rip it to shreds and burn the evidence. If I rip it up, I can deny its existence, and when asked by Dr. D-P for a status report on my "irons in the fire," as she calls them, I can tell her I haven't heard anything. She's lately begun to intimate that I should have a few more irons in the fire and that I shouldn't be putting all my eggs in one basket. She's a woman who likes to communicate in short bursts of energy and often uses clichés because they get the point across with a minimum of explanation. But every once in a while, when she suspects she's lost my attention, she'll drop a little bomb and then sit back and examine her nails. Like last week, we were talking about the fact that in the last three weeks I've only managed to send out one résumé, and Dr. D-P suggested that this might be construed as not making enough of an effort. To which I challenged that I was waiting to see what happened with the *Post-Gazette* before I planned my assault on the restaurants of

Pittsburgh. To which *she* added that putting all my eggs in one basket seemed to be an issue with me. I'd done it before, hadn't I? I'd put everything into Grappa and into my relationship with Jake and look where it had gotten me. I'd spent all of my emotional capital, when what I'd really needed to do was keep something back, just for me. It may be why, she hinted, I feel so lost and empty all the time.

I told Dr. D-P that a marriage is like a soufflé, a labor of love, requiring the taming of plenty of temperamental eggs, under precise conditions and under the direction of a skilled and talented chef. It seems to me that if you can't put all your eggs in the marriage basket, then you ought to just forget it and order takeout. Actually, I hadn't told her that, I just thought of it, but now I wish I'd said it.

Today, still stinging from the *Post-Gazette* rejection, I decide that my homework assignment will have to wait. I'm supposed to be putting together a list of restaurants where I'd be interested in working and researching the Pittsburgh catering scene, neither of which, I've decided, I have any interest in doing.

Later, when I tell this to Dr. D-P, she nods and asks why.

"Look," I tell her, my tone defiant. "I managed and owned a successful New York restaurant. I'm way past the point in my career where I'm interested in working for someone else. And in case you haven't noticed, I don't play particularly well with others."

She laughs. "So open a new restaurant, Mira. It doesn't have to be a four-star 'serious' restaurant. It can be a tearoom, a deli, a breakfast joint, you decide. That is, after all, the point. You get to decide."

I thump my fists into the cushions of the couch, exasperated. We have had this conversation before. "I-I just can't get excited about something new."

She tilts her head and gives me a quizzical look. "That isn't really true, is it? You've been very excited about the possibility of doing some food writing, some restaurant reviewing. That would be a new venture for you."

Something about my body language must have alerted her to the possibility that this is no longer an option, because she's all over me in seconds. "So, have you heard anything from the *Post-Gazette?*"

I don't answer her right away. I fidget and look up at the ceiling. "They are not interested at this time." My voice is tight and formal, just like the letter, and I feel a sudden heat behind my eyes.

"I see," she says quietly. She doesn't say anything else, but moves forward in her chair. "I know that's a real blow, Mira. I'm sorry." And I think for a second she's going to say something about eggs in baskets, but she doesn't.

I'm crying, ridiculous as it seems, sitting with my fists clenched in my lap crying real tears because I've received a three-sentence form rejection letter for a job I knew I had no real chance of getting.

She considers me a moment, chewing thoughtfully on her lower lip before handing me a Kleenex.

"What was the biggest obstacle you encountered in running Grappa?"

I blow my nose. The biggest obstacle? Who knows, there were so many. "There were obstacles every day. Running a restaurant isn't easy. Starting up was nightmarish—there were weeks on end, before we opened and then right after, when I don't think I slept more than a couple of hours a night."

"But you succeeded, against improbable odds, didn't you?"

"Yes, we did, but there were two of us. We were in it together. I can't do this alone." A deep, guttural choking sound escapes me, and I look up self-consciously. I can't believe I've become someone who cries in her therapist's office.

"Mira, don't let Jake take this from you, too." She says this softly and, reaching over, puts both her hands on top of my own clenched fists. Her voice is low and soft, but there's an urgency there and an undercurrent of something that sounds like anger.

chapter 19

In the lobby of the Highland Towers there is a little deli called the Brown Bag. I had planned on treating myself to a nice lunch at Casbah, and had even briefly entertained the possibility of calling Richard and asking him to join me, but I'm emotionally spent from my life coaching appointment and can barely make it down to the deli on the first floor. I order a grilled Reuben sandwich and some steak fries the instant I'm seated, without even looking at the menu.

The waitress shouts my order to the line cook and fills my water glass, slopping some onto the chipped Formica table. When the cook grumbles that it's almost two o'clock, she fixes him with a withering look.

"After two, it's only pie, coffee, and fountain drinks, but don't worry, hon," she says to me. "It's only five till."

She's wearing a brown polyester uniform with a white collar and cuffs. Her nails are long, artificial talons, painted a frosted pink, and her fingers, all ten of them, are crusted with cheap silver rings. I try to imagine myself in a greasy white apron and a hairnet, grumpily manning the grill, taking orders from a waitress old enough to be my grandmother.

"Thanks," is all I can manage.

"Coffee?"

I nod, too exhausted to speak.

Dr. D-P has earned double her fee this afternoon in a marathon cheerleading session. The latter half of the therapy hour was devoted to something she calls "Leapfrog Theory." According to Leapfrog Theory, it apparently doesn't matter that I have no experience writing restaurant reviews; if it's what I decide I want to do, then I should just go for it and not let a little thing like Enid Maxwell's rejection put a damper on my plans. The initial rejection is best viewed as merely an obstacle, she tells me, one that may or may not be easily leapt over. The point is that I won't know unless I try. And so I've agreed to telephone Enid Maxwell and extract some sort of commitment to meet with me so that I might share with her my expansive knowledge of the New York restaurant world. Like I'm doing her some kind of favor.

When I balked at this suggestion, Dr. D-P told me that she wouldn't have suggested it had she not known that I had it in me. "Whether you recognize it or not, Mira, one doesn't get to the top of one's profession without the liberal application of Leapfrog principles." When I tried to tell her that there's also a hefty element of luck involved, she reminded me of my iron-willed resolve in trying to hold onto Jake and Grappa. Sure, it hadn't worked out, but it hadn't been because I gave up too easily.

I devour the sandwich, a mountain of corned beef between two greasy slabs of marble rye, leaking cheese and Russian dressing all down the front of my sweater. It's delicious, and I don't stop eating until I've finished the last thick fry, which I use to mop up the remains of the sandwich. I need all the sustenance I can get for what I'm about to do.

I leave the waitress a hefty tip, which she tucks into the breast pocket of her uniform. "Thanks, doll," she calls, smiling at me and waving, her silver rings glinting in the afternoon sun.

An hour later, I'm sitting cross-legged on my bed, clutching the rejection letter, on which Enid Maxwell's phone number is prominently displayed, making it all too easy for me to call her. I've spent the last thirty minutes online on my laptop reading past Food section excerpts. At a minimum, it has given me second thoughts about having any association with the *Post-Gazette*. The recipes are uninteresting (cream of cauliflower soup made with frozen cauliflower, Velveeta Light, and canned tomatoes). In addition, they review a different fast-food freezer item each week. This week's offering, Amy's Vegan Black Bean Burritos, has been given two thumbs-up by the reviewers. Doesn't anyone in Pittsburgh cook?

I'm looking for excuses not to call, but the alternative—having to fess up to Dr. D-P next week that I hadn't been able to do it—is by far the more frightening prospect. Dr. D-P has made it seem as if my psychological well-being, not to mention my entire future, is riding on this one phone call. If I'm ever going to be able to move on with my life, I have to get over my fear of rejection, she said. It's as if Jake's rejection has seeped into every area of my life, polluting my sense of self worth so that now I live in constant fear of being spurned again, even by a newspaper that lauds the use of processed cheese products.

So, I'm stuck. Finally, I arrive at the psychologically comfortable compromise of calling after five and leaving a message. I'm counting on what I can remember from episodes of *The Wire,* that newspaper editors are seldom at their desks and rarely answer their land-line phones. So I prepare and rehearse a confident-sounding message, gently challenging Enid's provincial sensibilities and offering to meet with her to discuss the rise of the Pittsburgh restaurant.

I dial the phone.

While it's ringing I rehearse my message. I take a deep breath. I want to sound relaxed and confident. "Hello, Enid. This is Mira Rinaldi. Listen, I just wanted to touch—"

"Pressroom." The voice that answers is gruff and masculine.

"Yes, hi. I just wanted to leave a message for Enid Maxwell." There is a deafening noise in the background.

"Who? I can barely hear you."

"Enid Maxwell," I yell.

"This is the pressroom. She must have forwarded her phone. Hang on, I'll find her."

"No!" I practically scream into the phone. "I mean, that's okay, don't disturb her, I'll just leave a mess—"

"Oh, wait a sec, she just walked in." The background sounds suddenly become muffled as the man puts his hand over the receiver and yells, "Yo, Enid, phone."

I'm seized by a sudden urge to hang up—and I'm about to—when an irrepressible, irrational thought suddenly flashes through my wearied brain, as irrational thoughts have a habit of doing when you are tired, stressed, and genetically predisposed to paranoia. Newspapers probably have caller ID on their phones—making it easier to identify informants calling in with anonymous tips. Enid could easily identify me as the caller, and I would be busted for hanging up on her.

"Yeah, Enid Maxwell," she barks.

"Enid, this is Mira Rinaldi. I—"

"Who? Listen, you're going to have to speak up. We're running a test sheet in the pressroom, and I can't hear you."

I try again, feeling ridiculous. "It's Mira Rinaldi," I yell into the phone.

Suddenly, whatever had been causing the deafening noise in the background stops dead, leaving the echo of my shouted name reverberating in the empty air.

"Oh, Mira, the aspiring food critic." Her voice has returned to its presumably normal tones.

I'm shocked that she remembers me from the three-sentence rejection letter, which I'd assumed was just a form letter, prepared and signed by some underling. "Yes, that's me."

"Okay. What's up? Make it quick if you can. I'm rushing to meet a press deadline, which means I have about thirty seconds to talk with you."

"Well," I begin, taking a breath, trying to force some air into my constricted chest. "I got your letter and I, I was wondering if we might be able to meet. I think I have something to offer that you might have overlooked in my—"

"Look," she interrupts. "I read the review you enclosed. Your restaurant, what is it called, Limoncello, Vino, something like—"

"Grappa."

"Yeah, right. Well, Grappa sounds like a wonderful restaurant, and *Gourmet,* I know, did not bestow its praise lightly. Clearly you and your husband are talented chefs, but what makes you think that you could be a restaurant reviewer?"

Her tone is condescending, and I hate to be condescended to.

"Ex-husband. And you want to know why I think I could be a restaurant reviewer? One: I have spent the last twenty years eating great food. Two: I have a well-developed palate. Three: I've also run a successful Manhattan restaurant, which is no small thing, as I'm sure you know. I know what it takes to make a restaurant successful," I tell her.

"Yes," she sighs, "but you have to be able to *write* about it. Look, do you think just because you read *Gourmet* you can suddenly become Ruth Reichl? How are your writing skills? Do you have a sample to submit?" She sounds just this side of irritated.

Let's see. Jake and I had written our own wedding vows that, in a fit of rage after the separation, I had torched with the portable gas flame we used for doing crème brûleé. I'd written a few papers while at the Culinary Institute, but most of them were cost analyses and technical explanations. How to make a brown veal stock. The pros and cons of using a blond versus a brown roux.

"Well, I have some writing from school. I had to write some papers at the Culinary Institute, but they're several years old. I guess I—"

"The CIA? You went to the CIA?" For some reason she sounds impressed.

"Yes, I did."

Suddenly the deafening noise is back, and once again Enid has to shout to make herself heard. "Look, I've got to go. Get me a writing sample and we'll talk."

I'm about to hang up when the noise once again stops abruptly and Enid continues, her tone softer and resigned. "This is not New York, Ms. Rinaldi. Do you know how often *Gourmet, Bon Appétit,* and *Food and Wine* have featured a Pittsburgh restaurant? Exactly never. Go ahead. Send me a sample, and if I like it, I'll give you a try, but don't get your hopes up. You may find that you are the one who is disappointed."

"So, do you want the short version or all the gory details?" Ruth asks when I arrive on her doorstep a full hour late to pick up Chloe. I'd tried calling in the interim, but Ruth either had turned off her answering machine or was on the phone and hadn't picked up, I'd even stopped at the Smallman Street Deli on the way over to pick up Ruth's favorite corned beef sandwich and a couple of kosher hot dogs for Carlos as a peace offering for being late, but she doesn't even mention it. Instead, she drops the bag on the counter without even looking inside and ushers me into the family room where Chloe and Carlos are sitting on the floor in front of a video gnawing on frozen bagels. "Sorry," Ruth says when she catches me looking around at the toy-strewn room and at Carlos's and Chloe's glazed and glassy-eyed expressions, clear evidence of TV coma. "You know I don't usually park them in front of the TV, but we are definitely talking extenuating circumstances here."

She hands me a box of tissues, when I was really hoping she'd offer me the other half of her corned beef sandwich. "What are these for?" I ask innocently.

"Just wait until you hear this. Trust me, you'll need them. By the way, I hope you can watch the kids a week from Thursday," Ruth says. I nod, even though she hadn't really been asking. "Oh," Ruth continues, "and do you think you could help me make a couple dozen rugelach? It's very important that they be good and mine; well, suffice it to say I have a problem with anything that involves a rolling pin. And in this instance, props are key."

"Props?"

"Yes, the machine has been put in motion!" Ruth says, leaning toward me, her face pink with excitement. A pool of saliva has begun to accumulate in the corners of her mouth that, coupled with her flushed face, makes her appear vaguely rabid.

"What are you talking about?" I ask, looking at her with alarm.

Ruth stops short and looks at me with surprise. "Can you really be this dense?" she asks.

"Apparently so," I tell her, removing my coat and taking a seat on the sofa.

"Clearly, you're going to need the long version," Ruth says, plopping down on the ottoman next to me.

I'm barely settled on the sofa before Ruth launches into her story. While the kids were napping, she got a call from Leah Hollander inviting her to join them for their weekly mah-jongg game at Rona Silverman's house the following Thursday afternoon.

"Okay, so while we're on the phone, Leah asks me how long I've been divorced, and when I tell her that I've never been married and that Carlos is adopted, she says something about what a good mother I must be to take all this on alone." Ruth looks over at Carlos, whose face is covered in masticated bagel, which he is in the process of smearing onto Ruth's expensive Persian rug. "Hmm, well, anyway," Ruth continues, turning back to me. "She then proceeds to tell me all about her poor son, Neil, whom she would love to see settled, particularly with a woman who is so clearly interested in being a mother."

"I'm beginning to get the picture," I tell her.

"I thought you might," Ruth says, getting up to retrieve the deli bag from the kitchen counter. On the way back, she grabs two beers from the bar fridge. "You can't drink wine with corned beef, right?"

"Definitely not," I tell her, accepting the Stella Artois she offers me, along with a sheaf of napkins and the other half of her corned beef sandwich.

"Okay, so then, completely unsolicited, she tells me all about Neil's wife. How much they wanted kids and how hard they tried to get pregnant, how Neil has wanted to be a father since he was a little boy. Finally, she gets pregnant and midway through the pregnancy discovers a lump on her breast. Obviously they remove it, but she has to choose between getting an abortion and delaying treatment until after the baby is born. She waits until just after Eli is born to start treatment. My God," Ruth says, popping the lid on her beer and taking a sip, "can you imagine giving birth and then having to go through that kind of treatment when you have a newborn and are probably already feeling sick, hormonal, and depressed?" Ruth grabs a Kleenex from the box and blows her nose. "Anyway, at first it seemed like the treatments were working, but then it turned out it was started too late. When Eli was about six months old they discovered the cancer had metastasized to her pancreas and liver. She died two months later."

"What was her name?" I whisper, plucking a Kleenex from the box.

"Sarah. Her name was Sarah," Ruth sobs, and both children turn to look at us. Chloe begins to cry. I cross the room, sweep her into my arms, and hold her close. I rub my face into Chloe's fuzzy head, drink in her smell, revel in the grasp of her small fingers around my neck, all the while thinking about how much Sarah must have wanted this, how brave she must have been, and the wrenching sadness she must have experienced when she realized everything she would miss. Ruth bends to hug Carlos, and we carry the kids to the sofa where we sit, holding them until they begin to squirm. We put the children down and reach for each other's hands.

"What a tragedy, huh?" Ruth asks, her voice still husky with tears.

I nod.

"That was almost a year ago. Poor Neil. Poor Eli," Ruth says, squeezing my hand.

"Poor Sarah," I say, and Ruth looks stricken.

"God, what an awful person I am," Ruth sobs, burying her face in her hands.

"You're not awful," I tell her, while I hold her, rocking her gently as she weeps heaving sobs into my shoulder. Carlos toddles across the room to lay his head on his mother's knee. He wraps his arms around her legs, his sweet brow furrowed as he makes his mother's sadness his own.

I teach Ruth to make rugelach: cinnamon, walnut, chocolate, and apricot, along with mandel bread and strudel. Afternoons, while the kids nap, we take out one of Mrs. Favish's recipe cards and dissect the recipes one by one, meticulously wrapping our efforts in foil and plastic wrap and placing them in the freezer in anticipation of Game Day. At first, Ruth is a zealous pupil, ready to follow the rules and even displaying an academic interest in understanding the "whys" of baking—why the eggs needed to be room temperature; what advantage there was in softening the butter in one recipe, while in another it needed to be cold. But soon after our first lesson, she loses interest in the process, marveling that people would spend so much time making something that could be duplicated by someone else and bought for a few bucks.

"There's a bakery right down the street that sells artisan bread! What would be the point?" she asks me when I suggest that next time we might try making a loaf of bread. "And besides, my arms hurt from rolling out that dough," Ruth complains, flexing a bicep.

"Toned arms are nice, don't you think?" I ask her, rolling up my sleeve to display my own firm upper arm. Years of toting heavy roasting pans, lifting crates of produce, and rolling out pasta dough have left my upper body toned and muscular, without ever having to set foot in a gym. Ruth gives my arm a poke and shrugs, unimpressed. Pressing a fingertip into my upper arm, I'm surprised to find that it now feels a bit like the bread dough I've just suggested we make; maybe it is time to start looking into that gym membership.

When not overseeing Ruth's culinary education, I spend the better part of the week searching through boxes and papers for a writing sample to send to Enid Maxwell. I open every box and rifle through reams of old stuff, most of which lies strewn in random piles all over the attic. Finally, I find something stuffed into an old journal, but after reading it, I realize that it's probably not what Enid had in mind. It wasn't even what my teacher had in mind— I'd gotten only a B minus.

No, I need to write something completely new, something designed specifically to impress Enid, not only with my writing skills, but with my discerning palate and capacity for brilliant food analysis. How hard can that be?

Actually, pretty hard. After wasting an entire Ruth-babysitting afternoon sitting in front of my dad's computer waiting for inspiration to hit, I chalk it up to writer's block and give up. Figuring that maybe cooking something new might inspire me, I spend the next couple of hours looking through my cookbook collection. I pick up *Tastes of the Caribbean,* which reminds me of the review I'd read in the *Post-Gazette* a couple of weeks ago—the one I thought the reviewer had bungled. After a few minutes on the *Post-Gazette* Web site, I finally find it: Koko's Caribbean Bistro.

It's an exceptionally daring move—taking on an established reviewer, not to mention a restaurant that's already been reviewed and found to be lacking. But if I do it right, I just might get Enid's attention.

Thinking it might be fun to take the kids out to dinner (the real test of a waiter is how he or she deals with fussy babies), I decide to invite Ruth to come with me. However, one look at her exhausted face when I arrive to pick up Chloe, and I know this will be an uphill battle.

"Come on. It's only five thirty. We'll be back before eight. I promise. My treat?"

She slumps her shoulders and gives me the "I'm too tired to move" look. She says, "I'm just looking forward to getting Carlos fed and to bed."

"The stimulation of a new place, new food, might be good for him. He'll fall right asleep as soon as you get home."

Ruth laughs. "*I'm* the one who doesn't need the stimulation. Besides, I thought reviewers were supposed to be low-key, anonymous-like. Believe me, going to a restaurant with Carlos will do nothing to preserve your anonymity. They'll be talking about you for weeks."

On the way home I try Richard. He answers the phone just as the machine picks up and tells me, over the answering machine's recorded message, that he's just on his way out the door.

"Hey, perfect. Glad I caught you. Want to have dinner with two gorgeous women? Chloe and I want to try this new Caribbean bistro, and I'm on assignment, sort of. How about it?"

Richard doesn't say anything, but I can hear another voice in the background. "Well," he finally says, "I'm actually on my way out to dinner. Tonight isn't going to work. How about I call you later?"

Richard doesn't sound like himself. Apart from his lack of effusiveness, he didn't even pick up the bait when I told him I was on assignment. Obviously, he's seeing someone and, judging from the sound of his voice, it isn't going well. I remember his cryptic comment last week about not wanting to ruin the afternoon with talk of his love life, but because Richard is such a private person, at least when it comes to his romantic liaisons, I know it would be fruitless to push.

The next morning I set off early thinking Chloe and I will do some shopping in the Strip and then have lunch at Koko's. We stop for coffee and biscotti at Bruno's and, because it's still a little too early for lunch, we sit a while. Bruno is here this morning, perched on a stool in the back, hunched over a large ceramic bowl of bis-cotti dough. His hair is completely white now, his nose and ears bigger and his frame much smaller than I remembered. The knuck-les of his hands are ruddy knobs, the fingers bent with arthritis at unnatural angles, and his movements are palsied. His face is ex-pressionless, the practiced countenance of a person used to being in pain.

When we first came in, I hovered by the counter, hoping that Bruno would look up. Eventually he did, smiling at Chloe and me, but I knew from his filmy gaze that he didn't remember me and probably wouldn't even if prodded. His son, or perhaps even his grandson, handles the heavy lifting now. I watch as the young man gently wrests the bowl of dough from Bruno and in one fluid move-ment turns the heavy bowl onto the counter, scrapes out the con-tents, and dusts it with flour. He stands there a moment, watching as Bruno sinks his hands into the dough. He's probably thinking he could do it better or faster. Finally, he smiles and pats Bruno gently on the shoulder, sending a thin cloud of flour into the air.

Chloe pushes her chubby board book at me and smiles. I take her onto my lap and read to her about sheep in a jeep while she drinks her milk. She follows along, pointing to the pictures, cooing and gurgling, her voice mimicking the rhythm and cadence of my own. We're so engrossed in the story that at first I don't notice the man standing at our table. When I finally look up, it takes me a sec-ond to recognize Ben Stemple, Fiona's nephew.

"Hey," he says. "I thought that was you. Wasn't sure though. You look different in clothes. How's the sink holding up?"

"Great, thanks," I stammer, remembering the rapidly dissipat-ing bubbles, my hastily wrapped towel, and the humiliating Pippi Longstocking hairdo. I feel a blush creep up from the collar of my shirt to stain my face.

Ben is holding a bag of biscotti and a paper cup of coffee. With his foot, he moves Chloe's wooden highchair over so that there is room to sit. "Do you mind?" he asks, hooking another chair with his foot and dragging it over to the table.

"No, not at all," I tell him, not really sure if I mean it. I hand Chloe her board book. He opens the bag of biscotti and holds it out to me. "They're cornmeal. My favorite. Wouldn't think a corn-meal cookie would be good, but I love 'em. Can't get enough."

I take one from the bag, break it in half, and offer Chloe a piece. "Do you live around here?" I ask him.

"No. Bloomfield, not far, but I'm working around the corner," he says, removing the plastic lid of his coffee and swiping at the foam with the tail end of his biscotti. "I'm a sub in the new loft development on Smallman Street. You know, the pickle factory? Those lofts are going to be beautiful, but I swear I can still smell vinegar. Must be psychological. All the guys think I'm nuts."

Ben reaches into the bag for another biscotti. His hands, I notice, are small and neat with short, trimmed nails. They're the sort of hands you might expect to see on a musician, or a teacher, someone accustomed to using his hands for more delicate purposes. They seem too fine for the rest of his body and are unusually clean, given the type of work he does.

I feel as if I should say something about his aunt, who is, after all, the only real connection we have, but what is there to say? Instead, I ask him about the lofts.

"Do a lot of people live around here?"

"Some. More than there were six months ago. We did another property last year, further up the street, the Cigar Lofts. They're all sold."

"Did they smell like tobacco?"

Ben wads up the now empty biscotti bag and tosses it into the wastebasket. He appears to seriously consider my question, looking up at the ceiling as if trying to summon an olfactory memory. He finally shakes his head. "Nope. Can't say that they did." He gives me a sideways glance, trying to figure out if I'm making fun of him.

"I've always wanted to live in a loft, but in New York you can't touch them." I'm not sure why I've told Ben this.

"If I had some money, I'd buy one, for investment. I think they're really going to take off. You ought to come and see them. If you have time to come now, I'll give you a tour."

I look at my watch.

"You have somewhere to be?" he says, the barest trace of a smirk on his face. Now it's my turn to wonder if he's making fun of me.

"Well, no, actually Chloe and I are just having lunch at Koko's."

"The Caribbean place? Is it any good? I pass it every day and think I should go in and give it a try. I'm not totally sure what Caribbean food tastes like, but what the hell, it looks interesting."

"I don't know. I've never been. I'm actually writing something about it." I've told him this just in case he really was making fun of me. Fiona has probably already told him that all I do is lie around the house, guzzling brandy.

"What are you writing?"

"Well, it's sort of a review. I'm working on a piece for the *Post-Gazette* Food section."

"Wow. You mean like the Nibbler, the reviewer in the paper?" He seems surprised and impressed. "Aunt Fi didn't mention that. That's really cool."

"Well, it's sort of a test piece." Now I feel ridiculous.

After an awkward silence, Ben says, "Feel like some company? I'm waiting on some fixtures, and the delivery won't be until after one, so I've got time." His eyes flash, and he smiles at Chloe, giving her a chuck under her chin. "Besides, it's no fun to eat alone." I'm not sure if he is talking about himself or me.

"How are you going to refer to me in the review?" Ben asks, while reaching for the last of the conch fritters we ordered as an appetizer. It's only after citing "truth in journalism" as justification for my having the last fritter that Ben agrees to even split it with me.

"What do you mean?"

"Come on—you've read the Nibbler reviews in the paper. He always refers to his dining companion as BFON—Best Friend of Nibbler or MON—Mother of Nibbler. You know, 'EXSOON found the salad to be too heavily dressed. . . .' Like that."

"EXSOON?"

"Yeah, ex-significant other of Nibbler."

"You read the restaurant reviews?" I ask.

"Sure, sometimes. I mean, the Nibbler's no Frank Bruni, of course, but still they're entertaining."

"Frank Bruni?" I ask.

"Surprised?" Ben answers, his eyes narrowing.

"No, it's just that I haven't really given it much thought," I tell him, trying not to offend him any further.

"Well," Ben says, smiling at me, "my point is, you ought to come up with something that will distinguish yourself, some kind of gimmick. It'll make your piece a little more interesting."

"Yeah, thanks, I'll think about it," I tell him. What's even more surprising than his being an occasional reader of restaurant reviews is the fact that he also seems to have spent some time thinking about them.

Over lunch he talks a lot. In addition to offering a running commentary on the food, he also finds time to disclose that he makes his own beer, plays the bass guitar in a grunge band, and was formerly married to his high school sweetheart, but it hadn't worked out. Finally, over dessert, a pineapple crisp with a buttery brown sugar glaze, topped with homemade coconut ice cream, which we decide to share, Ben says, "So, what about your ex? What kind of a guy was he?" His eyes shift to Chloe, who has fallen asleep in her stroller. What he really means is, what kind of a guy leaves a little baby? But I don't want to talk about Jake.

I don't say anything and instead reach for another bite of the pineapple crisp, which is delicious. "You just want me to keep talking so that you can finish the dessert. Well, forget it," I say lightly, spearing the last slice of pineapple with my fork.

Ben scoops a spoonful of the ice cream and gives me a speculative look. "Okay. Sorry. Forget I asked."

I can't. I don't know why it's so much easier to talk while you eat, but now that the pineapple crisp is gone, there doesn't seem to be much more to say. I signal for the check.

"He's an okay guy, I guess. He just didn't want to be married to me anymore. He didn't want to be a father to Chloe." In search of a distraction, I scrape the dish with the tines of my fork, trying to loosen the remaining caramel, which is stuck resolutely to the bottom of the ramekin.

Ben leans forward in his chair, rests his forearms on the table, and clasps his small hands. "That doesn't sound like an okay guy to me."

chapter 20

Deadlines are an unavoidable fact of life for a journalist, and already I'm having trouble meeting them. Although I lost no time in eating at Koko's, it's taken me almost a week to write the review. I took Ben's advice and tried to come up with a gimmick that would make my piece unique and finally had come up with "BITER"—Buddy I Take to Eat in Restaurants—who in this case, I write, is a guy on a diet who orders only a small mango and jicama salad with the dressing on the side and then proceeds to eat everything in sight, starting with the bread basket and culminating in a near stabbing over the last forkful of the pineapple crisp. I'm hoping it's cute.

Because I wanted to run my review by Dr. D-P before e-mailing it to Enid, I stayed up ridiculously late last night to finish it. Dr. D-P is pleased with my progress and even takes a few minutes out of our session to read my review, which I present to her the instant I sit down, before I even take off my coat. I watch as she takes out her pen and begins making corrections in the margins.

"These are just little things, Mira. Sentence structure and, well, spelling. Doesn't your computer have spell-check?" she asks, without looking up.

"Some of them might be island words. Those aren't in spell-check," I tell her, craning my neck, trying to see what she is writing.

"Hmm. You also might want to rethink BITER. It's a bit of a stretch, don't you think?" She scribbles some more on my review and then hands it back to me without further comment.

"Look at it later, Mira. This is fine, and the things I marked are all easy to fix. Now, let's talk about your next steps."

I don't want to talk about my next steps. I'm not exactly sure what I wanted from Dr. D-P on the review, although something more positive and encouraging might have been nice. But as usual, she isn't deterred, running on about interview techniques and follow-up notes should Enid happen to call before our next appointment. Our session runs ten minutes over, and despite her more than usual dose of helpful hints and useful strategies, I leave feeling unsatisfied. I'm halfway to Ruth's to pick up Chloe before I realize why. I hadn't talked with Dr. D-P about what was really on my mind—my lunch with Ben. How for the first time I hadn't choked on my words when talking about Jake.

The day before the big mah-jongg game, Ruth phones me at 7:00 a.m. just as I'm feeding Chloe breakfast. We'd planned on meeting at Gymboree later in the morning and talked about possibly taking the kids to lunch afterward so that I might quiz her on baking techniques and ingredients, in case anyone asks her about her recipes.

"I don't know what it is this time," she says. "He was fine when he woke up, but now he's covered in hives." Carlos, Ruth has discovered, is an allergic kid, breaking out in hives whenever he tries a new food. "The only things he had to eat yesterday were Cheerios, a couple of Kraft Singles, and some ham, all of which are on the Carlos-approved list." I'm glad we're on the phone so Ruth can't witness my shudder. "Maybe it's me," she continues. "I read an article about someone who was allergic to another person, except it was a husband who was allergic to his wife. They had to get divorced. Do you think Carlos could be allergic to me?"

"No, he's not. It's probably something in the air, or dust from the carpet or something. He's fine."

"Well, anyway, the point of all this is that I can't go to Gymboree today, which is probably just as well," Ruth says, groaning. "I stayed up too late last night studying that damned card, and I've got circles under my eyes that extend beyond my kneecaps. I look like shit."

Ruth had ordered the latest official mah-jongg card from the National Mah Jongg Association. "Leah asked me if I had the 2011, so I lied and said yes. I just hope it comes in time," she had told me last week. It had, but barely, arriving only yesterday. Since receiving it Ruth had tried to enlist my help in learning the various mah-jongg combinations, but I kept mixing up the cracks and the bams, not to mention the flowers and the dragons, so she quickly gave up on me. "You should probably stick to food," she said. "That's your strong suit."

Maybe I should be insulted, but the truth is I admire Ruth's academic approach to dating. I'm impressed by her desire to learn to cook and to play mah-jongg, not to mention her sifting through reams of fashion magazines and "how-to" books, culling for information designed to make her optimally attractive. "Look," she says when I point this out to her. "I've been in school over half my life. I'm good at research. It's what I know." But it makes me think about my own approach to love that, at this point, is nonexistent. I have never been particularly good at studying, and the few things I know outside of cooking, I've learned from experience, not from books. Maybe I should give the academic approach a try. If there's a self-help book out there for me, Ruth probably already owns it.

"Besides," Ruth continues, "I don't think Neil's even going to be there today. When Leah called to confirm the time for the mah-jongg game, she mentioned Neil was going to be out of town on business this week. Oh, hey, can you come over after Gymboree? You've got to quiz me on these combinations."

"I thought you told me I should stick to food."

"You probably should, but I'm desperate."

"I don't get it. What's the point of learning these when you just have to relearn new ones next year?"

"The point is an end to my spinsterhood. That's the point."

* * *

Although Chloe always seems to enjoy the Gymboree classes, in the last few weeks it seems as if she's come to anticipate them as well. This morning as we make the turn onto Forbes Avenue and head toward the JCC, her little body strains, and she begins giggling. Then, when we get out into the gym, she looks around intently, searching for Carlos most likely, who by now, because of my growing friendship with Ruth, has become a regular fixture in her world. It seems that Chloe, if not her mother, has begun to build a life in Pittsburgh.

This morning they've set up what they call a "water center," really just a plastic baby pool with some Dixie cups, a bunch of floating Ping-Pong balls, and a few rubber duckies. I'm in the process of wrapping Chloe in a waterproof smock when, to my surprise, we are joined by Eli, who rolls up his sleeves, grabs a smock from the hook, and toddles toward his father, who is by the door filling out a name tag. Funny, hadn't Ruth mentioned that Neil was out of town on business?

Perhaps it's because I now know his story, but there's something incredibly touching about seeing Neil, a tall man, on bended knee with his arms wrapped around his son. I watch as Neil gently guides Eli's head through the neck of the smock and ties the strings in the back. Then, before he stands, he kisses the top of Eli's head and ruffles his red curls. Neil's hair is a sandy color, flecked with silver, making me wonder if Sarah had red hair.

Neil and Eli join us at the water table, where Chloe is in the process of hoarding all of the rubber ducks. Eli approaches the table and makes a gentle attempt to wrest one from her tight-fisted grasp. When I move to intervene, Neil stops me. "No, don't. You've got to respect the Toddler's Manifesto."

"The Toddlers have a Manifesto?" I ask, surprised.

"Yes. It starts: 'If I had it first, it's mine.'"

"What's the rest?"

"If I want it, it's mine. If it looks like mine, it's mine. If I had it five minutes ago and I want it back, it's still mine. If you lose it and I find it, it's mine. The toddlers express it much more elegantly, of course, but you get the idea. I'm surprised you don't know it," Neil says, looking down at me with a smile.

"No, they really have to start inviting me to their meetings. And anyway, technically, Chloe's still an infant," I tell him, taking two of the rubber ducks from Chloe and offering them to Eli. Chloe wails in protest.

"Well, then, you've got yourself a precocious child, I see."

I smile at him.

"You're Mira, right?"

I nod.

"I'm Neil," he says, offering his hand, which I take. His palm is cool and dry.

"Of course, I remember." Just then, Neil's phone begins to ring. He releases my hand and reaches into his pants pocket to answer it.

It's a business call. Neil covers the receiver with his hand and mouths, "Excuse me," while I join the kids at the water table and make a show of splashing around with them and pretending not to listen. After a few minutes, Neil hangs up and rejoins us.

"Haven't you heard, you shouldn't keep those in your pocket?" I ask him, bending low to reroll Chloe's damp sleeves.

Neil hangs his head and laughs. "Yes, just don't tell my mother. She's got her sights set on additional grandchildren."

Without really intending to, the four of us spend the rest of the class together. I tell myself it's because, despite their initial tussle over the ducks, Chloe and Eli seem to get along very well.

"What can I say? He's a day care kid. He plays well with others," Neil tells me when I comment on what an easy child Eli seems to be.

"It's nice you can at least take part of the day off to do this, though."

"I've worked part-time since Eli was born. Well, not really part-time, full time, actually, but I work out of my house. One day a week my mother watches Eli, two days he's in day care here at the JCC, and I have him the other two days. He's a good kid. He's got some separation issues, but I suppose that's to be expected under the circumstances. I'm guessing you know my story?"

I nod. "I'm sorry about your wife."

Neil nods, his lips pursed. "Thanks," he says. "I assume my mother told you? She's put out an APB among her network of Jewish mothers. I'm sure she's preparing a feature article for *The Jewish Chronicle* just in time for the Passover issue extolling my virtues and advertising my availability. I suppose I should give up being embarrassed about it. You can't stop the machine." Neil smiles wryly and then leans his head back and rests it against the cinderblock wall of the gym while we watch the kids roll around on the yoga balls in front of us.

"I'm sure Sarah was a wonderful woman."

"Thank you," Neil says, looking over at me, his eyes searching my face, startled perhaps, that I've said her name. It just slipped out, and the instant I say it, I regret it. It's too personal, too invasive, but ever since Ruth told me about Sarah, I haven't been able to stop thinking about her. "Thanks for saying her name. People don't like to. I think it makes them uncomfortable, but it's nice to hear it," Neil says, giving my hand a brief squeeze.

As soon as "The Bubble Song" begins to play, Eli, Chloe, Neil, and I join the other moms and kids to sit in the parachute circle. Even though Neil apparently didn't mind, I'm still embarrassed to have intruded on his grief, and I make a point of not sitting next to him. Instead, Chloe and I choose a place on the other side of the circle. It's warm in the gym, and the wafting of the parachute lends a welcome, cool breeze. The kids take turns crawling in and out while the instructors blow bubbles and the adults move the parachute up and down, its thin silk casting shadows of red, blue, and gold on our faces.

In the coatroom after class, Neil seeks us out. "Eli and I are going to have a latte at the Coffee Tree. I don't suppose you ladies would care to join us?"

"I, ah, I mean *we'd* love to—Chloe's a bear without her morning latte." Neil's smile is warm. "But, actually, I've promised my friend Ruth that we'd stop over." At the mention of Ruth's name, I feel my body deflate with the sudden realization that I've just wasted fifty-seven minutes of prime opportunity to help advance Ruth's agenda.

"I just figured since the kids seemed to have such a nice time playing together, you know?" Neil says.

"You remember Ruth. She was here a couple of weeks ago? She has a little boy, Carlos?" Maybe it's not too late.

Neil nods, absently. Silently, we gather our things, diaper bags, stray mittens, and boots.

The four of us are on our way out of the coatroom when we are intercepted by Rona Silverman, who's headed for the ladies' locker room. She's wearing a stylish brown and black pareo over her swimsuit and is in the midst of removing her bathing cap and shaking loose her frosted hair.

"Why, Mira, Neil!" Rona says, stopping mid-shake.

"Mrs. Silverman," we say in unison.

"What I wouldn't give for those curls," she says, running her manicured hand through Eli's thick curls. Eli buries his head in Neil's neck.

She looks at Chloe's nearly bald head and gives it a rub. "Don't worry, dear, it will grow," she croons. "Besides, Eli's older, isn't he, Neil? He's what, almost two?"

"Yes, in June," Neil says.

"Although, as I recall, he had a full head of hair from the moment he was born. Isn't that right, Neil?"

But Rona doesn't wait for Neil to answer. "I've got to run," she says, glancing at the waterproof watch displayed on her tanned wrist. "I've got a bridge game in half an hour." She's halfway through the locker room door when she stops and turns back. She looks from Neil to me, surveying us coolly, and says, "Oh, Mira, dear, please tell your friend Ruth that we're so looking forward to mahj tomorrow."

"Okay, give it to me one more time. What happens if you declare mah-jongg in error?"

"With or without exposing your hand?" Ruth asks, eyes narrowing, as if I'm asking her a trick question.

"Without."

"That's easy. If a player declares mah-jongg in error and does not expose her hand, and providing all other hands are intact, then play continues without penalty," Ruth says.

"Okay, smarty-pants, what if the player exposes all or part of the hand?"

"Well, it depends, of course. Are we talking about the player who declared mahj in error or one of the others?"

I scramble to decipher the small print on the back of the card.

"Never mind, I know it. If the person who exposed her hand is the person who mahjed in error, then her hand is declared dead and play continues, assuming all other hands are intact. If they're not, then the game cannot continue and the one who mahjed in error pays everyone double."

"Since when is mahjed a verb?"

"Since now. Okay, now ask me one more time about the pair exception."

"Can't we be done now? I'm mahjed out," I groan. But Ruth doesn't even wait for me to ask.

"You can never call a tile that's part of a pair, unless it is for mah-jongg."

"Jesus, what a ridiculous game!" I say.

"No, it's not. It's actually fun."

"It's unnecessarily complicated. We've been studying for two hours, and I don't even know what a 'pung' is and it's all over this card!"

Ruth rolls her eyes. "A pung is a three and a kong is a four, silly."

"Never ask me to play this game, okay?"

"Okay, I promise," Ruth says. "More wine?"

"No, thanks."

We've ordered a pizza and are just finishing off the last of the wine while the kids nap. I'm not used to drinking wine in the afternoon, and it's given me a headache. I would have refused, but by the time Chloe and I arrived at Ruth's she had worked herself into such a frenzy over tomorrow's game that she needed it to calm her down. Ruth pours the last sip into her glass and tucks her feet up on the couch.

"Thanks," she says. "I feel better."

"Good," I tell her, massaging my temples. Ruth gets up and leans across the kitchen bar to reach into the cabinet. "Here," she says, handing me a bottle of Advil. "You look like you have a headache."

"Thanks," I tell her, taking two.

"Hey, I didn't even ask you, how was Gymboree today?"

"Fine, it was fine. They had a water table, just a baby pool with some toys, but the kids loved it."

Please don't ask me if Neil was there. I can still remember the pressure of his fingers on mine and a complicated mass of feelings wells up in me, aided and abetted by the headache, the afternoon wine, the pepperoni pizza, and a hefty measure of guilt over the idea that somehow I'd given Neil the wrong impression.

I look away, afraid to meet Ruth's eye.

"Water table, huh? Sounds like fun," Ruth says, yawning.

"It was," I tell her, recalling Neil's teasing about the Toddler's Manifesto. I look around the room, anywhere but at Ruth, at the empty pizza box on the coffee table, and then at our children sleeping at our feet, wrapped in their little blankets. Their lives are not very complicated. And the rules are clear. I envy them their simple lives.

chapter 21

I dip Chloe's hand into a tin pie plate filled with turquoise paint. She squirms, as if she isn't entirely enjoying the sensation of the squishy paint in between her fingers, and gives me a searching look. I put her hand to the paper and press gently. Once Chloe sees the print her hand has made, she stares transfixed, barely noticing as I dip her hand into the pie plate for another application of paint.

On Sunday, she will be a year old. The party will be very small, so I really don't need to send out invitations, but I'd gotten the idea from *Parents* magazine and thought it looked cute. We make them for Ruth, Carlos, Fiona, Dad, Richard, and Ben. I also make a couple extra, thinking they might be nice to have for Chloe's scrapbook.

I hold Chloe's hands under the warm water, gently rubbing the creases of her tiny palms to remove the excess paint. She's perched on the side of the sink watching me intently as I rinse her hands, her eyes warm and trusting. She's a calm and stately baby, yet there's an intensity about her, a quiet intelligence. I often have the sense that, if she could speak, she would offer up slowly, and with great gravity, some profound commentary on the state of the world.

Chloe can stand unassisted, although she has yet to take her first steps. She has a favorite book, prefers squash to sweet potatoes, and, ever since she was an infant, has slept on her back with her arms raised over her head in a position of complete surrender. But she will remember none of these things when she is older. One day, in the not too distant future, she will ask me what she was like as a baby and, like all kids, will delight in my reminiscences, either real or embellished. Will I remember *this*, I ask myself, struggling to hold onto the moment, or will it vanish like the turquoise paint, swirling in gentle eddies down the drain of the porcelain sink?

One day, too, she will ask me about Jake. And I'll have to decide what to tell her. It's been a blessing, perhaps, that Jake and I divorced when we did. She never had a chance to know him, and that will make the loss easier for her to bear. But one day she may want to know why there is no daddy in her life, and it will fall to me to tell her some palatable version of the truth. And there's always the possibility that, even knowing whatever masticated version of the truth I've given her, she might one day want to know him anyway. I try not to think of the other baby, Jake's other child, who I imagine is close to being born now, and hope that there will be some way to protect Chloe from the knowledge that her father has chosen to love another child instead of her.

We hang the prints to dry on the clothesline over the laundry sink, and I hold her hands as we walk together up the basement steps.

My father is on his back under the kitchen sink, a wrench poised in his hand, a tea towel over his stomach, the top of which is scrunched under his neck.

"The sponges were damp," he tells me, when I ask him what he is doing. "Fiona went to get a new sponge from the bucket in the back of the sink this morning, and they were damp. There must be a leak somewhere."

Fiona emerges from the utility room carrying a bucket, a plunger, and a rag.

"Can you see it? Can you see where it's leaking? Shall I turn on the water?" Fiona says, bending low to offer my father the rag.

"No and no!" my father cries. "I'll get wet."

Fiona throws her hands into the air and turns to look at me.

"Men. Helpless. Can't live with them. Can't shoot 'em. Well, don't worry about it. I'll ask Ben to stop by and take a look." She bends down and gives my father a playful squeeze on the knee. "Come on, Grandpa, let's get moving."

My father, who has recently become as domesticated as a neutered tabby cat, replaces the wrench with unconcealed relief as Fiona bustles around the kitchen, filling a bottle with juice and checking the diaper bag for diapers and wipes that I have already packed. To give me some time to get a few things done for the party, he and Fiona have volunteered to take Chloe to the zoo today. He helps her into her coat and slings the diaper bag over his shoulder, as Fiona holds out her arms for Chloe.

Once the invitations are dry, I write little notes on the back of each one and tuck them into the envelopes. I plan to deliver them this afternoon on my way to the market. I leave Ben's invitation on the counter next to the sink, because Fiona called him before they left for the zoo. Ruth and Carlos aren't at home, which doesn't surprise me because it's Saturday morning, their therapy morning. Carlos and Ruth are seeing an "attachment therapist," someone who is supposed to be helping them build their relationship. I leave their invitation in the mail slot, thinking I'll call Ruth when I get home. We hadn't had a chance to fully debrief about the mah-jongg game Thursday; it ran long, and Carlos had a dermatologist appointment they were rushing off to, or maybe it was the allergist. Carlos has quite a medical team, and sometimes it's hard to keep them straight.

Next, I hop a bus and head over to Richard's shop. Although it's after ten, the storefront is dark. I hang around for a while drinking coffee at the Three Goats, but when he isn't there by ten thirty I walk over to his house a few blocks away. I could have just left the invitation in the mail slot, as I had Ruth's—both of them already knew about the party anyway, so the invitation was really just a formality—but I've been worrying about Richard lately. He doesn't seem himself. Throughout our relationship, Richard usually has been the one to call me, leaving clever messages on my answering machine, designed to make me think he is dying to speak to me, waiting by the phone for my return call. But lately my phone calls have gone unanswered or, on the rare occasions I've managed to catch him in, he has seemed distracted and fidgety.

Richard lives in a restored brownstone on Copeland Street, a tall, narrow house, painted the color of seashells, with a perfectly tended front garden, complete with picket fence. His car is parked on the street, so he must be home, but the house is dark and no one answers the bell. Richard's cat, Katherine, is sitting in the front window languidly licking her paws. She's undisturbed by my ringing, but when I try Richard from my cell phone—I can hear the phone ring inside the house—she jumps down from the window and heads for the phone. She likes to listen to the voices on the answering machine, walking rings around it while the message plays, nuzzling it with her fluffy face and purring. I'm surprised when Richard answers, his voice groggy and thick sounding.

"Richard?"

"Umm, yeah."

"It's Mira. Hey, do you know what time it is?"

There's no response at first, and then a slow groan escapes. "Shit, is it really after ten?"

"Yes, it is. I stopped by the shop and got worried when you weren't there. Is everything all right?"

"Fine. Fine," he says, clearing his throat. "Where are you?"

"I'm standing on your front steps, as a matter of fact."

Silence.

"Give me a minute. I'll be right down." He doesn't sound thrilled.

"Okay. Take your time. I'll run across the street and get you some coffee. You sound like you could use a cup."

"Bless you, my child. Make it a double."

When Richard lets me in a few minutes later, he's dressed, but there's at least a day's worth of stubble on his cheeks, and his face has a droopy look, heavy in the jowls. He takes the coffee from me and then, without a word, turns and makes for the kitchen at the back of the house, Katherine at his heels.

"Aren't you having any?" he asks, his head buried in the refrigerator from which, after some rummaging, he emerges with a container of milk. He pours the coffee into one of his own porcelain

mugs, empties about half a carton of milk into it along with a handful of ice cubes, and downs it in a couple of long, thirsty gulps.

He doesn't seem to notice that I haven't answered him.

"No, thanks, I've already had mine," I finally tell him, eyeing the
two glasses in the sink, oversized wine goblets I recognize from
Richard's collection of crystal barware.

He reaches up with the back of his hand to wipe the milky froth
from his mouth, and I notice that his hands are trembling. The
tremor is slight, but because I've already figured out that Richard
has been drinking, I'm alert for the tiniest change. He holds my
gaze evenly, defiantly, as if daring me to say something.

I've known Richard for over twenty years and in the whole of
that time I've never known him to take a drink. He went through
hell to quit, I know, from stories he told me on several occasions
when he thought I was being too hard on my mother, who had
never been able to stop. Those were the only times I ever saw him
get really angry. "You don't know," he would say, his voice low and
cold with fury. "You don't know what it is like." And that voice and
that look would be enough to stop me dead.

He stands in front of me, his arms outstretched on the kitchen
counter, holding its rim in each fist, the knuckles white with effort.
The rest of his body, though, is a study in practiced nonchalance. I
sit hunched over on the kitchen stool, our eyes locked. He looks
away first, a stray upward glance, but I hear the creak in the upstairs floorboard, too. Someone is there. Suddenly Richard's face
widens into a loopy grin.

I stand up, pull the invitation out from my coat pocket, and
hand it to him. "Chloe's party. It's tomorrow. I hope you can still
make it." My voice is hoarse.

"Of course." He takes the invitation and, tucking it into his
front shirt pocket, gives it a small, reassuring tap. And then, he
cups my face in his hands and kisses me on the forehead. I want to
say something to let Richard know that I'm worried. That I love
him. He pulls me closer to him and rests his chin on the top of my
head.

"Don't worry," he says. "I'll be there."

*   *   *

I walk home the long way, down Shady to Forbes, stopping at the market for some fruit and the paper store for party hats, streamers, balloons, and some cute, but expensive, birthday candles in the shape of farm animals that I know will delight Chloe, all the while ruminating about Richard. Whomever he's seeing obviously isn't good for him, but because Richard has seldom shared those particular details of his life with me, it's awkward bringing it up. He dated a nice architect named Steve for a couple of years, whom he brought to our wedding, but it hadn't lasted. Since then, he's mentioned no one.

I turn down Fair Oaks, my father's street. It's a beautiful, winding road, so typical of Pittsburgh streets, hilly and tree-lined. There are buds on the oak trees, that precious yellow-green of early spring. Even though I've lived my whole life in places where seasons change, I'm always vaguely surprised when spring finally puts out its gentle feelers. There's a silver BMW parked in front of the house, and I think for a minute that it might be Ruth's, but it isn't. I'm midway up the front walk when I hear the car door open behind me and a voice calls, "Mira?" I stop my trek up the front lawn and turn around. To my surprise, Neil is standing there with a small stuffed bear I recognize as belonging to Chloe.

Neil tucks the bear under his arm and takes a bag from me. "Looks like you could use a hand," he says.

"What are you doing here?"

"I came to return this," Neil says, holding the bear out to me. "Eli must have put it in our bag while we were talking in the coatroom the other day. I thought Chloe might be missing it. You know how kids can be."

"I don't think she even realized it was missing," I tell him, taking the bear. "What about the Toddler's Manifesto—if you lose it and I find it, it's mine? Shouldn't Eli get to keep it? After all, a manifesto is a manifesto."

Neil pauses, as if seriously considering my question. "Well, as you pointed out, Chloe isn't officially a toddler yet, so technically she isn't bound by the Manifesto." We are now standing on the front steps of my father's house. I glance across the street at the Silvermans' house, which mercifully looks vacant at the moment.

"Hey, how did you know where I live?"

"Do you think the Jewish mothers' network of spies is immune to infiltration? Although I must admit that your case posed a bit of a challenge. You're not Jewish," Neil says.

"No, I'm not."

"That made it extremely classified information. I had to go pretty deep."

I smile at him. "Where's Eli?" I ask.

"With my mom. I'm on my way to pick him up now. I just figured, since I was in the neighborhood . . ." Neil's voice trails off as he deposits the shopping bag on my father's front step and turns to leave.

Neil's mention of his mother triggers an idea. "Wait a minute," I tell him, running in the front door and grabbing one of the extra invitations I made from the kitchen table.

"Here," I tell him. "I thought of inviting you, after the kids had such a good time the other day, but I didn't know how to get it to you. Not being Jewish, I'm not hooked into the network."

"Thanks," he says, taking the invitation and opening it.

"It's going to be a small party. Mostly just family and my friend Ruth and her son Carlos. You met them at Gymboree. She's now your mother's mah-jongg partner, you know. Maybe your mother mentioned it?" I ask hopefully.

But Neil doesn't seem to be listening. Instead, he is studying Chloe's tiny handprint on the front of the card, running his fingers over the rough paint.

"We'd love to come," Neil says, smiling at me. "I guess we'll see you tomorrow." He turns to leave, but turns back halfway across the lawn. "And by the way, there are no partners in mah-jongg. It's every woman for herself."

chapter 22

"I thought you'd be pleased!" I tell Ruth, who is in the process of wailing into the phone.

"But it's tomorrow! My hair's a mess, and I have nothing to wear. I can't possibly be ready in time," she groans.

"Of course, you can—you're ready now. And it's a kid's birthday party, not an actual date!"

Ruth sighs. "So, where did you say you ran into Neil?"

"On the street. Near Rona Silverman's house," I tell her, not exactly a lie.

"I wonder what he was doing there," Ruth asks. I say nothing. It wouldn't be as much of an issue if I'd just told Ruth in the first place that Neil had been at Gymboree that week. It was a silly omission, and I now wonder why I held out. There really was no reason *not* to have told her, but to reveal it now would be awkward. Then, I remember Neil's comment about mah-jongg yesterday, and I feel my face get hot.

"Why don't you see if you can get your hair done on Sunday before the party? I'll watch Carlos." I can't believe I've just volunteered to babysit Carlos.

"Really? Don't you have stuff to do?"

Of course I do. "Not too much really, and besides Fiona and my dad are going to help with the decorations, so I'm in good shape. Just drop him off early," I tell her.

"Well, maybe, if you're sure," she says. Ruth calls back a while later and arranges to drop Carlos off a few hours early so she can get her hair and nails done before the party.

On Sunday, Richard is the first to arrive, bringing with him a huge kitchen set, complete with an impressive assortment of kitchen implements and life-size plastic food, that will likely take my father and me most of the afternoon to put together. He chats effortlessly with Fiona and even remembers to ask my father about his latest grant proposal. In fact, he's so much his usual, jovial self that I find myself studying him closely, wondering if perhaps I'd imagined the shaky hands, bloodshot eyes, and the droopy, hangdog look yesterday. Not to mention the two wineglasses in the sink.

Nevertheless, I've promised myself that I will look for an opportunity this afternoon to talk to Richard alone, so I lose no time getting him in the kitchen under the guise of helping me finish the fruit salad. But once we're there, I have no idea how—or where—to begin.

"Richard," I say.

"Oh, Mira, I can't believe I forgot," Richard says, wiping his hands on a dish towel and disappearing into the mudroom at the back of the house. He emerges a few seconds later carrying a small, velvet jewelry box. "It's Chloe's real present. I hope I have the distinction of giving Chloe her first piece of jewelry," Richard says formally, taking a beautiful, antique sterling silver baby bracelet from the satin-lined box and offering it to me for inspection. He has had HAPPY BIRTHDAY, Chloe's initials, and the date engraved along its underside.

"Richard, it's beautiful. Thank you," I tell him, reaching up to kiss his cheek. I put my hand on his shoulder and begin again, "Richard, I—"

Once again we are interrupted, this time by Ruth who, weighed down by a large floral arrangement, is rapping urgently at the kitchen door with her elbows.

"Sorry about the elbows," she says when I open the door. "My nails are still wet. Here, these are for you," she says, handing me the flowers. "No one thinks to give the parents a birthday present on the kid's birthday, but after all, it's a milestone for you, too. The day your life changed forever. Happy Chloe's birthday, Mira," Ruth says, hugging me.

"Isn't that the truth, speaks the man with no progeny!" Richard says, helping Ruth out of her coat and introducing himself. He quickly ushers her into the dining room, where I can hear him waxing enthusiastic over the unusual hue of the calla lilies in the flower arrangement as he pours her a glass of punch.

Ruth is right. Today is a milestone. A year ago Jake and I were still together. He'd held my hand, fed me ice chips, and rubbed my back as I labored to bring our baby into the world. His anguish over my pain had been real, as had his joy at Chloe's birth. I never would have imagined back then that a year later he wouldn't even make the guest list.

Ruth comes in, brushing crumbs from her blouse, and asks, "Was Fiona a snake charmer in another life?"

"Not that she's mentioned. Why?"

"She's got Carlos on her lap, and she's feeding him grapes. He hates grapes!"

"She does have a way with kids. Chloe loves her," I tell Ruth, realizing that it's true.

"So, do I look okay?" Ruth asks, nervously turning a full circle in front of me.

"Better than okay, actually. Your hair looks fabulous." Ruth has had her hair blown dry, and it looks full and pretty. She is wearing a long silk tunic and a pair of designer jeans she's clearly taken to the dry cleaner—the creases look sharp enough to slice steak.

"Want me to finish that while you go change?" Ruth offers.

"I am changed," I laugh. I'm wearing my Gap jeans and an oversized button-down shirt that had once belonged to Jake. "Besides, I'm the cook. I need to be comfortable." Ruth takes the knife from my hand and orders me upstairs to change my clothes. "At least put on a sweater or something. You're going to be looking at these pictures for the rest of your life."

I keep the jeans, but swap the oversized shirt for a blue sweater.

I let my hair down and brush it. When I come downstairs, Neil and Eli are standing in the front hall. Richard handles the introductions, while Ruth sucks at her punch. Everyone turns to look at me.

"Neil, Eli, welcome! Neil and Eli are our friends from Gymboree class," I tell everyone. Neil bends down to help Eli out of his coat, no easy task since Eli refuses to relinquish the large, brightly wrapped package he's holding.

"Go on," Neil whispers in Eli's ear. "You know what to do with that, don't you, Eli?" We all watch as Eli approaches Chloe, who is sitting on the living room rug, pulling at the party hat Fiona has placed on her almost bald head.

"How precious," coos Fiona, setting Carlos down and picking up the camera. "The package is almost as big as he is," she says, snapping a picture. We all watch as Eli makes his way laboriously to the middle of the room. He's within drooling distance when suddenly he's intercepted by Carlos, who tackles him, causing the corner of the package to poke Eli in the eye.

"Carlos!" shrieks Ruth, rushing to intervene, just as Neil scoops up Eli, who is, for a second, too stunned to cry. Ruth picks up Carlos and whisks him off to the kitchen mumbling ominously about "time-outs," just as Eli begins to wail.

"How about some ice?" Fiona says to Neil, who is trying to get a look at Eli's eye.

"I'll get it," I tell her, hurrying into the kitchen to check on Ruth. She's in the pantry, trying to gain control of a hysterical Carlos, who is writhing mightily in a kitchen chair.

"I give up," Ruth says miserably.

"Forget about it. Calm him down and get back out there. Eli's fine," I tell her.

I fill a plastic bag with ice and wrap it in a dish towel for Eli, although by the time I return, he's stopped crying. He's sitting on Neil's lap watching transfixed as my father entertains him with his one and only magic trick—the separating thumb.

Mercifully, the rest of the party proceeds uneventfully. When it's time to open the presents, I sit Chloe on my lap while Dad mans the video camera. Fiona has gotten Chloe a pink plastic purse, complete with a play cell phone, a large key ring of brightly colored keys, and a dozen sparkly bangle bracelets. "Thanks, Fiona," I tell her.

"I figured since she's always digging in mine, she should have her own," Fiona says, bending down to give Chloe a hug. Neil and Eli have given her a tub of crayons and a whole slew of water toys. Ruth and Carlos have given Chloe a tiny tricycle.

Fiona and Ruth help gather the empty wrapping paper while Richard, Neil, and my dad break down the boxes. "Oh, Mira, you forgot one," Ruth says, holding out one last gift, buried under a pile of discarded paper.

"Oh, that's from us," says Neil, "although it's really for Mira, not for Chloe. You can open it later if you—" But I've already begun removing the paper. It's a book. *What to Expect: The Toddler Years.*

"Thanks," I tell him. When I meet his eye, I'm surprised by the intensity of his gaze.

"Hey, I have this book," says Ruth, leaning over my shoulder. "I loved the series. Of course I really didn't need the *What to Expect When You're Expecting*, but I thought the one about the first year was great."

"Me too. During that whole first year my wife and I referred to it as 'the Bible.' " At the mention of Neil's wife, Ruth falls silent. Neil clears his throat.

"I've never read a parenting book," I tell them.

"Really?" Neil and Ruth ask in unison.

"Not a one. I guess I should have," I say, judging from their incredulous expressions.

"Surely you read T. Berry Brazelton? You must have," Ruth says, shocked.

I shake my head, trying to remember why I hadn't. Running a restaurant had been an exhausting business. By the time Jake and I crawled into bed at night after closing up, it was too late to do anything but sleep. Remembering how little time Grappa had left for anything else, I wonder how different Chloe's life would be now had we stayed.

Richard jumps to my defense. "How could you? You didn't

even read the newspaper! The moment you stopped moving you fell asleep." Neil and Ruth are unimpressed. I give Richard's arm a grateful squeeze and pick up the book. It's a hefty tome. How much invaluable parenting advice have I missed already?

"Time for cake, everyone?" Fiona asks, handing Chloe to my father and adjusting her party hat.

"Don't forget to read the inscription. It concerns an addendum to the Manifesto," Neil whispers over my shoulder as we move into the dining room for cake and ice cream.

"What manifesto?" Ruth asks, innocently.

I tuck the book under my arm and follow Fiona into the kitchen. Richard dims the lights, and Fiona readies the camera. I bring in the cake, a homemade vanilla sponge cake with real buttercream icing. I've decorated it like a pasture with green coconut grass and a corral made of licorice. Inside, an entire farm's worth of animal candles are grazing. Chloe is charmed.

Food. As I've long suspected, it is my greatest parenting accomplishment.

To Ruth's chagrin, Neil and Eli leave shortly after we finish the cake, pleading nap time, but Ruth suspects it's the prospect of free playtime with Carlos that has chased them away.

"Seriously, every time Carlos sees Eli he goes into attack mode. It's like he's gunning for the poor kid!" Ruth says, exasperated. "You've got to admit, this doesn't exactly bode well for the Brady Bunch future I've been envisioning," she says, helping herself to another slice of cake. "It's a good thing I've already got an in," Ruth continues. "Did I tell you? Leah asked me what I was doing for Passover. I think there's a chance she might invite me—I mean us," Ruth says, looking down at Carlos. He's sitting on a blanket at her feet, gnawing on the cow candle. "Carlos! Enough of that," she says, picking him up and sitting him on her lap. I hand her a napkin. "Look, a hive! There must be red dye in those candles. Mira, can you get the Benadryl? It's in the living room in the diaper bag."

My dad's in the process of putting together the kitchen set from Richard, and the living room is littered with hundreds of plastic pieces. It takes me a while to find the diaper bag. When I return to the kitchen with it, Ruth is no longer at the table. She is standing at the kitchen counter. She looks up when I come in, and the expression on her face is pure pain. Her mouth is set in a grimace as if she's about to cry.

"Mira," Ruth whispers. "How could you?"

I look down at the book open in front of her on the counter, the one Neil had given me. On the inside cover he's inscribed the following message: *The Parents' Manifesto—If you want her, let her know. All's fair in love, war, and mah-jongg. Will you please go out with me? Neil.*

Of course I try to explain, but Ruth tells me she's in no mood to hear it. "All this time, I thought you were helping me," she says, her voice cold and low. I try to tell her that I hadn't done anything to encourage Neil. I was trying to help her. But none of it makes any difference. The sound of our arguing chases my father and Richard from the living room. Fiona takes Chloe upstairs. I follow Ruth and Carlos out to the car, but Ruth still refuses to talk to me, refuses even to look at me.

Back inside, the house is quiet. I grab a picnic blanket from the mudroom, wrap it around myself, and head outside to the front porch where I curl up on the porch swing, furious with myself for letting things get so out of hand. Why hadn't I anticipated this would happen? What had I been thinking? The problem is I've never been the type to think too far ahead, which might explain why I've never been any good at games. Unlike Ruth, I'm incapable of developing anything resembling a strategy.

It's starting to get dark when Fiona joins me on the porch. She scoots my feet over to make room for herself on the end of the swing. "May I, Mira?" she asks, her voice gentle. She takes out her knitting, spreads her pattern over her knees, and dons her glasses.

"Richard left. Said for you to give him a call later. Oh, and Ben called," Fiona tells me. "Water main break in Bloomfield. He worked all day. Asked me to tell you he's sorry to have missed the party."

I nod.

"He's got a little gift for Chloe, though. He wanted to bring it by, but I told him he'd better wait for another time." She looks down at me over her reading glasses. "I figured you'd had enough entertaining for one day." I lay my head against the back of the swing, listening to the comforting click of Fiona's knitting needles.

"You know, Mira," Fiona says, laying aside her knitting and turning to look at me. I can feel her eyes on me for several seconds, and when I return her gaze, she smiles at me. "Ruth will come around."

"I'm not so sure," I tell her.

"Of course she will. She just needs to realize that you didn't do anything wrong. Right now she's angry at you because it's easier to blame you than blame herself."

"But Ruth didn't do anything wrong! Besides, they're much better suited to each other than Neil and me."

Fiona laughs. "In my opinion he's not ready for either of you. Neil's got to get over Sarah first." I look at her, surprised. "Ruth filled me in on a few of the details while you were upstairs changing. Sooner or later she's going to realize that the route to the altar does not run through Leah Hollander's back door. When she does, she'll be back," Fiona says, picking up her knitting. "Mira, you can't make someone love you. Just like you can't help who you love. Look at your father and me. Who would have thought? He's so smart, and I have to take off my shoes just to make change." Fiona removes her feet from her sandals, wiggles her fuchsia-stained toes, and giggles.

I can't believe I ever thought Fiona shallow. When she leans over to pat my hand, I take hers and clasp it in both of mine. Then I lay my head on her shoulder and begin to cry.

chapter 23

Figuring that Chloe needs a twelve-month checkup, I finally break down and make an appointment for her with a doctor in the pediatric group Ruth uses. According to Dr. Brent, Chloe is healthy, happy, and developmentally on schedule. She seems pleased with her progress, applauding my choice of Gymboree class and even complimenting me on the wide variety of foods Chloe has been exposed to, telling me that I am setting the pattern for good lifelong eating habits.

"Give yourself a pat on the back," she says.

"What can I say?" I tell Dr. Brent, hoping I don't sound too smug. "Food's my thing." Then, as we are leaving the office, she gives me a list of reading materials; number one on the list is *What to Expect: The Toddler Years.*

I turn on my cell phone and check my messages, hoping that Ruth has called. But there's only one message, and it's not from Ruth.

Enid Maxwell wants to meet with me, according to the message left on my cell phone at 11:16 this morning. I hadn't heard a word from her since I e-mailed her my review a couple of weeks ago and had assumed she wasn't interested. I lose no time in calling her back and am surprised when a young woman, who seems to be expecting my call, answers the phone. "Yes, Ms. Rinaldi," she says, as

If she knows me. "Ms. Maxwell is available to meet with you this afternoon at two o'clock. Would that be convenient?"

No, it wouldn't, unless Ms. Maxwell wouldn't mind if I drag my sleep-deprived toddler to the meeting. Now, since my fight with Ruth, I've lost my regular babysitter. "How about Wednesday afternoon?" I suggest. My dad's office hours are on Wednesdays. Maybe he wouldn't mind letting Chloe take her afternoon nap in his office. That, or maybe Fiona would be willing to watch her during her lunch hour.

"Let me check her schedule." I hear clicking sounds. "Ms. Maxwell can see you at one forty-five on Wednesday."

"Perfect," I tell her. Prime napping time.

I call Ruth again and leave yet another apology on her answering machine. By the time I hang up the phone, I'm exhausted. I put my feet up and flip through this month's *Bon Appétit,* marveling that someone who used to live action-packed eighteen-hour days is now wiped out by a trip to the park and a pediatrician appointment.

I flip absently through the magazine, at least until I get to page sixty-eight, where a tiny two-sentence blurb catches my eye. It's in the "Up and Coming" section and announces the opening of a small enoteca in the financial district. "Il Vinaio," the blurb says, "is brought to us by the owners of the popular West Village trattoria, Grappa. In addition to an extensive collection of wines, overseen by sommelier Nicola Cabot and partner Jake Shaw, Il Vinaio will serve a selection of small plates."

Sommelier? Since when is a slut who drinks too much a sommelier?

The phone is in my hands before I can stop myself. Renata doesn't answer, but her machine picks up immediately. "Why didn't you tell me?" is all I can manage.

I'm unable to call Ruth who, were she speaking to me, would undoubtedly have something calming to say or, at a minimum, would be willing to Google the restaurant and filter the reviews, picking out only the bad ones. In desperation I call Dr. D-P. When her machine picks up, I leave a message telling her that I've just heard from Enid and asking her to call me back. I figure when she does, I might be able to wheedle some free therapy over the phone.

I hang up and within minutes I manage to work myself into a frenzy of gargantuan proportions.

"How can Jake do this?" I wail hysterically, when the phone rings a while later.

"Do what, Mira?"

"Open another restaurant! The time and energy—not to mention the money! Do you have any idea how difficult it is? How expensive?" Dr. D-P is silent while in between sobs, I fill her in.

Finally, she says, "Mira, this isn't really about the money, is it?"

"The bastard couldn't even pay me child support. Now he's having another baby *and* opening a new restaurant!" I tell her, hiccupping loudly into the phone.

"What you really mean is how could he have moved on, don't you?"

I recoil as if I've been slapped.

"What you need right now is an attitude adjustment," Dr. D-P says, her voice clear, steady, and purposeful. "For starters, let's turn that statement around. How about instead of asking 'how could he,' we ask a different question. How about we ask, 'how could *you?*' "

"How could I what?"

"We are going to put you in an 'I'll show him' frame of mind," Dr. D-P says.

The assignment is to stand in front of the bathroom mirror and imagine that I've just run into Jake on the street. What do I want him to see and what do I want him to know about my life?

So, I stand there, staring into the bathroom mirror with my cell phone jammed to my ear, my blotchy, tear-stained face staring back at me. What do I want Jake to know? I have no idea. Nothing. Not a single thing comes to mind.

The thought of one's ex moving on and prospering might be enough to cause some people to get out there and really give it a go. Make a stab at showing their exes just what a good deal they threw away. "How did I ever let her go?" they ask themselves in our fantasies. Was I missing that particular gene or something? That "I'll show him" gene?

I groan. "I don't know what to say."

"Have that conversation, Mira."

"I feel like an idiot," I wail.

"It's an important exercise. Brush your hair and put on some makeup. Remember what you say and how you say it, and we'll talk about it tomorrow. Besides, it will also be good preparation for your meeting with Enid. You're really going to need to sell yourself. Remember, feelings follow behavior, Mira. If you pretend to be relaxed and confident, eventually you will become relaxed and confident."

"I know, I know," I tell her. And after I hang up, I take another stab at it, although it takes several attempts before I can start the conversation without crying or looking like I'm about to. But once I get started, I find I have plenty to say, none, or almost none of it, true. I tell Jake that I've opened another restaurant; perhaps he had caught the review in last month's *Food and Wine?* That, and I'm here in New York City to pick up my James Beard Award for my latest book, the newest collection of my food writings. I've even come up with a title for it: *With Fork in Hand, and Tongue in Cheek: A Chef's Guide to Eating Around the World.* I also tell him Chloe is a terrific kid and that he really missed out.

By the time Renata calls back, I'm in bed, going over my review in preparation for Wednesday's meeting with Enid Maxwell. "I swear, I thought about telling you, but Michael talked me out of it," Renata says.

"Fine. It's fine. I'm better now."

"You sounded awful."

"I was just surprised. That's all."

"I know. I'm sorry."

"Don't be. It was just a bad moment."

"So, how are you? How's Chloe? Did she get our birthday present?" Renata and Michael had sent Chloe a bottle of port, to be opened on her twenty-first birthday.

"Thanks. She loved it."

There's so much that I want to ask her, but I don't know if I should. Aside from not wanting to appear obsessed, I'm really not sure I want to know when Jake's baby is due. "So, has Jake's baby been born yet?" I blurt out.

Renata hesitates. "She miscarried. Or at least that is what they're telling people, or the few people who knew, anyway. It never really was public knowledge, if you know what I mean."

"What do you mean, at least that's what they're telling people?"

Renata doesn't reply right away, and I can tell she's deciding what to say. Whether or not I can handle it.

"Well, it just didn't make sense. The sommelier thing? She went away to do it. A four-week course in Las Vegas, with closed registration and a long waiting list. I checked. You don't go registering for a sommelier course when you know you're pregnant. Not unless you're an idiot—that's a hell of a lot of wine to be spitting out—or unless you never intended to have the baby."

"You think she had an abortion?" I ask.

"I don't know, Mira. All I know is that she came home from Las Vegas and suddenly they're obsessed with this idea of the enoteca. It's not exactly the time to be opening a new restaurant, you know. They bought this little tapas place that was going under. On Fulton Street. They moved right in and turned it around in record time."

"Where did they get the money? Jake made it seem like they were really strapped after the Grappa buyout."

Renata exhales softly into the phone. "First of all, why you would believe anything that man had to say is beyond me. But now that you mention it, I did hear a rumor a few weeks ago that Jake has hooked up with some serious investors, some sort of restaurant collaborative, based in Vegas."

"Vegas? Why would they be interested in Jake?"

"I don't know, but Tony told me that Jake is moving over to Il Vinaio, and Nicola installed a new executive chef at Grappa, who's also from Vegas."

"What! She can't do that! What the hell is Jake thinking?" I yell into the phone. "That place doesn't need Jake. Since when is tapas haute cuisine? I told you she would run Grappa into the ground, didn't I?"

Renata is quiet.

"Well, didn't I?" I demand.

Renata softly clears her throat. Finally, she says, "Look, *cara*, forget I said anything. Come on, Mira, I want to hear about you. How are you doing?"

Before I know it, it's as if I'm back in front of the bathroom mirror, spouting the made-for-Jake lies. In fact, I barely recognize the chic, hip life I'm describing to Renata, including my foray into the world of food writing—I think I even referred to Enid Maxwell as "my editor."

Renata is impressed. "And what about love, Mira?" she asks me. "Are you ready for that again? It's time."

I tell her I've been too busy to think about love. We hang up, but only after I have made several vague promises to come to visit sometime soon, the moment there is a lull in my schedule.

I toss my cell phone onto the bed and head to the bathroom where I splash some cool water on my face. Could it be true? Not just the part about Jake's ceding control of Grappa to someone I didn't even know, but the part about the baby? If Jake had reconsidered fatherhood yet again, his timing was only slightly better (or slightly worse, depending on how you looked at it) this time. With a pang I remembered Jake's hand on Nicola's belly as I passed them on the way out of the lawyer's office months ago. He had seemed so proud. How could anyone—even Jake—be so ambivalent? But what surprised me almost as much was that Nicola had agreed. Even if Jake had told me that he had second thoughts when there had been time to do anything about it, I'd never have chosen to get an abortion.

Or would I? If I'd known then that I'd be making a choice between Jake and Grappa on the one hand, and a nameless, faceless baby on the other, would I have been brave enough to choose the baby? For that matter, if I were Sarah could I have made the courageous decision she did?

It's like a spasm, sudden and involuntary. I'm standing at the foot of Chloe's crib, watching her breathe, panic rising, as if those previously unacknowledged thoughts had assumed a shape and a form and were lingering in the darkness ready to take Chloe from me the instant I close my eyes. I lean down next to her head, feeling her sweet, milky breath on my cheek, and softly stroke her forehead. I will never doubt that I made the right choice.

Perhaps it's no coincidence that they chose to open Il Vinaio so shortly after losing their baby. Could it be that Jake believed he had to choose between fatherhood and his career as a chef? Couldn't he have found room in his heart for both?

Maybe to be really good at either one, you do have to choose. After all, I'd made a choice, too. Just like Jake had. We'd chosen differently, and it had driven us apart.

The phone rings. I run across the room and make a dive for the bed before the second ring can wake Chloe. It's a wireless number I don't recognize.

"Hello?" I answer warily. It is almost eleven. No one I know, here anyway, would call so late.

"Mira, jeez, did I wake you? I hope I didn't wake Chloe."

"Who is this?" I whisper so as not to disturb Chloe, who I can hear stirring in her crib.

"It's Ben. Ben Stemple. Look, I'm sorry to be calling so late, but something actually came up and I needed—"

"How did you even get my number?" I ask him.

"Aunt Fi gave it to me. Sorry about the party, by the way. I hope she gave you the message?"

"Yeah," I say.

"Listen, if you're sleeping, I can just talk to you in the morning."

"No, that's okay. What's up?" I ask him, sitting up in bed and adjusting the pillow behind me.

"I need some advice. Some cooking advice, actually."

"Wow, you eat late."

"What? Oh, yeah." Ben laughs. "No, it's actually for a meeting I have tomorrow morning. Do you remember those lofts I'm the plumbing sub on? Well, one of the real estate agents, a guy I know pretty well, has a client who's a gourmet cook and wants some advice on putting in a top-of-the-line kitchen, a professional-grade stove, and something called a pasta spigot, whatever that is. Marble countertops, the whole nine yards. Money apparently is no object."

"It's a faucet on the wall by the stove. For filling big pasta pots."

"Huh?"

"A pasta spigot. That's what it is."

"Oh." Ben seems to consider this tidbit. Out loud. "Why not just fill them at the sink and carry them over?"

"Well, you could. But the deep pots sometimes don't fit under ordinary faucets. And besides, they're heavy to lift."

"Jeez. How much pasta is this lady gonna cook? Anyway, it's a plumbing nightmare. The water lines are all the way across the kitchen island! Good thing money's no object."

Ben, I guess, is a practical sort of guy.

"Hey, it's not your money. You can charge her whatever you want. Think of it that way."

"Yeah, I guess. Anyway, she isn't even here yet. She's moving here from Texas. Took some executive job at Del Monte. There's only one unit left, at the penthouse level, and she needs to know what kinds of things will fit in the space, what she might have to add, before she makes an offer. I mentioned to Skip, my friend, that you might be able to help lay it out for her because you used to be a professional chef."

Used to be.

"Sure," I croak, attempting to clear the lump in my throat. "Spending someone else's money is always fun."

I agree to join Ben and his friend Skip for their meeting at the loft tomorrow morning at nine. I hang up the phone and lie there in the dark listening to Chloe breathe. Although it's barely April, the attic is close, the air heavy and thick with heat. I'll need to buy a new air conditioner soon. I open all the windows and climb back into bed, trying not to think of what Ben said about my having been a professional chef. What am I now?

When I arrive at the lofts the next morning, Chloe in tow, Ben is waiting for me in the lobby with a latte from Bruno's and a bag full of biscotti. He's also brought Chloe's birthday present, a little Fisher Price peg board with a hammer and big chunky nails.

"Hey, thanks for coming on such short notice," he tells me, handing me the coffee and fishing a biscotti out of the bag for Chloe. "This woman is hot to get this deal done. Another unit sold over the weekend, and this is the only one left. Skip will be here in a couple of minutes, but we can go on up and get started. He faxed me a copy of the wish list," Ben says, reaching into the front pocket of his work shirt and shaking it out with a flourish.

On the way up, Ben shows me the list: a Gaggenau six-burner gas range, a wall-sized electric convection double oven, a SubZero professional refrigerator and freezer, warming tray, pasta spigot, and a built-in Jura-Capresso espresso machine; in fact she proposes a whole coffee station, including a sink with a built-in water filtration system and a top-drawer fridge for storing coffee, milk, and cream.

Three sinks in three separate areas. Ben will have a field day. The space is bigger than most traditional New York loft spaces. There's a large, partitioned area for a bedroom and another sleeping loft suspended over the living room, which is reached by a narrow, wrought iron staircase. Because it's a corner apartment on the top floor, there are six big, arched windows wrapping around the apartment on two sides. The walls are exposed brick, and the floor a rich, dark stained hardwood. There are some low built-in bookcases running along the back wall under the stairs, and someone has set out a couple of sofas, a comfortable-looking easy chair, and a reading lamp. Standard model apartment furniture. It's a pretty apartment, light and airy, but the best thing about it is the kitchen, which is open to both the living and dining areas. Even without the appliances, the kitchen dominates the space. Standing in the middle of the kitchen, you can see and be seen from just about any place in the whole apartment.

"A second bedroom or a home office," Ben calls to me from the sleeping loft. "Not bad, if you aren't too tall," he says, stooping slightly while trying to stand in the middle of the room.

I spread out a blanket from the diaper bag, give Chloe the peg board to play with, and head for the kitchen, where I'm joined by Ben. He pulls out his tape measure and a pad of graph paper, and we get to work. We try the stove where it's already been roughed in, and the dimensions work, give or take an inch, which Ben assures me they can shave off on either end of the cabinetry. But the problem with a stove of this size and power is that you need a significant ventilation system, so I suggest moving it to the opposite wall, an idea Ben likes, as it means the pasta spigot will be closer to the main sink and disposal.

When Skip arrives a while later, Ben and I have a sketch to show him. Skip, who had barely given me a nod when Ben introduced us, looks at the sketch and almost instantly begins shaking his head.

"Nope, this won't work," Skip says.

"What do you mean, it won't work?" Ben asks.

"Well, for starters, what's this?" he says, pointing to the large rectangular block we've drawn just above the stove.

"That's the ventilation hood for the stove. You need one for a stove this size," I tell him, trying to sound official. After all, I've been asked here in a somewhat professional capacity.

"Well, that's going to be an issue. She wants the stove on the island. She's planning on installing a wall-sized flat-screen TV over there"—Skip points to the long wall by the foyer—"and she wants to be able to watch it while she's cooking."

"Well, she could put it on the island, couldn't she, Mira?" Ben asks.

"Well, I—"

"Just nix the hood," Skip says.

I shake my head. "You need something, and a downdraft won't do it for a stove this size."

Skip lays the sketch on the plywood countertop and considers it. After a while he takes the top of his pen and begins cleaning out the dirt from under his fingernails. "How much we talking anyway?"

"I've had some experience with professional appliances, so I've taken the liberty of preparing a rough estimate," I tell Skip, handing him a sheet of paper on which I've tallied the approximate costs. "This, of course, doesn't include installation, or the cost of materials for cabinetry and countertop. I know she wants marble counters, but—"

"This is just for the appliances?" Skip has suspended his excavation efforts and is now distractedly running his fingers through his hair.

"Yup. Ben can give you a rough idea of the installation costs."

"Shit, I had no idea," Skip says.

"Well, the good news is," I tell him, "your client probably does. Presumably, she knows something about the brand names she's suggested. Anybody who knows Gaggenau, knows it's very high-end."

"Is this $3,600 for a coffeemaker? That can't be right! No coffeemaker should cost that much," Skip says, pushing Ben's sketch aside and fixing me with a withering stare.

"Look, I didn't pick the machine. She did. That's what they cost. Me, I get by just fine with a little stove-top *macchinetta* at home, but we had a Jura at the restaurant, so I know how much they cost. Most good coffee places have something similar. But you have to want to serve lots of really good coffee to justify one."

The edges of Skip's lips are white as he whips out his cell phone. "Okay, I'll give her a call." He doesn't even say thank you.

While Skip is breaking what does, in fact, turn out to be surprising news to his client, and Ben is trying to make an appointment with the general contractor to firm up his estimates, I give the kitchen another once over. If it were mine, I decide, I would do all open shelving, no top cabinetry. Poured and stained concrete for the counters, with a small, marble, inset pastry station. I'd keep my little *macchinetta* and instead use the coffee station space for a second oven with a warming tray underneath.

Chloe had been happily hammering away at her peg board, but now begins to fidget. Ben and Skip are still on the phone, so I walk Chloe around the apartment, checking out the views of the river, until my back begins to hurt. I lead her over to the sofa, a good vantage point from which to observe the kitchen. I decide that I agree with Ms. Moneybags, the stove should be on the island, but I'd angle the island in the opposite direction, toward the river view on the far wall. By going with a slim, streamlined hood, we could avoid unduly obstructing the view.

"Hey, be careful she doesn't get anything on that sofa. It's white, you know," Skip whispers loudly, putting his hand over the microphone of his hands-free phone. It's a nice sofa. Impractical for kids maybe, but it's slipcovered, and the fabric looks washable. Much nicer than the sofa I have in storage in New York, the red mohair with a loose spring in the middle cushion that Jake and I had found on the street one day and dragged home under cover of darkness.

Skip and his client are haggling over the costs. Apparently, she hadn't done her homework on the appliances and is balking at the cost of the professional-grade kitchen. It turns out that she has a family living in Dallas, a husband and two teenaged children, and is planning on commuting between there and Pittsburgh for the next four years, at least until the last kid is out of high school.

"Hey, you, Mary, is it?" Skip says, snapping his fingers to get my attention. "How much you figure she'd save if she decides to downgrade to electric?"

"Gaggenau, so far as I know, doesn't make an electric version." They do, but no real cook would want one. Soon we are down to a GE Monogram electric range and a Starbucks Barista–model espresso maker. She steadfastly refuses to yield on the marble countertops, insisting that they will look classy with cherry cabinets. "Very Tuscan," I can hear her say, with a heavy Texas drawl. I feel like grabbing the phone and telling her that cherry is not Tuscan. Chestnut, pine, or cypress maybe, but definitely not cherry.

You shouldn't buy a loft because the real estate agent is an annoying jerk who doesn't take you seriously. You also shouldn't buy a loft because the woman who's about to make an offer is loudly insisting on putting totally impractical marble countertops in what you are now thinking of as your kitchen.

I write a number on a piece of paper and slide it over to Skip. He pushes it out of the way without even looking at it. I push it back. "Hang on a second," he tells Ms. Moneybags.

"What's this?"

"I thought you were a real estate agent. It's an offer. To buy this place."

"An offer from whom?"

"From me."

I've offered the asking price, which is considerably higher than the offer Ms. Moneybags is proposing. It also represents a significant chunk of my divorce settlement, but for the first time in almost a year I can envision, even if it's only the tiniest glimpse, a life without Jake. I can see myself making a cup of espresso in my little stove-top *macchinetta,* my vintage Italian posters hanging against the old exposed brick, Chloe playing contentedly in the cozy space under the stairs, her toys and books filling the long, low shelves. Intoxicated by the vision, I'm suddenly willing to spend whatever it takes to make it mine.

"I'll call you back," Skip tells Ms. Moneybags.

chapter 24

By the time the paperwork is done it's almost noon. I'm ravenous, so Ben, Chloe, and I go across the street to Primanti Brothers. We order two Primanti specials, mine with extra coleslaw, Ben's with extra fries and a fried egg on top. When the waitress puts the overflowing red plastic basket in front of me, the sandwich topped with glistening French fries, I dig in with both my hands.

"Hey, wait a minute," Ben says. "I propose a toast. To a masterful negotiation and a wise investment."

I respond with a groan. "I don't think the deal I made would qualify as either masterful or as negotiating," I tell Ben, swallowing painfully. "After all, I paid the asking price. Who does that?"

"No, no, it was masterful. *You* were masterful. And actually, you paid five thousand dollars more than the asking price." Unfortunately, Ben is correct. After I offered the asking price, Ms. Moneybags quickly countered with an offer a thousand dollars higher.

"You had to once she matched your offer. That jump plus your big down payment is what got Skip on board and killed the prospect of an extended bidding war. And the look on his face." He laughs and swipes at his beard. "I've known the guy twenty years and I've never seen that look!" he says, a string of cheese hanging from his mouth.

I have to admit I had enjoyed Skip's sudden about-face. He'd gone from being a condescending finger snapper to someone respectful, deferential, and subservient as soon as I whipped out my checkbook. Someone who took me seriously. Since giving up Grappa I've become accustomed to people not taking me seriously, and I relished Skip's rapt attention as he chatted amiably about my new neighborhood, how up and coming it was and how it took a real New Yorker, someone as sophisticated and savvy as myself, to recognize the true value of this investment.

"I, ah," I start to speak, but no words come out. The bottom line is I have no job and only one slim prospect. I have a child to raise, and I've just bought an impractical penthouse apartment in a city where, until an hour ago, I had no future plans.

Ben puts his sandwich back in the red plastic basket and wipes his mouth. "Come on. It's a good investment. You're a successful businessperson. I'll bet you would have had to pay five times as much for a similar place in Manhattan."

"Ten times, more like," I tell him.

"See, you've made a wise business decision. These loft apartments are going to take off, you watch." Ben shakes a fry at me to emphasize his point. "You're just not thinking down the road. I'll bet you make a bundle."

"I can't believe that I'm taking long-term investment advice from you." I look up at the ceiling of the restaurant, open wooden rafters stained to a dark patina from years of grease and smoke. Light a match, and the whole place would probably go up in flames.

Ben looks hurt. "Hey, what's that supposed to mean?"

I gesture to the sandwich, the second half of which is already poised in Ben's hands. "Anybody who eats this stuff is clearly not thinking long-term."

He smiles at me, the lines around his eyes, which I hadn't noticed before, making tiny craggy creases underneath his lids. He covers his mouth, disguising a delicate belch, and gestures to the waitress for some more water. She pretends not to see him.

"You're one to talk," he says, his mouth full of sandwich.

"What's that supposed to mean?"

"Well, you did just buy a three hundred thousand dollar apartment on impulse. Good investment or not, that's not exactly planning ahead."

I'm not sure if it's the Primanti sandwich or the beginnings of buyer's remorse, but I have a pain in my stomach, a burning sensation that's begun to radiate down my left arm. I take a deep breath, and the pain shifts from my arm to deep in my esophagus. I remember reading somewhere that heart attacks begin like this.

"I've always wanted to live in a loft," I tell him, my voice sounding hollow and unconvincing. I put a hand to my chest. "Who am I kidding—I don't even have a job! I have no idea what I was thinking." Ben leans forward and looks concerned. He reaches into the pocket of his work shirt and pulls out a roll of Tums. He unravels the package, hands me two, and takes two for himself.

"Look. You misjudged me," he says, waving the Tums. "I planned on having lunch at Primanti's today. Who says I don't think ahead?"

Between several calls to and from Skip, not to mention my financial advisor, Avi Steiner, in New York, I spend most of the afternoon on the phone, with each call becoming more deeply entrenched in the Pittsburgh real estate market and the inexorable march toward home ownership. I've exhausted my supply of Tums, having consumed the rest of Ben's, plus another entire roll that I bought on the way home from lunch. When the heart palpitations begin, I shut off my phone and lie face down on the bed and try to think quieting thoughts. Can you die from an overdose of Tums?

I'm too nauseous to eat dinner, but I sit with Chloe while she happily devours her chicken and peas. Eventually, I pour a glass of wine, hoping it will calm me enough to listen to the messages that have accumulated while my phone was off. Eight missed calls.

Two each from Avi and Skip, the substance of which is that my money has been transferred and the remaining paperwork completed; one from the contractor supervising the finishes on the building, Ben's boss, who wants to set up a meeting with me to discuss paint, flooring, and fixtures; one from Ben calling to check on me and to tell me to put in a good word for him when I meet with his boss. And one from Ruth.

"Mira, listen. I'm sorry I was so horrible. I know you were trying to help. It's not your fault that Neil likes you. You can hardly blame the guy. You're pretty and funny and a great cook. Besides, I must have been a real ass to think that playing mah-jongg with Leah Hollander was going to get me anywhere. I have a Jewish mother, and I would no more take dating recommendations from her than I would from my cat. Anyway, tomorrow is Gymboree day, and I wanted you to know that I hope you'll come."

The final message is from Neil, telling me he is looking forward to seeing me at Gymboree tomorrow and wondering if I have plans for Saturday night. The sound of his voice, so earnest and hopeful, fills me with panic, and I delete the message without even listening to the rest of it, then wish I had.

Ruth answers on the first ring. "Mira, thank God! I was beginning to think that I'd totally blown it and that you'd completely given up on me. I'm sorry."

"Me too. I really wasn't trying to steal Neil."

"I know, I know. You only left me about eight messages." Ruth sounds like she's been crying. "I talked to my therapist and realized what an idiot I was being. I hope you can forgive me."

"Of course, if you can forgive me."

"Done." For the first time since Sunday, my stomach has stopped churning. It's nice to have my friend back.

"Hey, guess what?" Ruth says, sounding more cheerful. "I made my mother's brisket recipe—the one with the Coke in it. It wasn't quite as good as I remembered. I was worried that if you stopped being my friend I was going to have to learn to cook! Thank God that's over." Then she asks, "So what have you been up to?"

"I bought a loft."

"Wow. Congratulations! You didn't even mention you were looking," she says.

"I wasn't," I tell her. Ruth is silent. Stunned no doubt. "Come on," I tease. "Haven't you ever bought something on impulse?"

"A pair of shoes, yes. Real estate, no."

"So, did I completely screw up? I still can't believe I—" I exhale sharply; the palpitations have started again.

"No, not necessarily," Ruth says, quickly. "It's a good time to buy. I'll bet you got a great deal."

I change the subject.

"About Gymboree tomorrow, I can't make it. I've got an interview at one forty-five with Enid Maxwell, the food editor at the *Post-Gazette*. I've got to spend the morning assembling my dossier."

"Good for you! What are you going to wear?" Ruth asks.

Wear? I haven't even thought about it. It's been a good ten years since I've interviewed for a job, and never once have I been interviewed in an office setting, so I'm unsure of the protocol.

"A suit's a must, understated makeup, no open-toed shoes. And stockings—it doesn't matter if it's eighty degrees outside. Stockings are standard job interview protocol," Ruth counsels. I never wear makeup, so understated is, well, an understatement. The only suit I own is the one I wore to my meeting with Ethan Bowman and later, my arraignment, so I consider it bad luck. Ruth offers to lend me one of hers.

"Come on over before the interview. I'll get you dressed. I've got a beige crepe suit that will look great on you. I'll watch Chloe. It's actually easier with two."

"Great. I'll bring lunch," I offer.

"Don't bother. We can have brisket sandwiches," Ruth says.

"My treat. I insist."

"Chicken," Ruth mutters.

"Good idea," I reply.

I'm on my way out Ruth's front door the next afternoon, in a pair of her high-heeled pumps that are a half size too big. "Go get 'em!" she calls, tossing a tube of sheer pink lipstick to me. "Just a dab. You look great," she says, balancing Chloe on her hip. I smile and flash an enthusiastic thumbs-up before picking my way down Ruth's cobblestone walk. I feel shaky on my feet—and it isn't just the big shoes. It's been ages since I've wanted anything this badly and, for a moment, I don't recognize the sensation, the gnawing at your insides, the quavering hunger that comes from sheer want. Or perhaps it's the residual effects of yesterday's indiscriminate expenditure. Tucking Ruth's lipstick into my briefcase, I pull out a fresh roll of Tums and stuff a few in my mouth on the way to the bus.

Enid Maxwell is a small, neat woman with expensively cut and carefully styled short hair, the color of a brightly buffed and polished nickel. When the secretary knocks on the wall of the cubicle, Enid stands, offers me a cool, manicured hand, and instructs me to have a seat. Before sitting down herself, however, she stands on her tiptoes, settles her glasses atop her nose, and surveys her domain. Apparently satisfied by the bustling chaos outside her cubicle, she sits back down, rests her forearms on the desk, and says, "Well, Mira."

I've brought along a copy of my résumé and several copies of my restaurant review in a thin leather portfolio I've borrowed from my father. I pull out a copy of the review and prepare to slide it across the desk at her, but she shakes her head at me.

"I've got them. Don't bother," she says.

From a file folder on her desk Enid pulls a copy of my résumé, along with the *Gourmet* review and a couple of other things I'm pretty sure I didn't send her. "Well, well, Mira," Enid says again, readjusting her glasses. "You are quite a talented chef. *Gourmet, Bon Appétit, Saveur, Food and Wine*," she says, leafing through the file on her desk. Enid, apparently, has done some research on me. "Grappa has been mentioned in every one of them, mostly quite favorably." She leans forward and whispers conspiratorially, "By the way, I have it on good authority that Grappa has suffered in your absence. A friend at the *Times,* who I called while assembling my dossier on you, let it slip. You might watch the food section in the next few weeks." She sits back in her chair, studying me, waiting for a reaction.

Ever since my phone call with Renata and hearing the news that Jake was jumping ship to Il Vinaio, I've dreaded hearing news of Grappa. But there's still a part of me that is secretly thrilled by the knowledge that Grappa has suffered in my absence. I know it's selfish, but I can't help it. Public affirmation that I had mattered to Grappa. I wish I didn't need it, but I do. I want nothing more than to pump Enid for the details, but of course this isn't exactly the time. I swallow hard and do my best to return Enid's speculative gaze with a level one of my own.

Once again she reaches into the manila folder, this time removing a photocopy of a newspaper column. "But even before Grappa, you were noticed. This," she says, looking over her glasses at me, "you may recall from *New York* magazine, February 1995. 'Under the direction of talented chef Francis Barberi and creative sous-chef Mirabella Rinaldi, Il Piatto has reopened to rave reviews.'"

Il Piatto was, in fact, the last job I'd interviewed for. I left there after five years to open Grappa. It was also the first time I'd seen my name in print, and I feel strangely nostalgic and unexpectedly touched that Enid has ferreted out this small, mostly insignificant, accolade. I'm impressed that she has so thoroughly researched my career, but more than a little puzzled.

"In fact, ever since you graduated from the Culinary Institute you've done well for yourself. You apprenticed in Abruzzo and then in Bologna, where undoubtedly, you perfected *la cucina Italiana*. You've amassed an impressive set of credentials thus far in your relatively short career," she says, rifling through the file once more. I think for a moment that Enid will pull out my third grade report card, but instead, she gathers the papers, puts them back into the folder, and sets them aside.

"Look, Mira, Ruth Reichl, Barbara Fairchild, Frank Bruni, even me," she says, with a slight, self-deprecating inclination of her head, "all of us are passable cooks. We can all give a damn good dinner party, but we don't have the gift that you have. And, by the way, you don't have the gifts they have, either, but that's beside the point. So the question is," Enid says, swiveling in her desk chair and chewing thoughtfully on the earpiece of her glasses, "why would someone like you want to become a food writer?"

"I didn't get to where I am in the food world without having a well-developed palate. I know—"

Enid holds up her hand. She wasn't really asking me. "I know, I know. You've already told me that. But that isn't the real reason. You want to be a food writer because it is convenient. Do you know how many people apply for a job like this? Some are writers who think they would like to be paid to go out to dinner, but couldn't identify celeriac in a lineup of root vegetables. Some people are foodies with no writing skills who think their knowledge of the food world is enough for them to get by. I've actually hired some of those—but I'm getting too old to rewrite their columns."

"Look, Ms. Maxwell—"

"My point, Mira, is that cooks need to cook. You won't be happy writing for a living, and you won't get rich either." Enid sits back in her chair and gives me a speculative look. She appears to be considering something. She hesitates before continuing. "You think I don't understand what it takes to be a chef? I was at the CIA a couple of years ago. Took a two-week course for business people who want to become restaurateurs. I *know* how hard it is. I could never have cut it. The difference between those of us in the fake course and the kids we saw running themselves into the ground, besides a whole lot of talent, is the drive to cook. They *need* it. The threat of a bad review of Grappa in the *Times* bothered you. I could see it in your face. A restaurant like Grappa gets into your blood. You don't go from that to this," she says, gesturing to the papers on her desk and the short walls of the cubicle. "Face it, you've missed it."

"Missed it? The eighteen-hour days on my feet? Dealing with suppliers and linen sales people on my 'off' time? Replacing line cooks on a weekly basis? There's a lot more to the restaurant business besides cooking. Loving to cook isn't nearly enough." My voice is rising to an uncomfortably high pitch. Despite Ruth's perfectly tailored suit and a liberal dose of Bare Naked lip gloss, I've somehow gotten off on the wrong foot here. Before I'd even walked in the door, Enid seems to have made up her mind that I'm not cut out to be a food writer. So why bother interviewing me? "And besides, what makes you think I don't cook? I cook every day. For my family. Real cooks find ways to cook."

Enid holds up her hands in mock surrender. "Yes, you're right. That is precisely what I'm suggesting, Mira. Listen, I don't know how much time you've spent looking at our food section since you've been back in town, but it's in the process of undergoing a much needed transformation. We're trying out a bunch of new ideas. Maybe you noticed a couple of weeks ago we did a feature article on 'Five Ingredient Wonders'? We're considering continuing something like that once a week, publishing a few recipes on a theme: "Beat the Heat with Easy Summer Meals in Minutes." She gestures as she speaks, blocking out chunks of the title with her hands, as if it's written on a billboard.

I groan involuntarily.

"What?"

"No—nothing."

"Come on, you groaned. Did you see the article?"

"No. Well, yes, yes, I did. And if I'd been the editor I might have changed the title to '101 Uses for Cream of Mushroom Soup,'" I tell her, uncharitably blocking out those letters on my own personal billboard.

Silence. I've blown it, I think, holding my breath. When the hell am I going to learn to control myself?

Enid laughs. "Touché, Mira, Touché. I told you before, *Bon Appétit,* we're not—that's where you come in."

"Me?"

"Well, the way I see it is I've got two choices. One, I sign Campbell's on as a corporate sponsor, so that someone, even if it is only some slob in their PR department, is reading the Food section; or two, I hire you to develop some new recipes. Something to wake up those tired Pittsburgh taste buds. People here are ready for something new, but they lack the knowledge about where to go or what to cook. The recipes in the *P-G* need to offer something quick and easy enough for the average cook to put together, but unique. What do you say?"

I'm stunned. "Are you offering me a job? I mean, a real one, a paying one?"

Enid smiles. "Damn, Mira, you're quick. Well, are you interested?"

"Well—I—"

"It'll just be part-time, of course. The Food section is only weekly, but occasionally there are some Sunday special recipes you'll be asked to consult on. We don't have a test kitchen, so you'll have to work out of your home. How about ten hours per week, thirty bucks an hour, to start, all expenses paid?"

I certainly won't get rich doing it, but this isn't New York City, and part-time would leave me plenty of time for Chloe. But the best part is I'll be cooking again.

"Let me think about it, and I'll get back to you."

Enid seems surprised that I haven't immediately accepted the job. I will, of course; it's just that, for the moment at least, I'm enjoying seeing her a little off-balance. But, shrewd newspaperwoman that she is, she quickly regains her composure. "So what's for dinner?" she asks.

"Excuse me?"

"You said you were cooking for your family. Can I ask what a professional chef feeds her family, or is that some deep, dark secret?"

"Curried prawn chowder, black sea bass en papillote with baby artichokes and red pepper coulis, frisee salad with shaved Asiago," I tell her, even though the only thing currently in our refrigerator is the other half of my Primanti's sandwich.

"I love sea bass. What time is dinner?"

So, I'm being wooed by Enid Maxwell.

chapter 25

Richard is standing in the middle of the loft holding a tape measure and frowning at the white slipcovered sofa. "You don't want that. The scale is wrong for the room, and it's not a good white. It's also totally impractical."

"It's washable, and, besides, I like it," I tell him.

"No, you don't. You just think you do, because it's here and it's easy and because you can't imagine any other possibility."

I know Richard means this literally, that he's talking about sofas and not lifestyles, but because I'm not yet completely at home with the idea that I've bought this place, I snap at him.

"That's ridiculous. I can imagine lots of possibilities!"

Richard tosses his tape measure onto the sofa and looks at me.

"Okay, tell me what you see," he says calmly.

It is easier than I thought to tell Richard what I see, the apartment I'm envisioning, the furniture, the lamps, dimly lit, casting deep shadows on the brick walls, and the dishes, the only things I recognize as anything that I actually own, stacked neatly on open shelves in the kitchen. So why do I feel as if I'm on the outside, my nose pressed against the window of someone else's life?

Richard listens carefully, occasionally nodding in response to a particular detail, and he smiles when I tell him I've always wanted to live in a yellow house.

When I finish, he says nothing, but studies me, the vestige of a smile clinging, despite itself, to his handsome face.

"I really don't care about the sofa," I tell him, picking up his tape measure and tossing it to him, not because it is true, but because I cannot bear to look at Richard a moment longer. In the couple of weeks since I've last seen him he's changed, though someone unused to living with a drunk might easily miss the signs. His arms and legs look thin under his custom shirt and carefully tailored trousers. He smells heavily of peppermint, yet his breath has the slightly acidic twang of mouthwash and stale coffee, and he has the nervous shifty gaze of a man who wants only to be alone with his next drink.

Although I'm hurt and disappointed that Richard apparently doesn't trust me enough to share whatever crisis has brought him to this, what hurts almost as much is the thought of intruding so completely and with such finality on his carefully guarded dignity. He is, after all, still holding down a job and maintaining his relationships, at least after a fashion. He pockets the tape measure and makes a few notes on the inside of a yellow manila folder, which is neatly labeled "Mira's Loft." He's taking my request for some decorating guidance very seriously. And his advice, despite whatever personal turmoil he is experiencing, is practical and direct.

"My recommendation is that you take only your Heywood-Wakefield dining table and chairs. And the framed artwork. Leave the rest of your stuff for that Hope person." He wrinkles his nose in a paroxysm of disgust, though I'm not sure whether it is at the vision of Hope or of my assorted odds and ends of furniture.

I nod, deliberately avoiding his eye. "Thanks. I'll arrange to have them shipped."

Richard looks at me for a moment, as if he's considering saying something, but instead, takes out his phone and checks his voice mail for the second time in the twenty minutes we've been here.

He listens to his messages, smiles, and clicks his phone shut.

"You wouldn't happen to be free for dinner Thursday night?"

Richard ought to know that I've been free for dinner for, oh, roughly the last six months. "Sure," I tell him.

"Good. There's someone I'd like you to meet."

"I liked the one with too much ginger. Isn't there any of that left?" my father calls from the refrigerator.

"No, Chloe is eating it for breakfast. But there's plenty of the 'not enough orange zest,'" I tell him. My father pulls out several carefully marked containers of soup from the refrigerator and dons his reading glasses. "Peanut? Is this right? I don't think I even tried this one."

My first assignment, which Enid e-mailed me three days ago, is a column entitled "Soup Suppers." I'd selected two Grappa stand-bys, a roasted pappa al pomodoro and a lentil and sausage with red wine. But the third, a vegetarian carrot soup, had given me some trouble. I'd easily tried a dozen variations in the last couple of days, most of which are stacked, uneaten, in Tupperware containers in the fridge.

The clear winner had been the cumin-scented carrot with co-conut milk and cilantro, the recipe for which I'd e-mailed to Enid, along with the rest of the column, early yesterday morning. She nixed my discussion of how to prepare soup stocks from scratch, but allowed me to keep in the recipe for baguettes, a simple one, involving only flour, yeast, and water and no specialty gadgets. "You've got to pick your battles, Mira," she told me. "You can't ex-pect people to make their own chicken and vegetable stocks *and* their own bread."

The column will run tomorrow. In the end, I was pleased with my efforts, but now that it's out of my hands I'm nervous about seeing it in print. Not that I have a byline or anything, just a small mention at the end of the column: "Recipes courtesy of Chef Mirabella Rinaldi, formerly executive chef and owner of Grappa, New York," which I'm sure most people won't even read.

"Dad, take the rest in for lunch, otherwise I'm going to throw them away. Forget the peanut, though. It was terrible. I don't even know why I saved it."

"No, I think I'll pass," my father says, frowning at his palms.

"Do they look orange to you?" he asks, holding out his hands to me. They do.

"Too much beta-carotene. Hey, don't worry, you'll live longer and see better," I tell him, giving him a kiss on the cheek.

While Chloe is finishing her sliced bananas, I clean out the refrigerator, tossing entire disposable Tupperware containers unopened into the trash. I need the space so that I can begin working on my next assignment, which Enid gave me moments after I e-mailed her the final version of my piece. This time, the assignment is a column on kid-friendly food, entitled "Cooking With and For Kids."

Enid has given me several suggestions—three of them involving processed cheese products—so I can already tell that there will be some major theoretical differences. My philosophy is that kids shouldn't be played down to. Introduce them to complex flavors early on, and they'll develop sophisticated palates. It's worked so far with Chloe, whose list of green vegetables, in addition to the standard ones, includes mizuna, artichokes, and rapini. The problem is, I don't know too many other kids. None really, except Eli and Carlos. I don't know much about Eli, but Carlos survives on nothing but Kraft Singles, oranges, macaroni and cheese, and Cheerios.

Because of the column, Ruth has been pulling double duty in the babysitting department lately. So when she calls for the third time this morning to ask if, in addition to the apple juice and fruit snacks I'm already picking up, I could also buy some nail polish remover, I owe it to her to dredge up my extra reserves of patience.

"According to *Vogue,* brown nails are in, but I think they look too punk. I used half a bottle just getting it off two fingers. I look like a freak. Better get the large bottle, okay? Oh, and I don't suppose you have any more of that carrot soup, the one with the peanut butter in it?"

"Sure," I tell her, fishing the Tupperware container out of the trash and rinsing it off. "I'll bring it over."

Just as Chloe and I are on our way out the door a few minutes later, the phone rings again. Sure it's Ruth, I don't pick up, figuring she can make me a shopping list when I drop off Chloe.

* * *

"What's this?" Ben asks, sitting down to eat. He's come on his lunch hour to install my pasta spigot, but because the loft is basically empty, we've had to make a table out of the large plywood crate that, until earlier this morning, had contained my professional series Gaggenau range. The lone stool is Ben's tall Craftsman tool chest.

"This? This is Carlos's Three-Cheese Casserole." In between my appointment with Dr. D-P and my trip to the loft to supervise the installation of the range, I'd run home and gathered some ingredients from my father's pantry, intending to break in my new stove and play around with my kids' cooking assignment. I'd used tricolor bows, mixed with a combination of cottage cheese, Gruyère, the end of a piece of hard cheese I'd found in the back of the fridge, and a couple of eggs. I baked it all in a hot oven and served it topped with a fresh tomato basil sauce.

"Hmm. Pretty good. Who's Carlos?"

"I'm a journalist now. I can't divulge my sources."

"A mystery man, huh?" Ben gives me a curious look.

"Actually, he's a kid I know."

"Oh."

"It's for a column on kid-friendly foods."

"You think a kid would eat this?"

"A kid does eat this."

"No kid would eat this."

"Why not?"

"Because for one thing, kids don't like Swiss cheese."

"It isn't Swiss, it's Gruyère."

"Okay, way worse than Swiss."

"It's delicious, loaded with calcium, and all that I had in the refrigerator."

"Aha! So the recipe from your mystery kid did not specifically mention Gruyère?"

"No, not exactly."

Ben helps himself to another serving of Three-Cheese Casserole.

"I'll bet the original recipe called for cheddar," he says, taking another bite. "Kids would like it better with cheddar."

"Actually, it was Kraft American Singles."

"I rest my case," Ben says, looking smug.

"Oh, yeah? What do kids know?"

It's nice of Ben to install my pasta spigot. For one thing, he isn't charging me, preferring instead to barter his services in return for food. When he tells me that he'll have to come back to hook up the water lines, he suggests that maybe I could make something on my new stove for dinner one night. For us.

"Maybe we could even scare up another chair. You know, both of us eating at the same time." Ben widens his eyes, as if he's just suggested something as daring and improbable as eating al fresco on the dark side of the moon.

"Sure, but I warn you I'll still be working on this kid column, so you're taking your chances. It might be hot dogs, or peanut butter and jelly sandwiches," I tell him, flustered by his flirting.

"Nah. Too obvious. You'll come up with something, something probably way too exotic. You could always ask Aunt Fi. She has all kinds of kid recipes. My cousins were very picky eaters, so if she wanted them to eat something besides peanut butter, she had to get creative. She had a recipe for brownies made with tomato soup. You almost couldn't taste the soup," he says, depositing his empty plate in the sink. "Thanks for lunch," Ben says, giving my arm a squeeze.

By the time we get home, it's almost supper time. I'm making dinner, another version of the casserole, this time with cheddar and mild tomato salsa, when I notice the answering machine light blinking. The first and only message is from Richard. "Mira. I guess you're not there." There's a long pause, as if he'd hoped I'd hear him and pick up. "I need you to do something for me," he says, only the "something" comes out as "shomething." Another long pause. "Call me, all right?" Richard doesn't say good-bye, but before the connection is broken I can hear the sound of the phone being clumsily hung up, as if he tried to place it in the cradle and missed, causing it to fall over on the table. And then, a static fumbling accompanied by a halfhearted "shit."

From the automated voice on my dad's machine I know that the call had been received at nine forty-five this morning, which means it had been Richard, and not Ruth, who called as we were on our way out. I haven't spoken to him since the day at the loft when he'd invited me to dinner to meet his mystery guest. Ordinarily, I'd have called him and tried to worm some additional details out of him, but I've been so busy working on my column that I hadn't given it much thought. I call him back, first at home, then at the shop, and finally, on his cell, where I leave a message.

After Chloe is in bed, I try him again, this time also leaving messages at his home and office from my cell phone. I replay his message several times, studying his diction and trying to talk myself into believing that he just sounds sleepy, and not drunk.

Finally, in search of a distraction, I fool around with some more kid recipes, concocting a breakfast cookie out of oatmeal, honey, raisins, and wheat germ that probably no kid would eat.

Maybe no adult either. When my father comes home, I give him a couple of the cookies with a cup of tea, and he innocently inquires if my next column is cooking for pets. "There aren't enough good dog biscuits around," he says, surreptitiously wrapping the remains of his cookie in a piece of paper towel.

I'm in bed reading Fiona's copy of *Good Housekeeping,* trolling around for ideas for kid-friendly foods, when my cell rings. It's Richard's ring tone.

"Richard, thank God. I was worried about you," I say.

"Mira Rinaldi, please," a voice, not Richard's, asks.

"Speaking. Who's this?"

"My name is Nate. You're a friend of Richard Kistler's?"

"Yes, yes, I am. Who's this? Where's Richard?"

Nate takes a deep breath, audible and unsettling, and I can feel the rush of blood to my ears. "I'm calling from the hospital. Well, actually from outside the hospital. You know how they are about cell phones in hospitals." Nate laughs nervously. I can hear the wail of an ambulance in the distance.

"Where's Richard? Is he all right?"

"There's been an accident," Nate says. His voice, very young sounding, is throaty and hoarse.

"Where is he?"

"Shadyside Hospital." And then he mumbles something that sounds like "car accident" and "ICU."

I throw on a pair of jeans and a sweatshirt and wake my father to tell him what's happened and that I'll call as soon as I know anything. When I arrive at the hospital, I give the attendant at the front desk my name and Richard's. She directs me to the fifth floor, the ICU.

"Are you family?" she asks, her face a mask, as she fills out a pass that will allow me access to the unit.

"Yes. How is he?"

"The nurse will let you in and can give you information on Mr. Kistler's condition. How are you related?" she asks, her pen poised over the pass.

How are we related? He helped my mother. He's been like an uncle. We made a pact at AA. We are blood brothers. "Richard is my brother," I tell the woman. She hands me the pass.

"Fifth floor. Make a left out of the elevators. Ring the buzzer at the double doors."

The nurse who opens the door to the ICU suite is dressed in pink, her hair covered by a paper, elastic-rimmed cap. The lights are low, her voice a whisper.

"Ms. Rinaldi?" the nurse says, squinting to read the name on my pass.

I nod. "This way," she says, darting a furtive glance in the direction of the waiting room, a small alcove off the main area, where a man in a black leather jacket is stretched out on the loveseat, his arm covering his face.

She leads me along a wide, dimly lit hallway, stopping outside a large room separated from the corridor by a wall of glass. "What happened?" I ask her. "How is he?"

"He's unconscious, but stable for now. He's only a couple of hours post-op, so we're still watching his vitals."

"My God. What happened?"

"He passed out behind the wheel and crashed head-on into a section of guardrail on Bigelow Boulevard. The surgery was to repair a ruptured spleen and to stabilize a splintered sternum. He also sustained a severe head injury and hasn't regained conscious-ness." She places a hand on my back and gently pushes me inside.

"Squeeze his hand and talk to him. He may be able to hear you, and your presence will be comforting to him." She moves toward the bed. The lights are dim, and the person in the bed, who I can hardly recognize as Richard, is covered in bandages. I'm unable to move. My legs are leaden, and I can feel the whooshing of the blood in my ears again.

"Richard, Richard," the nurse calls to him, her voice loud and authoritative. "Mira is here. We found her. She's here with you now." She's bending over him, shouting into his face, but Richard, who doesn't like loud noise, who doesn't like people invading his personal space, doesn't react at all. She gestures for me to join her on the other side of the bed.

"I'll be back in about ten minutes," she says, her voice once again a whisper. "Ten minutes every hour are for visiting. The doctor should be around in a while and will want to speak with you."

Richard is hooked up to a host of machines, wires and tubes dangling from several places. His face is bruised and swollen, his chin slack. I take his hand, gingerly wrapping my fingers around his, not wanting to upset him, unlike the nurse whose grasp had been firm, even rough.

"Richard, I'm here. I love you," I whisper into his ear, bending low to brush my lips against his forehead. "I'm sorry. I'm so sorry I didn't answer the phone. I should have been there. I'm here. I'm here now." There's no sign that Richard has heard me, no encour-aging pressure on my hand, no murmuring lips. I lean down into the bed, over the railings to rest my head against his, stroking his hand and whispering to him, until the nurse comes to the door and gestures to the clock over the bed.

"I need to go in and check his IVs and fluids. You can have a seat in the waiting area. The doctor will be with you shortly."

The waiting alcove is empty, the sleeping man gone, perhaps spending his precious ten minutes in another of these horrible rooms, at the bedside of a wife, a parent, or, God forbid, a child.

I try to remember everything I can about Richard's family. His parents live somewhere in the South, Florida maybe, but I have no idea how to reach them. The door to the ICU buzzes, but the nurses' station is empty. The buzzer goes off again. This time I see a man craning his neck to look through the narrow window into the lounge. When he sees me, he holds two Styrofoam cups up to the window, as if to indicate his hands are full. Although I haven't seen his face, I recognize the leather jacket. He's the man who was sleeping on the couch when I arrived.

"Mira?" he asks, when I open the door. I nod, and he hands me a cup of coffee. "Here. I figured you could use this. I'm Nate." He puts his coffee down on the table and begins emptying packets of various non-dairy creamers and sweeteners from the front pockets of his jeans.

"I didn't know what you take in it, so I just brought everything." Nate sits down on the mauve sofa, opens two packets of sugar, and empties them into his coffee. "I wasn't sure it was you, when you walked in. I should have said something. I guess I'm just not thinking too clearly. I'm sorry."

"That's okay. I'm not thinking too clearly myself." I take a seat opposite Nate and watch him stir his coffee. "I can't believe this. When did it happen?" I take too big a sip of the coffee, which is so hot it scalds the roof of my mouth.

"Tonight, around six, I guess."

Nate hangs his head, cups his neck with two delicate hands, and massages the nape.

"Were you with him?"

Nate looks up sharply, but he doesn't answer; instead, he runs his hands from his neck up through his dark hair, encircling a lock in between his fingers and tugging gently. It's a languid and luxurious gesture, as if he's just awakened from a nap, sleeping off the chill of an autumn afternoon. His face is expressionless, with clear white skin and a hint of a dark beard. His eyes are too blue to be real, his features finely sculpted, high cheekbones, a small pointed chin, full lips, smooth and pink and bloodless. He's young, probably no more than twenty-five or twenty-six. For an instant I see him as Richard must, his face a mesmerizing combination of man and boy.

"He wasn't wearing any shoes, for God's sake. I don't know

what he was doing. He was drunk." Nate's voice is low and angry. "He called me this morning because he thought I took something that belonged to him. We argued, and he threatened to come to where I work, so I went over to his house. I thought I could calm him down. But when I got there he was in the front yard, shoeless and drunk, shouting at me. I left, but he kept calling me on the phone. For hours he wouldn't leave me alone. I finally told him to stop calling me or I would report him—get a restraining order or something when he"—Nate's voice grows softer, his anger reduced to a dull whine—"when he crashed. I heard the whole thing."

"You left him like that? When you knew he was drunk and upset? What were you thinking?"

Nate inhales slowly, once again meeting my gaze, the harsh and artificial blue of his eyes flashing defiantly in the dim glow of the waiting room.

"What was I supposed to do? He was being abusive."

"I don't believe that. That's not Richard. He isn't—I mean he doesn't—" Overwhelmed by the picture Nate has drawn, I have trouble finding words to describe just how unlike Richard any of this is. All I seem to be able to focus on are the absurd details of this story, and I finish indignantly, "Richard doesn't walk around in his yard barefoot!"

Nate looks at me strangely, his full, bloodless lips set in a pitying smirk.

"Listen," Nate says, picking up his jacket and standing up. "Now that you're here, if you don't mind, I'm going to leave. I really don't belong here. Not anymore. I'll come and see him later."

"Wait a minute," I say, holding my arm out to keep him from leaving. "How can I get in touch with you?" He reaches into the pocket of his jacket, takes out a pen, writes his phone number on a crumpled sugar wrapper, and hands it to me. Even though it's warm in the ICU, his hands are cold, the nails tinged with blue.

He turns to leave, presses the buzzer to open the unit doors, and steps out into the hallway. I follow him to the elevators and watch as he jabs the button accusingly.

"Nate?" I call. He turns toward me. "I need Richard's phone or address book. There are people I need to call."

Nate reaches into the front pocket of his leather jacket, takes out Richard's phone, and hands it to me. "Here," he says, glancing at me. "But I already checked, his parents aren't in there. You are his emergency contact."

I take the phone and slip it into my pocket. There's a sudden draft as the elevator doors open, and Nate steps inside. As the doors glide shut, I stick out my arm, causing them to bounce back abruptly, as if recoiling from my touch. Startled, Nate leans back against the wall, looking as if I meant to strike him. "What was it that Richard thought you took from him?" I ask. He stares at me for so long I think perhaps he hasn't heard me. I'm about to repeat myself when he says, in a voice that is slow and clear, "Everything."

chapter 26

I spend the better part of the next two weeks at the hospital, becoming a semi-permanent fixture first in the ICU and then later in Richard's regular room, which he shares with an older-looking asthmatic man named Jonas.

Richard's progress is slow, and it's only because I'm here every day that I can gauge his progress at all, watching vigilantly as gradually his body begins responding, first to light and then to noise. Then, one day, almost two weeks after the accident, there's a faint pressure at the squeeze of my hand and a fluttering of his eyelids at the sound of my voice. The doctors don't say much, and when I press them, they concentrate on the positive, telling me things like that his incisions are healing nicely and he's lucky to be alive, and that his splintered sternum was millimeters away from piercing his heart. I want them to tell me when Richard will wake up, but this they don't seem to know. All they seem willing to say is that head injuries take time, and it's still too early to tell.

As far as I know, Nate hasn't stopped by to see Richard, as he said he would. Even so, when I first felt the slight pressure in Richard's grip and what I thought might be a smile at my calling his name, I called Nate and left him a message. Since then, I've called every couple of days, leaving upbeat, yet business-like updates on Nate's answering machine. Not that I really expect him to show up.

One day, Richard opens his eyes, looks at me, and groans.

"Hey," I say, coming around the side of the bed to grasp his hand. The muscles of Richard's face struggle to arrange themselves in a smile, but only the right side of his face is cooperating, and the effect is more like a grimace. He opens his mouth and tries to speak, but soon grows exhausted by the effort. Still, I can tell by looking at him that he understands me. I brush the hair from his forehead, moisten his lips with a clean sponge, and massage his fingers as I fill him in on the details of his life over the past almost two weeks. He makes no further move to speak until I ask him if he can remember the accident, at which point a small sob escapes as he tries to turn his face away, the light in his eyes flickering dangerously. I tell him the doctors are confident that he will recover fully, and point out the blooming bromeliad in the corner of the room that his parents (or, more likely, the social worker from the nursing home in Boca Raton) sent to cheer him up. I managed to track them down through an entry in Richard's checkbook to the Palm Gardens Senior Center.

Despite himself, Richard is making progress. By the end of the following week he's strong enough to be transferred to a rehabilitation facility. It's a more hopeful place, with cheerful murals, a lovely solarium, and much more liberal visiting policies, meaning that I can now bring Chloe, who greets Richard in the mornings with a delighted squeal, which seems to cheer him. This morning Chloe and I have brought him breakfast, a Maytag blue cheese and apple soufflé, fresh croissants, and a large thermos of café au lait.

"Here, I bought you a present," I tell him, tossing a large plastic bag onto the bed and struggling to keep a straight face. Inside are two cheap sweat suits, one blue and one brown, which I bought because the physical therapist overseeing his rehab told me he'd need comfortable, loose-fitting workout clothes. Richard, I happen to know, owns nothing that isn't perfectly tailored, so I'd gone to Walmart and gotten the pair.

"What is this hideous dung-colored thing?" Richard asks, pulling the brown sweatshirt out of the bag and holding it between his thumb and forefinger. It takes several seconds for him to enunciate this particular little gem, but the accompanying sneer is unmistakable. I let loose a loud cheer, grab Chloe, and do a victory dance around his bed, thrilled that the Richard I know and love, clotheshorse, style hound, and incredible snob, is on his way back home.

"I can't believe you bought those," Richard says.

"I thought the green racing stripe down the leg would look nice with your hair," I tell him, flopping down on the bed next to him and making Chloe giggle.

He snorts. "This material feels like spun straw," he says, holding the sweatshirt at arm's length. I take the sweatshirt from him and hand him a mug of coffee.

"It's what your physical therapist told me to get. Besides, I can't really see you incorporating the sweat suit into your fashion repertoire, so I figured I'd just pick up a couple of cheap ones. We can burn them later, if you like."

"Yes, on the front lawn. We shall build a pyre to the gods of good taste." Richard raises his mug of café au lait in mock salute and then, taking a long sip, rolls his eyes upward. "Mmm. Delicious. You are forgiven." Then, he takes my hand and raises it to his lips. "Thank you, Mira," he whispers.

Because I've been so preoccupied with Richard the last couple of weeks, neglecting almost everything else except Chloe, the move to the loft has been put on hold. My new bedroom set and Chloe's crib were delivered last week, but I've yet to set them up. The Gaggenau man has left several increasingly agitated messages on my voice mail wanting to schedule a time to install the hood to my stove. Even Ben has threatened to send me a bill because, although he still hasn't been able to hook up the water lines, he finished installing the pasta spigot weeks ago and I haven't yet made good on my promise to cook him dinner. Even Dr. D-P has been put on hold. The only thing I've done, apart from taking care of Chloe and visiting Richard, is work on my columns, mostly because I'm afraid of Enid, but also because I've found the cooking, and to my surprise, the writing, to be restorative.

I'd almost missed seeing my first column, which had come out the morning after Richard's accident. It wasn't until I listened to my voice mail the next evening, which included congratulatory messages from my father, Ruth, and Ben, that I even remembered it at all. My second column, the one on kid-friendly foods, had also escaped my notice until one morning, arriving at Richard's with Chloe in tow, I find him holding court at one of the round tables in the solarium, the *Post-Gazette* Food section spread out in front of him. He's surrounded by a bunch of little old women, whom he is filling in on the sordid details of my past.

"So sorry, dear, but bully for you for taking matters into your own hands," a small, bent gnome tells my kneecap.

"Who needs a man?" says another, presenting me with a pen and a newspaper folded neatly around my column, which she asks me to autograph.

It's hard to be angry at Richard, who doesn't look the least bit contrite in his dusty adobe-colored sweat outfit. "Actually, you ought to thank me," he says, when I threaten to withhold his morning cappuccino. "It's good publicity for you. A *real* celebrity chef story. You could be a sort of female Anthony Bourdain," he tells me. "But even better. *You've* actually been to jail. Come to think of it, I'm not sure Bourdain was ever arrested. And if he was, it was drugs. Your story is definitely more colorful."

"Thanks, but no thanks," I tell him, feigning annoyance.

Physically, Richard is making good progress. He's walking with the aid of a walker and slowly regaining the use of his right side. Yet there are times when he seems to curl up into himself, when he can't or won't communicate, sitting for hours at a time, his eyes glazed over. It's as if someone's hung a "closed" sign across his face. I like to think that Richard has gone somewhere more interesting than the Shadyside Rehabilitation Center, but not so interesting that he won't eventually come home.

The doctors have diagnosed depression and are plying him with all sorts of drugs, but it will be some weeks before they can judge their effectiveness. When Richard's health insurance runs out after two weeks, it seems too soon to think of sending him home, but the social worker tells me that they can arrange for a nurse to come daily and even stay overnight in the beginning, if necessary. But

Richard's house is two stories, and I worry about his managing the stairs or tripping over the cat, so I tell her to arrange instead for a hospital bed to be delivered to my loft. He can recuperate at home with me.

"You're getting out tomorrow," I tell him the next afternoon.

He puts aside his crossword puzzle and raises an eyebrow.

When I tell him the plan, he protests. "I will not have you following me around, force feeding me, fretting over me. It's annoying."

"Well, too bad, Richard. It's time you got back to work. You promised to decorate my apartment, and the only way I can think for you to do it is to make you live there. When it's finished, you can leave."

Richard turns away from me and doesn't say anything more. I start to worry that I've made a mistake by initiating this forced dependence on me, but soon he begins to squirm in his wheelchair, trying to get his right side to cooperate as he struggles out of his sweatshirt, the dung-colored one. He balls it up and tries to toss it to me, but it lands inches from his seat. Then, exhausted and panting with the effort, he says, "Prepare the bonfire."

I shove the last of the unopened boxes into the space under the stairs, into the space that should be Chloe's cozy nook. I've spent the last twenty-four hours scrambling to get the apartment set up and prepared for Richard's arrival and have been too busy to unpack all but the most essential items: the Diaper Genie; Chloe's kitchen set and Fisher Price farm; my pots, pans, copper sauciers, and assorted kitchen implements, although the dough hook is missing from the KitchenAid mixer and the shallow olive-wood bowl has somehow gotten separated from its matching mezzaluna. I have no idea where my toothbrush is, but I've spent the last half hour unwrapping and washing my china, a vintage set for twelve from the fifties by Russel Wright, because I've missed it—the elegant sweep of the cup handles, the delicate glaze, a blue so clean and light it appears almost iridescent. I like looking at it, spread out on the open shelves in the kitchen. It makes this place, or a small corner of it anyway, feel like home.

Earlier in the day I'd been dispatched to Richard's for all his necessary items: his cashmere lounge suit and paisley silk robe and slippers; his favorite antique Wedgwood coffee cup; his collection of Steelers Super Bowl highlight DVDs; and the TV from his kitchen to watch them on; and Katherine, his elderly seal point Siamese, who had taken up temporary but reluctant residence with Richard's neighbors, a young working couple who had found it a chore to soft boil Katherine's daily egg. I open a bag and spill some fresh litter into Katherine's box and slide it into the small remaining space under the stairs. Katherine approaches, circling my legs, a trembling purr caught in her throat. She looks at me, then at the litter box, and then with a grace and agility that belies her fifteen years, jumps into the potted palm, a housewarming gift from my father and Fiona, and pees.

Richard is snoring in the hospital bed by the window, his headphones askew. In the last few weeks his hair has lost its sheen, and it now hangs in wispy, dust-colored tufts over the earpieces. The Steelers DVD, a replay of their 1975 Super Bowl victory, has ended, and the television screen is filled with black and white static. Not for the first time this week do I marvel at what I've gotten myself into. The Richard I know wears thousand-dollar suits, has his hair professionally highlighted, and drinks his morning coffee from an antique Wedgwood cup. He does not wear sweat suits or have bad breath.

I turn off the television and remove his headphones. Richard stirs, and I nudge him a little more urgently, until he opens one eye and looks at me. The expression on his face is one of nearly complete disorientation.

"Do you have to go to the bathroom, Richard?" I ask him. He hesitates. Richard refuses to use the bedpan, or the potty chair next to his bed for that matter, and I know that if I don't help him he'll try to do it himself after I'm asleep, which is dangerous given his still limited mobility. "Let's go. I'll help you." He looks down toward the end of the bed and then around at the room before returning his focus to my face. He missed a spot shaving this morning, and there's a stubborn patch of whitish hair growing just under his chin. He reaches up and begins to pick at it distractedly as, slowly and sadly, he nods.

We make our way to the bathroom, and Richard, now fully awake and leaning heavily on me, tells me a joke.

"Three notes walk into a bar: a C, an E flat, and a G. The bartender says he doesn't serve minors. So the E flat leaves, and the C and the G share a fifth between them."

Richard leans forward and steadies himself by placing one hand on the back of the toilet. He's a tall man, and the toilet is one of those low, one-piece models, making the angle awkward and uncomfortable. Richard's right side is still stiff and bruised. With his weakened hand he struggles to free himself, while I support him, my eyes just about level with his penis, which I try not to look at. Richard hunches over the toilet. My neck and shoulders are wedged under his arm, my head discreetly angled away. I'm sure we look ridiculous, like two teenagers playing Twister. We stand there for several moments, waiting for him to go.

This time it's my turn. "What did the grape say when the elephant sat on him?"

"What . . . did the grape say?" asks Richard through tightened lips.

"Nothing. He just let out a little wine."

Richard lets out a guffaw. He's startled by the stream of urine suddenly escaping his body and struggles to bring himself under control.

"I don't think I've ever heard you tell a joke before," Richard says, as the two of us hobble back to his bed, exhausted.

"I don't think I've ever told a joke before, at least not as an adult," I say.

Richard stops and turns to look at me. "Well, you have fine comedic timing, my dear. Where did you come up with that one?"

"*The Big Golden Book of Jokes,*" I tell him.

"You bought a book?"

"Yup, I sure did. At the variety store."

We arrive at the side of the bed. Richard begins to pivot a fraction of a second too early, landing on the bed with a thud and bringing me down on top of him. His face is grim, but he wraps his arms around me and kisses me roughly on the top of my head.

"I hope you bought the unabridged edition. I think we're going to need it."

Chloe wakes early the next morning. The move and the new surroundings have unsettled her. I bring her into bed with me, hoping she'll go back to sleep, but she doesn't, which means neither can I. Chloe has been out of sorts for the last several days. She, like Richard, is a creature of habit, wanting order restored to her baby world but being unable to ask for it, instead communicating her desire in tetchy cries, shortened naps, and fitful sleeps. Today is Wednesday, Gymboree day. Unfortunately, though, the move has put me behind in my research—three hundred and fifty words and four recipes on low-fat Southwestern favorites due on Monday—and I really should spend the day cooking and writing. But we haven't been there in almost a month, and I wonder if Chloe misses it.

I haven't left Richard alone yet, except to run across the street to the market, but Gymboree is across town so we'll be gone at least a couple of hours. When Richard awakens, I feed him and Katherine their morning eggs, and we spend some time reviewing the buzzer system, so that Richard can let his physical therapist in at noon. I tuck his cell phone and a bottle of water into a small canvas bag attached to his wheelchair. Richard wheels himself over to where he has his set of Steelers DVDs spread out across the entire length of the twin-sized hospital bed.

"I'm looking for the San Diego game, from the '75 season. See if you can find it for me, will you?"

"Are you sure you're going to be okay?"

Richard doesn't answer, but nods, fumbling with his headphones.

"What if you have to go to the bathroom?" I ask, worrying about the sixteen-ounce bottle of water I've just tucked into Richard's bag.

"I won't," he says, trying to untangle the cord to the headset.

"You don't have to wear those. No one else is here."

"I know. I like them," Richard says, putting them on.

"But you might not hear the buzzer if your therapist comes early."

Richard looks up at me and smiles sweetly, holding his hand to his ear and pretending not to have heard me. "I'll be fine. Go. Please," Richard says too loudly, having found and inserted his DVD.

In the month since Chloe's last Gymboree class, her sense of balance has become more refined. To my surprise and her delight, she is now able to climb the five steps of the slide holding on to me with only one hand. When she positions herself at the top of the slide, I hover near her, my arm outstretched, careful not to touch her, but she soon grows impatient with my hovering and reaches over to push my arm away.

"No," she says, frowning at me.

"A clear and assertive 'no.' Quite unlike her mother, I see." I looked around the gym at the beginning of class and didn't see Neil and Eli, so I'm surprised when I turn around to find them standing right behind me.

"Hi," I say, surprised. "I didn't see you."

"We're starting on potty training. We've spent most of the class in the little boys' room," Neil says, placing a hand on the small of his back and stretching. "Man, those potties are low."

I smile at him, feeling suddenly awkward.

"I've left you several messages," Neil says. "And I haven't heard from you, well, unless you count the thank you note. I guess I should take the hint."

Since I deleted Neil's message a couple of weeks ago, he's called me three more times, calls which, largely because of Richard, I've been too busy to return. "I'm sorry. A friend of mine had—"

"I know," Neil says. "Your friend, Ruth, mentioned it. I'm sorry about Richard. We met at Chloe's party, remember?"

I nod.

Ruth hadn't mentioned that Neil was asking about me, hardly surprising given the circumstances. Although Ruth and I had made up, we seem to have agreed tacitly not to mention Neil, and I haven't been to Gymboree since the accident. In the scope of things, the life and death matters of the last few weeks have overshadowed any potential romantic entanglements. Still, it must have been painful for Ruth to have had to field Neil's questions.

"I've been preoccupied," I tell him. "I'm sorry."

"Well, at least you were able to get those thank you notes written," Neil says, with a tight smile.

I'd written the notes while sitting at Richard's bedside waiting to see if he would ever emerge from his coma. When Eli begins tugging urgently on Neil's pant leg, he gives me a curt nod. "Excuse us," Neil says formally. "Nature calls. Again."

We avoid each other for the rest of the class.

During "The Bubble Song," I sneak little glances at Neil, who steadfastly refuses to look in our direction. Eli, who looks nothing like Neil, sits on his father's lap and rests his head on Neil's chest. Apart from noticing Eli's red hair and freckles, I hadn't really realized how little they resembled each other. How does it make Neil feel to look into his son's eyes and see his wife? Does he find it comforting or is it a constant reminder of his loss? I cannot presume to imagine which, but it makes me thankful that Chloe looks like me.

chapter 27

The primary responsibilities of a sous-chef are to anticipate the chef's needs and to do all the uninteresting tasks competently and without complaint. Richard is failing miserably. His physical therapist noted on his progress report that he needs to be using his right side more and that anything I can do to encourage him would be beneficial. So I've put him to work soaking corn husks and ripping dozens of little strands with which to tie low-fat tamales.

"I couldn't do this before my accident. What makes you think I should be able to do it now?"

"Stop complaining. If you were in my kitchen, I'd fire you."

"I am in your kitchen," Richard says petulantly. "Besides, I don't even like tamales."

"Too bad. It's what's for dinner. I've got to get this column finished, and I need to test these recipes."

He ruins the next two husks, deliberately, I suspect. His lips are set in a grim line, and his hands curl into small, loose fists as he weakly pounds the table. "Okay, okay, I think that's enough. Thanks, Richard," I tell him.

He removes his apron, dusts off his paisley bathrobe, and tries not to look smug as he wheels himself over to the window where he begins pawing through a stack of library books Fiona has brought him.

I'm just in the process of filling the last of the corn husks with the masa harina when the door buzzes. It's Ben Stemple, a tool chest in one hand and a couple of brown paper bags in the other.

"I was in the neighborhood and I remembered that I never activated the water lines on that pasta spigot. I thought I'd stop by, hook 'em up for you. I've given up on your promise to cook me dinner, so I brought my own," Ben says, depositing the two large, grease-stained paper bags on the counter. "I'm willing to share, but I'm warning you, it's not up to your standards. I got it from that little Oriental cart on Twentieth. I'm not exactly sure what it is, though. My Chinese is a little rusty. And since I had no idea what kind of wine you drink with Chinese, this is what I came up with," Ben says, pulling a six-pack of Sapporo from another brown paper bag. "I figured Japan was close enough."

He stops short when he sees Richard in his bathrobe in the wheelchair. "Oh, I didn't know you had company."

I make the introductions.

Richard sits up a little straighter in his chair, runs a hand through his wispy hair, and adjusts his paisley robe before shaking Ben's hand.

"If this is a bad time . . ." Ben says, looking from Richard to me, a puzzled expression on his face.

"No, not at all," Richard says. "Hurry up on that spigot and maybe I'll be spared the low-fat tamales."

Ben looks at me.

"No, really, it's great," I tell him. "The kitchen is a bit of a mess, but do a good job and I'll pay you in tamales."

"Deal, but you have to promise at least to try the stir-fried pigeon. It's a real delicacy, and besides, you'll be doing your part to help keep the neighborhood pest free," he says, winking at me.

After dinner, Ben does the dishes while I put Chloe to sleep in the upstairs loft. When I come downstairs, Richard is propped up in bed reading *Lord of the Flies.*

"I'd forgotten what a perfectly vile book this is," Richard calls from the living room, mid-yawn. "I can't believe they assign this book to children. It's a wonder teachers don't have more sense." He holds the book at arm's length, examining the cover.

"Where did you get that?" I ask.

"It was in the bag of books Fiona brought. I told her I wanted to read some of the classics, but I was thinking more along the lines of Henry James or Tolstoy," he says, peering at us from over the rims of his reading glasses.

Ben, who is in the midst of drying dishes, studies Richard with a slightly bemused expression. Throughout dinner, a mismatched hodgepodge of ethnic food—Mexican, Chinese, and Italian—I'd gotten the feeling he was trying to find out who Richard is.

By the time we've finished the dishes, Richard is snoring, gently riffling the pages of *Lord of the Flies,* which lies open on his chest, with each prolonged exhale. I should be working on my column, a draft of which I'd hoped to finish tonight, but when Ben pops the lids on the last two beers, I take the one he offers me and lead the way out onto the balcony.

"The tamales were great," Ben says, stepping outside. "The pigeon, not so good."

I don't have any furniture outside yet so we sit on the floor, our backs up against the wall, our feet stretched out against the railing. Ben leans over and shuts the balcony door with the toe of his work boot. "So we won't disturb your, ah, friend?" he asks, gesturing toward Richard, who is sleeping just inside the doorway.

"Richard? You won't disturb him. Not unless you're planning to release a nuclear weapon. He's a very sound sleeper," I tell him.

"Aunt Fi mentioned you've been friends for years, but is he—are you—?" He waits, hoping, I suspect, that I will fill in the blank. I don't. Ben sips his beer and peers thoughtfully at me.

"I've known Richard most of my life. He's an old friend," I tell him, smiling. I'm deliberately being evasive because I'm enjoying the fact that Ben seems to be working so hard to find out.

"Just an old friend?" Ben asks.

"He had an accident and lives alone. It's easier for him to recuperate here with me and Chloe."

"You're a really good friend," he says, moving toward me. Ben's lips are dry and warm. and his kiss is teasing, his soft lips brushing mine, then pulling away. He kisses me again, lightly, gently, burying his face in my neck and my hair, before returning to my mouth. I can taste beer, breath mints, and something deeper, sweeter, like carrots maybe, and it seems the most delicious thing I've ever tasted. I want to give in to it, to eat my fill of him. Suddenly, he breaks away, and we part, like boxers in a ring leaning back against the brick, panting.

"I'm sorry," Ben says quietly. "I've wanted to do that ever since the day I first met you. It was those damn bubbles."

Despite the fact that I've enjoyed flirting with Ben, looked forward to it, really, his kisses have taken me by surprise.

I've gone years without another man besides Jake being interested in me, and I'm flustered by the sudden attention. I'm not sure how I feel about Ben and the possibility of anything more, but I owe it to him—and myself—to try to figure it out.

"Ben, I don't know if—" The words leave my mouth reluctantly, as if I'm speaking a harsh and unfamiliar language.

When I'm unable to finish, he sighs. "Who am I kidding? I'm not in your league." His tone is nonchalant, but I can tell he's hurt. "You know I Googled you," he says, sitting back against the wall and picking up his beer.

"You did?" I ask, surprised. "Why?"

"I wanted to get the scoop on you. You know, you're not exactly forthcoming with the personal details." He looks at me, juts his head in Richard's direction, and shrugs. "Read a bunch of articles about you. Checked out Grappa. You're pretty big-time." He drains his beer and stands up. "I better get going. Gotta hit the slag heap early tomorrow. Thanks for dinner, Mira," Ben says. He offers his hand and pulls me to my feet. I'm hoping he will kiss me again, but he doesn't.

After Ben leaves, I make myself a cup of peppermint tea to try to quell the churning in my stomach. I turn on the computer and pull up the draft of the column I'd begun earlier, but it's no use. I can concentrate on only one thing, and it isn't low-fat tamales.

But, no matter how much I'd enjoyed Ben's kisses, I couldn't bear the thought of running into him at various birthday parties, holidays, and family occasions if things didn't work out between us. Because, however mismatched, the relationship between Fiona and my father seems to be thriving. Since I moved out last week, it's pretty obvious that Fiona has moved in. When we stopped over the other day, I couldn't help but notice my mother's china cabinet has been totally emptied and is now filled with Fiona's rather peculiar collection of crockery, plates, shot glasses, salt and pepper shakers, and other assorted knickknacks collected from her various travels. There's no trace at all of my mother's antique china, which I'd never really liked. Even so, it's a little hard to stomach its being replaced by a "What Happens in Vegas Stays in Vegas" commemorative nut dish.

And as if that wasn't reason enough, there's this: Despite my recent real estate purchase, I still haven't given up the thought that Chloe and I will return to New York someday. Even with overseeing Richard's recuperation, working on the column, and caring for Chloe, there's a certain restlessness I can't deny. Enid had been right; something's missing.

Earlier, Ben had said he found me by Googling me. I'm no stranger to Google, but I've never Googled myself, so before tackling my column I type in my name and hit Enter. Eighty-four hits. I click on the first one. Sure enough, there's a picture of me, a younger, fitter Mira, along with a short, and now significantly outdated, bio. There's also a picture of Grappa, taken from the street in springtime. The window boxes are in bloom. It was before we'd made much money, so I'd planted them myself. Though you can't see them in the picture, mixed in with the flowers are herbs and other edibles, thyme, rosemary, purple basil, and nasturtiums, whose cascading leaves hid tiny pockets of orange buds.

I click on the picture and peer at the screen, needing to see the pits in the front door that became more visible when I painted it with a glossy paint by mistake, and the brass kick plate I installed myself because Jake has always been hopeless with a screwdriver. I hadn't remembered those things until I looked at this photograph, and suddenly I'm afraid that I will forget them. I hadn't taken enough pictures of Grappa, and I feel grateful to have stumbled upon the gift of this outdated photo lingering in cyberspace, almost as precious as any baby picture of Chloe's.

Next, I Google Jake. There's a picture of him, a recent one. His hair is longer and swept away from his face. Underneath his bio are links to both Grappa and Il Vinaio. I click on the Il Vinaio link and find a picture of Jake and Nicola standing in an unfamiliar dining room. It looks like any of a hundred restaurants I've been to in my life, but despite the fact that I have no real connection to the space, I still feel a pang, a catch in my chest at the sight of Jake smiling into the camera, his arm resting across Nicola's shoulders. Nicola's face looks softer, rounder than I'd remembered it.

Once I start, I cannot seem to stop, Googling everyone I can think of: Richard, smiling in a yellow shirt and paisley ascot on his Web page; Dr. D-P, who, I learn, is president of her synagogue and a squash player. Even my father has a bio listing two of his most recent publications alongside a picture that looks like it could be from his high school graduation; he's still got hair and is wearing heavy black-framed glasses.

No one bothers to update a Web page with bad news. You don't fill in "I got fired" in between your job as chef de cuisine of the French Laundry and your next position as president of the Culinary Institute of America. You wait for the next best thing to happen to you before you update your Internet bio, each of us stopping at our last, best time. Ruth, Enid, Neil—all can be Googled. The only person I can think of who can't be Googled is Ben. Even Fiona, in a fuchsia sweater and matching lipstick, is smiling from the CMU Chemistry Department staff page. I try Ben, Benjamin, even the name of his plumbing company, Stemple Plumbing, but there's nothing. No record of his last, best time, and for that I envy him. He can fall asleep each night thinking maybe it hasn't happened yet.

Contorni

Now by cookery I swear,
Which doth make us whole again,
Cooks surpass all other men!

—Jean Anthelme Brillat-Savarin

chapter 28

So far, I haven't written a column that Enid hasn't edited the hell out of. I always get the food stuff right; in fact, I know much more about food than Enid does, but I'm no writer. As a result, Enid requires that I e-mail her each column several days before the actual deadline. However, because I often feel the need to challenge authority, I've taken to sending them in later and later with each passing week. I intended to e-mail it to her before I went to bed, but by the time I finished Googling everyone I could think of it was well after midnight, and within minutes I fell asleep on the couch, my laptop resting on my knees. So, when I awake to the ringing phone the following morning, a line of drool as fine as dental floss escaping from my open mouth, I know, without even having to check the caller ID, that it's Enid calling to reprimand me.

"Okay, okay, I'm hitting 'send' right now," I offer in lieu of a greeting.

"What? Mira?" asks a voice, not Enid's.

My stomach lurches, releasing a surge of bile that tastes like beer and salsa.

"Oh, shit, I didn't wake you, did I?"

"Ah, no," I say, sitting up and looking wildly around the apartment. Could I be dreaming? I crane my neck to peer behind me at the clock in the kitchen. It's barely seven o'clock in the morning.

"Jake?" I whisper.

"Yeah."

"Ah—" My mouth is open and fulminating, my brain a vacuum; nothing, not a sound, not a thought, can escape.

"I know; it's been a while. How have you been?"

I sit up and look over at Richard, who is snoring in his hospital bed by the window.

"I'm fine. We're fine," I tell him.

"Good. That's good," Jake says.

"What do you want? Is something wrong?" I ask, cutting to the chase.

"What makes you think I want something?" Jake asks. "Can't I call to see how you're doing? How Chloe's doing?" He lowers his voice to a whisper. "I know I—I missed her birthday."

"Yeah, you did."

He must have the phone jammed to his ear because I swear I can hear him swallow. "How is she?" Jake asks, his voice hollow and distant, as if we're talking on two tin cans strung together across some great divide.

"She's perfect," I say, my voice catching.

The silence on the other end of the phone feels like a black hole.

"Listen," Jake finally says, "I've got something really big on the front burner here—a real deal . . . that I thought you might want—"

"I already know you've opened a new restaurant. I read about it."

Jake pauses. I don't know if he's expecting me to congratulate him on his latest venture or what, but if that's what he's waiting for, then he can wait. I'd rather chew tacks.

"You thought I might want what?" I ask him. Coffee. I need coffee. I head into the kitchen and loudly begin scooping espresso into my *macchinetta*. Richard stirs in the corner.

"I thought you might be interested in a business proposition, that's all," Jake says.

I set the *macchinetta* on the stove, turn on the gas, and go to the refrigerator for milk.

"But you just opened another restaurant. Clearly you didn't need me," I tell him, pouring the milk into the saucepan and setting it to simmer.

"Look, Mira, we're not just talking about Il Vinaio here. That's small potatoes compared to what we're envisioning."

"We? Really. By the way, is it true you're moving from Grappa? And who's this executive chef from Vegas you're bringing in?" I demand, my voice fueled by the impending arrival of caffeine in my system.

"Who told you that?" Jake asks, instantly suspicious. "Never mind," he continues. "Just hold on and let me explain. A lot of the top guys, Batali, Keller, Lagasse, have all opened satellite places in big American restaurant markets like New York, Vegas, LA, even Orlando, all of which, I'm sure I don't have to tell you, have been tremendously successful. Look, it's not just another restaurant I'm opening, it's a whole restaurant syndicate we're talking about here. When these guys approached me—"

"Who approached you?" I ask.

"Look, they're good guys. Smart business people. And they want to talk to you."

"Me?" I ask, surprised. "Why would they want to talk to me? Who are these guys?"

"Philippe—he's the guy I tabbed to run Grappa just until I got Il Vinaio up and running—is Nicola's cousin. Used to be a banker, but he got tired of the life and moved to Vegas and apprenticed himself to Paul Bartolotta. Always wanted to cook. Anyway, he introduced me to the group. He used to work with one of the guys in the conglomerate when he was in finance," Jake says.

"Well, I have it on good authority that this guy—what's his name—Philippe isn't doing such a great job," I tell him, remembering Enid's comment several weeks ago.

Jake is silent.

"Jake, why wouldn't you let Tony run Grappa?"

"I'm getting to that," Jake sighs. "Nicola and I are in as founding investors in this restaurant syndicate, and I've offered Tony a share as well. He's in—a small share—but he's in," he says. I can hear the strike of a match as he lights a cigarette. He coughs discreetly. "Nicola wants to go back to Vegas—eventually," Jake says, quietly.

The milk, which I've been simmering on the stove, erupts in a hissing, bubbling volcano, spraying scalding liquid all over my hand. I shut off the gas and run my hand under the water, but after a few seconds, I pull it away. I *need* to feel the throbbing. I need to know this conversation is real, not part of some alternate dream universe into which I've somehow fallen.

"Look," Jake continues. "You've got the money from the buy-out, and I thought maybe you'd be getting tired of not working and might be looking for something to do. This is a fantastic investment opportunity. You won't believe the returns—"

"Why?"

"What do you mean why? I just told you it's a great return—"

"No, why are you suddenly so willing to help me?"

"Mira, I don't hate you. I never have. I have a lot of respect for you. You're a talented chef and a good businesswoman, and I want Grappa to succeed. I just wasn't ready to be..." Jake can't continue. He clears his throat and takes another long drag on his cigarette. "What you wanted me to be," he finishes quietly.

"You mean a father?"

Jake doesn't answer me.

"Jake—are you offering to give me back Grappa?" I ask.

He hesitates. "No," he finally says. "I'm offering to let you buy into the restaurant syndicate that will own Grappa and several other restaurants. We will all make far more money than just by owning Grappa alone. You and Tony, if you want, can move in and take over the management of Grappa. You'll have the autonomy to run it however you want, although technically, you will report to the syndicate—of which you will be a member. How much you buy in will determine your voting share."

"How much are we talking?" I ask.

"You have enough. Listen, these guys are in from Vegas this weekend and they'll explain all the details to you. Lay out the specs on the deal. Come to New York; meet them. See for yourself. They want to fly you out—top-notch, all expenses paid."

"Jake, it's been six months. I've started to build a life here. I've got a job and an apartment. What makes you think I can just pick up—"

"I know about your job," Jake says. "It's a waste of your talent, in my opinion. Come on; you've missed it. I know you, Mira. I can't believe you haven't," Jake croons, his voice low, teasing, taunting.

Enid had said the same thing the first time she met me. Why? Are chefs like ex-addicts who never stop craving the buzz—our need to cook advertised somehow in our faces, our bodies, like an addict's wild-eyed desperation or trembling hands? I'd told Enid then that real cooks find ways to cook. But was cooking for my family and testing recipes for the culinary neophytes of Pittsburgh enough? Not long-term. Jake is offering me another chance at Grappa. I'd be a fool not to at least hear him out, wouldn't I?

"Just promise me you won't do anything rash," Ruth says when I tell her my plan.

"Who, me?" I ask her, smiling sweetly and batting my eyelashes in her direction.

Ruth fixes me with a withering stare. "Very funny. I'm serious, Mira. Who are these investors? You don't even know who these people are."

"I promise I'll be sure to get all the details when I meet with them on Saturday, okay?" I tell her.

Ruth and I have taken Carlos and Chloe to the Children's Museum, which nobody except Chloe seems to be enjoying. Carlos has gotten himself stuck inside the yellow snake slide for easily the fifth time this morning. He gets about halfway down before he starts screaming and doesn't stop until Ruth crawls into the snake's gaping maw to retrieve him. When I suggest to Ruth that maybe we should move on to the puppet theater, she refuses.

"It's important for me to try to follow Carlos's lead," she says, before climbing back into the round yellow tube. "He needs to know that I'll respond when he needs me," she says.

"What is it with Carlos and tubes?" I ask, remembering a similar experience at Gymboree.

"Our therapist says that Carlos is trying to recreate the birth process as a way of bonding with me. Hey, speaking of therapists, have you talked this trip over with yours?"

Because I suspected she'd try to talk me out of going to New York, I'd cancelled my last appointment with Dr. D-P. "No, it really isn't that big a deal," I lie. "I'm just going for the weekend. I'll hear what they have to say, take a few notes, and tell them I'll get back to them."

"You really need to do some research first. Promise me you won't sign anything, okay?"

"I promise," I tell the yawning yellow snake, which appears to have eaten Ruth and Carlos.

I can hear Ruth slowly inching her way down the slide. She emerges with Carlos behind her, his arms wrapped around her middle, his face buried in her back. When they get to the bottom, she pulls him onto her lap and kisses the top of his head. In the last few weeks, Carlos has grown noticeably calmer, his cries less shrill, his giggles a little easier to coax. Ruth and I exchange a smile.

"So," she asks, "how was it hearing his voice? Was it weird?"

Ruth's question startles me, despite the fact that I'd been able to think of little else since Jake's phone call three days ago.

"A little, I guess."

Ruth studies me carefully. "Hmm. More than a little, I'm guessing," she tells me.

I look away, uncomfortable with the scrutiny. The truth is that after all these months of not hearing his voice or seeing him or hearing about him—or living in the city where I have to face remnants of our life together at every turn—I've gotten to the point where there are things I actually relish about no longer being with Jake. Like, going out to breakfast—which Jake hated and I loved—or being able to fold back the pages of the newspaper willy-nilly, instead of in an origami-style trifold, without inciting some exasperated comment from Jake. Small things to be sure, but still, I notice them.

And then there is Ben, who makes me laugh, who likes to eat. Who likes me.

But all of it, months of work, hundreds of therapy dollars, had seemed to evaporate at the pull of Jake's voice on the telephone.

I've arranged to meet Michael and Renata for dinner Friday night at a new Belgian bistro in Tribeca called Moulin Bruges. I arrive in New York in the late afternoon and, since I'm not due at the restaurant for a couple of hours, I drop my bags at the hotel and head downtown.

I don't know what I'm expecting, but Il Vinaio is a small and insignificant space, sandwiched between a grocery store and an Indian restaurant on Fulton Street near Dutch. From the outside at least, it seems like a poor stepsibling to the hipper, more artfully designed Grappa. There's only one small sign above the industrial-looking front door, with the name *il vinaio* in lowercase letters written in a font meant to imitate a small, neat, handwritten script. I peer inside. The place is already crowded. When a pack of brittle, stressed-out-looking financial-types rounds the corner, I allow myself to be jostled inside with them. After all, I'm considering becoming an investor. Isn't it due diligence to check it out? Also, I promised Ruth I'd do some research.

I keep my head down and my sunglasses on, thinking how much I don't want to run into Nicola—who could be here somewhere—or, for that matter, Jake, who's probably in the kitchen. I scan the room, but there's no sign of either of them. There are a couple of seats left at the bar—a glitzy brass and glass affair, an upscale, over-amped version of what you would find in a typical Italian enoteca—but I can't bring myself to sit down.

I pull the collar of my blazer up over my neck and turn to make my way back out the door. I'm not sure why, but I'd expected visiting Il Vinaio would be easier, less emotionally costly, than visiting Grappa. After all, I have no real connection to this place, which is much too glitzy on the inside for my taste anyway; it's hard, in fact, to see Jake's hand in here at all. But there's a sickening knot in my stomach. Why did I assume that wandering into Jake and Nicola's new life would be easy?

The outside air hits me in the face, a warm, heavy blast that makes me gag. I'm relieved to have escaped undetected, but my relief is short-lived as I see Jake standing across the street, trying to light a cigarette, his face angled to the side, his hand cupping the struggling flame.

I quickly turn away and walk at a good clip in the opposite direction of where I need to go, hoping Jake is too bent on lighting his cigarette to have noticed me. I cannot resist a final backwards glance as I turn the corner. Jake is standing squarely in the middle of the sidewalk, the cigarette unlit between his fingers, staring after me like he's just seen a ghost, or a mutant, or some equally improbable act of nature, something that even if it's standing right in front of him, he can't be sure he's really seen.

"Well, at least the *cagna* wasn't there," Renata says, later, at dinner. *Cagna*, loosely translated, means "bitch" in Italian. Renata, as it turns out, has her own independent reasons for not liking Nicola, which she's in the midst of enumerating. Shortly before Il Vinaio opened, Nicola abruptly switched suppliers and fired Renata, right after rejecting as unusable several cases of expensive imported olive oil, which she'd opened and claimed were rancid. (They weren't.) When Nicola refused to pay her, Renata called Jake, with whom she has done business for years and who, at one time at least, had counted her as a personal friend. He had not even returned her call.

"*Puttana!*" sings Michael, raising his glass of Belgian ale. Michael has been busy studying Italian, taking courses at the Berlitz school uptown twice a week. He and Renata are planning a trip to Italy in the fall, to meet Renata's family, and Michael wants to be able to communicate with his in-laws.

"*Is that what they are teaching you at that expensive school?*" she says to him in Italian. When Michael doesn't answer her, she rolls her eyes and gives me an exasperated look. "Besides," Renata says, raising her glass of Riesling, "a *puttana* she is not. *Puttana* is too good for the likes of her."

A *puttana* is an Italian whore, and in Italy whores have a somewhat more reputable standing than they do elsewhere. For centuries they've been glorified in both classic opera and popular song. Among their many noteworthy attributes, Italian whores are reputed to be responsible for the development of a much beloved pasta sauce, pasta puttanesca, a spicy and salty dish made with capers and anchovies. Its chief attraction, aside from its wonderful flavor, is that it can be prepared quickly—in other words, between clients.

Michael launches into a rendition of the "Drinking Song" from *La Traviata,* which he sings with wide, sweeping arm gestures, causing Renata to look around embarrassed. Michael isn't drunk, just silly, relaxed, and in a good mood. He's just landed a plum assignment, editing a book by the Berkeley cooperative responsible for improving the quality of California school lunches, which will mean lots of trips to Berkeley, several opportunities for meals at Chez Panisse, and even the prospect of a meeting with Alice Waters, who is a member of the co-op and one of Michael's idols.

"More herring, anyone?" Michael says, raising the almost empty crock of smoked herring pâté we've ordered as an appetizer with our drinks. I shake my head. My impromptu trip to Il Vinaio has put a bit of a damper on my appetite, and I've ordered only an endive salad for dinner. Renata and Michael, on the other hand, have ordered half the menu, moules marinières for Renata and roasted potato and leek soup for Michael, then carbonnade à la flamande and chicken waterzooi, which they are planning to share.

Michael and Renata fill me in on the latest New York gossip until the starters arrive. Michael tastes his soup, pronounces it excellent, and offers Renata a spoonful, which he feeds to her, delicately holding his napkin under her chin as she sips. It is the type of intimate gesture, sweet and touching, that makes me slightly squeamish to watch.

"Oh, this is wonderful. Mira, you must try some. Michael, give her a taste."

"So, Mira, what's this about a new business venture?" Michael asks, offering me some soup.

"Jake's grand plan to take over the restaurant world, you mean?" Renata pipes in. Michael shushes her.

"Well, I'm not exactly sure," I tell them, wiping a trace of soup, which happens to be delicious, from my chin. "But from what I understand, a group of investors is interested in backing Jake in a multi-venue package that would encompass Grappa, Jake's new enoteca, and a large restaurant venture in Vegas. They're looking for some additional investors and have asked me to take over Grappa."

"Wow, that's pretty impressive," Michael says, spreading some pâté on the heel of a baguette.

"Ill-advised, in my opinion," Renata says. "I always knew Jake had an egomaniacal streak."

"I don't know," I tell her. "Lots of the big-name chefs are doing it."

Michael says, "Mira's right, and every one of them has been successful. There are some unsaturated markets out there; it makes good business sense to move now, while prices are depressed. Wait too long, and you could get shut out."

"You want to know something?" Renata says, looking from me to Michael and shaking a butter knife. "Jake is not big-time."

Even though she has just finished ranting about Nicola, Renata's ire surprises me. "Since when are you so angry at Jake?" I ask.

"Mira," Renata says, ignoring my comment, "what you loved about Grappa is the intimacy, the fact that you recognize the people you're feeding. Cooking is an intimate act, or at least it should be. I shouldn't need to remind you that the notion of the chain restaurant is not Italian."

"Come on, Renata," Michael says, leaning forward and wiping the remains of his soup with another piece of baguette. "We're not necessarily talking Olive Garden here."

"Feeding people and getting rich are two different things. One is a noble calling, the other pure gluttony," Renata says.

"Look. No one is suggesting opening up an all-you-can-eat buffet. At least I don't think they are. I guess I don't really know," I tell them, remembering the arrival of the FedEx man at my door Thursday afternoon bearing a first-class ticket to New York on USAir, a voucher for a suite at the Trump Soho, and an official-looking letter from the AEL Restaurant Syndicate inviting me to a meeting on Saturday morning. Beyond that I don't know a single thing about these people, or their plans for this supposed restaurant syndicate.

"Besides, since when are getting rich and feeding people mutually exclusive?" Michael asks. "What Mira should be interested in is getting Grappa back. Everything else is incidental. If she gets rich in the process, so be it. Call it an occupational hazard."

"Amen to that," Renata says, raising her glass of Riesling. "And to our renewed business relationship," she adds, turning to me. "I hope I'm not being presumptuous, but I assume you will be needing my services once you are back in command at Grappa?" The waiter places a large plate of mussels in front of Renata, who immediately scoops a few onto my bread plate.

"Oh—of course, but wait a minute here—I'm not, I mean I haven't committed to anything yet. The meeting isn't until tomorrow. I'm not really in a position to—"

"Do me a favor," Michael interrupts. "Just let us know how the meeting goes. It's the kind of thing we might be able to throw a little capital toward, provided the returns look decent."

Renata raises her eyebrows.

"You know I've always wanted to own a restaurant," Michael says, turning sheepishly to Renata. "And besides, even you told me you thought it was a good idea."

"Maybe so, maybe in the abstract it is, but Italians don't do business with people they don't like. And I don't like Jake or that, that—*cagna*."

"Down, girl," Michael says, smiling. "I love that she's so loyal," Michael says to me, as he reaches over to pinch Renata's cheek. "But if we don't change the subject, my darling Renata will develop a good old case of *l'agita*. See," he says, winking at me and turning to Renata, "I am learning something in that expensive school."

Renata mumbles something in Italian that I don't quite catch.

"So, Mira," Michael continues, "tell us about Pittsburgh. Renata tells me you're doing some writing? I didn't know you had writing aspirations." Even though I get the sense he's just being polite, I've been dreading the question. Michael, after all, is a food editor. And because I've played up my role in the Pittsburgh newspaper world as part Bob Woodward, part Frank Bruni, I'm feeling, shall we say, a tad cornered.

"Well, it isn't real *writing*. I mean, recipes are different. It's more like just writing things *down,* if you know what I mean."

"Yeah, but still, cranking out a weekly column isn't easy." Michael gives me an admiring look, and I don't have the heart to tell him I'm really only developing and testing recipes and that, according to Enid Maxwell, I couldn't write myself out of a paper bag.

"Are you going to keep doing it after you come back here?" Renata asks.

I hadn't even thought about having to give up my column. Or where we'd live, or getting Chloe back into day care, which could take several months. I hadn't thought about a lot of things. All, it seems, I had thought about was Grappa—and Jake—and not necessarily in that order. Suddenly the room feels too warm. I pick up my water glass and drain it in a couple of long, thirsty gulps; it's instantly refilled by a hovering waiter.

"You know, there's no reason you couldn't try to get your column syndicated," Michael says later, over dessert and coffee. "In fact, I think it's a good idea. Didn't you say this editor wants you to wake up those tired Pittsburgh taste buds? Mira, most home cooks—and not just in Pittsburgh—are intimidated by things professionals take for granted. They view cooking as a necessity and a chore. Take Renata here," he says, patting her gently on the shoulder.

"Hey, what's that supposed to mean? I love to cook!" Renata says, slapping Michael's hand as he reaches for a bite of her lemon soufflé.

"Renata, my love, you are an assembler par excellence. You have impeccable food sense and you know where in New York to buy the freshest and best prepared food. In fact, no one can assemble a better meal than you. But when was the last time you actually cooked anything?"

"*Divino,*" Renata says, closing her eyes and tasting the soufflé. She drops a big spoonful onto my bread plate, resisting my half-hearted attempts to refuse. Turning to Michael, Renata says, "Why on earth would anyone cook when you can just come here and eat this?"

Michael smiles at her and says to me, "Why would anyone write anything after Hemingway, or compose a symphony after Beethoven, or paint a landscape after Turner? It isn't necessarily about doing it better. It's about *doing* it."

"Michael, that isn't what I meant. It's just, why should I slave away in the kitchen when I can just come here and pay for someone really talented to do all the work while I enjoy the results?"

"Tell her, Mira," Michael says, reaching back into Renata's dish for another taste.

I know what Michael means. If someone told me that I could travel anywhere and eat anything I wanted, choosing, if I so desired, to eat only in Michelin-rated restaurants for the rest of my life, but the price for such a gourmand's dream would be that I could never cook again, I'd turn it down without a moment's hesitation. It's about doing your best by a pile of mussels sweet from the sea, or holding a perfect tomato, warm, rosy, and smelling like summer, and knowing that there are a dozen ways that you can prepare it, each one a delicious *homage*. I look away, unable to answer Michael. Maybe it's seeing Jake again, or being back in New York, or talking food while eating a great meal with people you care about; whatever it is, it's been building since the instant I stepped off the plane at LaGuardia. Suddenly, I don't know how I have been able to resist it all these months, the raging itch to be back in a kitchen.

I shake my head and stand up. Michael and Renata, spoons poised, look up at me. "I've got to go," I tell them.

I grab my purse and deposit a kiss on each of their cheeks.

"Where are you going?" Renata calls after me.

"Michael's right. I've got to go. I'll call you tomorrow."

Before Chloe was born, Jake and I used to volunteer in a soup kitchen near St. Mark's Place in the East Village on our days off. Mostly, the food we prepared was simple stuff, making a couple hundred peanut butter sandwiches at a clip, or dumping a dozen cans or bags of stuff into a twenty-gallon soup pot, using whatever was on hand in the kitchen to feed as many people as possible. It wasn't the kind of thing that required any sort of culinary ingenuity or skill, but one look at the satisfied expressions on the faces of New York's cold, hungry, and homeless come supper time on a winter's night, and you would've thought we were Eric Ripert and Alain Ducasse dishing up *homard thermidor.*

The place is still there, and even though it's after nine, there's a line coming out the door. Despite the fact that it's June and the days have been warmish, the impending chill of a late spring evening threatens, and the place is full of people looking for a decent meal and a full stomach to help fend off the cold and the damp. It's been over a year since I've been here, but I enter through the alley door, don a stained and tattered apron, and join the volunteer cooks. "Yo, lady, long time no see," says a man wearing paper slippers, whose name is Boulie, as he raises his fist to mine.

"Hey, Bo, how are you?" I say softly, touching my knuckles to his. "What do we need?"

"I got some sammiches going on over here, and we got a big casserole over there, needs some finishing. Jump on in," Boulie tells me, wiping his hands on his apron and flashing me a smile. That's how it is here. No one ever assumes anything or expects you to show up, but there's always room for one more, and they're always glad to see you.

Tonight the kitchen crew consists of Boulie, a couple of white kids sporting dreadlocks and wearing NYU tee shirts, and an older woman named Mary, whose hair is dyed an unnatural shade of aubergine. Mary is probably pushing eighty, although she's taken some pains to conceal it. She smiles warmly at me when I show her how to chop the pile of old onions she's busy working on. The trick is, I tell her, to keep the root intact, anchor the tip of the knife on the chopping block, and move only the back end of the blade. Her mouth widens into a big, round "O" revealing no teeth, just a mouth full of tender, pink gums the color of pencil erasers.

We work more or less silently, the two young kids and Boulie moving to the steady beat of reggae music piped in through a small, cheap boom box stained and spattered with tomato sauce. I set to work chopping several heads of wilted celery. The casserole Boulie mentioned is several pounds of graying, chopped meat, browning in an ancient cast iron skillet and halfheartedly tended by one of the two boys. I sauté the mound of celery, throw in some of Mary's onions, and, a couple of carrots later, it's approaching palatable. Because little here is ever fresh, the challenge is to make something out of the donated castoffs. When I was at Grappa we, like many other successful restaurateurs, had done our part, donating bread and rolls and leftovers, things we couldn't recycle or sell, to the various soup kitchens around the city.

I wonder if Jake's kept up this practice, and if Boulie knows whether or not he has. More likely, consistent with the philosophy of never having any expectations, nobody here knows, or cares, where any of this stuff even comes from. It is a challenge to serve a meal here, but no more so, I suppose, than it is to eat it.

After a couple of hours, my legs begin to ache, unaccustomed as I've become to standing so long on my feet. The knife slips and I slice my finger, a ragged cut made worse by the dull blade. "Shit!" I cry, looking around for the nearest kitchen towel to staunch the flow of blood, but seeing nothing, shove my finger in my mouth. Boulie comes over and, laying a hand on my arm, leads me to the first aid station.

"Come on, lady, take a load off," he says, easing me into a plastic lawn chair. He dons a pair of latex gloves and crouches in front of me.

The taste of my own blood, gray and metallic, lingers in my mouth. Boulie swabs my finger with an alcohol wipe and brings it close to his face to examine the wound.

"This is some cut. On a regular person, this'd need a stitch," he says solemnly, holding my hand carefully in both of his.

Boulie takes my cut hand and gently forces it upward. "Keep it up, stop the bleeding," he says, standing to rummage in the first aid kit. "One of them butterfly bandages, that's what I'm looking for."

"What do you mean 'a regular person'?" I ask.

"You a cook," he says, opening the bandage and kneeling again at my feet. "Cooks is tough," he says, leaning close to apply the bandage to my finger. "Look at these," he says, reaching over to take both my hands in his. He turns them over and with one latex-sheathed finger traces a knife scar that runs between the thumb and forefinger of my left hand. And then, he edges the sleeve of my shirt an inch or so up my wrist, revealing the half dozen puffy red welts where I'd been spattered by the scalding milk a couple of days ago. Boulie takes off his gloves, tosses them into the wastebasket, and splays his fingers out in front of him, displaying his own large, scarred hands.

He stands and raises his apron to his face to wipe his brow. "Go on home. It's close to midnight, and you shouldn't get that finger damp. Give it a rest. Keep it up, know what I mean?" He gestures with his arm, raising it and patting the elbow.

"Thanks, Boulie," I whisper, standing on my tiptoes to kiss his cheek. "I'll see you again."

"I'll be here. As long as people keep eating, I'll keep cooking."

chapter 29

The meeting, scheduled for 10:00 a.m., is being held in a private residence at Trump Soho, just upstairs from where I'm staying. I wake early and force myself to be content with the in-room coffee service until at least seven thirty when I can reasonably call Hope. I'm hoping she will invite me over to my old apartment for coffee, but there is no answer when I call. I'm considering going out to the Beanery, or one of my other favorite breakfast haunts in the West Village, but then think better of it; I'm not sure I trust my resolve to stay away from Grappa, should I be that close, and after the pain of Il Vinaio last night, I'm not sure I'm ready. So, I order breakfast from room service and sit in bed flipping channels, munching croissants, and making crumbs all over the six hundred–thread count Frette sheets, until it's time to change into my J. Crew pant-suit and venture upstairs.

When I get off the elevator on the eleventh floor, I am immediately met by a tall blond woman wearing an expensive-looking sheath and sandals with five-inch heels the width of toothpicks. She greets me by name and ushers me through a door into a large, well-appointed living/dining suite. A long table is set with an enormous, oiled olive wood bowl filled with dozens of perfect looking green apples. A few fanned AEL brochures grace each end of the table. The sideboard is laid with a series of domed chafing dishes, cut crystal flutes, carafes of juices, and buckets of champagne. Without asking me, she pours me a glass of champagne, and then, hand poised over the selection of juices, she turns her megawatt smile my way and asks, "Bellini or Mimosa?"

Just then, the door at the far end of the room opens, and three men enter. Two men I don't know, and Jake. It hadn't occurred to me to wonder if Jake would be here—or worse, Nicola—although I suppose it should have. For a second I look around frantically, fearing she may follow him through the open door, but she doesn't. I reach for the flute. "Thanks, I'll just have it straight up," I tell her, taking the glass and downing a hefty sip as Jake and the two men advance upon me.

"Good to see you, Mira," Jake says, extending his hand and not quite meeting my eye. As I reach for his hand, Jake pulls me toward him and kisses me perfunctorily, once on each cheek. His lips feel foreign, abrasive on my face. Gone is the instant familiarity. He looks older, tired, tight around the eyes. But the oddest thing about him is the way he's dressed: pressed camel-hair trousers, a laundered white button-down, a beautiful cashmere sweater the color of a ripe cantaloupe, and a pair of well-shined Italian loafers. In fact, all three of them look as if they've stepped out of the pages of the Sunday *Times* Men's Wear section, dashingly rumpled. The Jake I know is just rumpled—hold the dashing.

"Mira, this is Marcus Drexler, head of the AEL Syndicate, and his partner, Jasper Hilliard. Marcus, Jasper, I'd like you to meet Mira Rinaldi," Jake says, "my ex-wife."

"Mira, what a pleasure. Thanks for coming," Marcus says, extending his hand. His manner is easy, as if we were meeting at a cocktail party, which, given the fact we are all holding crystal champagne flutes at ten o'clock in the morning, we might as well be. Once the introductions are complete, Marcus ushers us into the living room where he gestures for me to have a seat.

"Welcome home, Mira. I trust you were comfortable last night?"

"Yes, of course," I tell him. "Thank you."

"Nice little spread we have here, isn't it?" he asks, gesturing around me into the room. "Arthurs E. Lybrant has its accounting offices in the financial district, of course, but we actually prefer to meet with clients and potential investors here, where the atmosphere is more casual and intimate. We believe that food is a very personal issue and that each restaurant in our syndicate is a unique member of the AEL family."

Marcus then gestures to Jasper, who dims the lights and flicks a switch, which triggers the release of an overhead screen behind me. Jasper hands me a slick brochure, along with a leather portfolio containing a pad and a pen, in case, he tells me, I want to take some notes during the video.

The presentation is an expensively produced, half-hour montage with a music overlay and beautiful panoramic shots of the syndicate's various restaurant venues, only a few of which—Il Vinaio being one—are open yet. The theme, that our upscale restaurants will be successful in these exciting venues, is persuasive. I try not to sneak too many looks at Jake.

Once the video is over, Jasper appears behind me and flips through the brochure he has given me, pointing out the various restaurant "concepts," complete with floor plans, chefs' resumes, and proposed menus. It's impressive. Clearly they have been getting advice from industry professionals, people who understand Grappa's market—at least from the logistics end.

"Mira," Marcus says, standing up. "Let's sit and discuss some of the particulars over a little breakfast, shall we?" Suddenly, he is at my elbow. Jake walks ahead of him to the sideboard where he begins filling a plate.

"Please," Marcus says. "Help yourself."

"It's rather intimidating feeding chefs, you know, but we've done our best," Jasper says, with a self-deprecating smile.

And they have. Eggs Benedict, served in perfectly steamed artichoke hearts, with slices of thick-cut, grilled pancetta and a hollandaise sauce the color of a Cézanne sunrise; lush, tender strawberries with clotted cream and muscovado sugar; warm croissants; hand-cured smoked salmon; and coffee in heated mugs.

I've already eaten, but I fill a plate anyway, just to be polite. I take a seat across from Jake. I am instantly reminded of the last time I sat across from him at such a table—the day I lost Grappa. I push my plate away.

"We hope you'll have a chance to stop into Il Vinaio while you are in the city. The pictures in the video really don't do it justice," Jasper says, balancing a forkful of eggs.

I can feel Jake's eyes on me. "Great. I'll be sure to drop by," I tell him.

"Mira," Marcus begins, "I'm sure I don't have to tell you how difficult it is to run a successful restaurant these days, particularly in this challenging economy. There is an operating side to it where you and Jake are the experts—and there is also a business and marketing side. What our group does is remove the burden of business and marketing, and minimize the risks. Part of our job—what we feel we do best—is to identify the talented operations people, people like you and Jake, and make it easy for you to do what *you* do best. We organize the financial aspects. We buy restaurants, retool and reorganize, and identify potential investors, all with the goal of generating additional capital to invest in alternate ventures in untapped or unsaturated markets. Since we bought Grappa at the end of last year, its profits have increased substantially."

"Really, how interesting. I've heard—" I begin.

Jasper smiles. "I know, I know. You've seen the review in the *Times*. Look, Marcus told you part of what we do is retool and reorganize. It's a process not without its share of growing pains. The bottom line is that when you normalize the numbers by taking out the nonrecurring setup and organizational expenses, we've been able to increase Grappa's profit margin. Here," he says, opening a packet of papers in front of me. "Take a look at the normalized first-quarter earning statements; see for yourself."

I look at the highlighted portions of the spreadsheet, which shows a profit margin of forty-three percent.

"A ten-percent increase in profits in the first quarter. That's impressive," I tell him—and it is.

"And first-quarter profits, particularly in the restaurant business, are, as you know, typically the lowest, reflecting the post-holiday slump," Jake interjects.

Of course I'd known that. Who does Jake think taught him that? I stare at him, my eyes flashing. I'm also piqued because I now know where Jake got the money to buy me out.

Marcus continues. "By investing some of Grappa's capital, and with the help of some investors—Jake and Tony Marsden among them—we have managed to open Il Vinaio. And already at this juncture, we've been able to attract several additional investors, so that we envision being able to open three more restaurants within the next eighteen to twenty-four months: one in Vegas, one in Miami, and one in Napa."

The Napa Valley is the second greatest restaurant region outside Manhattan—and every American chef's dream. I'm momentarily overwhelmed with thoughts of Grappa's country home. A lovely kitchen garden overlooking a nearby vineyard, a small cooking school where I could retreat with Chloe during the winter to teach, sip wine, and pick fresh herbs.

"I can see that one got you, didn't it, Mira?" Marcus says, resting a hand lightly on my arm. "Look, what we see in Grappa and Il Vinaio is a brand, with you and Jake here as the primary concept people. By virtue of your initial investment, you will become a shareholder in the company—both as an owner and a manager at the restaurant syndicate that owns Grappa and Il Vinaio. Once we launch these other restaurants pulling on the Grappa/Il Vinaio brand, the profits will grow geometrically."

I sit back in my chair and consider Marcus, who has paused to spread some clotted cream on his croissant. He holds it aloft for a split second before popping it into his mouth, chewing with the abandon of one who enjoys his food. Where just a few months ago I'd glimpsed a life without Jake or Grappa in the nearly empty loft, I can now see myself, without the slightest effort, back here in the city. I roll the idea around, tasting it, savoring the latent burst of possibility lingering like a flavor in the back of my throat, the Napa offshoot, the cooking school Jake and I had dreamed of, my life here, in this city.

"Okay, here's the financial piece. The cash we are asking you to invest will be paid back within the first eighteen months. The financial plan calls for a cash down payment of only $72,000, plus a

$288,000 loan, for a total of $360,000. We are having a closing with the Sixth Street Bank at the end of this month. For our first-tier investors who join us now, we negotiated an interest rate of just 6.8 percent, so debt service is minimal—under $20,000 per year. Of course, we cannot make guarantees, but based on our projections, which have already been blessed by our accountants and the banks, within the first eighteen months you will have recovered your initial $72,000, plus covered initial debt service on the loan. After that, you will be getting returns on the bank's money. Assuming that you use that to pay down the principal on the bank loan, the entire loan can be paid down within four years. At which point you can sit back and reap pure profits."

Marcus is watching me intently. Slowly and delicately he removes a stray wisp of cream from the edge of his mouth and continues. "Listen, we know this is a lot to digest. Take a few days. Take a close look at the financials."

"I'm not a financial expert. I'd like to have my lawyer review them."

Marcus smiles winsomely. "We wouldn't have it any other way. Have your lawyer review everything. I'd also be happy to put him or her in touch with our financial people—the accountants who helped put this together. We think the papers speak for themselves. Just tell your lawyer not to delay. One of the reasons we flew you in on the weekend is because we've got less than two weeks left until the closing for first-tier investors, and we wanted to give you the opportunity to participate on the best possible terms.

"Of course, your investment will also yield you a voting interest. You will be in the unique position of being an owner, as well as an employee. We will of course pay you a salary as executive chef at Grappa, which should more than cover your living expenses pending the increasing returns you will enjoy as the syndicate grows. As a parent of a young child, I'm sure it will give you great comfort to know that the modest investment you make now will generate substantial returns for years to come. It could fund your daughter's college education, graduate school, a beautiful wedding—whatever the future holds." Marcus pulls out his wallet and slides over a sheaf of plastic-coated photos of three towheaded children. "I know my kids are first on my list," Marcus says.

"Mira," Jasper says, turning to me. "We are not just recruiting you to be an investor—with returns like this, recruiting investors is not our biggest challenge. We need you at the helm at Grappa. We never intended Philippe to be a long-term solution. He's a talented chef, but he doesn't represent the Grappa brand. You do, Mira. *You* are Grappa."

The meeting concludes shortly thereafter with the exchange of contact information. I've given them Jerry Fox and Avi Steiner's contact information and arranged to have the papers sent over first thing Monday morning. I've heeded Ruth's advice and agreed to nothing, other than to look at the various documents AEL has promised to send me. I make a mental note to call Jerry Fox the minute I'm alone.

"Mira, wait a minute," Jake says, stepping out to the elevators and pulling the door to the suite shut behind him. "There are some things I'd like to discuss—regarding Grappa."

"Yeah, like what?" I tell him, spinning around on my heels. Despite the headiness the offer has induced, I'm still stinging from the news that Jake sold Grappa to a third party right out from under me.

"Can we have dinner? Jasper told me you aren't leaving until Monday morning." It's true. Since Ruth, Fiona, and my dad agreed to watch Chloe and check in on Richard, I've arranged to stay in town an extra day to clean out the storage space in our old apartment.

I shake my head.

"Listen," he says, grabbing my arm. "I assume you saw the review?"

"Of course I have," I tell him, even though I hadn't. Early on in my work with Dr. D-P, she'd declared a moratorium on contact with New York, forbidding the daily monitoring of my old life, which had included reading New York newspapers and checking in regularly with Tony, Renata, and Hope.

"Jasper was right. Things aren't the same since you left. None of it is, actually," Jake says quietly. "Sunday night, the restaurant is closed. Come to Grappa. Please?"

Jake still has hold of my arm, although he has loosened his grip and allowed his hand to slide slowly down my forearm until it brushes gently against my fingers.

The touch of his skin on mine is electric. I feel as if I've been ripped loose from the shaky mooring of my life and hurled by a rapidly rising mistral into someone else's. Mine, but not mine. Since getting back here I've been looking for a foothold, something familiar to grab on to, some way to orient myself. I know I should get in a cab and head straight for LaGuardia, change my ticket, and get back to Pittsburgh.

"What time?" I ask him.

I run downstairs, change my clothes, and find the closest Internet café. I order a double latte and settle in at one of the worn wooden booths. Finally, I find it, one thin column buried deep within the Wednesday Food section several weeks back.

It's a bad review, written by a staff writer, right away a bad sign. If Frank Bruni writes you a bad review, people will still come to your restaurant, for a little while at least—if only to see if he was right. According to the reviewer, who I'd never heard of, many of the dishes seem tired, in contrast to the recently overhauled décor, which is uncharacteristically slick. The reviewer lauded the addition of a martini bar and happily noted that the wine selection also had been considerably enhanced. I am mentioned by name, a little two-sentence blurb near the end of the article: "with the departure of chef Mirabella Rinaldi, the pasta specialties have suffered mightily." The reviewer cites as evidence a gluey cream sauce and an uninspired chard-filled ravioli. While it might have been the public affirmation I was after, it still makes me sad.

I consider Jasper's comments at the meeting this morning. He said *I* am Grappa. Me, not Jake. Yet, at least at one time, we were good together. The problem is, if I come back to manage Grappa and Jake is at Il Vinaio, we will still, at least according to Marcus, be part of the same brand, which will, I imagine, entail some working together. And then there was Jake's comment as he brushed his hand against mine and invited me to dinner. What exactly had he meant that "none of it" is the same since I left? Where is Nicola in all of this? Since Renata is on the outs with both Jake and Nicola, I have no hope of getting any scoop from her, but I am not above pumping Tony for information tonight, when we meet for dinner. If anyone knows anything, he will.

On my way back to the hotel I call Jerry Fox. Of course, I get his voice mail, so I leave a message telling him to expect a package from the AEL Restaurant Syndicate on Monday morning, along with my authorization to review the materials.

Next, I call Ruth who, unlike Jerry, answers on the first ring.

"Well, how did it go?" she asks.

"Amazing, actually," I tell her. I fill Ruth in on the details of the meeting, omitting only the tidbit about my interchange with Jake. By the time I finish I'm nearly breathless. "Oh, and did I mention the Napa Valley?"

"Yes, you did."

"Do you have any idea what that means? We could join the ranks of Cyrus, Ad Hoc, the French Laundry, America's greatest restaurants!"

"That sounds like some pretty stiff competition, if you ask me," Ruth says.

"I admit it would be hard work, but people who don't call the requisite two months ahead for a reservation have to eat somewhere, don't they? If we could just get an in—"

"Mira, please tell me you didn't sign anything, did you?"

"No. A promise is a promise. But I did have the financial statements sent over to my lawyer. They've given us full access to their accounting firm and—"

"Why not let me have a look at those financial statements? In case you've forgotten I've got an MBA from Wharton, which at the moment is gathering dust. I'd love to have a look."

"Sure," I tell her, embarrassed that I hadn't thought of it before. "If you're sure you have time."

Ruth sighs heavily into the phone. "Oh, it will be a struggle, but I'll pencil you in between nuking the microwave Easy Mac and our trip to the park. You can pay me in food. Hey, I've exhausted my freezer stash and have had to resort to Lean Cuisine, which, by the way, doesn't taste as good as I remember. I think you've ruined me," she laughs.

"Don't worry. Help is on the way. I'll be home on Monday."

Ruth fills me in on Chloe and Richard, and I promise to call Marcus right away to arrange for Ruth to receive a copy of the financial statements. We're about to hang up when Ruth says, "Look, Mira, I know this is exciting, but just—" She hesitates.

"What?"

"Be careful, okay?" Ruth finally says.

"Of course, I'll be careful," I tell her. "But this is a once in a lifetime opportunity. I'd be investing only a portion of what I got out of Grappa, but I'd be an owner again, and the returns would be more than I've ever made before. They also promised me a creative say in the restaurant syndicate. That they have the confidence in us is pretty incredible. We could be the next Jean Georges—it's almost too good to be true."

"Yeah, that's what I'm afraid of," Ruth says.

I've arranged to meet Tony for dinner at the Blue Ribbon restaurant after he gets off work, around midnight. Once I decided to come to New York and hear out Jake's investors, I called Tony, who confirmed that he'd been in touch with the AEL syndicate and told me that I'd be crazy not to jump on the next plane and sign on the dotted line.

"They're offering you Grappa on a silver platter, Mira. What the hell are you waiting for?" Tony asked.

From the inside, the Blue Ribbon looks like any of a hundred other dimly lit restaurants in Manhattan, but what makes it unique is the line that begins to form after midnight, often snaking all the way around the corner onto Spring Street. It isn't a fancy place, but the food, although simple in concept, is innovative: tender veal meat loaf, celeriac mashed potatoes, lobster mac and cheese. It may not be the only place you can go in New York City to eat cheese fondue at four in the morning, but it is the best. Although it's usually full throughout the evening, it doesn't really get lively until well after midnight when, after the close of dinner service most everywhere else, New York's chefs go out to eat.

Jake and I got into the habit of coming here at least once a week when we first lived in the city, before we opened Grappa. It was the mid-nineties, and a young Mario Batali, the West Village's rash and innovative chef, commanded a large table in the back, often buying out the entire raw bar and threatening to drain the wine cellar dry. Jake and I often waited in line an hour or more for one of the white linen-covered tables, dreaming of the day when we would be invited to join New York's cooking legends for a raucous, candlelit supper. Even after Mario and his crowd stopped coming, Jake and I would still sometimes go, take a seat at the bar, and share a dozen blue point oysters and a bottle of wine.

Tonight, because I've gotten here early—just a little after midnight—I've been able to secure a plum table in the back. I order myself a glass of Gewürztraminer, thinking, as the bright-eyed waiter takes my order, what strange lives chefs lead. By necessity and for convenience, most of your friends are chefs. Who else besides another chef would want to share a four-course meal with you at two in the morning? It isn't that chefs are inherently more fun than nurses, or pharmacists, or off-duty cops, or other people who work night shifts. It's just that often what you want to talk about is food. Odd perhaps, that after putting in a twelve-hour day surrounded by the stuff, you still want to talk about it, your ideas for reviving a tired sherry reduction, or a particularly innovative use of foie gras. No one besides another chef wants to do that in the middle of the night.

A few minutes after I arrive, Tony comes in. He looks exactly the same as last time I saw him, the same leather bomber jacket, the same white chef's tunic, the same shaved head, glossy and brown as a freshly baked brioche. Tony greets the bartender, a short, well-muscled guy named Bob, who gestures toward my table in the back.

"Hey," Tony says, depositing his knife satchel on the extra chair and approaching my side of the table to envelop me in a hug. He smells of sweat and food, of tobacco and browning onions and fried things.

"You look great," Tony says, pulling away and studying my face.

"Thanks. You too," I tell him, giving his thick arm a squeeze.

Tony waves away the menu the waiter offers him. "I want a steak, bloody, an order of fried leeks, and the blue cheese mashed potatoes," Tony tells him. "A glass of Cab with dinner and a double Grey Goose martini as fast as Bob over there can make it."

"Tough day?" I ask him.

"Aren't they all?" says Tony.

Over his martini, Tony fills me in. He's been working under Philippe, who, in Tony's opinion, is a competent cook, but will never be a chef. "Wouldn't recognize a creative spin if it bit him on the ass. You know the kind," Tony says, taking a hefty gulp of his drink.

I do. Jake and I had worked for plenty of them in our time. But, given the mediocre review in the *Times*, and what I'm sure is Tony's accurate assessment of Philippe's stewardship in the kitchen, how is it that profits are up ten percent? Something doesn't quite add up.

"So," I ask. "What gives?"

Tony shakes his head. "Seriously, Mira, these guys may be fucking geniuses. First, they've replaced some—make that all—of the expensive suppliers. I assume you've heard about Renata, right?"

I nod.

"Eddie, too. But that's only part of it. They've cut staff and pay, considerably beefed up the wine list, and added a froufrou martini bar. The markup on the wine is huge, and the martinis are exotic, interesting, and expensive. Suffice it to say, we are attracting a slightly different type of clientele. But we're still crowded every night and booked a couple weeks out on the weekend. We are making more money than we did this time last year, so it's not all bad, you know?"

Not all bad? Even though Marcus and Jasper had mentioned making changes, I hadn't really focused on precisely how those changes impacted Grappa. "Tony, how is any of that good? People can get good booze anywhere in this city!"

Tony holds up his hands in mock surrender. "I know, I know," he says. "Obviously, the downside is that, if steps aren't taken to address the drop off in food quality, we may be living on borrowed time. Which reminds me, I brought you a present," Tony says, his eyes flashing mischievously. He reaches over to rummage through his knife case and pulls out a small Styrofoam container. "Here you go. *Buon appetito,*" he says, smiling. I open the container. Inside is a small portion of gluey-looking gnocchi and a handful of limp morels. "I figured if you were having any doubts about coming back, this would put you over the top."

I spear a a piece of gnocchi, which offers more resistance than it should. Right away I can tell, without even tasting it, that it will be too tough. "The dough's been overworked," I tell him, laying the untouched pasta on the edge of my bread plate. Tony picks up another from the container with his fingers and pops it into his mouth.

"Yeah, and the flavoring is too overpowering. The morels are completely lost. It's crap," Tony says. "Yes, I like the restaurant syndicate concept, and the numbers are pretty hard to ignore. But in terms of maintaining Grappa's quality, we need you back soon. You're right; people can get good booze anywhere, and sooner or later they are going to realize that the food is no longer great. It's already started. Some of our longtime customers are coming around less frequently. But, if you come back soon, we can turn it around. Speaking of good booze . . ." Tony drains the rest of his martini. He turns around and waves a finger in Bob's direction. "Look, I had my lawyer review the papers from AEL. He says everything looks kosher. I've already put in about half of my sabbatical fund at this point, and I'm planning to invest the rest, but only if you're in, too. What do you say? When are you moving back?"

I hesitate. There is still so much I have to figure out. I want to ask Tony about Jake and Nicola, but I don't quite know how. Luckily, Tony anticipates my question.

"Jake's pretty much full-time at Il Vinaio. He's hardly ever at Grappa now, you know," he says. "With the pay cuts, there's been a lot of staff turnover as well. Freddo's long gone. Zoe, too," Tony says, shaking his head.

"Zoe? We hired her right out of cooking school! She was there six years." Zoe was one of the line cooks at Grappa, a tall, healthy-looking kid from the Midwest who worked the grill. Her kind of loyalty, not to mention longevity, was a rare thing in the restaurant business. I'd had a run-in with her shortly before I left the city. It was on one of the last days I'd worked. I was tired and stressed, and I can't even remember what it was about; I just remember yelling at her, as she stood, towering over me, struggling not to cry.

Tony shrugs.

"What happened?" I ask, taking a bite out of the shaved artichoke and Pecorino salad the waiter has just set down in front of me.

For some reason, my question has surprised Tony, and he shifts uncomfortably in his seat. Just as I think he's finally about to answer me, the waiter brings his steak and sets it in front of him. Tony leans back and allows the waiter to rearrange our table to accommodate the huge plate. At first, I think he's just being circumspect. The New York culinary world is a notoriously gossipy one, and I assume he doesn't want the waiter to hear what he's about to say. But after the waiter leaves Tony cuts a piece of his steak and spears it with his fork. He raises it midway to his mouth where it remains, poised in midair, dripping blood.

He still doesn't say anything.

"What happened, Tony?"

"Nicola made her life a living hell. That's what," Tony says quietly.

"Why?"

"I swear I thought you knew. I figured Renata would have told you."

"Knew what?"

Tony exhales, a slow, painful-sounding wheeze. "About Zoe and Jake."

I stare at Tony, not really understanding.

"What about Zoe and Jake?"

Tony lays down his knife and fork, carefully arranging them on his plate before answering me. He does not meet my eye. "They had a thing a few months back," he says.

The waitress sets down Tony's second martini, and I take a sip, welcoming the burn in my throat as I digest this fascinating morsel.

Six months ago, five—hell, maybe even two months ago news like this would have filled me with hope. Now, I'm not sure what to feel.

"It was when Nicola was away. In Vegas." Tony says.

"What happened?"

Tony stops eating, his knife and fork poised limply over his dish. He drops his utensils and pushes his plate away.

"Jesus, what does Jake have that I don't have, you know? Women going wild over this guy, I just don't get it, but whatever. Nicola's back about fifteen minutes before she figures it out. Big showdown in the kitchen. Right in the middle of service she tells Zoe to pack up and get the hell out. Zoe looks at Jake, who just stands there, his mouth hanging open like a fucking steamed clam. Zoe yells back that she isn't going anywhere; she'll sue their asses if they fire her. Then, Nicola drags the both of them back into the office, and they're in there for about a half hour—completely quiet— while we're down two cooks and the rest of us are trying to keep the line moving. It was a hell of a night. Next thing you know," Tony says, picking up his fork and knife, "Zoe's gone, Marcus and Jasper show up, and plans for Il Vinaio are spread out all over the back room."

"Where did Zoe go?"

"I heard she went back to Chicago—probably with a nice severance package."

"So are they . . . okay, Jake and Nicola?"

It's the first time I've said her name, and I can't help wincing. Tony watches me carefully. Finally, he shrugs. "I don't know, Mira. Like I said, Jake isn't around much. Both of them are at Il Vinaio most of the time now." Tony leans forward and lays a beefy hand on mine. "Look, Jake doesn't have a clue how to fix Grappa, Mira. You do. Forget about him. He's not in your league anymore. Never was, in my opinion." Tony wipes his mouth delicately and deposits his napkin on the table as he turns and signals for the check.

"Come back, Mira," Tony says.

"I'm thinking about it, Tony."

chapter 30

I spend a good chunk of Sunday afternoon going through my storage space in the basement of my old apartment building on Perry Street. Most of it is stuff that I never should have saved in the first place: boxes of old cooking magazines, irrelevant now that everything is available online; mismatched mugs and dishes; two broken vacuums; and a wardrobe of size four jeans that will never be worn by me again in this lifetime.

There's also a ton of Jake's stuff.

After the police had carted me away in handcuffs the night I discovered them *in flagrante*, Jake had come home and packed a single duffle bag of clothes before moving in with Nicola. At some point, I'd expected him to ask me for something, anything—his electric toothbrush, a razor, his fleece slippers when the weather turned cold—but he never did. Apparently, anything that had been in our apartment and shared by me was tainted and needed to be abandoned posthaste, like nuclear waste or anthrax-tainted stationery.

When I finally realized Jake wasn't coming back, I'd packed up every trace of him, his books, tools, high school yearbook, childhood photos, the boutonniere from his senior prom (he'd taken Lindsay, a mousy blonde), even his high school track jersey, half intending to put it out on the curb with the trash, but I never had the guts to follow through. At the time, the fact that he could walk away from years of accumulated memories both amazed and horrified me, but now, knee-deep in the murky basement, where, in the pauses in my work, I think I hear ominous scurrying coming from the deep recesses of the storage unit, abandonment definitely seems like the better part of valor.

Hope invites me in for coffee around two o'clock and offers me a sandwich—bologna and cheese, which I thought nobody ate anymore—and I eat it sitting at my own dining table, which Hope has covered with a red and white plastic-coated picnic cloth. In all the disruption surrounding Richard's accident, I'd never arranged to have it shipped.

"I suppose you're going to want this back," she sighs, lifting the corner of the tablecloth to reveal a provocative flash of sleek, walnut table leg. I've just finished telling her about my meeting with AEL and the likelihood that Chloe and I will be moving back soon. Understandably, she's skittish about my being back in the apartment; I know she's afraid I'm going to want to cancel our sublet agreement.

"I'm not sure," I tell her. "You can keep it for a while."

"My subletters can't move out before the end of the summer," she finally says, offering me a plate of fudge stripe cookies.

"I know," I tell her.

After lunch I cart the boxes to the dumpster in the alleyway. I've saved only the two boxes of Jake's stuff and one box of old *Gourmet* magazines, thinking they might be collector's items one day. I'll tell Jake tonight that he has one last chance to reclaim his memories or they will be gone with the next trash. I take the stairs, trudging up the four flights to place the key into Hope's itching palm. "Here," I tell her, taking her hand and closing it tightly around the key. "It's yours. Stay as long as you like," and for the first time all day, Hope's face relaxes into a smile.

And I mean it. Chloe and I will find a new place to live. A pretty, light-filled apartment in a different neighborhood, a place to make a fresh start. Together, Chloe and I will find a new favorite coffee bar, a dry cleaner, a grocery store, and especially a happy day care center. I haven't accumulated too much in Pittsburgh; other than the apartment, which shouldn't be too hard to sell now that all the other units are taken, there really isn't much to tie me there. My dad can visit of course, and soon Richard will be mobile again, back to his own house and his work. For the first time, I understand something like the sense of freedom Jake must have felt at walking away from everything—voluntarily—and starting over.

I take my time heading back to the hotel, winding in and out of the streets of the West Village, scoping apartments, writing down the phone numbers of rental agencies, and taking notes on which sections to avoid. The phone rings in my bag. It's Ruth.

"Hey. Everything okay?"

"Where are you? Didn't you get our message? Can you believe it?"

"What message?" I look down at my phone and see the tiny sealed envelope icon on the bottom of the screen. "I was in the basement all afternoon. No cell reception. I haven't listened to it yet," I tell her.

"Big news. Fiona and your dad brought Chinese over to your apartment for lunch, you know, to keep Richard company, and when I dropped Chloe off there, they invited me to stay. So, we're all sitting around eating, and Carlos and Chloe are playing on the floor, and suddenly Chloe pulls herself up on the coffee table, grabs a fortune cookie, and *walks* back over to Carlos. She took like, five steps all by herself, until she noticed we were all staring, at which point she fell down, crushed the fortune cookie, and started crying. But hey, she's officially taken her first steps! Go, Chloe!"

I stop short in the middle of Christopher Street, stunned. Chloe had taken her first unaided steps, and I had missed them. I'd worried about her being late to walk, had trekked untold miles with my fingers caught in her tightfisted embrace. But whenever she sensed I'd been about to disengage myself, she'd tightened her grasp, pulling me closer, lower, nearer to her. Now she's done it. And I missed it.

I can picture them all sitting in my living room watching her. Did Chloe look around for me? Did she wonder where I am?

"Oh, shit," Ruth finally says. "Mira, I'm so sorry. We called you right away and left a message. I can't believe I've been so insensitive," she sighs. "I guess it's just that I've had to reconcile myself to the fact that Carlos sat up and rolled over and got his first tooth before I adopted him, and maybe I've conditioned myself into believing it's not that big a deal. I'm so sorry. I didn't mean to upset—"

"No, no, it's okay. Go, Chloe! Plus, I love the fact that she was going after a fortune cookie," I tell her, but my voice breaks, and I know Ruth is not convinced. Neither of us is.

"Okay, no more walking until you get home. I will glue her booties to the floor if I have to," Ruth says.

I hang up and then listen to the message, which is from all of them—Fiona, Richard, my dad, Ruth, Carlos screeching in the background. Richard tells me not to worry, he's managed to capture it on video with his phone. Fiona adds that she's going to buy Chloe her first pair of dancing shoes, and I can tell from her breathless voice and Chloe's muffled giggles that she's dancing with her around the apartment. Then, she presses the phone to Chloe's ear and says, "Tell Mama hello," and Chloe, expecting to hear my voice, coos expectantly into the other end. Poor Chloe, who will now have to get used to my not being there for ballet recitals, school plays, orthodontist appointments, and teacher conferences because I'm too busy managing my restaurant empire.

I'm not due at Grappa until eight, so on my way back to the hotel I stop at the grocery store and buy a half bottle of wine. I intend to soak away the afternoon of grime I've accumulated, not to mention the heaps of maternal guilt, while sipping a glass of wine in the tub. I'm also hoping it will relax me. I'm nervous about tonight. Not just about being alone with Jake, but about being at Grappa. I haven't set foot in there since Jerry escorted me out the back door and drove me to the courthouse to turn myself in. I wonder if it's possible to have some sort of post-traumatic stress reaction the instant I set foot in the place. What if I start foaming at the mouth or writhing in psychic agony?

I take a deep breath and swallow, remembering all at once something that Dr. D-P told me early on in our therapy. It was after I first saw the blurb in *Bon Appétit* about Il Vinaio, and Dr. D-P had coached me through the exercise in the bathroom mirror. At our next session, she'd suggested that whenever I found myself in a tight spot emotionally, I should try to consider myself "an anthropologist on Mars."

"A what?" I'd asked her.

"An anthropologist is a person—"

"I know what an anthropologist is."

She looked at me like she was considering asking me for a definition.

"What's your boss's name again?" she asked, trying another tack.

"You mean Enid Maxwell?"

"Yes, Enid. Pretend you're writing a report of what you're observing, editing out all the extraneous details. Just give her the facts, not the emotions. I think you'll find it a useful technique for helping to keep your feelings under control in difficult situations."

So, I practice all the way to Grappa, taking note of the precise hue of the yellow cabs, which really are more orange than yellow, the bent street sign at the corner of Leroy Street, the man dressed in a clown suit swinging an expensive briefcase, his cell phone pressed to his ear.

I stop short on the corner of Bedford and Grove. From here I can see Grappa, which is in the middle of the block. The black and white awning looks freshly scrubbed, and pots of blooming hibiscus trees flank the front door, which, as I move cautiously closer, I see has been replaced; the worn wooden one I'd painted with glossy paint by mistake has given way to a deeply stained chestnut one. The restaurant looks dark. I linger at the top of the steps, gathering the courage to venture down the three steps and try the front door.

Jake must have come up through the alley, because suddenly he is behind me. I can feel him even before he speaks; the hair at the back of my neck prickles as I catch the familiar scent of his cologne. I turn around, and there he is, dressed in jeans and a blue button-down shirt that looks as if he's napped in it, an apron slung low on his hips.

"Around back," he says, smiling at me. I follow him down the alley, where he pulls out a key dangling from a chain underneath his apron, and watch as he unlocks Grappa's back door. He holds it open for me and allows me to enter first. I walk past the office, which mercifully is dark, and down the hallway, pausing just at the entrance to the kitchen. The summer sun, on the verge of setting, casts ribbons of golden light through the wrought iron bars on the half-windows, bathing the kitchen in a luminous glow. Apart from that, it looks almost exactly the same as it did on the day I left.

"Philippe and his crew left things more or less the same in here," Jake says, taking my sweater and hanging it on top of his jacket on the hook by the door. "The dining room, not so much. You won't like it. That's why we came in through the back," he tells me, simply.

"I know," I whisper. "I've seen it. On the Web site." Jake nods.

He places a light hand on my arm as he moves past me into the kitchen.

Jake has set the corner of the workstation with a crisp white cloth and two tall candlesticks, a small vase of tulips between them.

"Prosecco?" he asks. I'm about to decline; after all, this is supposed to be a business meeting, not to mention the fact that I've already drunk a half bottle of wine in the tub. But before I can even answer, Jake opens the walk-in, pulls out an already opened bottle of Prosecco, and pours two glasses. He hands me one. "Mind if I put you to work?" he asks.

"Not a bit," I tell him, grateful for something to do.

He smiles at me. "Okay, how about a salad?" Without even thinking about it, I reach to pluck a head of garlic from the braid by the prep station, the small whisk from the jar of utensils by the grill, and next to it, the salt box, everything, incredibly, exactly where I'd left it.

I whisk the vinaigrette together in the bottom of the wooden salad bowl, top it with assorted greens from the walk-in, and shave a few shards of Parmigiano-Reggiano over the top.

I turn around, but Jake's gone. I hear him in the office, and seconds later, the opening bars to *Gianni Schicchi* begin filtering through the sound system; on his way back in, he stops to check something in the oven. "Okay, what next?" I ask.

"Nothing. Everything else is done. I'm just finishing," he says, busying himself at the pasta station, where he unveils two perfect mounds of pizza dough resting on the marble block.

"Demeter's breasts," Jake says with a wicked grin. He raises his glass of Prosecco. "To Demeter, goddess of grain. No, seriously," he says. "To a fruitful and successful partnership. Thanks for coming, Mira," he adds, softly. I raise my glass and take a seat across from Jake at the pastry station. I watch as he takes one of the two mounds and caresses it into a perfect round pizza with nothing more than a couple of flicks of his wrists. I do my best to conjure Dr. D-P's anthropologist, but she is no longer on Mars; she is right here in this kitchen, watching, mesmerized as the muscles twitch beneath Jake's shirt, the bones of his wrists rotate smoothly in their sockets. He slips the dough onto a peel and slides it into the pizza oven.

With the slam of the oven door, the reverie is broken. I suddenly wish I'd kept my last appointment with Dr. D-P. How foolish not to have told her I was going, not to have left a lifeline, a trail of psychic breadcrumbs back to the land of rationality. I've left myself with little choice; I'm on my own.

"So," I say, while Jake busies himself with preparing topping for the pizza. "Interesting meeting yesterday."

"I thought you'd think so," he says. "I assume you're in?"

"Probably. I want my lawyer to look things over first, and assuming everything checks out, we'll send over an addendum to the proposal."

Jake looks up, his hand poised over some fresh arugula. "What kind of addendum?" he asks.

I shrug. "Hopefully, it won't rock the boat, but if I'm going to take creative control over Grappa, I need to know that I'll have the freedom to make the kind of decisions I need to."

Jake takes the warm pizza from the oven, spreads it with a wedge of softened, oozing Taleggio, scatters a few slices of fresh apricot, some prosciutto, and a handful of the arugula over the top. He anoints it with olive oil and a squeeze of fresh lemon. The combination is one of my recipes, and it's been a seasonal favorite at the restaurant for years. I wonder if Jake even remembers it's mine. He picks up his wine and the pizza, and we take our seats at the table.

"Bravo! This looks beautiful," I tell him as he places the pizza onto my plate.

"They won't be into redecorating. I can tell you that right now," Jake says, frowning.

"That's okay. The dining room is fine the way it is. I'm talking about staffing, purchasing, choosing suppliers."

"I know you're talking about Brussani Imports, but there are some things you should know—" Jake begins.

"Look, it's not just Renata, and I haven't made up my mind about anything yet. AEL has promised me creative control of Grappa, and I need to know I'll have the power to make decisions that I think are in Grappa's best interests. That's all."

Jake pauses and then nods slowly. "Good idea," he finally says. We eat in silence for a minute or two.

"I was cleaning out the storage unit at Perry Street, and I found a couple of boxes of your things. Do you want to come and get them?" I ask.

Jake looks up at me, surprised. "What? Oh, sure. Thanks for saving them," he says.

"No problem."

Jake leans his forearms on the table as if he's about to say something.

"So?" I ask.

"So what?" Jake says.

"What else do you want to talk about?" I ask. "You said yesterday you had some things you wanted to discuss."

Jake picks up his wineglass and pushes his wooden bar stool back a couple of inches. "Remember when we took that trip to Puglia?"

He knows that I do. We'd gone for our anniversary a few years ago. We had stayed on the top floor of a small hotel impossibly cantilevered over an expanse of rocky shore. We'd eaten burrata, a Pugliese specialty, every morning for breakfast, with a slab of bread—arguably the best in Italy, still warm from baking overnight in the dying embers of the ancient stone oven. The cheese would arrive each morning on a tray outside our room, still warm, and wrapped in the customary thick blade of grass, swollen like a ripe piece of fruit. I can remember the sun-dappled roof tiles outside our private terrace, where we'd made love in broad daylight overlooking the Adriatic Sea, licking the thick cream from each other's lips.

My mouth is suddenly dry. I reach for my wine, nodding, I hope not too vigorously.

"Do you remember Silvano's?" he asks.

"Of course, I do," I tell him. We'd eaten at Silvano's three times in our weeklong stay there. Usually, when we traveled we tried never to eat at the same restaurant twice, but we'd met Silvano on one of our first mornings in Polignano a Mare. He was picking mussels from the sea floor at low tide on the beach near our hotel. Jake and I stopped to watch him, and after a while we got to talking. We told him we were chefs on holiday. He told us he owned a tiny restaurant a quarter mile or so up the beach, and he invited us to come for lunch. By the end of the meal we were in the kitchen helping him prep for dinner. He did everything himself, from the cooking to the dishes, relishing all the tasks with the intensity of a person who is uniquely content with his life. We'd enjoyed his company and his food so much we kept going back.

"I was thinking," Jake continues, "about the concept of a cooking holiday. Not just a cooking school, but an actual working restaurant, where people come to work for an afternoon, an evening, even a week."

It's an interesting idea, but an impractical one. When I tell him so, he shrugs.

"Some people are fascinated by what we do, and I bet we could get them to pay big bucks for the chance to walk in our shoes for an afternoon. I think it might be an interesting idea for a television series, actually. Didn't you ever fancy yourself a star?" he quips.

"No!" I tell him, shocked at the suggestion. He laughs, and I finally figure out he's been teasing me. "Well, maybe," I say, smiling.

Jake reaches across the table and picks up my hand, tracing his finger over the butterfly bandage Boulie placed there a couple of days ago. "What happened?" he asks. The gesture surprises me, but the roughness of his calloused hands is familiar, exciting.

"Nothing, just a cut," I tell him, gently extricating my hand from his grasp.

"Don't move," he says, getting up from the table and crossing the kitchen. He hefts a large cast iron pot from the oven. He lifts the lid, cups his hand, and wafts the steam upward toward his face.

Even from across the room, the smell makes me want to swoon. Jake has made my favorite dish—his signature take on cassoulet, made with wild boar sausage braised in Barolo, cannellini beans, fennel, and sweet red peppers. I can hear the hollow snap as he breaks the delicate crust of toasted bread, garlic, and grated Parmigiano-Reggiano. He fills a shallow bowl and places it reverently in front of me.

"It's not exactly summer fare, but I know it's your favorite. I missed making it for you this winter. It actually works nicely with your pizza recipe, which has always been one of *my* favorites. We make a pretty good team, don't you think?" he says softly. "Go ahead, taste it."

"Aren't you going to join me?"

"Of course," he says, raising his eyes to meet mine. I watch as he fills his plate, picks up a bottle of wine and two glasses, and joins me at the table.

He pours us each a glass of red wine. "Well?" he asks, his eyes focused, unblinking, on my face.

I spear a piece of meat, which yields easily to my fork, and raise it to my lips. I take a deep breath and close my eyes. I give Dr. D-P's anthropologist one last desperate try, but all I can taste is Jake. The flavors are at once complex and earthy. I taste every ingredient: the thick, slightly gamy taste of the boar; the subtle undercurrent of the fennel, which, when braised, releases a delicate licorice perfume; the gentle creaminess of the beans; the smoky heat of the roasted peppers; the harmonious balance of the wine.

It tastes like love.

I open my eyes slowly. Jake is still watching me. I look away, embarrassed, shamed at what I've allowed him to witness.

"I'm not sure anyone appreciates my cooking quite like you," Jake says, his voice thick and low.

Suddenly, he's at my side. He pulls me to my feet, presses me to him, and kisses me, a deep, rich, extravagant kiss that reminds me of a bowl of late summer raspberries, warm, tender, lush, and tart. I can feel how aroused he is. He pulls my shirt free from my jeans and runs his hands across my bare back, pressing me into the corner of the counter. The pain is exquisite.

Just then a phone rings somewhere, the ringtone, Wagner's "Ride of the Valkyries." Jake's. And mine, although Jake probably doesn't know that. Months ago, in a fit of longing, I changed my ringtone to match his and never bothered to change it back. Jake pulls away, panting. His eyes flit to the hallway where our coats hang on hooks. He looks at me, looks away again. I pull myself up, run a hand through my rumpled hair.

"Hold that thought," he says, scurrying over to the hallway to fish his phone from his coat pocket. I reach for my wineglass and take a long, luxurious sip, but the wine lodges uncomfortably in my throat. I finally swallow, not because I want to, but because I need to remind myself exactly how bitter it tastes. The last time I tasted it was here, in this kitchen, almost a year ago. I grab the bottle and confirm what I already know. 1999 Tenuta dell'Ornellaia Masseto Toscano.

"Sorry, I missed it, and they didn't leave a message," he says, frowning. "Now, where were we?" he says, reaching for me again.

I drain the wine. "Nowhere," I whisper. "That's where we are, Jake. We are nowhere." It isn't until I say the words that I realize I actually mean them. It's like putting on a pair of eyeglasses you thought you didn't need. Suddenly, I'm calm, and like that anthropologist Dr. D-P had rattled on about, preternaturally tuned into the most insignificant details. Like the stain on Jake's apron that looks like the state of Florida, the pack of Merits in the front pocket of his shirt I hadn't noticed before, the wistful look in his tired eyes. "I'm sorry," I tell him. "I can't." He grabs my wrist, presses my palm to his mouth, and kisses it. I pull my hand back and turn abruptly.

Partly, it's the wine, but mostly it's the way Jake's body had tensed the instant the phone began to ring. I know, without Jake's having to tell me, that he isn't finished with Nicola—not nearly—and I can't see myself dodging phone calls, meeting clandestinely, being another in a long line of women wooed by Jake and his bag of recycled tricks.

I pick up my sweater on the way out the door. *Don't turn around,* I repeat until I'm safely out of the alley and onto Grove Street.

Regrets? A few, but the biggest one is that I didn't get to finish the cassoulet.

Dolce

I've set the board: henceforth 'tis yours to eat.
—Dante, *The Divine Comedy*

chapter 31

The great gourmand, Auguste Escoffier, once said, "Good cooking is the essence of true happiness." Did he mean that happiness is to be found in the act of cooking? Or in the appreciation of the result? If the former, it should follow that all good cooks are happy. But most of us aren't, at least the ones I've known. Most of the cooks I know are looking for something. The lucky ones, people like Boulie and Silvano, seem to have found it, while the rest of us soldier on, searching for love, or adulation, or affirmation, gathering scraps wherever we can find them.

Maybe what Escoffier meant was that true happiness is to be found in one's ability to satisfy a basic human need so spectacularly. Those of us content to take our happiness secondhand cook because what we want, what we crave, is to be needed. Nurturers extraordinaire, brokers of comfort, we hope to turn the tables on our own needs by filling the stomachs and souls of the world.

Jake had needed me. Maybe that was what I loved about him. We'd been companionable, compatible, in small ways; our dreams, professional at least, had been shared. Perhaps he even loved me, insofar as he was capable of loving, but I suspect what he really loved about me was my caring for him completely, loving him to the exclusion of everything else. Until Grappa; and until Chloe.

One thing I know for sure—Jake's infidelity won't end with Nicola and Zoe.

Some men are just built that way, I guess. It should give me some satisfaction, but it doesn't. It no longer even makes me angry. When I examine just what's worth salvaging from my life in New York, what I keep coming back to is Grappa, some reminder of the reason I became a cook in the first place. That, and Chloe, should be all I need.

Arriving home, I find that Richard has covered one wall of the apartment with irregularly shaped splotches of yellow. At least a dozen different shades, beautiful, rich hues—the deep golden of a mellow aged Gouda, the color of burnished wheat on an autumn afternoon. And not the whole wall, just a small section, maybe four feet square. Some of the splotches look like he has just waved the brush back and forth a couple of times, and one of them, the last one in the row, is just a single stroke of ochre, barely the width of the paintbrush. He's dumped the brushes in the kitchen sink without rinsing them and is lying on his bed in a paint-spattered sweatshirt, sound asleep with his shoes still on. He looks still and peaceful, his fingers interlaced, the tops of his knuckles smudged with paint.

He stirs as I remove his shoes. "Welcome home," Richard says, his voice raspy with sleep.

"Looks like you've been busy," I say, nodding toward the wall.

"I remembered you said you always wanted to live in a yellow house," he says, taking my hand. "Do you like it?"

I do, and the fact that Richard remembered this touches me. I put my arms around him and lay my head on his chest. "I love it. Yellow is a happy color, don't you think?"

"Yes, and there are many shades of happiness. You can take your pick," he says, sitting up and gesturing toward the wall.

"Looks like we've got plenty to choose from," I tell him.

"It's a miracle I was able to get anything done, what with the parade of hovering visitors you lined up to save me from myself," he says.

"I didn't want you to be lonely."

"Lonely would have been a luxury," Richard says, smiling.

"Hungry?" I ask.

"No, thanks. That nice young man stopped by and brought me some dinner." Richard reaches over and pulls a grease-stained bag from his bedside table and takes out half a corned beef sandwich. "A cup of tea would be nice, though, if you're making it."

"What nice young man?" I ask, getting up to put the kettle on.

"Ben. Fiona's nephew," Richard says, his mouth full of corned beef. "He's been working in the building, and he's taken to stopping by, probably on your orders, I'm guessing," Richard says, sitting up and donning his glasses, just so he can look superciliously over the top of them at me.

"I didn't tell him to come. Maybe Fiona did," I tell Richard.

"Or maybe it wasn't me he was coming to see," Richard murmurs, raising the newspaper to his face.

The last time I saw Ben was the night he kissed me on the balcony. It hadn't been much more than a week ago, but it felt like months. I was afraid I'd hurt him, which I probably had. Given where my life is now heading, for once in my life, I've managed to do the prudent thing.

Make that twice. I'm instantly reminded of Jake and our aborted tryst in the kitchen. Jake's kisses were so full of urgency—so different from Ben's, which had been tender, sweet, tentative. Nothing like months of fitful ruminating, and the elegant foreplay of a terrific meal designed, I can now see, to push all of my buttons. The difference? A long and complicated history—which actually had turned out to be the problem.

While I'm waiting for the water to boil, I stop to peek in on Chloe again, asleep in my bedroom. My flight had been delayed for several hours, and I'd gotten home too late to see Chloe awake. But, because I'd insisted, Fiona and my father had dropped her off and put her to sleep in my room. I didn't want her to wake up one more morning without seeing me. Back in the kitchen, I measure the tea out and put a few biscotti on a plate.

"Mira, I want you to do something for me," Richard says, startling me. I hadn't heard him get up and am surprised to find him standing at the kitchen counter leaning heavily on his cane.

"Of course, Richard."

"I want you to take me to an AA meeting," he says. It's the first time either Richard or I have acknowledged his, so far as I know, one and only period of transgression in over twenty years.

"Of course I will, Richard."

I keep Richard company at the kitchen table while he sips his customary nighttime herbal tea. It has wild nettle root in it, which Richard swears helps him sleep a deep and dreamless sleep. It also tastes like dirt, which is why I'm drinking silver-tipped Darjeeling with extra milk and sugar.

"Richard," I begin. "About Nate—"

"It's okay. It's over, Mira. It's been over," he says, reaching up with a paint-spattered hand to brush a piece of hair from his eyes. His hair is the color of dust, and the way it hangs over his ears in ragged tufts makes Richard look old.

"It's funny," he continues, resting his chin in his hands. "I think you get to a certain age, and what you want from someone becomes very different from anything you've ever wanted before. But it's hard to let go of your youthful sense of what love is. You want to hold onto it for as long as you can, even though it doesn't fit. Even though it is," he hesitates, "ridiculous. Let's face it, there's nothing romantic about Depends and three-pronged canes and sweat suits," Richard continues. "But I've got to start thinking about the long haul, Mira. My chief requirement should be someone who is willing to see me through to the end."

"Richard, what are you talking about? You've got years still. Besides, you've got me. Remember, we made a pact?" Richard rests his cool palm on my hand. His skin is translucent, the intricate network of veins running like tiny rivers beneath the surface, the remnants of a tired-looking bruise, left over from the IV, encroaching across the back of his hand, the bluish purple of a deep-water sea.

"So," Richard says, taking a sip of his tea, "when are you leaving us?" Richard raises his hand to my face and strokes my cheek. His eyes are sad.

I sigh. "I just bought this place. Even if I can get a loan to cover the initial AEL investment, I'll have to sell this place quickly to rent again in New York."

Richard flaps his palm at me. "Don't worry about it. If we stage it right, it'll sell in a minute. Who knows, I might even buy it from you," Richard says, looking around with his practiced decorator's eye, which finally comes to rest on the yellow wall.

"You?"

"Yes, it might be time for a change—for both of us," he murmurs.

"Richard—"

"I fully intend to get back out there and begin combing the geriatric wards for the unattached, the infirm, any eligible gay man of a certain age who can't outrun me. And I suggest you do the same—age and appropriate sexual conventions considered, of course," Richard says, raising his teacup. "You know, I think I like Caribbean Sunset," he says, flicking his chin in the direction of the living room wall.

"Which one is that?" I ask, shifting slightly in my chair in order to have a better view.

"The third from the left," Richard says, pointing.

"I don't know. I kind of like the one two down, the big splotch that looks like Texas. What's that one called?"

He consults the piece of notebook paper on which he has kept a record of his splotches, all of which are numbered, along with their corresponding names.

"Well, well. How appropriate," Richard says, laying his hand once again over mine. "New York Cheddar."

The next morning I awake before five and lie in bed for an hour contemplating, of all things, the blueberry muffin. Capitalizing on the tartness of the fruit is the key, I've decided. I'm thinking about muffins because it seems much easier to think about a relatively simple baking conundrum—namely, why there aren't more good blueberry muffins in the world—than it is to contemplate the enormity of what I am about to do. Namely, sell the apartment I'd managed to convince myself just a few short weeks ago was the ticket to my getting over Jake, and move back to New York to reclaim Grappa. Chloe and Richard are still sleeping soundly, and I won't be gone long. Quietly, so as not to wake them, I pull on jeans and a sweater, pad downstairs, and let myself out the front door. I buy several pints of wild blueberries from the guy on the corner, who also tries to talk me into buying yesterday's lettuce so he doesn't have to throw it away, which he knows he should. On my way home I stop in at Bruno's, which is just opening, for a caffè latte. Bruno's grandson fires up the espresso machine, and while I wait for my latte, I order a couple of croissants for Richard and a half dozen of the tiny hazelnut cookies I've lately fallen in love with.

On my way home, I see Ben coming out of Primanti's across the street, carrying a large paper bag and a huge Dunkin' Donuts plastic coffee mug. I wave, but either he doesn't see me, or his hands are too full to wave back.

"Hey, I know you," I call to him, darting across the street. "Had your fill of pigeon?" He gives me a halfhearted smile, but otherwise doesn't respond, although at least he slows his pace a little.

We walk in silence for at least half a block before he says, "Actually, I'm still working in your building. A couple of the last buyers changed the specs on the plumbing, and the other day some woman saw me carrying a toolbox and begged me for an estimate. Wants an upgrade on her shower and bathroom fixtures, too." He stops to shift his bags. "Looks like I'm gonna be busy servicing the ladies in your building for quite a while."

"Great. Richard says you've been stopping by. Come for lunch some day," I tell him.

"Why? Something needs fixing?" he asks, giving me a sidelong glance.

"You like that place, don't you?" I ask, gesturing to the Primanti's bag.

"Primanti's? Yeah, I do," he says, opening the bag and taking a fry. "Got them on the side today. Gotta shake things up once in a while." He holds the bag open and offers me one.

I shake my head. "I didn't know they served breakfast," I say.

"They don't. Same menu twenty-four hours a day," Ben says, munching another fry.

"*Gourmet* magazine did a piece on them a few years ago. Do you remember?"

"Yeah, I remember. Food Network, too," Ben says with a wry

smile. "For weeks afterward you couldn't get near the place. Yuppie suburbanites from six surrounding counties were lined up three deep at the counter." He shudders.

"Do you know," he says, turning to face me, "I've been going there practically my whole life. My stepdad used to take me there when I was a kid. We'd go early in the morning, sneak out while my mom was sleeping. We'd sit at the counter and eat these sandwiches for breakfast—always with the fried egg. Man, I could barely reach the counter, and my hands were too small to wrap around a sandwich. Whenever I think about him I remember the smell of stale beer and fried potatoes. Those were good times."

"What happened to him? Your stepfather?"

Ben doesn't say anything for a moment. "He and my mom divorced when I was about ten. We kept in touch for a while." He shrugs. "You know how it goes." He turns toward me. An edge has crept in and surrounded Ben's easy drawl. "This place is an institution. You want to be a food writer? Why don't you write about this—I mean the no-frills, real-life version of this place, not the high-end, food magazine, 'isn't it so cute we're slumming' version."

We walk back toward the lofts in silence. I want to tell him I'm sorry, that I hadn't meant to hurt him, but I've never really been good at that sort of thing.

"Hey, have you tried Bruno's hazelnut cookies? Trust me, once you try these, there's no going back." I open the bag and offer one to Ben.

He takes it, and even though it's only a little bigger than a quarter, bites off just a small piece. "Mmm. Good," he says, popping the rest of the cookie in his mouth. "Got any more?"

"You can have one more, but that's it. They are for research purposes only. I'm experimenting with the recipe, and I need to study the rest." I've already made a half dozen attempts at duplicating Bruno's recipe, but there's something about his version that conjures memories of Italy, of the *panetteria* off the square in Scanno, each morsel crumbly and sweet, the taste of the roasted hazelnuts thick and full on the tongue.

Ben chews his cookie slowly. "So, what do you think?" I ask him. "A hint of Frangelico? Or coffee, maybe?"

He shrugs. "Don't know. A dab of honey maybe, but not too much," he says, looking pleased with himself.

"Hmm, right. Good catch," I tell him, even though I'd already thought of it.

"You know, you could probably just ask Bruno for the recipe. I bet he'd give it to you," he says.

"No!" I exclaim, horrified. "That would be like calling the toll-free number for the *Times* crossword puzzle hotline. The whole point is being able to do it myself. I'm usually pretty good at stuff like this, and besides, I'm nowhere near ready to admit defeat."

Ben softens, smiling for the first time, a loopy, goofy grin, as if I've just said something incredibly silly.

"I'll get it in the end, or, who knows, maybe I'll come up with some version that I like even better," I add, defensively.

"So," he asks, "how's the newspaper biz? What's up next?"

"Barbeque Basics."

"Oh," he says, reaching into his bag for another fry.

Enid had e-mailed me the assignment while I was in New York, so I'm already a couple of days behind. This morning the FedEx package with the AEL financial statements is scheduled to arrive, and Ruth is coming over this afternoon to take a look at the documents, so I won't have much time today either. I've promised to cook her dinner, though; maybe while she is sorting through the documents I could whip up a batch of barbeque sauce, something with an interesting twist.

We're in front of the lofts, but Ben stops several steps before the front door. "Aren't you coming in? I thought you were working here."

"I am, but I can't eat inside. I'm just the hired help," he says. "I was going to eat by the river and watch the sunrise. Want to join me?"

"I'd like to," I tell him, and I would, but I've already been gone longer than I anticipated, and I'm worried Chloe will be awake. "But I'd better not. Chloe—"

Ben nods and then raises his hand, the one with the Primanti's bag.

"Do you want to come up?" I ask, but Ben has already turned away and is walking toward the river.

"Nah, too messy. And you'd probably make me use a plate." He turns around and walks backwards, squinting upward into the blue-gray dawn. "It's going to be a spectacular sunrise. It'll be over in ten minutes, max. Sure you won't change your mind?"

I shake my head. "I can't."

"Suit yourself." Ben shrugs.

Ruth is sunning herself on my balcony, which is so narrow that half of the resin lawn chair she has imported from her deck and dragged upstairs from the trunk of her Jeep is in my living room. Carlos and Chloe are playing on the rug in the dining area, and Richard is napping by the window, his sketchbook open on his lap.

"You know, if you really want to get some sun, we could just go to the Schenley Park pool," I tell her, handing her the Diet Snapple iced tea she has requested.

"No, this is great," Ruth says, getting up to reposition her chair. "And besides, I can't be seen in public without a cover-up yet. I'm taking this butt and abs class at the gym, but it hasn't started to kick in yet," she says, angling her chair so mostly just her legs are in the sun. She drags my coffee table, on which she has spread out a whole year's worth of AEL's financial reports, closer to her and dons the bifocal sunglasses dangling from a chain around her neck.

"So, what do you think?" I ask.

"Well, so far, it looks pretty good. They've got a two-year projection of increasing returns, based on their business plan."

"So it looks like a good investment, right?"

Ruth frowns. "Not sure yet," she says, biting the inside of her cheek.

"What do you mean? I thought you just said—"

"Mira, if this were a car you were buying, what I've done so far is the equivalent of walking around the chassis and kicking the tires. I know it's shiny, the tires are full, and all the chrome is polished, but I've yet to open the hood."

"So open the hood," I tell her. "We don't have much time. The closing is a week from Thursday!"

Ruth takes off her glasses and rubs her eyes. "I can't," she says. "Why not?" I ask her.

"The documentation I need isn't here. I need to know where the capital was generated and what the investment hierarchy looks like. They've just given us the summary financials."

"Here," I tell her, handing her a pad of paper and a pen. "Write down what you need to see, and I'll make the call." Ruth scribbles some notes on the pad and hands it to me. I call Marcus and leave a list of the information Ruth needs with his secretary, along with Ruth's address and phone number. Next, I call Jerry Fox, who has faxed over a copy of the addendum I'd outlined this morning. When I ask if he's had a chance to look at the financials, he tells me they'll be in touch as soon as Avi Steiner has a chance to review them.

"What's for dinner?" Ruth calls from the balcony as soon as I hang up.

"Barbequed chicken with a Spanish peanut sauce."

"Sounds fattening," Ruth says.

"It is. It's for work. You and Richard are the guinea pigs."

"Hey, do you think you could do a column on spa food next?" she asks.

"Maybe. Sure, I guess." I look over at Ruth, who is pinching a chunk of her thigh and frowning.

"Unless you don't mind my camping out on your balcony for the rest of the summer, it might be a good idea."

Richard asks me to give him a haircut, just a trim really, to neaten up the sides. He's been on edge the last couple of days, anticipating tonight's AA meeting. I think it's a positive development that he seems interested in his appearance, which almost convinces me to overlook his poor judgment in having asked me to do it.

"You can't use those!" he exclaims in horror as I advance upon him brandishing a pair of kitchen shears.

"Why not?" I tease. "I keep them sharp. Besides, these are not ordinary kitchen shears. They're Wüsthofs and probably cost more than that antique coatrack in the corner, which, by the way, doesn't belong to me."

"I know, I know," Richard says, reaching into his shaving kit for his pair of haircutting scissors and handing them to me. "But I couldn't get to the shop while you were in New York, and I had deliveries that needed to be accepted. Besides, it's only temporary," he says, looking around at the crowded apartment, which is starting to look like an antiques warehouse. Richard has just accepted his first assignment in months, and in the last two days, he has had all sorts of things delivered here. Swatches, paint chips, and his drawing board cover the breakfast bar, and now, instead of being perpetually plugged into his beloved Steelers videos, Richard is almost constantly on his cell phone, barking orders to delivery people or soothing his nervous client in dulcet, patrician tones.

I set him up on a stool in the kitchen and wrap a dish towel around his neck. I'm gearing up to take my first snip when Fiona enters the apartment carrying a large, covered saucepan. She has agreed to come over and watch Chloe while I take Richard to his AA meeting.

"Fiona, you didn't have to bring dinner with you. I already made—"

"I didn't," she says, depositing the pan on the counter with a bang. "I brought it over so you could tell me what is wrong with it." She slumps into the stool next to Richard. "I found that barbeque sauce recipe of your mother's you asked me to look for, and I've been practicing all day. Your father wants to have his new crop of advisees over for a welcome cookout this weekend, and I want it to be nice." She presents me with the tattered recipe card, stained with the evidence of her recent efforts. "I know she was quite a cook and I—" Fiona stops short and stamps her small, sandaled foot on the kitchen floor in a display of thinly concealed angst. "I just want to get it *right*," she finishes, frowning.

"Excuse me," Richard grumbles. "I hate to interrupt this cooking lesson, but you were in the middle of cutting my hair, remember?"

"Sorry, Richard," I tell him, but he has already picked up the scissors and handed them to Fiona. "Fiona can do it. I'm sorry, Mira, but every time you come near me with those scissors all I can think of is Sweeney Todd." He shudders.

"Come on, Richard. Let's go into the bathroom where I can do it right over the sink. It'll take but a minute," Fiona says, helping him up and handing him his cane. The two of them trail off toward the bathroom.

While they're gone, I taste Fiona's sauce and right away diagnose the problem—or one of them anyway. She has used poor quality vinegar, a distilled white vinegar by the taste of it. Checking my mother's recipe I note she didn't specify what kind of vinegar to use, so I pull down a bottle of aged apple cider vinegar from France from my pantry shelf. I pop the cork and give it a smell—fruity and intense with a hint of caramel. By the time Fiona comes out of the bathroom I've assembled most of the ingredients necessary for a new, and hopefully improved, batch of sauce.

"We can try making it when I get home," I tell her.

She stops and clasps her hands together. "Thank you, thank you, Mira." She looks like she is about to cry, and I have a sudden urge to put my arms around her.

"Nonsense," I tell her. "It will help me out, too. The column is due tomorrow, and I have to make it anyway. Besides, you're the one doing me the favor. Thanks for watching Chloe tonight."

"Don't be silly," Fiona says. "I'm glad of the company. Your father is interviewing a candidate for visiting professor tonight, so it will be just us girls," she says, stooping to pick Chloe up from the floor where she is playing. "What do you say, Chloe, how about we have a tea party?"

I watch as Fiona dances Chloe around the kitchen, completely unself-consciously, her bracelets tinkling, and her high-heeled sandals clicking merrily on the wood floor.

My mother, who never once danced with me, who was seldom silly, and whom I can't remember ever wearing bracelets, had been so different from Fiona. Watching Chloe giggling delightedly in her arms, I'm suddenly so thankful that Chloe has someone like Fiona, someone fun and silly and playful in her life. Fiona dances around the table toward me, and when she swoops Chloe in to kiss me, I envelop them both in a hug. "Thanks, Fiona. Thanks for everything," I whisper in her ear.

"Why, Mira dear, you're welcome," Fiona says. She looks at me, her eyes soft. "In case you haven't noticed, I love this little girl!"

At the last minute, Richard insists on walking to the car. I hand him his ebony-topped, curly maple walking stick, which he instantly rejects as being "too flashy," choosing instead the four-pronged, stainless steel cane his physical therapist brought and keeps urging him to use. He's dressed in a pair of khakis, a blue plaid button-down shirt and a dark windbreaker. He looks like a high school gym teacher. I know he's taken pains to appear unobtrusive, something that normally doesn't come easily to him. There's a code of conduct at AA, one even I remember from my brief stint at Al-Anon twenty-odd years ago: no last names, no flashy possessions, and no snap judgments.

In fact, no judgments at all.

On the way over, Richard is quiet. I suspect I know what he's thinking—probably the same thing I'm thinking. Twenty-three years ago, when we first met, he was at AA at the urging of his then lover. Although he stopped drinking, the relationship hadn't lasted. That history appears to have repeated itself is an obvious fact that neither of us mentions.

I pull into a handicapped parking space across the street from Wightman School and turn off the engine. We're ten minutes early. Richard is staring straight ahead, his lips parted in a half smile. He reaches over and takes my hand in both of his. "Do you remember the first time I saw you? You were standing under that street lamp over there," Richard says, pointing. "You were smoking a cigarette, and I could tell by the way you were holding it you hadn't been smoking long. Each puff looked like it hurt, but still you kept at it, sucking on that stupid cigarette, taking one long drag after another. I thought you were the angriest kid I'd ever seen."

Richard is staring at the streetlight as if he can see me there, his nostrils slightly flared, as if he is expecting to smell the smoke from my purloined Marlboro Light. "You were what, all of fifteen?"

"Barely," I tell him.

Richard is quiet for a moment, then he continues. "You know, I almost walked right past you. I had enough problems of my own—in those days it was all I could do to get myself to a meeting. I've spent a lot of time lately thinking about how different my life might have been if I'd just kept on walking. Who would have thought that angry kid would end up saving my life? But you have, Mira, and I just want you to know how grateful I am." Richard bends forward and kisses me tenderly on the cheek. "I know it hasn't been easy coming back here, but if you hadn't, where would I be?" He grabs my hand and squeezes it tightly.

Richard places his outstretched palm on the car window as if he's trying to keep the outside at bay a moment longer. And I let him. So we sit and watch the people trickle in, looking for ourselves in the group—the angry girl in the torn jean jacket, in some ways indistinguishable from the woman I'd become, in other ways barely recognizable; the well-dressed man with the haunted look. But the people entering Wightman School do so singly, quietly; it's only then that I realize how lucky Richard and I have been. To have found someone to help you traverse the rough bits, to tell a joke or hold your hand or whistle in the dark when life throws you a menacing curve. Suddenly, Richard throws open the car door and swings his good leg out. I hurry around to help him.

"Life is a banquet," he says, grandly sweeping his good arm wide. The gesture knocks him slightly off-balance, and, smiling, I grab his arm to steady him. Richard can keep himself unobtrusive only so long. "But the problem with being a cook, Mira, is you never get to be a guest at your own party. Go back to New York, rebuild Grappa. Find a great apartment and paint it yellow. But don't forget to pull up a chair and dig right in. You're ready. We both are."

"Thank you," I whisper.

I hand him his cane, and he takes my arm as we begin our advance upon Wightman School, where, behind heavy oak doors, demons are lurking. This time, though, we're both hopeful; if we tread carefully, hand in hand, we might just be able to leave them behind.

chapter 32

The meeting drains Richard, although apart from the minimal introductions required, he'd barely said a word.

When we arrive home, Fiona takes one look at him and says she thinks we'd better save our barbeque sauce tutorial for another day. Since my column is due to Enid tomorrow, I tell her I'll take a shot at the recipe and let her know how it goes. She pats my hand, kisses Richard good night, and is gone. I help him get ready for bed, and then, by the glow of a single tiny lamp so as not to disturb him, I tape my mother's recipe card to the hood of the stove and begin.

Although my mother was a talented cook, she wasn't a careful recipe writer; not all good cooks are. There is an art to the written recipe, I've only lately begun to discover. Assume your reader only knows so much. Deliver the information clearly and in small doses. Leave just enough ambiguity to allow for interpretation. Each cook needs to find the holes, the tiny gaps that allow her to improvise, to make the dish her own. My mother had left too much to the reader's imagination, a shortcoming that could be overwhelming to the inexperienced cook; I find that there is much I need to add, but I try to tread lightly.

Whether by chance or design, my mother hadn't allowed me to really know her, and so I've been left to piece her life together from the scraps she left behind. My mother hadn't taught me to cook any more than she had taught me to be a mother, but I take comfort in the fact that I've still managed to learn something from her by looking in the holes.

It's well after 2 a.m. by the time I've cleaned up the kitchen and e-mailed my column to Enid, but I'm not ready to sleep. I make a cup of tea and am about to grab a couple of Bruno's cookies when I notice a small brown paper sack propped up by the cookie jar, on which Ben has written the following in his neat block script: *Have you considered cacao nibs? I bet you haven't! Ben.* Fiona must have forgotten to mention he stopped by.

Inside the bag are a couple dozen hazelnut cookies and a small plastic bag filled with what looks like mouse droppings. I open the package and drop a couple onto my tongue. They taste a little like chocolate, deeply flavored, thick, and somewhat bitter. But the aftertaste is something entirely different, sweeter, fuller, and much more complex, something you couldn't have predicted from their first gustatory impression. I pop one of Bruno's cookies in my mouth. Ben just might be on to something.

Enid returns my column to me first thing the next morning, bloodied with red "tracked changes." But before I can so much as hit "accept changes," she is on the phone.

"Since when have you become an armchair philosopher?" Enid asks.

"I'm not allowed to be sentimental?"

"How about you stick to cooking?" Enid says, with a sigh.

"But I wrote three recipes."

"Which look fine, but why tell them to look for the holes? What holes? I don't get it. It's too abstruse. Cooking is not supposed to be abstruse," Enid says.

"Okay, I'll fix it," I tell her.

"No, I'll just fix it," she snaps. "It'll be easier."

"Okay. You fix it."

"Listen," Enid says quietly. "We need to meet. Next Monday, one o'clock. Bistro Rive Gauche. Do you know it?"

"Sure," I tell her, even though I don't. "Why? What's up?"

Enid hesitates. "Nothing. Nothing's up. Just be there, okay?"

I hang up the phone, trying to ignore the heavy feeling in the pit of my stomach. There was something in Enid's voice, something businesslike and distant, when she is usually friendlier in a brash, newspapery sort of way. I suspect I know what's coming.

I'm about to be fired.

Which, for some reason, troubles me. I am about to quit anyway, so there really isn't any reason why it should bother me.

Who am I kidding? I'm no writer. Enid has to rewrite practically everything I send her because I can barely string two sentences together. Most of the time, though, she's been reasonably pleasant about it, quietly correcting my errors of spelling, punctuation, and parallel construction—whatever the hell that is—like some good-natured grammar fairy.

Maybe it's the idea of failing at something, or letting someone down—particularly Enid, whom I like. Or maybe it's the completely unlikely fact that I actually like writing my columns. Until I started doing it, I didn't really feel like I had much to say. Now, the idea that people might open their paper on a Thursday morning, read one of my recipes, and head out to the grocery store, makes me happy. It's not the same feeling I get from nailing the missing component in a particularly complex recipe, or constructing a beautiful and perfectly balanced plate, but still it feels good.

I've been toying with the idea of trying to write the column from New York, as Michael had suggested, but I realize it will be too hectic, with moving back and getting settled, not to mention the fact that I'll have to hit the ground running at Grappa. I'll just beat Enid to the punch and resign. I think of calling her back and doing it over the phone, but it seems like the kind of thing I should do in person.

I'm up to my elbows in cookie dough when the bank calls to tell me I have been approved for my loan to cover the initial AEL investment, which is a relief because the closing is scheduled for now just a week away. I call Jerry Fox, who agrees to have his colleague review the settlement sheet before I sign it. He assures me that I don't need to attend the closing if the terms are approved and I return the signed and notarized papers in advance of the meeting next Thursday. We've just finished running down the last minute checklist of things to do and are about to hang up when Jerry says, "Oh, two boxes of documents showed up this morning from AEL addressed to you and somebody named—hang on"—I can hear Jerry rifling through his messages—"Ruth Bernstein. What's up with that?"

Marcus's secretary must have screwed up and sent the backup documentation to Jerry's office instead of to Ruth. I explain this to Jerry and ask him to forward the boxes to me.

"Mira, it is a lot of stuff. I'm not sure Avi will have the time to go through it before Friday. Not to mention it's going to be expensive to copy. Are you sure you need them?"

"Don't worry about the copies," I tell him. "Just go ahead and FedEx them to me. And no need for Avi to take a look. Ruth can fill him in on anything he needs to know." Why pay Jerry's firm five hundred dollars an hour, when Ruth has volunteered to work for food?

"This Ruth knows what she's doing?"

"She's got an MBA from Wharton," I tell him.

"Well, she's going to have to be fast. The closing is next week."

My next call is to Ruth. "What are you doing tomorrow night for dinner? How does chilled avocado soup followed by lobster paella sound?"

"Like it's not on my diet," Ruth answers.

"Okay, broiled oysters with chili and lime, steamed lobster, and avocado and grapefruit salad."

"You working on your spa menu?"

"Kind of," I tell her.

"What's for dessert?"

"Two boxes of documents."

Ruth laughs. "You figure out a way to make a sugar-free, fat-free, chocolate cheesecake, and I'm there."

Of all the marvels of the modern world, there are few things that can rival a well-baked cookie and a cup of tea, served in the part of the afternoon when the spirit begins to flag. Part respite, part distraction, part pure fun, it restores the body and soul and whets the appetite for the evening meal.

I've spent the afternoon working on duplicating Bruno's hazelnut cookie recipe and have finally found a version I like. I serve

Richard a few, along with a cup of tea in his favorite antique Wedgwood cup, then pack up a couple of dozen for Fiona and my father. And, because this version owes much to Ben, I put a few in a bag and pour a tall glass of iced tea and go hunting for him on the fifth floor.

It isn't hard to find him. The double doors on the corner loft are ajar, construction materials litter the entryway, and Bruce Springsteen is wailing from an iPod dock in the kitchen. No one answers when I knock, so I just walk in. Ben is sunning himself on the balcony, his feet up against the railing, reading the newspaper.

"Hard at work, I see," I tease, handing him the iced tea.

"Ah, the joys of being an hourly employee," he says, squinting up at me, his hand shielding his eyes from the sun. "Actually, I'm waiting for the plumbing inspector. He was supposed to be here half an hour ago. I thought you might be him. Hey, did you get my note?"

"I did, thanks."

"I was thinking, the texture's the key to that cookie. Sure, cacao nibs are ugly-looking, but they have an interesting texture. I had to look pretty hard to find them. Anyway, I thought it might be worth a try, that is if you're still hung up on recreating the recipe," he says.

"Here," I tell him, holding out the paper bag. "They're nothing like Bruno's, though." I smile at him.

Ben takes a cookie from the bag and holds it between his thumb and forefinger, examining it like it's a rare geologic specimen. "They're chocolate," he says, surprised.

"Actually, I flavored them with espresso powder. Like I said, totally different from Bruno's."

"But I thought that was the point—to duplicate his recipe," he says, taking a bite.

"It usually starts out like that, but experiment enough, let the ingredients speak to you, and you can end up with something completely different. Sometimes something you like even better."

He chews his cookie slowly, thoughtfully. "Complex, interesting; a cookie like this keeps you on your toes," he says, holding it aloft and looking at me, one eyebrow raised, his lips twitching as if he's trying not to smile.

He pats the small expanse of concrete next to him and holds out the bag to me. "Can you stay a minute? Is Chloe okay?"

"Sure, Richard's watching her for a few minutes," I tell him, sitting down.

"So, I never asked you, how was New York?"

I rest my head against the balcony's back wall. The late afternoon sun has warmed the bricks, and I can feel their heat in my hair and through the thin cotton of my shirt.

"It was—complicated," I tell him.

Ben turns sideways to consider me. "When are you leaving us?" he asks, taking a sip of tea.

"A few weeks, maybe. I'm not exactly sure when."

Ben nods. "Miss the big city, do you?"

I shrug. "It's my restaurant. I've got a chance to get it back. It's what I want. What I've always wanted," I tell him.

"Pittsburgh can't compare to New York, in terms of the dining experience." Ben winks at me as he raises his iced tea glass to his lips, his pinky outstretched at an exaggerated angle.

"Pittsburgh has its share of great restaurants. It's no New York, but there's more to it than meets the eye," I tell him. "It's a great town. Look at Bruno's—one of the truly great bakeries in any city. There's—"

"Look, you don't have to sell me. I live here, remember? And where else can you be right in the middle of the city and be this peaceful? It's a good life," Ben says, stretching his legs so his feet are dangling over the edge of the balcony. "It suits me just fine." He rummages in the bag for another cookie and pops it into his mouth. "Gotta say, the nibs were a good call. Like a nut, but not a nut. Keeps you guessing, you know?"

"I know. It was an inspired idea. Thanks."

Ben draws his legs in toward his chest and rests his elbows on his knees. "Not that you asked my opinion, but I don't think you should go."

I turn to look at him, surprised. "Why not? This is a huge opportunity. I'd be nuts to pass it up."

Ben looks away. "Well, we'd all miss you for one thing," he says.

"I'll miss you, too," I tell him, although as soon as the words leave my mouth, I regret them. Aside from not wanting to give him the wrong impression, I'd glossed over the fact that he'd said "we," not "I."

Ben smiles. "Especially Aunt Fi. She's crazy for Chloe, and Chloe loves her, too. But that's not the only thing. I mean, you've got an interesting job, an opportunity to influence how people cook and eat."

I lean against the bricks. "I worked so hard to build Grappa. From nothing. I can't imagine letting it go again. Besides, I think I'm about to be fired from my very interesting job."

"What? That's bullshit! They can't fire you. You've got a following!"

"Well, I don't know about that—"

"Jesus," Ben says, grabbing the newspaper. "If they fire you what's left? The Nibbler? Listen to this." Ben folds the newspaper in two and begins reading. "The dining experience was significantly diminished by the lack of accessible parking." Ben pulls the newspaper down and grimaces at me. "What does parking have to do with dining?"

Ben gathers up his newspaper and stands. He drains the rest of his iced tea and hands me the empty glass. "Thanks for the snack," Ben says, offering me his hand and pulling me to my feet. "Good luck with Grappa, Mira."

"If you are ever in New York, come to Grappa and I'll take care of you," I tell him, although we both know he never will.

"If I'm ever in New York," he says, laughing.

"This can't possibly be fat free," Ruth says, scraping the bottom of the ramekin with the tine of her fork.

"It's not. It's *lower* fat. It's impossible to remove all the sugar and all the fat. It would be tasteless. But don't worry, it's filled with protein and not too terrible for you."

"In that case," Ruth says, eyeing my unfinished dish.

I push it toward her. "Knock yourself out. I owe you big-time for this one," I tell her.

Ruth digs into the documents after dinner while I get the kids ready for bed, but even with a double espresso, by eleven o'clock she is starting to nod off. So we pack the two boxes of documents and the sleeping Carlos into her Jeep. "I'll finish them over the weekend," she says, yawning.

"Do you know there are two thousand five hundred pages in a box of documents?" Ruth asks, when I call her early Monday morning to see how it's going. "You can check it on Wikipedia."

"But the closing is on Thursday. Jerry has to have the signed settlement sheet no later than Wednesday, which means that I have to mail it tomorrow at the latest to get it there in time!"

"Calm down. Go ahead and sign it and put it in the mail. I'm through the first box and halfway through the second and so far everything looks good. I'll have it done by tomorrow."

"I can't even watch Carlos this afternoon. I've got a meeting with Enid at lunch today. Fiona is watching Chloe. But how about if I take them both to the pool tomorrow?"

"Sure, that would be great," Ruth says. She hesitates, and I can hear her rifling through paper. "You know, it's just starting to dawn on me that you're actually leaving. I'm going to miss you, Mira."

"Me too. But we'll visit. You and Carlos will just have to come to New York."

"And you'll come back here, for holidays, right?"

"Right. It won't be so bad; you'll see," I tell her. Never mind that with Grappa I probably won't have a single holiday to myself for the next ten years.

Bistro Rive Gauche is a tiny new restaurant in the Cultural District that calls itself a bistro, but really isn't. Bistros are casual, homey kinds of restaurants, and within seconds of stepping inside I can tell this is the kind of place that takes itself a little too seriously. It isn't busy, and I'm seated immediately.

On the bus over I'd scribbled a few notes on the back of an envelope—points I wanted to make sure to cover in my resignation speech. I pull them out and slip them into my lap so I can refer to them during lunch. I'm no longer sure why it seemed important for me to resign before Enid fires me or, for that matter, why I'm suddenly so nervous I can barely catch my breath. So, while I'm waiting for her, I study my script, mouthing the words, hoping the couple sitting a few tables over doesn't think I'm talking to myself.

Enid breezes in fifteen minutes late.

"Here," she says, dropping a stack of papers onto my bread plate. "Some more fan mail. And these are just the snail mail letters," she says, taking off her jacket and hanging it neatly over the back of her chair. "Most of the old timers still write letters. One of them," she says, picking up the stack and reaching for her glasses, "looks like a marriage proposal, which if you don't answer, I might. The guy sounds nice. Old, but nice. Called you 'my dear' and signed it 'with respect and admiration.' They're all good or, I should say, mostly. My favorite is from the woman who substituted three of the ingredients and then blamed you for the fact that her muffins didn't rise. And after your compelling dissertation on the dangers of substitutions in baking. Honestly!" she clucks.

Within seconds of Enid's arrival, a waiter approaches, bearing menus that he presents with a flourish, and begins reciting a litany of specials. Today's offerings include grilled tuna in a soy wasabi marinade, and a pan-roasted squab with curried apricot chutney, neither typical bistro fare. It makes me think wistfully of compound butters and pestos of fresh herbs and toasted nuts, of mushrooms and lardons, eggs and roast chicken, none of which appear anywhere on the menu.

I order myself an appetizer portion of mussels and a side of frites to start and a green salad. After an extended cross examination of the waiter, Enid orders a beet and goat cheese salad and the veal chop with Roquefort butter.

Enid scoots her chair closer to the table and gives the bread basket a once over. "So . . ."

"So?" I echo, picking up a roll and buttering it while Enid gives me a hard look. Even though I've spent the last fifteen minutes rehearsing my speech, so far I've barely been able to manage much more than a trained parakeet.

"Listen," Enid says. "I'll get right to the point. You're doing a good job, Mira. It's been a long time since the Food section has attracted this much attention," she says, gesturing to the stack of letters on the table. "I mean the Nibbler gets his fair share, but let's face it, most of it's hate mail. That son of a bitch is hard to please." Enid gives her immaculate silver pageboy a small pat before picking up one of the rolls and giving it a contemplative squeeze. "Not warm and definitely not baked on the premises. Certainly not worth the carbs," she pronounces, tossing the roll back into the basket.

So much for getting right to the point.

The waiter brings Enid's salad and my mussels. Enid picks sulkily at hers.

"I hate it when they serve the dressing on the side. Salads should be dressed lightly but thoroughly."

"And not too cold," I add. "I hate it when the salad is too cold. You can't taste the greens."

"Mmm, right," Enid says with an approving smile. She puts down her salad fork and fixes me with a penetrating stare.

"Mira, are you happy?"

"What?"

"I mean at the *Post-Gazette,* doing what you're doing?"

"Enid, listen, I've got something to tell—"

"Okay, some doctor tells you tomorrow that you've got a year to live, and you're okay with leaving behind a newspaper file of 'Bistro Favorites for the Home Cook' as your legacy?"

"No, as a matter of fact—"

"Aha! I knew it!" Enid signals the waiter and orders a carafe of house wine. "Listen. I'm fifty-six years old, today as a matter of fact," she says, raising her water glass, "and I've been dreaming of having my own restaurant for the last thirty years. If it doesn't happen soon, it's never going to. Running interference for the Nibbler—Jesus, what a ridiculous name!—and figuring out if oleo should be capitalized and editing your columns on barbeque basics—you think that's what I want my legacy to be?"

We sit in silence for a moment while the waiter pours our wine. This strange talk of legacies and of happiness, not to mention my relief, however misplaced, that Enid isn't going to fire me, has suddenly made me ravenously hungry.

Enid watches me eat. "How are the mussels?" she asks, her fork hovering in between her plate and mine.

"They're okay," I tell her, nudging my plate toward her. "Mussels are almost impossible to screw up, especially nowadays when the quality is uniformly good. Throw them in a pan with a little garlic, olive oil, and wine, and they're done. But, bistros live and die by their frites, in my opinion."

"Well?" she says, gesturing in the direction of my frites.

I offer her one.

"Just as I suspected," she pronounces mildly. "Soggy. So," Enid says, after a beat, "what do you think?"

"Well, to make really good fries you have to fry them twice and these—"

"No!" she says, rolling her eyes. "What do you think I've been talking about?"

Enid might just as well have been conducting this whole strange lunch in Japanese. I honestly have no idea what she's been talking about. She carefully lays down her knife and fork and leans forward, her voice low and soft. "What do you think about opening a restaurant? With me. You do the cooking, menu development, etcetera. I handle the business and maybe put in a couple hours a week in the kitchen, if you're willing to have me. What do you say, Mira?"

"A restaurant?" Enid has caught me completely off guard.

"Yeah, what do you say?"

"Enid, I can't. I've been trying to tell you. I'm going back to New York. I'm going back to Grappa."

Enid sits back in her chair and carefully lifts a hand to smooth her hair. "Oh," she says, raising her napkin and dabbing delicately at her pursed mouth. "I had no idea you were thinking about leaving. If you were unhappy, you should have said something," she says, her voice prim and clipped.

"I'm not. I wasn't. It's just that it's a great opportunity. It came up totally unexpectedly."

Enid drains her wine and refills both our glasses. She eyes me speculatively. "I waited too long. I should have guessed. I didn't think you'd be happy for more than a couple of months doing this crap." She swipes at her mouth with her napkin and drops it beside her plate.

"No, I've really enjoyed writing the column. I appreciate the chance you've given me." I lay a hand on top of Enid's. "Thank you."

Enid sits upright in her chair and coolly removes her hand from mine. "So, tell me about it. Grappa wants you back? How did you manage that?"

I fill her in on the details, even going so far as to suggest that if she wants to own a restaurant, there still might be room to buy into the syndicate.

"Oh, no," she says. "I was hoping for a more hands-on experience. I'll just have to throw more dinner parties," she says, sipping her wine, her eyes dark.

"You know, Enid. It sounds romantic, but when you own a restaurant, you live, eat, and breathe it. There's room for nothing else. You have no idea what it entails. I do. The headaches, the frustrations, not to mention the time."

Enid looks over at me. "So why are you doing it?"

"Because it's always been my dream. I can't *not* do it."

Enid sits back and considers me. "How do you know it's not my dream, too?" she asks.

I hesitate. "I don't." Who am I to tell Enid not to pursue this? "If it is, then I think you should go for it. It will be hard, though," I tell her. Enid looks crushed. I change the subject: "I'll stay on for a couple of weeks. I'd like to write a farewell column, if you'll let me. I've been thinking about it and—"

Enid waves her hand dismissively. "Of course. Write whatever you want. But Mira, are you sure? Isn't there anything I can do to change your mind?"

I shake my head. "I've got the papers all signed and ready to mail." I pull the FedEx package from my purse and set it on the table between us. "The closing on the deal is Thursday."

Enid calls the waiter over and waves a hand over her plate. She has hardly touched her salad.

"Cancel my veal chop and bring me a large piece of your best chocolate dessert instead. And two forks. Did I mention it's my birthday?" Enid asks, turning to me.

I raise my wineglass. "Happy Birthday, Enid."

"Congratulations, Mira," she says, touching her glass to mine. "To dreams fulfilled," she adds, her eyes wistful.

chapter 33

On the way home from lunch with Enid I stop at the Federal Express office to mail the signed documents back to Jerry. Once the envelope is swallowed up by the postbox, I feel like the tiny hourglass in Dad's beloved Scrabble set has just been flipped. As a kid, whenever I played with him and he thought I was taking too long, he would flip the hourglass. But the rapidly draining sands made me too nervous to come up with any decent word, and I almost always ended up doing something stupid, or just traded in my letters. As soon as I get home, I call Ruth to tell her she should forget about finishing the documents; if she hasn't found anything in the first box, she probably isn't going to find anything in the second.

"But I want to finish. It's really interesting how this is all put together," she says. "I hadn't realized how much I missed the world of high finance," Ruth tells me.

The next morning I stop by to pick up Carlos. Fiona, Dad, and I are taking both kids to the Schenley Park pool so Ruth can continue her review of the documents in peace.

"I promised myself I wouldn't get mushy, but I'm going to miss you—and not just the food," she says, looking up from her work. Her dining table is littered with paper, an old-fashioned adding machine spewing miles of white tape.

I hand her the insulated lunch box in which I've packed her fresh tuna and avocado salad.

"Thanks," she says, getting up from the table to put her arms around me.

The professor Fiona works for is summering in the south of France, so she is at liberty to use the twelve weeks of vacation she has accumulated over the past several years, which basically has amounted to her having the summer off. She has also somehow managed to get my father to take advantage of the lighter summer schedule at the university and work only three days a week.

We've agreed to meet at the pool. When Carlos, Chloe, and I exit the women's changing room, I see that Fiona and my dad are already there. They've managed to secure three chaises and are encamped in prime real estate by the baby pool, Fiona, a glowing bronze goddess in a bright yellow bathing suit and my dad in plaid bathing trunks I can remember from my childhood, his bald head covered in sunscreen and glistening like a greased melon.

"I like your bathing suit, Fiona," I tell her, approaching.

"Thanks," Fiona says. "Your father likes me to wear a bikini, but I don't think it's appropriate when I'm with my gr—my Chloe," she finishes shyly.

"Honestly, Fiona!" Dad says. "That's not something I think Mira needs to hear—"

"I think Dad's right; you should wear a bikini. You've got a great figure," I tell her.

Six months ago I would have been horrified that my father actually had a preference for Fiona in a habit and wimple, never mind a bikini—or that she'd been about to refer to Chloe as her granddaughter.

My father looks at me, his eyes narrowing slightly as he squints into the sun. I smile at him, and he winks at me. He reaches over and pats Fiona chastely on the arm. "See, baby, what did I tell you?"

Fiona places her hand over my father's and sighs. "For a woman of my age, maybe."

Although she has never even hinted at her age, Ben once told me she is fifty-five. "For a woman of any age," I say, and I mean it.

She smiles as she swings her tanned legs from the chaise, moving to help unstrap Chloe from the seat of her stroller. I sit down on the lawn chair next to her, fish Carlos's things from the beach bag, and begin the arduous process of wrestling him into his water wings. Even though Carlos is afraid of water, Ruth had made me promise I'd put them on.

"How did the barbeque go last weekend?" I ask.

Fiona beams at me. "It was terrific, thanks to you, Mira." I'd given Fiona the test batch of sauce I'd made, which had actually turned out to be excellent. "One of your father's students recognized your name from the paper and asked him if you were related. Tell her, Joe."

"Reads your column every week, she said," my father says, looking up from his novel. "She said to tell you she's cooking more, thanks to you."

"Your father is very proud of you, you know. You're kind of like a celebrity. Pittsburgh's own celebrity chef."

Fiona lowers herself into the baby pool and scoops Chloe onto her lap. Chloe instantly begins flapping her arms and splashing. Carlos and I sit on the grass, a couple of feet from the edge of the pool. "No waaer," he says, burying his face in my arm, when Chloe's flat-handed splash launches an arc of water that lands within an inch of us. I pull Carlos close and gently pat one water-winged arm. "Okay, buddy. We'll just sit." The last time Ruth and I had taken the kids to the pool, the furthest Carlos had gotten was submerging one of his big toes in the shallow end.

"How about I take Chloe for a swim in the big girl pool, give you and Carlos a little space?" Fiona says. I nod, and Carlos and I huddle together on the edge of the towel, watching as Fiona and Chloe head off hand in hand.

Fiona sets Chloe down on the edge of the pool, and, placing one hand gently on Chloe's stomach, eases herself down the ladder until she is standing just underneath her. Then, I watch amazed as Chloe scoots herself off the edge and hops into Fiona's waiting arms. The two of them bob easily around in the deep water, and I can tell by the way she allows Fiona to swing her around that

Chloe's not the least bit afraid. One day she will be a good swimmer, and I will have Fiona to thank.

"You know, it's a mitzvah to teach your child to swim," Ruth told me the last time we'd taken the kids here, when Carlos sat screaming by the edge of the kiddie pool. A mitzvah, Ruth explained, is a basic precept of Jewish law, somewhere between a good deed and a commandment. Fulfilling a mitzvah is considered a blessing. "Too bad, too," Ruth said, turning to look at me, the helplessness in her eyes piercing. "It makes a lot of sense to me. You need to teach your child to survive in the world because one day you won't be there."

Based on a few offhand comments Ruth has made, I know her mother didn't approve of her decision to adopt Carlos or raise him as a single parent. It makes me angry at this woman, whom I'd never met, for undermining Ruth's confidence as a parent, when she needs all the building up she can get. It also makes me appreciate my father and Fiona who, incredibly, has managed to be just the right blend of friend, maternal figure, and doting grandparent.

I am blessed, I think.

A couple of hours later, when the sky clouds over and the rumbling of thunder is heard in the distance, we load the kids into the car and drive to Eat'n Park on Murray Avenue.

Fiona has just finished telling me about a lead she thinks Ben has on a buyer for my apartment.

"Someone who already owns one apartment in your building, I think," Fiona says, piercing a rippled dumpling. She furrows her brow. "Or maybe someone from work. I forget. You'll have to ask him."

The kids sit on booster seats, eating macaroni and cheese with their fingers, Chloe between my father and Fiona and Carlos next to me.

I pick at my grilled chicken salad. It's raining now in earnest, and outside the window I can see people rushing down Murray Avenue, umbrellas raised. A man trailing an old-fashioned shopping cart behind him and a young mother wheeling a stroller, its tiny occupant completely encased in plastic, approach each other from opposite directions. They meet just outside our window, and I watch as they lower their respective umbrellas and embrace.

"You know, we never even had a housewarming party," Fiona says. "With Richard being sick and all. It's bad luck not to have had at least one party there. Let's throw you a going away party."

"I'm not going," I say.

"It's your party, you have to go," Fiona says, laughing as Chloe picks a piece of dumpling from her plate.

"No, I'm not *going.*"

Is there ever a single moment of clarity, when everything comes together, when drums sound, bells ring, lightbulbs glow? If I were directing a movie of my life, I'd be tempted to bathe the people outside the Eat'n Park window in a soft, apricot glow, close in on their quickening steps as they run forward to meet each other. The lowering of umbrellas, the spray of rain on the glass, the way the woman had stepped delicately around the stroller and laid her hand on the man's arm as she moved to embrace him. But it was actually a perfectly ordinary moment. The truth, I realize, is that I made up my mind a while ago. It was as if I'd written it down on a scrap of paper, shoved it in a drawer, and forgotten about it, only to happen upon it some time later, the message in my handwriting something I'd always known but didn't quite remember writing down.

My first call is to Jerry Fox. I need to tell him to tear up the signed contracts before I change my mind again. My cell phone begins beeping ominously just as his secretary tells me he's in a meeting. As soon as I finish telling her to have him call me immediately, my phone dies completely, which means I have to get home to my charger before he calls me back.

I fly up the stairs to Ruth's townhouse, Carlos and Chloe in tow. The three of us burst in through the open screen door. "I'm not going. Stop. Forget about it."

Ruth is pacing in the dining room, her cell phone cradled to her ear. "Where have you been? I've been trying to call you!"

"My cell phone died. My charger is at home," I tell her.

"Here, plug it into mine," Ruth says, fishing her phone charger out of the drawer of the buffet. "Wait a minute, what do you mean you aren't going?"

"I changed my mind. I don't know. I realized that it's unfair of me to take Chloe away from everything she has here. Our lives will be so much more difficult. I'll never see you, or Richard, or my dad and Fiona. Or Ben. I'll miss you all. I like writing my column. There are a million reasons."

"Thank God," Ruth says, clicking her cell phone shut and clutching it to her chest. "That's what I was trying to tell you," she says. "I found something. In the documents."

"What are you talking about?"

Ruth leads me over to the dining room table. "I assumed eventually I'd be able to nail down the source of all the capital used in the projections."

"You mean where they are getting the money? I thought they were getting it from me. You know, the investors."

Ruth hesitates. "It's not exactly that simple—or at least it shouldn't be. The source of capital really refers to AEL's investment strategy. They have to have some way to grow the money enough to cover the projected returns, right? Take a look at the number of investors and the payouts. Twenty percent returns in thirty days, pretty atypical even for high-yield investment programs. The number of re-investors is ninety percent. Again, atypical, although not unrealistic, given the high rate of returns. But since the restaurants won't be showing that kind of profit, where does the money for the large payout come from? That's where the investment strategy comes in. Think of it like a recipe. AEL pools everyone's money and invests it in some funds or series of funds. Twenty percent of the pool in X fund for thirty days at a projected return rate of ten percent. Thirty percent of the pool into Y fund for sixty days at twelve percent. Like that. But I got all the way through the first box and couldn't find how AEL would sustain the promised returns. They've only provided backup for the projections for the first two years. That raised a red flag."

"But they've been paying people."

"Exactly," Ruth says. "It's early yet, and new investment money is coming in. So I'm deep into the second box, and I see that they have planned at least two more layers of investors—essentially doubling the number of investors. Although nothing in the documents explicitly shows it, if you extend the restaurant profit projections beyond the two years, and then compare that with what will be required to meet projected payouts, the math only works as long as they continually expand the pool of new investors. You can only maintain that kind of strategy for so long before it all comes crashing down. You remember Bernie Madoff? This has the earmarks of a classic Ponzi scheme."

My cell phone rings. It's Jerry.

"Jesus, Mira, what do you mean rip up the documents? The closing is tomorrow!"

"Listen, Jerry. Ruth thinks she found something."

"Well, she better have, and it better be big. You want AEL to sue you for backing out at the last minute?"

I hand Ruth the phone.

While she is filling Jerry in, I put the kids down for a nap.

Ruth spends the next hour on the phone, first with Jerry, then with Avi Steiner. By the time she hangs up, Jerry's secretary is booking her on a flight to New York first thing in the morning to go over things in person. I follow her around the apartment, watching as she pulls a navy blue suit from a plastic dry cleaning bag and inspects the heels of a pair of brown Jimmy Choo pumps. "Hopefully, I'll be home tomorrow night," Ruth says. "You'll watch Carlos?"

"Of course. You're the one doing me the favor, remember?"

"You keep saying that, but I don't know, it feels like the other way around," Ruth says, rummaging in the back of her closet. "Aha! There it is!" she says, her voice muffled. She emerges holding a large, tattered box.

"I didn't think I'd be using this any time soon," she says, throwing off the lid and pawing through inches of tissue paper. She pulls out a beautiful briefcase. "It's vintage Hartmann," she says, stroking the glossy leather. "It belonged to my father." Ruth has never mentioned her father, but I can tell by the wistful look in her eyes that she adored him.

"I know I originally planned on taking a year off, but I'm thinking about going back to work part-time. I think it might make me a better mother. Does that sound crazy?" she asks, opening her suitcase. Even though she'd spent most of the last thirty-six hours hunched over financial documents, she looks bright eyed and more relaxed than I've ever seen her.

"Not one bit," I tell her.

Enid answers my call on the first ring.

"Don't suppose you've changed your mind?" she asks.

I hesitate. The eagerness in her voice is nearly overwhelming. "I have, but not about the restaurant. I'd like to stay on—writing for the Food section, if you'll still have me. I've decided to stay in Pittsburgh."

"I'll take that as your opening offer. I accept."

"Enid, I'm not ready on the restaurant. I don't know when I will be."

"Just promise me you'll at least think about it."

"I will, but—"

"That's good enough for me. I don't want to push you, but I'm here, Mira, when you're ready."

"*If* I'm ready," I add.

"Okay, I get it. If."

chapter 34

Ruth returned from New York having managed to convince Jerry and Avi that what she'd uncovered in AEL's financials merited a call to the authorities. Since then, Ruth has also been interviewed by an SEC investigator who found what she had to say pretty interesting. Any remaining question about the legitimacy of AEL disappeared when, one week into the investigation, AEL's outside accountant—who turned out to be the *only* accountant in the agency—disappeared without a trace. It then came out that he'd previously been investigated in regards to a similar pyramid-style scheme discovered several years earlier in which he allegedly had only a peripheral role and claimed not to have known about the fraud.

Tony may be out most of the fifty thousand dollars he initially invested, but because of Ruth's eleventh-hour rescue, he was able to save the rest of his sabbatical fund.

It was too late to save Grappa. The restaurant was so heavily mortgaged that when the scheme collapsed, a trustee was appointed to oversee the orderly shutdown of the restaurant. After Grappa folded, Tony went to Italy to cook for a year. He took Grappa's loss hard. We both did. As for Jake, I have spoken to him only once. I called him after I heard about Grappa's closing. Virtually all of his funds were invested with AEL, and he lost everything. I have no idea if he and Nicola will remain together, although I somehow doubt she's the type to stick around after the money has run out. Jake now has no choice but to look for a job in someone else's kitchen. He'll find one—a talented chef always can find a place to cook. Before we hung up, he offered me his recipe for cassoulet. "I'll write it down and send it to you," he said. "I'd like to think of you enjoying it, Mira."

True to her word, in the weeks that followed Enid didn't bring up the restaurant again. Not once. Until yesterday.

After I e-mailed my latest column to her, she called me to follow up on the changes and to discuss the Thanksgiving spread. "It's only a month away," she said. "Here's what I'm thinking. Each of the four remaining weeks we choose one dish, stuffing, gravy, cranberry sauce, and focus on it. Teach the method and give a bunch of different interpretations. What do you think?"

"Great," I said. "I'm on it."

Then she asked me if I've given the restaurant idea any more thought. When I told her I was still thinking about it, she said only this: "Okay. Fair enough. I won't mention it again; I promise." This has been bothering me. I can't stand the feeling that my own inertia could cause this idea to wither and die, yet I'm having a hard time mustering the energy to do anything about it.

Lately, I've found myself remembering Grappa's early days, the most difficult parts: the huge start-up costs; the losses most restaurants experience the first year—if they even survive the first year; dealing with banks and financial types—which I hated; the hiring and rehiring of cooks and notoriously unreliable dishwashers; finding a decent laundry service.

It isn't that I'm suffering from a dearth of ideas—I've got plenty of those, from breakfast joint to tapas bar, from sandwich shop to enoteca, each of which I approach with an all-consuming intensity, rather like a case of twenty-four-hour flu. Then, when the fever has run its course, I discard the idea as being too much like Grappa— or not enough.

* * *

"Listen to this," Richard calls out to me from the living room, where he is poring over *What to Expect: The Toddler Years.* "It says what she's doing is completely normal."

I've just attempted to give Chloe pasta with peas and a nut-free pesto, which she's eaten before and liked, but which tonight made her wipe her tongue with her bib and gag. Tired of her crying, I gave up, boiled her some plain noodles, and served them with a boring tomato butter sauce.

"Kids' palates are sensitive, and most kids go through a picky phase around the age of two," he reads. "So our Chloe is precocious, just as we've always suspected," Richard says proudly. In the months he's been living here, I've been surprised to discover that Richard has a real paternal streak. As his recuperation has progressed, he's taking an increasingly active role in caring for Chloe; he's always happy to read her a story or help with her bath, even change the occasional diaper. I love that Richard takes pride in Chloe's accomplishments, dubious though this one may be. The phone rings, and Richard calls, "Do you have it, Mira?"

At the moment I'm holding Chloe, who is covered with tomato sauce, attempting to remove a piece of ziti from her grasp. As I answer the phone, balancing it in between my shoulder and chin, Chloe loses interest in the piece of ziti and reaches her saucy hands toward the receiver.

"Hello, Mira? It's Ben. Are you busy? I need a favor."

"I'm about to give Chloe a bath," I tell him, as Chloe's tomatoey hands settle in my hair.

"How'd you feel about flipping some burgers for a couple of hours? A friend of mine had an accident. He burned himself in a small grease fire at his restaurant, and he's totally freaking out. He just opened this place in Bloomfield, and if he can't find someone to help him out he'll have to close for the evening. It's Saturday night, and he can't afford to lose the business. I'll even help. How about that? The best offer you've had all evening, right?"

"Ben, I'm sorry. I've got Chloe."

"Not to worry. I already thought of that. I called Aunt Fi, and she said to drop Chloe off at your dad's on the way over. We can pick her up after we're done. Come on, what do you say? Please?"

"I didn't know you had a friend who owns a restaurant," I say, thinking it funny he hadn't mentioned it before.

There's a knock at the door, and when I go to open it, Ben is standing there with his cell phone to his ear.

"Oh, yeah," he says, still holding the phone. "He's my buddy Jim's brother, Dave. Jim is the heating and cooling guy from Bessen's." We hang up our respective phones, and Ben makes his way to the kitchen, where he picks absently from the pot of ziti on the stove.

Richard walks into the kitchen and holds out his arms for Chloe. "Hello, Ben," Richard says, patting Ben on the arm. "You know, I could have watched her, Mira," Richard says.

He probably could have. Although Richard still isn't driving, his recuperation is just about complete. He's taken to going into the shop a few days a week and has hired an assistant to handle the overflow. He's really ready to go home, but I think he's staying for me; he's worried that I'm not ready to be alone. Maybe I'm not.

"Aunt Fi needs Chloe so she can finish Chloe's Halloween costume anyway," Ben says. Fiona has been working on Chloe's costume for weeks, an ear of corn made out of felt.

I put Chloe down, and she makes for the living room. "Richard, would you mind giving her a quick bath and putting her in her pj's while I change?"

"Done," says Richard. "Ben, would you mind helping me corral this urchin?"

I've changed into a chef's tunic and a pair of drawstring pants and am in the kitchen packing my good knives into my leather knife case when Richard and Ben emerge from the bathroom with Chloe, pink cheeked and freshly pajamaed.

"What are you doing?" Ben says. "The guy owns a restaurant. He's got knives."

"Chefs are picky about their knives. If I'm going to be cooking in a strange kitchen, I should have my own knives. It's a comfort thing."

"Nice outfit," he says, giving me the once over. "Very official. Come on, we better get going," Ben says, picking up my knife case and the diaper bag.

Chloe and I kiss Richard good night. "Don't wait up," I tell him.

Delano's is a local Bloomfield watering hole sandwiched in between an Italian groceria and a little take-out stand called Paula's Pierogie Palace. In addition to the worn wooden bar, they've got a half dozen tables, most of which are empty, so I'm guessing not too many people come here to eat. Ben walks us through an alleyway to the delivery entrance at the back of the restaurant.

The kitchen is small and the remains of a grease fire over one of the grills still apparent. A kid, with just a wisp of whiskers under his chin and a soiled apron slung low on his hips, is halfheartedly cleaning the fire extinguisher chemicals from the hood over the large griddle. He looks up, raises a rubber-gloved hand in greeting, and says, "I got two orders up for burgers. I told them it would be a while. These chemicals stick like a bitch."

"Forget the grill. We can clean it when we shut down for the night. We'll use the oven, broil the burgers, and, if things pick up we can fry them on the stove over here," I tell him, shooing him away from the griddle so that I can check out the oven underneath. He looks at me for a moment, clearly wondering who this crazy lady brandishing a knife case is, but I take advantage of his hesitation to further seize control. "Grab me a couple of broiler trays and fire up this oven," I tell him. "And dump all those condiments and start chopping some new ones."

I look over at Ben, who has found himself a clean apron and is already grabbing the bins of lettuce and tomato for the trash.

The kid, who is wearing a chef's tunic bearing the emblem from the local culinary academy with his name, "Ryan," embroidered over his chest, quickly gets on board, fires up the oven, and delivers me a tray of thin, premade burgers.

In less than ten minutes the burgers are out the door, each with a side of onion rings that Ryan tells me are the house's singular specialty—thin, crispy, and coated only with a light dusting of flour. They are, judging from the prepackaged soups and premade iceberg salads stacked in individual bowls three deep in the walk-in, the only thing, besides the burgers and the frozen chicken wings, requiring any real preparation.

Around nine thirty or so, the orders pick up. People sitting around drinking tend to get hungry eventually, and by the time they do, Ryan, Ben, and I are working more or less harmoniously. I've reorganized the kitchen and given each of us a station to cover. Ben finds a small portable CD player, and we flip burgers to Santana's "No One to Depend On," while Ben occasionally belts out lyrics in fake Spanish.

There's a rhythm to cooking, even flipping burgers. That's part of what I love about it. Because chefs are almost constantly in motion, we learn to be parsimonious with our movements, instinctively conserving them, stirring the sauce with one hand, flipping the contents of the sauté pan with the other. Each movement is precisely choreographed, according to the particular beat of the kitchen; the key is knowing just how long the buns need to rest atop the griddle to achieve a particular shade of gold, and when to take the food, in one simple flick of the wrist, from pan to plate. While Ben claims to be a competent home cook, it's clear he hasn't cooked professionally. He makes several unnecessary trips from the condiment station to the deep fryer, each time placing his hands lightly on my waist so as to move past me without bumping my hand or my arm, and each time flustering me, disrupting my rhythm, and once causing me to toast the buns to an unacceptable shade of umber.

The orders keep coming steadily until last call. Ryan goes out to help wipe down the tables and to get himself a beer. Only when I have stopped moving do I realize that it's almost two in the morning and I've totally forgotten about Chloe.

"Oh, my God! It's almost two!"

"Relax," Ben calls from the sink, where he has dumped two large cheese-encrusted sheet pans. "When things started picking up, I called Aunt Fi to tell her we'd be late. She said to tell you they'll keep Chloe overnight. No sense waking them now. Besides, this way you get to sleep in tomorrow. When was the last time you did that? After tonight you're going to need it. I don't know about you, but I'm whipped." Ben's hair is rumpled, and his apron bears spots from several run-ins with errant condiments, but otherwise he seems to have held up well. I, on the other hand, feel like I could run a marathon. There's an honest ache in my legs from being on my feet, but I'm upbeat and exhilarated like I usually am after a busy night in the kitchen. It reminds me of my Grappa days, of Jake and me working this late, the kitchen larger and the food more complicated, but the feeling's the same. I've missed it. I just hadn't realized how much. I turn away, startled to find there are tears in my eyes.

Suddenly, Ben is standing behind me, his hands lightly massaging my neck. "Thanks, Mira," he whispers. "You were great."

I don't know whether it's Ben's hands on my neck or his breath in my hair or the exhilaration of being back in the kitchen, but I'm suddenly in Ben's arms kissing him, and I'm pretty sure that it was my idea. He presses his body into mine, which is a good thing because my legs are suddenly weak, and were he to let go, I'd surely fall, but he doesn't. Instead, he reaches behind me and grabs a handful of my hair in his hand and gently, effortlessly removes the clips.

Ryan makes a lot of noise coming back into the kitchen and says loudly to no one in particular that he thinks he'll be going now.

Richard is still sleeping in my living room, so we go to Ben's apartment, which is much closer anyway. We only half undress before we start making love in Ben's living room, frantically gasping and clutching at each other. Afterward, we both fall into an exhausted sleep on the couch. When I awake the next morning, I'm alone. It's early; the sun is still on the rise, sending its diffuse rays through Ben's old glazed windows. He has covered me with a blanket and slipped a pillow underneath my head. I feel such a sense of relief, both physical and sexual, and I'm tempted to give in to it, to roll over and fall back asleep. But I can't. Chloe will be awake soon, and I don't want her to wake up wondering where I am. I throw off the covers and search the floor for my clothes, which I can't even remember removing, trying not to think about having to explain to Richard, who will be waking soon, where I've been.

"Don't move," Ben says from the doorway, holding a tray, the morning papers tucked beneath his arm. I have no idea how long he has been standing there watching me. "I've been up for an hour, making breakfast for us. You have no idea how intimidating it is cooking for a chef."

I'm suddenly shy, and then, remembering my lust last night, I feel my face begin to color. Embarrassed, I draw the blanket up around my breasts.

Ben sits down next to me and lays the tray on the coffee table in front of us. He doesn't look at me, but instead busies himself with its contents, sorting silverware and plates.

"I couldn't move you," he says. "You were out, and I couldn't sleep, so I got up and cooked. I figured you'd be hungry." Ben pours me a cup of coffee and hands me a chipped china mug.

"Thanks," I whisper, my voice breathless and scratchy. I sit up and arrange the blanket to cover myself.

"Don't," Ben says quietly, reaching over and gently pulling the blanket from my breasts. "I didn't get to—last night, I mean. I didn't get a chance to look at you." He reaches over and traces my nipple lightly with one finger, and I moan softly as he cups my breast. The breakfast is forgotten. Ben takes the lead now, taking me by the hand and leading me to the bedroom where he makes love to me again, this time slowly and carefully.

"You know, this would have been much better if we'd eaten it hot," he says later, munching a forkful of eggs. We're lying together in a tangle of sheets, the remains of the breakfast, now cold, lying on top of us.

"That's okay. You're really good at making"—I pause for effect and gaze lasciviously at Ben—"coffee."

"Thanks. You were great last night, by the way," Ben says, leering at me in return, "... in the kitchen."

"Touché," I say, pulling the covers up over me.

"That's really what got me going. You made it all seem so easy. You were formidable, commanding, quick. It was very, very sexy," Ben says, softly nuzzling my neck and kissing me lightly on the ear.

"Hey, how come you never mentioned before that your friend's brother had a restaurant?" I ask.

Ben pulls away and busies himself sorting through the morning newspapers we'd scattered in a heap on the floor. "I don't really know the guy," he says, picking up the Food section and tossing me the rest.

Confused, I raise myself on one elbow to look at him.

"Okay, look, he didn't actually call me. Well, he did, but not about the restaurant exactly. Jim and I were supposed to play racquetball last night, and he called to say his brother had this accident and that he was going to take him to the emergency room instead. When he told me what happened, I suggested you might help. I thought it would be good for you to get back into a kitchen."

I should have suspected as much. Ben had been doing me the favor, not the other way around.

"You aren't angry, are you?" Ben asks, kissing me.

"No. Well, maybe. I haven't quite decided," I tell him, feeling a little silly that I allowed myself to be so easily fooled. Partly, I'm relieved. I haven't cooked professionally since Grappa, and it felt good to prove to myself that I still can, even if it was only burgers and onion rings. I'm also touched that Ben took the trouble to help me like this. But mostly, I think, reaching for him, I'm grateful, grateful that cooking isn't the only thing I haven't forgotten how to do.

"Hey, did you see this?" Ben says.

"No. What?"

"The Nibbler strikes again! Jesus, what a bastard! Listen to this—first of all, get a load of this headline: 'Bistro Rive Gauche Only Half-Appropriately Named.'" Ben looks over the paper at me, an expression of mock horror on his face. "'FON'—that's Friend of Nibbler—'ordered the mussels. The mussels, one of the few authentically bistro items on the menu, were decent, but it is hard, some might say impossible, to ruin mussels, given the overwhelmingly excellent quality of the farm-raised product. The veal chop was overcooked, and over-sauced, but worst of all, the frites, the signature item on any bistro menu, were soggy, the result of the chef having used only a single fry method.'"

I lean my head back against the pillows and let out a laugh, a guffaw so raucous that Ben puts down his newspaper and looks at me with alarm.

Of course, I should have guessed.

"I don't get it," Ben says. "This is the kind of thing that should outrage you! Some poor slob pours his heart and soul—not to mention his last dime—into a restaurant and then gets a review like this one!"

"So, maybe he deserved it. Look, it's a tough market out there, and there's room only for the best. Bad reviews don't close restaurants. Bad food does. You shouldn't open a restaurant unless you know what you are doing."

"Well, then," Ben says, taking me in his arms, "what are you waiting for?"

chapter 35

"Okay, I'm in," I tell her.

"I knew you would be," she says calmly.

"Well, at least we can be assured of one good review," I tell her.

"No," Enid laughs. "I'm afraid the Nibbler is hanging up her lobster bib. *Our* good review will have to be earned. But that shouldn't be too hard for you, my dear. Congratulations."

We discuss the details, such as they are at this point, which amount to little beyond the fact that Enid has already begun working on the financial end. She has a friend who is connected with investments at Northwest Bank, and with whom she previously discussed financing. In addition, she's been looking for space and has already lined up a couple of possibilities that she wants me to see. My job is to decide what type of restaurant we will have, and what sort of space and equipment we'll need. As to what type of restaurant, Enid has an open mind, or so she says.

"But no tearooms, okay? My mother used to eat at tearooms. The tea is always weak, and the food unimaginative. Oh, and no retro shit. If I have to eat at another revamped diner serving chicken a la king, I'll—"

"Relax, Enid. No tearooms, no diners."

I share my news with no one. Not Richard, who doesn't seem to have noticed that I didn't sleep at home Saturday night, and not my father or Fiona, whose generosity in watching Chloe extended to breakfast and a trip to the zoo. Not even Ben, who calls not long after I hang up with Enid to invite me out on a date. If I tell anybody, it should be him. But I don't. In fact, I don't even answer the phone when he calls; instead, I cower in the bathroom while the machine picks up, listening to Ben's sweet and slightly stilted invitation to have dinner with him.

"Hello, Mira? I was, ah, wondering if you're busy tonight. I would love to take you out to dinner. Anywhere you like. You pick the place. I'll even wear a tie. Call me back, okay? Oh, this is Ben, by the way."

Yes, Ben, who I can't even imagine owning a jacket and tie, much less wearing one. I'm not completely sure how I feel about our backwards relationship, where the dinner invitation is issued after the fact—and with all the formality and forced cheerfulness of a date to the prom. Now that I've committed to the idea of a Pittsburgh restaurant, I'm committing to staying here, which means that any sane and reasonable person would proceed with extreme caution. Which is why, I suppose, I let the machine pick up when he called.

As soon as Enid gave me a list of the four properties she and her contact at Northwest Bank determined we could afford, I knew, sight unseen, the one we'd lease. Still, I've done my due diligence, trekking along with Chloe, Enid, and the real estate agent to look at the first three, paying about as much attention as my eighteen-month-old daughter and politely pretending to listen as they discussed the details of financing, offers, and contingencies.

The fourth space belonged to Bruno. He bought the building next to the bakery years ago, intending to expand his business, but somehow had never gotten around to it. He offered us a good deal on the building, but it was the location that had me sold—a long narrow space sandwiched in between Bruno's and the Pennsylvania Macaroni Company. It isn't big, but the ceilings are high, and there are two eight-foot double-paned windows that open onto the street in front. There's even a small courtyard separating the space from the bakery, just enough room for a couple of tables, a few plants, and maybe a whimsical iron fountain.

Before we'd even signed the papers, Bruno gave me the key, wrapped my fingers around it with his own trembling hands, and told me to keep it. Since then, I've been coming here in the early mornings with Chloe, the two of us getting up just as the sun begins to rise over the city, walking slowly, hand in hand, across Smallman Street to Penn Avenue, watching our neighborhood come to life.

This morning, outside Nordic Fisheries a couple of delivery guys are unloading lobsters and crabs by the case, pausing in between loads to sip coffee from Styrofoam cups. Across the street, on Penn Avenue, the green grocers are busy stacking crates of vegetables and fruits, arranging them into a still life to showcase their most beautiful produce: heads of red romaine, their tender spines heavy with the weight of lush, purple-tinged leaves; a basket of delicate mâche, dark green, almost black, and smelling like a hothouse garden; sugar pumpkins of burnished gold; new Brussels sprouts, their tender petals open like flowers.

At this hour the world belongs to those noble souls who devote their lives to food. Cook, grocer, butcher, baker, sunrises are ours. It's a time to gather your materials, to prepare your *mise en place*, to breathe uninterrupted before the day begins. Chloe and I enter the restaurant from the alley, which shares a loading dock with Penn Mac. A large truck is already backed up to a delivery bay where a man is unloading fifty-pound sacks of fine grain semolina onto the floor of the storeroom. He piles the sacks, one on top of the other, sending clouds of flour into the air. Judging from the number of sacks on the floor, he's been at it a while, and the entire alley is white with flour, hanging in the air like snow. It's come to rest on his bare forearms, on his hair and eyebrows. He nods to us and smiles at Chloe, who holds out her hands and watches, fascinated, as particles of flour settle into her small palms. I catch a few grains and rub them in between my fingers, all at once remembering what it feels like to coax a pasta dough to life, the precise moment when you feel its first breath as it relaxes and expands in one long sweet inhalation into your yielding hands.

The weather has been unseasonably warm this year, and even though it is the week before Thanksgiving, humidity hangs in the air, custard-thick and heavy. Before turning on the lights, I switch on the air conditioner, which sputters and groans before finally kicking in. The din is tremendous, so I switch it off and open the windows instead. A breeze moves in, bringing with it the smell of Bruno's baking bread and the sweet and slightly pungent smell of discarded lettuce and cabbage leaves that have fallen from delivery crates to litter the alley. The old Venetian blinds covering the windows flutter in the breeze, casting inky shadows on the walls and on the odds and ends of furniture, six wooden tables, each with four mismatched chairs, left over from whatever this space used to be.

I'm taking very seriously Enid's suggestion that I be the one to decide what kind of restaurant we will have. This is why I've been coming here in the early mornings to stand in the open space and let my imagination wander over the possibilities, each one a new and different incarnation. But there's one I keep returning to, one vision that, over the last several days, has begun to assume a more specific size and shape, one that feels just right to me.

Spuntino will only serve breakfast and lunch, my willing sacrifice to motherhood. Homemade pastas, frittatas, beans and greens, soups thickened with semolina and with ribbons of egg, a pappa al pomodoro made with a bread I'm planning to coax Bruno into baking especially for me, a thick crusty Florentine loaf with no salt. No big menus, no fancy wine lists. In fact, courtesy of Pennsylvania's antiquated liquor licensing procedures, no wine at all for at least the first six months. A place with an open kitchen and a counter where people can sit and talk to me while I prepare their breakfasts and lunches, because it would be nice to know the people I'm cooking for. Rustic wooden tables that encourage spreading out, maybe a low banquette and some comfy chairs gathered around a fireplace. One day I imagine Chloe stopping here on her way home from school to eat a bowl of soup and do her homework on one of the long wooden tables, chatting easily with the regulars, all of whom will love her.

I've been gone from Grappa for almost a year, and most of that time I've spent thinking about what I missed, idealizing it because it had been ours—mine and Jake's. But it had been replete with the sorts of compromises, big and small, that make any joint venture successful. Only recently have I begun to think about what I would have changed, if I'd had the chance. *Spuntino* ("snack" in Italian) will be my chance to do something different. Enid's given me complete creative control, so why not have some fun? How often do we get a second chance?

Ben has promised to help with the repairs—a good thing because, judging from the puddles of water pooling under the air-conditioning units, there's considerable work to be done. Since Richard moved out a couple of weeks ago, Ben's been around for two dinners, three lunches, and one breakfast. Neither one of us is thinking long term, at least not yet, but our relationship is developing like a slow and steady braise. A braise might not look like much to start with—throw a bunch of ingredients into a pot, add a little broth and wine, and simmer over low heat for several hours—but the technique tends to produce the most complex and full-bodied flavors in food. One of the most wonderful things about a really good braise is that the end result is often so much more than the sum of its parts.

Chloe has pushed one of the chairs along the floor until it has come to rest against the back wall, and the exertion has dampened her curls and cast a furrow in her brow. Now that her work here is finished, she's impatient to leave. She turns to face me, raises her arms, and calls, "Mama!" I cross the room and pick her up, holding her close to me despite the heat, nuzzling her hair, still flecked with flour dust. I know she will probably resent Spuntino for taking me away from her. I hadn't intended to do this until Chloe was older, in school. And Ben—I hadn't really planned on that either. But I think that Chloe will learn to share me with Spuntino and will forgive me for doing what it seems I am meant to do.

It won't be easy. There's a kitchen to plan, menus to write, a thousand details to attend to, but it's still my cook's morning. I take a seat at one of the empty tables, pull Chloe onto my lap, and breathe in the smells that make up my tiny slice of the planet, the alley, the oven next door at Bruno's, and the apple pie sweetness of my lovely daughter as she lays her head against my chest and relaxes into my arms.

Dear Reader,

Here you will find the recipes for a five-course Italian-inspired meal—suitable for a potluck book club dinner or any other occasion. (Don't forget the wine!)

I've included recipes from Grappa's fictional kitchen, as well as some of my own favorites. *Nota bene:* I am not Mira. I'm an untrained, albeit incredibly enthusiastic, home cook. That said, I'd like to think I've learned a few things from my research and testing for this novel—Mira has been a fine teacher. Please don't hesitate to improvise and make the recipes your own, because cooking, at its best, is both an expression of self and a gift of love.

Buon appetito,

Meredith

P.S. Please visit me at www.meredithmileti.com. I'd love to hear about your culinary adventures!

Antipasti: *Seasonal Tastes*

One of the hallmarks of Italian cuisine is great ingredients, minimally treated so as to showcase the natural bounty of the season. Ideally, an antipasti should open the palate for the rest of the meal. These combinations each target several of the major tastes—sweet, bitter, salty, sour, and / or umami.

Summer. A small slice of perfectly ripe peach, a shard of sharp Pecorino Romano, and a fresh basil leaf. Stack all the ingredients and wrap with a wafer-thin slice of prosciutto.

Fall. Half of a ripe fig, a shard of sharp cheese (smoked provolone, extra-aged Piave, or Beemster), and a sprig of peppery watercress. Roll all in a thinly sliced piece of smoked duck breast.

Winter. A Majool date, pitted and stuffed with a mixture of cranberry or mango chutney and softened mascarpone cheese. Add a smidgen of good Dijon mustard and top with a toasted walnut.

Spring. Purée some cooked fava beans with lemon juice, garlic, and a couple of tablespoons of olive oil. Garnish with a little fresh mint. Serve with spring radishes and endive stalks for dipping.

PRIMI: *White Pizza with Tallegio, Prosciutto,*
Apricots, and Arugula Salad

Pasta often follows the antipasti course, but I think this pizza is a knockout. We make this all the time on our gas grill, but the stove works just as well.

Buy pizza dough from your favorite pizzeria or local market or, if you have time, make your own. My favorite recipe can be found in Jim Lahey's wonderful book, *My Bread*.

Ingredients

Pizza dough for two
  10-inch pizzas
¾ pound softened Tallegio
  cheese
Shaved Parmigiano-Reggiano
  cheese
½ pound prosciutto

2 ripe apricots, pitted and sliced
  (or substitute a few slivered,
  dried apricots)
2 large handfuls fresh arugula,
  washed and dried
Olive oil, kosher salt, and black
  pepper
Lemon juice

Heat a large cast-iron pizza pan for about 10 minutes on high.

Divide the risen dough in half and roll out into two medium disks, placing each onto the pizza pan. Cook a couple of minutes until it just starts to brown. Flip and cook on the opposite side for another couple of minutes. Remove crust from pan and set on wooden board. Spread softened Tallegio cheese onto crust, top with a few shards of Parmigiano-Reggiano, and slide onto heated pizza pan, being careful not to burn yourself!

If using grill, turn heat high on one side and medium low on the other. Cook on low-heat side with grill cover closed. If using oven, place under broiler. Cook until the cheese is bubbling and crust is as crisp as you like it.

Top pizza with prosciutto and apricots. In separate bowl, toss arugula with drizzle of extra virgin olive oil, kosher salt, black pepper, and squeeze of lemon juice. Top pizza with salad. Shave a few more shards of Parmigiano-Reggiano over the top and serve.

SECONDI: *Jake's "Tastes like Love" Cassoulet*

This Italian take on a French classic incorporates fennel and roasted peppers. It can be prepared in advance and tastes even better the next day.

Ingredients

½ loaf day-old baguette (or substitute 1 cup bread-crumbs)
Olive oil
1 large sweet white onion, diced
1 fennel bulb, sliced
2 leeks, white and light green parts only, cleaned and sliced
2 carrots, finely diced
4 cloves garlic, minced
1 red pepper, diced
1 teaspoon smoked paprika
2 teaspoons each fresh thyme and oregano, chopped
Kosher salt and pepper
2 tablespoons tomato paste
2 slices bacon

2 pork tenderloins, cut into 2-inch cubes
1 pound wild boar sausage (or substitute a not-too-spicy Italian sausage). If sausages are longer than 6 inches, cut into 6-inch segments.
2 cups red wine
2 cups chicken stock
1 28-oz. can crushed tomatoes
3 cans white cannellini beans, drained and rinsed
½ jar roasted red peppers (approximately 2 whole peppers)
⅔ cup freshly grated Parmigiano-Reggiano
Chopped parsley

Cut baguette into 1-inch cubes, drizzle with olive oil, and toast in 400-degree oven for 10 minutes, or until golden brown. Substitute bread crumbs for baguette if you prefer to skip this step.

Heat 1 tablespoon of olive oil in a sauté pan. Sauté onion, fennel, leeks, and carrot until softened. Add 3 cloves of minced garlic and diced red pepper. Sauté for a minute or two more. Add paprika, thyme, and oregano. Season with salt and pepper to taste. Add tomato paste and sauté until the paste begins to brown. Remove from heat.

Dice bacon. In large, ceramic-lined Dutch oven, sauté bacon over medium high heat until fat renders and begins to crisp.

Add pork tenderloin and sauté until golden brown. Do not crowd the pan—you may have to do it in batches (if meat sticks to pan, add a bit of olive oil). Remove browned meat to separate plate and repeat with sausage until golden brown.

Deglaze pan with 1 cup of red wine, scraping up all brown bits. Add remaining wine, chicken stock, and canned tomatoes to Dutch oven and bring to a boil. Add back the browned meat and vegetable mixture.

Bake covered casserole in 350-degree oven for approximately 1 hour, or until meat is fork tender.

Add two cans of beans and stir. Purée remaining can of beans with roasted peppers and add to casserole.

Grind bread cubes or crumbs in food processor with remaining clove of garlic and pulse until finely ground. Add grated Parmigiano-Reggiano cheese and moisten with tablespoon of olive oil.

Distribute crumb mixture over top of casserole and bake uncovered for 45 minutes, until crust is browned and casserole is bubbling.

Garnish with chopped parsley, and share with eight people you love.

CONTORNI: *Mixed Green Salad with Basic Vinaigrette*

No meal in my family is complete without a salad, preferably served Italian style—after the main course. I make this salad dressing by the cup, and it lasts us all week. I like escarole and romaine, mixed with a little radicchio for color, but use your favorite combination of mixed greens.

Vinaigrette Ingredients

2 cloves garlic	⅔ cup extra virgin olive oil
1 teaspoon kosher salt	Freshly ground black pepper
Juice of two lemons (or as many lemons as will yield ⅓ cup lemon juice)	1 teaspoon Dijon mustard

Slice garlic and sprinkle with kosher salt. Mince, scraping knife back and forth over mixture to abrade the garlic, and form a paste.

Squeeze lemons to generate ⅓ cup juice. Add olive oil and whisk to combine. Add garlic paste, a few grinds of black pepper, and Dijon mustard. Whisk until dressing is emulsified. Store refrigerated.

Coat wooden salad bowl with dressing and top with washed greens. Salad can be made in advance and tossed just before serving.

Dolce: *Mira's Cacao Nib Cookies*

Ingredients

1 cup all-purpose flour
¼ cup unsweetened cocoa
powder
1 teaspoon instant espresso
powder
¼ cup confectioners' sugar
½ teaspoon baking soda
½ teaspoon kosher salt or
fleur de sel
1 stick butter at room
temperature

½ cup light brown sugar
1 teaspoon vanilla extract
1 tablespoon Frangelico liqueur
⅓ cup cacao nibs (or, if you
can't find them, chocolate-
covered espresso beans,
coarsely chopped)
Optional: ⅓ cup toasted hazelnuts

Preheat oven to 350 degrees. Mix dry ingredients (flour through salt) together in a mixing bowl.

Cream butter and sugar in the bowl of an electric mixer until fluffy. Add vanilla and Frangelico and mix to combine. Add the dry ingredients a little at a time and stir to combine. Stir in the cacao nibs and toasted hazelnuts. The dough will be crumbly. Take a teaspoon of the dough and roll into a ball approximately the size of a walnut. Place on baking sheet lined with a Silpat mat or parchment paper sheet and flatten slightly.

Bake 12–15 minutes. Remove from oven and let harden a few minutes before cooling on a wire rack. Enjoy with coffee or tea.

AFTERTASTE

Meredith Mileti

ABOUT THIS GUIDE

The suggested questions are included to enhance
your group's reading of Meredith Mileti's
Aftertaste.

Discussion Questions

1. *Aftertaste* is presented as "a novel in five courses." In what ways does the story arc parallel the courses in an Italian meal, and in what ways is it different?

2. Which of Mira's character traits do you most admire? Which traits do you find least admirable?

3. Mira observes, "Sometimes I think my only chance for happiness is in a kitchen, that any life I live outside is destined to be a shadowy, half-lived sort of life." Do you think that holds true throughout the book?

4. At one point Mira says of her mother, "I've been left to piece her life together from the scraps she left behind. My mother hadn't taught me to cook any more than she had taught me to be a mother, but I take comfort in the fact that I've still managed to learn something from her by looking in the holes." What does Mira mean by this? What do you think she's managed to learn by "looking in the holes"?

5. Richard tells Mira that the problem with being a cook is that you never get to be a guest at the party. Is this an occupational hazard or a character flaw?

6. The preparation of food is described in detail in various parts of the book. What purpose do these descriptions serve?

7. Many of the characters in the book (e.g., Mira, Jake, Renata, Michael, Fiona, Ruth, and Enid) display different attitudes toward food. What do those attitudes tell us about their personalities?

8. When you cook, how much do you follow a recipe and how much do you improvise? How well does that predict any other characteristics of your personality?

9. In this novel, food and its preparation often serve as a proxy for emotion. To what extent do you feel this is true in real life?

10. Are Ben and Mira well suited to each other? What is the chance they will end up together in the long run?